A
TRAITOR'S
LOYALTY

A TRAITOR'S LOYALTY

A NOVEL OF INTERNATIONAL INTRIGUE

IAN C. RACEY

vantage
POINT

Vantage Point Books and the Vantage Point Books colophon are registered trademarks of Vantage Press, Inc.

FIRST EDITION: May 2012

Published by Vantage Point Books
Vantage Press, Inc.
419 Park Avenue South
New York, NY 10016
www.vantagepointbooks.com

Manufactured in the United States of America

ISBN: 978-1-936467-31-0

Library of Congress Cataloging-in-Publication data are on file.

9   8   7   6   5   4   3   2   1

Cover design by Victor Mingovits

For my grandfather, Alf Massey (RAF 1940-1946), who first introduced me to British spies, the Second World War, and so many other of the elements that make up this story

Desdemona: Beshrew me, if I would do such a wrong for the whole world.

Emilia: Why, the wrong is but a wrong i' the world; and having the world for your labor, 'tis a wrong in your own world, and you might quickly make it right.

—William Shakespeare
Othello, Act IV, Scene iii

PROLOGUE

WHEN HE regained consciousness, the only sounds Simon Quinn heard were the dripping of a drainpipe and a stray cat or dog rummaging through the garbage. He lay on his left side, and his right shoulder ached dully. His head and upper torso lay in a puddle of something wet and sticky.

He opened his eyes. He was in a dark alley, in a pile of refuse against the side of a rubbish bin. The cat was nosing around in the garbage at his feet. He had no idea how he had gotten here, and he wondered why his right shoulder ached.

He took a deep breath and rolled onto his back. Without

warning, pain exploded in his shoulder and surged out through his entire body, overwhelming any other sensation. His vision blurred and darkened at the edges, and he contracted into a fetal ball. The cat screeched and ran off, but he did not notice. Now he remembered why his shoulder hurt.

He felt the bullet punch through his shoulder, a freight train slamming into him from behind. A fraction of an instant later, barely long enough for his brain to register that he had been hit in the first place, it exploded through the front of his jacket in a small shower of bone and blood. His pistol dropped to the ground. The bullet's impact knocked him to the side and carried him forward, one step, two steps, three, and he fell over the railing and plunged into the open air beyond.

When the pain had receded, he took a deep preparatory breath, closed his eyes and pushed himself up against the wall till he was on his feet. At the first sign of movement, the pain burst forth once more, assaulting his senses and threatening to overwhelm him again, but he was expecting it this time.

He was on his feet. The alley's nearer end led out onto the River Spree, from where he had staggered up before collapsing here and losing consciousness. At the other end, a few hundred yards away, light spilled into the alley from the street beyond.

He took another deep breath and pushed off, heading towards the street. Sweat had plastered his hair to his forehead, and he leaned against the brick wall, letting it support his weight. He held his hand clamped over his shoulder, but it did very little good. Blood continued to gush from the wound at an alarming rate; he would have to see to it soon.

He paused for a moment to check his watch. It had stopped working just after half past ten.

Quinn sat on the park bench across the street from the exit to the

U-bahn *station and checked his watch again. He had been sitting here for over an hour now. Karl was almost half an hour late. About twenty minutes ago, a green-uniformed Orpo street cop had asked him what his business was, but the sight of his false Gestapo ID had been enough to scare him off.*

A glimmer of movement across the road caught his attention: someone coming up the steps from the U-bahn station. It was a man, short, stocky, wearing a hat and a heavy dark coat, with his head bowed down as if to divert attention from himself. Karl. He emerged from the station, looked around, spotted Quinn, stared at him for a moment to confirm who it was, and started across the street.

A sudden thought struck Quinn. He reached into his pocket, his fingers searching desperately. His heart skipped a beat as he thought he might have lost it in the river, but after a moment he found it. His fingers closed over the roll of photographic film with relief.

Karl sat on the bench next to Quinn, still looking around nervously. "Do you have it?" Quinn asked.

Karl nodded. He reached into his pocket and pulled out a small object, which he handed to Quinn without making eye contact. Quinn took the photographic roll and dropped it in his jacket pocket. Karl's eyes continued to dart about.

Quinn collapsed against the wall and peered round the alley corner. The street was dark and deserted, lit at well-spaced intervals by streetlights. A few hundred yards down the road, a trio of long-haired teenage boys slouched against the wall in the shadows of a shop's awning. No sign of any lone skulker who might be Gestapo. Unless the teenagers were Gestapo, of course.

There was a telephone box across the street. Quinn stared at it for a moment. The far side of the street seemed a hundred miles away, but he had to make it. He took a deep breath, pushed off from the wall, and staggered in the box's direction.

His breath came in ragged gasps; his shoulder screamed at him to stop, give up, collapse. His vision blurred as tears clouded his eyes.

"What's wrong?" Quinn asked.

Karl blinked, shook his head and stared at his feet. "I don't know. It's just..." His voice trailed off, and he suddenly started looking around again. "I feel odd. Like it went too well. They didn't even check my security pass when I was leaving the building."

Quinn shrugged. "Just be thankful for small blessings. Look, you know what to do. Get the bus to the British embassy, and you'll be fine."

Karl nodded, took a deep breath, and squared his shoulders. "Yeah. Yeah, OK." He was staring straight ahead.

Quinn patted him on the arm. "I'll miss you, Karl. See you around."

He stood, looked around, and walked away in the direction of his car. Behind him, he heard Karl get up and walk in the opposite direction.

The car waited a hundred yards down the street, parked on the curb next to the sharp fifty-foot drop down to the river. He was almost there when he heard the screeching of a car's wheels down the road behind him, and everything ahead of him was suddenly thrown into eerie relief by a car's headlights.

He spun around to see what was happening, but the headlights glared so brightly that he had to throw his hands up in front of his eyes to shield them. All he managed to catch was a glimpse of Karl, standing transfixed in the headlights' beam.

With a final, Herculean effort, Quinn staggered forward and fell against the side of the telephone box. He caught a fleeting glimpse of his reflection, ghostlike, in its glass wall: black hair plastered to his sweaty forehead, eyes lost in shadow above a beaklike nose highlighted by the streetlights. His knees buckled and finally gave out from underneath him, and he slid slowly down the side of the box, leaving a trail of crimson smeared across the glass. He crouched on his hands and knees in front of the telephone box, struggling to get air into his lungs, as his vision blurred and a cold sweat beaded on his forehead and chest.

After several minutes, he clawed the door open and crawled inside, then pulled himself up onto his feet and, leaning against the wall, dug into his pocket for the few pfennigs the call would cost. He dialed a number from memory.

Somebody answered at the other end, even before the first ring had finished. "This is Aiello," a tense voice said.

"Lancelot," Quinn identified himself. His voice came out a tortured rasp.

"Jesus Christ," said Aiello at the other end, "what in hell happened to you? The SS bands have been jammed with traffic for two hours. We thought you'd been shot."

"I'm on Holsteinstrasse, across the river." He strained to make out the street number on the nearest shop. "In front of number thirty-seven. Bring a first aid kit."

"What—erm, right. Give me twenty minutes."

"Ten," Quinn said and hung up the phone. Then, closing his eyes and letting out an agonized groan, he collapsed against the door. It opened under his weight and he fell out, hitting the ground with a heavy thud. He lay sprawled on the pavement.

He turned back around, preparing to run for his car, but there was somebody coming from that direction too. The Gestapo had found them.

Quinn had his pistol in his hand in a second, as he turned back towards the first car and fired two quick shots at its windshield. He must have hit it, because it swerved out of control with a shriek of tires and crashed into a streetlight. But more came behind it, heading for Karl.

"Karl!" Quinn shouted. "Run!"

He glimpsed Karl heading down the tunnel into the U-bahn as he turned and started running himself. He had only one chance—he had to make it to the river before the Gestapo got to him. Behind him, he could hear the cars screeching to a halt and their occupants getting out. There were shouts in German and the sound of gunfire. He felt the bullets whiz past him.

He was almost there—just a few more feet. Then, suddenly, another gunshot. He felt the bullet punch through his shoulder, and he fell over the railing and plunged into the open air beyond.

He came awake with a start. He was sitting with his back against the telephone box. How long had he been out? He checked his watch, forgetting momentarily that it wasn't working. He looked down the street. The adolescent boys had gone.

He had to try to keep himself lucid. The shop front nearest him belonged to a record store, and in its window hung a giant poster. He focused on the poster, studying it in detail. It was a black and white image, a photograph of the Führer receiving the Beatles, presumably during their goodwill tour of Europe the previous summer. A bright, sunny day, the Reichstag visible in the background, festooned with swastika banners. John and the Führer clasping hands, smiles all round—beaming Beatles, beaming Führer, behind them an excited, beaming crowd of blond teenage Aryan girls and boys waving small paper swastika flags and Union Jacks.

A car came round the corner and started driving slowly up the street. Quinn tensed for a moment, expecting it to be a Gestapo Focke-Wulf sedan, but it was a nondescript little black Volkswagen. As it drove past, Quinn saw who was in the driver's seat—red hair, mid-twenties, American air-force uniform: Aiello. He waved. The action sent waves of pain radiating through his body. Cold sweat ran down his back and his throat felt dry.

Aiello saw him wave and pulled up next to him. He got out of the car. A look of shock passed over his face.

"Christ, man, what the fuck happened?" He hurried over and helped Quinn to his feet. "We've gotta get you outta here." He put Quinn's arm over his shoulder and together they staggered over to the car. Aiello opened the back door and helped Quinn in, then got back into the driver's seat.

"Did you get the first aid kit?" Quinn asked, as they pulled out into the street.

"Sure thing." Aiello grabbed the kit off the front passenger seat and tossed it back to him. Quinn started to strip off his coat and shirt. It was not an easy task in his current state, and every bump in the road multiplied the pain a hundredfold.

The car radio was tuned to the Western diplomatic frequency.

"The Gestapo put up road blocks on all the major routes out of the city as soon as all this started," Aiello said. "Now they're barricading the entrances to the NATO embassies and consulates. Unless you have somewhere else you can go, we'll have to leave the city by one of the little roads and hope they haven't blocked it yet."

"All right," Quinn said. "South, and get on the autobahn as soon as we get out of the city. For Dresden." He had started cleaning the wound now. He inhaled sharply as he daubed the antiseptic against the ragged, discolored edges of his flesh.

"What the hell happened tonight, anyway? What went wrong?"

"We were ambushed," Quinn said. "Somebody must have tipped off the Gestapo. They knew exactly where we would be making the exchange." He cut himself a bandage from the roll in the kit.

"Did you get what you needed?"

"Yes. Has there been any word on my contact? He was supposed to go to the British embassy."

Aiello shook his head. "Nothing. He never showed up. But the Germans don't have him, either. Or if they do, they're putting on a really good show over the SS frequencies of continuing the search. As far as anybody knows, he's just vanished."

RICHARD GARNER, standing on the roof of the British embassy, took a puff of his cigarette and stared through his binoculars at the sight of the capital of the world's most powerful empire at night. The bright lights and immense size of the city contrasted starkly with the first time he had seen Berlin, from the cockpit of a Halifax bomber, almost twenty-five years ago. But now, somewhere out there was the man he was looking for—cold, tired, overdue, and certainly very, very scared. Garner couldn't say he blamed him.

He lowered the binoculars, setting them down on the low brickwork wall that ran along the edge of the roof, took off his glasses and pinched the bridge of his nose. Without his glasses on, the street below was just a dark blur, punctuated every few hundred yards by pools of orange light from the streetlamps.

He pulled a handkerchief from his pocket, breathed heavily on each of his glasses' lenses to mist them over, and started to wipe them. A shiver ran down his spine. The night was chilly, and being this high up meant that a harsh breeze was blowing.

The radio operator, a freckle-faced lance-corporal from the

Royal Corps of Signals who could not have been more than twenty, sat on a wooden stool a few yards behind him. Garner could hear him now, fiddling with his equipment. He turned around and watched the young man. The lad pressed his headset against his ear, obviously receiving a message.

"It's the American embassy," he reported at last, his voice strong with a Scottish burr. "The Gestapo have blocked them off."

"That leaves who?" Garner asked. "Just the Canadians and the Greeks—and us?"

The corporal, hunched busily over his radio, nodded and responded distractedly, "Yes, sir."

Garner put his glasses back on and turned back around to the view of the city. The Royal Marines sharpshooter stood a few feet away, staring out at the surrounding area through a pair of binoculars, as Garner had been a few moments before, with his assassin's rifle leaned against the brickwork wall.

Garner took his cigarette from his mouth and exhaled a large puff of smoke, studying the Marine. He was in his middle twenties, about five foot eleven, with short, fair hair and a good build. Like both Garner and the corporal, he wore dark, nondescript civilian clothing. Garner would never have pegged him as a professional killer, but he had learned long ago that, in this business, appearances always deceived. He could not, for the life of him, remember the man's name.

The Marine had noticed his scrutiny now and had turned to face him. "Sir?" he asked. "Is something wrong?"

Garner shook his head no. "What was your name again, Lieutenant?" he asked.

The lieutenant had turned his attention back to the street. "Barnes, sir."

Barnes. Yes.

Garner checked his watch. A quarter to two. That meant it was just under three hours since the target had been due to arrive at the embassy, and four since all hell had broken loose over the SS frequencies.

With a tired sigh, he put the cigarette back in his mouth and the binoculars back to his eyes and began scanning the street below again. As long as it didn't come over the SS frequencies that he had been captured, they would have to continue searching.

A flicker of motion out the corner of his eye caught his attention. Instantly, he brought the binoculars to bear. There it was again—a few blocks down, somebody lurking in the shadows at the mouth of an alley. As Garner watched, he darted from the alleyway to the shadowy recess of the entrance to a building, taking care to avoid as much as possible passing through the bright pools of light beneath the streetlights. He looked fortyish, short and stocky, and he had on a hat and a long dark coat.

"There's our man," Garner said. "South, about three blocks away. Hiding in the shadows."

Barnes dropped to one knee and laid his binoculars on the wall, grabbing his rifle and bringing it instantly to bear in the direction Garner had indicated. "I see him," he said after a moment.

The figure was slowly making his way towards the embassy. Garner's heart quickened. Despite everything, this operation was actually going to come off.

Something was wrong, though. He could not pinpoint it at first, but then he realized: sirens. The sound of sirens, very faint, far away, but slowly drawing closer.

"The SS are coming," he breathed.

Barnes nodded without looking in his direction. "I hear."

The sirens were getting louder very quickly; they must have been traveling at breakneck speed. The man in the street had heard them, too—he had quickened his pace and forgone carefully shrouding himself in darkened alcoves in favor of making it to the embassy that much sooner.

Garner glanced down at the embassy gates. Two uniformed Royal Marines stood in the guard box, each with a rifle. With them waited a nondescript man in plain clothing—an MI6 agent, there to meet the figure when he arrived.

He spoke over his shoulder to the radio operator. "Have them open the gate. They need to be ready to meet him."

"Yes, sir," the operator said. He removed his radio headset, picked up the receiver of the in-embassy telephone sitting next to him, and dialed the front-gate extension.

Garner watched as the MI6 man picked up the telephone receiver in the guard box. Behind him, the radio operator relayed his instructions. The MI6 man said something, hung up, and spoke to the Marines. Immediately, they unlocked the front gate and swung it open.

The figure was less than half a block from the embassy now, still across the street, but the sirens were almost upon them. Then, suddenly, their source burst into view around a corner: an armored troop carrier, closely followed by two Gestapo Focke-Wulfs with flashing lights on top.

The figure burst into a sprint, heading straight for the open embassy gate. The armored car and the Focke-Wulfs came to a screeching halt. The Focke-Wulfs' doors swung open and two Gestapo got out of each, pistols firing. With an anguished scream that reached Garner as nothing more than a thin whimper in the cold air on the embassy roof, the figure clutched his right thigh and sank to the ground.

"Sir," said Barnes, but Garner ignored him.

The figure was still crawling towards the gate, dragging himself on one elbow and one knee while the other hand clutched at his injured leg. He was not six feet from the embassy entrance. The two Marines and the MI6 man stood right at the gate waiting for him, but they went no further. They knew the rules: as long as he was on German soil, they could not help him. He had to reach embassy territory before they could offer him asylum.

The four Gestapo and the Waffen-SS platoon from the troop carrier were hurrying towards the figure. "Sir," Barnes's voice was becoming more plaintive, "we haven't much time."

Garner did not respond. He stood transfixed, staring at the horrible scene that was unfolding inexorably before him. So close. They had come *so close*.

The SS were almost upon him. "*Sir!*" Barnes hissed.

Garner came out of his reverie with a start. "What? Yes, man— fire!"

Barnes's finger squeezed the trigger. A shaft of orange flame spat eighteen inches from his rifle muzzle. Down in the street, the figure's head exploded into a chunky vapor of blood, brains, and bone fragments. The nearest Gestapo was only a few feet away; he skidded to a halt and threw his arm up over his face to protect it. The figure's headless body collapsed to the ground, twitched for several moments and lay still.

Garner took the cigarette from his mouth and flicked it onto the ground. It landed next to his feet, smoldering. He ground it into the dust with his heel.

PART 1

CRISIS

If you can bear to hear the truth you've spoken
Twisted by knaves to make a trap for fools,
Or watch the things you gave your life to, broken,
And stoop and build 'em up with worn-out tools

—RUDYARD KIPLING, "If"

CHAPTER I

PRÉVEZA, GREECE

QUINN JERKED up in bed at the alarm clock's shrill shriek. His left hand fumbled about on the bedside table, his fingers probing till they found the clock, and it abruptly fell silent. He lay back in bed, a little disturbed at how on edge his body seemed to be. His heart pounded in his chest; his hands felt clammy; he was sweating and breathing shallowly.

He swung himself out of bed and moved across his cramped cabin into the tiny lavatory. He flicked the light switch on, blinking in the sudden harsh, colorless florescent light. He turned on the tap and splashed some cold water on his face to help wake himself up, then stared at his reflection in the mirror. A pair of sharp mahogany eyes stared back at him beneath a head of disheveled black hair, but it was the prominent nose that dominated his face. Quinn ran a hand over his chin. He needed a shave, but it could wait. He ran his fingers through his hair to straighten it, then flicked off the lavatory light.

A glance at the clock as he came back into his cabin showed that the time had just reached seven. A small chest of drawers stood against one wall. Quinn opened the top drawer and took out a small shortwave radio. He extended the antenna and flicked the radio on, to be greeted by a burst of static. The radio was tuned to the correct frequency, so Quinn took a slow step to the side to find the signal. From the static emerged the sound of chimes fading away. A voice followed a moment later.

"You are listening to the BBC World Service," the announcer said. *"The time is oh-six-hundred Greenwich Mean Time, oh-seven-hundred British Summer Time, Tuesday, the 27th of May, 1971. And now, the news."* A pause. *"Our top story: The German Government announced this morning that Adolf Hitler, Führer and Chancellor of the Greater German Reich, has died in Berlin at the age of eighty-two."*

Quinn had been holding onto the radio with one hand while the other slid another drawer open and began to rifle through it for some clothes, but now he stopped and gave the radio his full attention. He held onto it with both hands and straightened up. The news commentator's voice erupted into static at the movement, and Quinn straightened his arms and held the radio a little higher to regain the signal.

"—reveal the exact cause of death, but Western experts have believed for some time that Herr Hitler suffered from Parkinson's disease. As the German nation mourns, the greatest question arising from his death regards the Nazi succession. Herr Hitler has made no public

provision for his heir since the death of his previous designated successor, Reichsmarschall Hermann Göring, in 1947. His wishes are believed to be contained within his last will and testament, which, by his own order, will not be unsealed until following his funeral, set to take place in three days' time, on Friday, in the city of Linz in the German province of the Upper Danube. Who will be responsible for the administration of the German government in the meantime remains unclear at this time. We'll have more, including the reaction to Herr Hitler's death in Berlin, London, and Washington, later in the broadcast.

"In other news, fierce fighting continues around the city of Kharditsa in northern Greece, where British positions are under heavy attack from Croatian and Italian divisions. A Greek armored battalion—"

Quinn switched the radio off. For a moment he continued to stare at it, then, shaking himself slightly as if waking from some deep meditation, he collapsed its antenna, tossed the radio onto the bed and went back to the clothes drawer.

He dressed in a plain grey sweater, denim jeans, and a black leather jacket hung on a peg on the back of the cabin door. When he was dressed, he returned the radio to the top drawer and took out a small, snub-nosed pistol that he slid into his jacket's inside pocket. He went to close the drawer but paused, his hand hovering in mid-motion, then picked through the other items in it. There were two passports—one British, one Sicilian—and, at the bottom, a pair of small, rectangular leather cases. The first was embossed with the tiny letters MM, the second, VC.

Quinn removed the second case, sat down on the bed, and opened it. He looked at the medal inside, the deep maroon ribbon and the small, shiny gold cross with the inscribed legend "For Valour." The Military Medal in the drawer was his own, but the Victoria Cross he held in his hand was his brother's. Tenderly, he flipped the medal over and read the date inscribed on the back: 12 July 1944. Almost twenty-seven years ago now.

Quinn replaced the medal and snapped the case shut, then, on impulse, slid it into his pocket instead of replacing it in the drawer. He stood, opened his cabin door, and climbed up on deck. The day was bright and sunny, the air filled with the sound of cawing seagulls and the bustle of men at work on the docks. He squinted in the sunlight and covered his eyes. He had a pair of sunglasses in his jacket breast pocket. He took them out and put them on.

A squat, thickset figure sat with his back to Quinn and his legs dangling over the edge of the railing, fishing rod in hand. He had long, curly, black hair, and the sunburnt skin of his bare back was red and flaky.

"Morning, Giglio," Quinn called.

The large man turned towards him. A pale yellow scar ran down the left side of his face—a memento from when his ship had been dive-bombed by a Spitfire during the battle of Malta. He grinned.

"*Buon giorno, Signore!* A fine day, no?" His English carried a thick Sicilian accent.

"A fine day," Quinn agreed. "The others in town?"

"*Si, Signore.* We'll be leaving this afternoon?"

"I'm supposed to meet Kanellopoulos at eleven. He'll give us the location where we'll rendezvous. We should get underway right after that."

Giglio nodded. "*Si, Signore.* "

"Have you had breakfast, Giglio?"

The Sicilian shook his head. He nodded to his fishing rod and grinned ruefully. "Breakfast, I had planned to catch myself. But—" he shrugged, "—the fish do not seem to like my plan."

Quinn grinned. "I'm going ashore. I'll be back soon."

"Right, *Signore.*" Giglio turned back to his fishing.

Quinn climbed over the railing at the edge of the cabin cruiser's deck and jumped the five feet onto the jetty to which it was tethered.

The docks were still fairly quiet this early in the morning, but soon they would be bustling. Already there were signs of activity, as workers loaded and unloaded cargo at a few ships and a boy stood on a street corner selling newspapers. A pair of coast guard speedboats patrolled out in the bay. Quinn started walking along the waterfront, away from where the cabin cruiser was docked.

A low rumble from the sky made him look up. Three fighter jets, American, were flying overhead. They were headed out to sea, no doubt returning to their aircraft carrier after an early morning patrol. One had an ominous trail of black smoke pouring from one of its engines; no doubt these three had tangled with the Luftwaffe this morning.

Quinn crossed the road and headed down a street running perpendicular to the docks, leading into the city. Three blocks later, he bought some hot baklava from a street vendor and sat on a nearby bench to eat it. He gripped the piping-hot pastry lightly between his fingers and took only small nibbles until it had cooled down a little. While he sat, he gazed up at the vapor trails of the three fighters, the one mixed with a trail of smoke.

It was a silly little war, this war in Greece. Technically, most of its combatants were not even at war. The British and American forces were merely aiding their ally, Greece, against Croatia, while the German and Italian troops that they fought were doing the same for Croatia against the Greeks. That way, British and Italian infantry could slaughter each other, and American and German fighters could clash in the skies, while all four countries remained at peace with each other. Hundreds of young boys, still in their teens or early twenties, died every day to preserve that peace.

And in a very real sense, Simon Quinn was directly responsible for all of it.

He did not notice the car with darkly tinted windows pull up to the curb, nor did he notice the old man get out. When the old man sat down next to him on the bench, he gave him only a momentary glance before going back to his baklava.

It took a few moments for recognition to set in. When it did, he whirled around in disbelief and stared at the apparition from his past.

The old man regarded him coolly. "Hello, Simon," he said, his public-school accent tainted ever so faintly by foreign birth.

Quinn found himself speechless for several seconds, staring at the small, dignified old man sitting next to him holding a burnished hickory cane and leather valise. Very few people even knew this old man existed; nobody knew his real name. Friends and enemies alike regarded him with a mixture of fear and respect—even awe—simply as Talleyrand. He had earned the nickname for the zeal with which he maintained his power, for the cunning and ruthlessness with which he manipulated the lives of countless others for his own inscrutable ends, and for his apparent agelessness. For as long as anyone could remember, he had been Her Majesty's spymaster, the Director-General of the Secret Intelligence Service, and he showed no sign of relinquishing the position anytime soon. Quinn had never before heard of him leaving Great Britain, but now he sat next to Quinn on a public bench in a decaying port city in northern Greece.

"You," Quinn managed. At first his voice held only astonishment, but now venom appeared too. "What are *you* doing here?"

"Now, now, Simon," Talleyrand chided. "Is that any way to greet an old friend?"

"You're not a friend," Quinn said.

"Well, it's nice to see you too, my boy."

Quinn stared at him a moment longer, then tossed aside the rest of his baklava, got up, and walked away.

Talleyrand stood as well and called after him, "You've been recalled to life." Quinn stopped dead in his tracks. "Yes, old boy. There's a task that your country needs you for."

Quinn did not react at first. Then, slowly, he turned back to the old man. "No," he said. "I've washed my hands of you. Whatever stew it is you've made for yourself, you'll have to get yourself out of it this time." And with that, he turned purposefully on his heel and strode quickly away.

Talleyrand stared after him. "Fair enough," he murmured at last, and got back in the car.

Quinn walked back down the street in the direction of the waterfront. He was a little over a block away when he heard the sound of sirens coming up from behind. Everyone in the street turned and watched as three police cars and a van, lights flashing, screamed by toward the docks. When they reached the end of the street, the vehicles turned the corner and were gone. The onlookers went back to whatever they had been doing before.

Everyone except Quinn. He had seen only a flash of the figure sitting in the back seat of the last car, staring sullenly out the window, but he had recognized him instantly.

Kanellopoulos. His contact.

A shudder of dread ran through him. He stood transfixed, staring after the police convoy, praying they would turn in the opposite direction when they reached the corner. But no—they turned and headed straight in the direction of his cabin cruiser.

He broke into a run, heading for the docks. He rounded the corner and came skidding to a halt, looking down the waterfront towards his boat. Already it was crawling with police. He could see Giglio between two policemen as they escorted him to one of the police cars. Two coast guard boats sat a couple of dozen yards out in the bay, ready to catch anyone who might try to swim for it.

Even as Quinn watched, a policeman emerged from below decks, triumphantly holding aloft a machine gun. The hold carried forty-nine more just like it, all destined for the Greek guerrillas fighting in the north behind the Croat lines, and all illegal.

CHAPTER II

FOR LONG, endless minutes, Quinn watched the police crawl over his boat. A crowd had started to gather at the perimeter the police had set up at the head of the jetty, prevented from encroaching any further by half a dozen policemen stationed at the periphery of the scene.

After a while, the car pulled up to the curb next to him once again, and the back door opened. Talleyrand got out and waited, standing a few feet behind Quinn and watching the scene at the jetty from over his shoulder.

At last the old man said pleasantly, "What do you suppose the penalty is for gunrunning? Greece is at war, fighting for her very existence. I'm sure that at a time like this, it must be rather severe."

He let the statement hang in the air, then suggested, "Perhaps you would like to reconsider my offer?"

Quinn still stared at his boat, refusing to turn and meet the old man's gaze. "Those guns were destined for partisans behind the Croat lines, fighting for the *Greek* cause. And you know it."

"So you say now," Talleyrand said solemnly. "Of course you do. But how can the authorities know that? Especially since that young man Kanellopoulos they picked up this morning will no doubt testify that those weapons were intended for Croat guerrillas—in exchange for a pardon."

There was another silence, Quinn unwilling to concede defeat. But he knew he had no choice. At last, he turned to face Talleyrand. "All right," he said. "What do you have to say?"

The old man looked about, spotted a bench facing out onto the water and gestured to it with his cane. Quinn walked over and sat down. He stared out at the sea while he waited for the old man to follow. To the north lay the port's crowded docks; to the south, the headland curved away where the Gulf of Árta opened into the Adriatic Sea.

Talleyrand settled himself next to Quinn. "Don't worry about your boat or your crew," the old man reassured him. "They'll be held in custody until you've completed your mission, then released. It shouldn't take more than a few days."

"And my cargo?"

"Ah, yes." He pursed his lips. "Your cargo, I'm afraid, will have to be, ah, confiscated for the Greek war effort."

Quinn stared at him bleakly. "At no compensation to me."

"The price of doing business, I'm afraid," Talleyrand said, sounding not at all repentant. "Now, to the business at hand." He removed a large manila envelope from his valise and handed it to Quinn. Quinn opened it and pulled out a series of black and white photographs of a man in his middle forties with a receding hairline, greying dark hair, and a pair of horned-rimmed glasses.

"Richard Andrew Garner," Talleyrand explained. "Born in Hamburg, 1925, the son of an Irish importer. He was educated in England and enlisted in the RAF in 1943. He went through officer training and spent the last eighteen months of the war as a navigator on a Halifax bomber over Germany. He was demobbed a year after the Corunna Armistice and spent a term at Birmingham University before we recruited him. He started off working for us in Hamburg, then we moved him to the Berlin Station in 1956. He's been there ever since; he's now Assistant Chief of Station. He speaks English and German fluently."

"So what's the problem?" Quinn asked. Despite himself, he was falling back into the familiar rhythm of things—running over all the information in his mind, finding the holes he needed to fill and the questions he needed to answer.

"Three days ago, Richard Garner left the British embassy in possession of some highly sensitive documents and hasn't been seen since."

"You think he's turned?"

Talleyrand nodded. "That does seem the most likely scenario. If the Germans get their hands on those documents, it will mean some very bad things for Britain."

Quinn frowned. "If? You don't believe they already have him?"

"No," the old man said. "We'd know if the Germans had him. It would have come over the Gestapo communications that we can monitor, or something like that. No, though we don't know why he's disappeared, it seems clear it was not part of a pre-arranged plan with a German operator. Perhaps he had intended to turn later, and something has flushed him out ahead of schedule. Our best guess is that he's holed up somewhere, waiting to make contact with the SD."

Quinn was still staring at Garner's face, memorizing every detail: the jowly cheeks, the businesslike, straightforward look in his eyes. "So you want me to locate Garner and retrieve the documents?"

Talleyrand shook his head. "I want you to destroy the documents and eliminate Garner."

Quinn looked up sharply from the photograph. "You want me to kill him? You don't even want him questioned? You're not even sure he's turned."

"It doesn't matter. I cannot stress how sensitive these documents are, Simon. If they fall into the wrong hands, British national security will be irreparably compromised. The fate of the entire nation rests on the apprehension of Richard Garner. And as I say, he does not appear to be following a plan or acting in concert with an enemy agency. He's certainly unstable, and most likely very scared. Scared men are unpredictable, and unpredictable men are the greatest danger of all."

Quinn considered. "Why do you need me for this?" he asked at last. "Why can't you find this Garner yourselves?"

"Ordinarily, we would," the old man said. "But events of the last twelve hours have added a new dimension to the situation."

Quinn pursed his lips. "You mean Hitler's death?"

"Ah, you've heard. Precisely. The original situation was unstable enough, but now events have become completely unmanageable. The German government, the military, the Gestapo, the European satellite states—they'll all be in a state of complete disarray and impossible to predict. And so they'll stay for at least another three days."

"When Hitler's successor is named. After his funeral."

"Yes."

Talleyrand took a pack of cigarettes from his pocket, stuck one in his mouth and lit it. He offered one to Quinn, who shook his head.

"What's more," the old man continued, "if Garner is going to defect, he'll have to act now. He knows we're looking for him. Without this unfortunate incident, he could have lain low for a couple of weeks, until the coast was clear, and then made his move. But, as long as the next ruler of Germany is in doubt, those documents he has will give a strong advantage to any of the leading figures in the German government who will be looking to influence the succession. Garner will have to move now to make use of them. Given a short while longer, we would have been able to locate him ourselves. But now, we do not have that short while."

"All right," Quinn said. He gave the photographs another brief look, repeating the name, "Richard Garner," then replaced them in the manila envelope. A thought occurred to him. "You say he's been in Berlin for fifteen years?"

"Yes."

"Was he at all involved in... in my final operation?"

Talleyrand hesitated momentarily, nodded. "Yes, he was."

Quinn said nothing, acknowledged the information with a fractional nod of his head. Silence hung in the air.

He stared out at the sea once more. Trapped. No hope of escape.

Talleyrand produced more documents from the valise and handed them to Quinn: a German passport and an SS ID. Quinn shook himself out of his reverie and inspected them both. They identified him as Matthias Kaufholz, a thirty-six-year-old native of Vienna. He was an *obersturmbannführer* in Amt III of the SS. Amt III was the SS's internal security service, charged with maintaining loyalty within the government, the military and even the Gestapo itself. If Germany and Europe lived in fear of the Gestapo, the Gestapo lived in fear of Amt III.

"When you've completed your assignment, go to the British embassy in Berlin," Talleyrand told him. "Ask the desk clerk for the Gatekeeper. The Gatekeeper will see to your transport back here."

"Fine," Quinn said.

The old man stood up and began making his way over to where his car still sat by the curb, its engine running, but paused when he saw Quinn had not followed. "Come now, Simon," he said.

Quinn had risen when Talleyrand did, but had stopped to take a last look at his boat. The initial commotion was over, and the crowd around it had thinned. Policemen and ominous-looking plainclothes officials were carrying the crates containing the guns up from the hold and loading them onto an armored police truck. Reluctantly, he turned and followed Talleyrand to the car. The old man had the back door open, and Quinn climbed in. Talleyrand followed. As soon as the door was closed, the driver pulled away from the curb and started off.

"We're on our way to the local airfield now," the old man continued. "You'll fly from here to Athens. From there, you'll get to Berlin through a connecting flight from Zurich." He checked his watch. "It's a quarter past eight now. You should land at Reitsch Airport by noon. In the parking garage of the Lufthansa terminal, on the ground floor in the first row of cars opposite the lift, a grey Focke-Wulf will be waiting for you. In the boot will be an SS uniform, a change of clothes, a handgun, and what should be enough money to last you for a stay of a few days."

He held out his hand. "You're carrying a gun now," he said. It was not a question. "You won't get through Swiss customs with it."

Quinn stared into those hard grey eyes. Once he did this, he knew, he would be irrevocably committing himself. Finally, reluctantly, he reached into his pocket, took out the pistol and placed it in Talleyrand's hand.

CHAPTER III

THE CLOCK had reached half past twelve by the time Quinn got through customs at Hanna Reitsch Airport outside Berlin. The first thing he did was find a phone and dial the French embassy. A secretary answered.

"Maurice Beauchamp, please," he said, hoping Beauchamp was still in Berlin.

"Whom shall I say is calling?" the secretary asked.

"Johann Kreuz," he said. It was an alias he had used when he had been stationed in Berlin, four years ago; Beauchamp would recognize it.

"One moment, please," the secretary said, and the line went dead.

A few moments later, there was a click, and Beauchamp's voice came over the line. *"Allo?"* The voice was tentative.

"Hello, Maurice," Quinn responded.

"Jesus Christ," Beauchamp exclaimed, suddenly agitated. "Is it really you?"

"Yes," he said, "it's really me."

"What the hell do you want?"

"I don't think we should talk about it over the phone," Quinn said. "Why don't we meet?" He checked his watch. "Outside the— outside the Purification Museum, in about an hour?"

"Meet?" Beauchamp repeated incredulously. "You mean you're *in Berlin?"*

"The Purification Museum," Quinn said. "In an hour. Half past one. You'll be there?"

Beauchamp sighed in resignation. "I'll be there," he said. "This better be good, Johann. I'm risking my life to be there."

Quinn hung up the phone and made his way to the parking garage. The car waited exactly where Talleyrand had said it would be, the key in the ignition. Quinn checked the boot to make sure the SS uniform and the other change of clothes were there and put the handgun and some of the money—a roll of one hundred Reichsmark notes—in his pocket. Then he got in the car and left the airport.

He had not known how he would react, being back here after all this time. Now, as he drove through the familiar streets for the first time in four years, he felt no overpoweringly strong emotions, either positive or negative. Instead, there was only a curious detachment, a bland numbness in his chest. His eyes took in the landmarks he knew so well, but all his mind could do was note them clinically.

In a way, this bleak emotionlessness was mirrored in the city around him, but for different reasons. The people on the streets went about their tasks mechanically, staring glassy-eyed off into space as if their bodies were going through the motions, while their conscious minds had seemingly shut off. For almost four decades, their every action, every thought, had been controlled and directed by a single person, a single human will, and now that will was suddenly and unaccountably *absent.* Quite a few probably perceived him almost as a god. Many had probably begun to half-believe he would never die. Quinn secretly suspected that he had been among those.

Traffic was thick, and it was slow going across the city. He was initially surprised that there were so many people out, going about their business; he would have expected the government to declare today a Day of National Mourning. Most likely there was no one with both the authority and the confidence to have put that in motion. With the succession in such doubt, there were certainly quite a few at the top who were angling now for power. No one would want to seem to be gathering power to himself for fear of being the foe against whom other pretenders to the throne would unite.

And who *would* be the next Führer? Hitler had never married, and though he had kept a string of mistresses—the most significant to him, Eva Braun, had committed suicide over twenty years ago—he had never fathered a child, declaring that any child of his would never be able to emerge from the shadow he cast.

His most likely successors therefore came from his inner circle, the potentates who had been the rulers of Germany for thirty-six years: Bormann, Himmler, and Heydrich. Martin Bormann was Hitler's personal aide and head of the Nazi Party. Heinrich

Himmler, *Reichsführer* of the SS, ruled the Nazi state's labyrinthine secret police apparatus; his gaze—and his grasp—reached every corner of Germany and her European satellites. And Reinhard Heydrich, once Himmler's protégé and now his greatest political rival, as Reich Commissar-General of the East, ruled the strife-ridden conquered territories of what had once been the Soviet Union essentially as his own personal fief.

Additionally, there were several other high-ranking members of the Party or the SS or the government, men like Remer, Kaltenbrunner, and Hanke. And then there were the war heroes and military leaders, such as Skorzeny, Gollob or Barkhorn.

Joseph Goebbels, who had perhaps been the key figure in the regime after Hitler for so many years during the war and afterwards, had died in 1963. Göring had died in 1947. When he had first named Göring his successor, the Führer had also named Party deputy Rudolf Hess as second-in-line—but the British had captured Hess in a bizarre episode in 1940, and he had sat in the Tower of London ever since. His captivity was only one of the many issues left unresolved by the Corunna Armistice that had ended the war in 1946; in the years since, no real attempt had ever been made for a proper peace conference to clear them up.

Despite the traffic, Quinn arrived at the Aryan People's Racial Purification Museum a few minutes after one o'clock, almost half an hour before he was due to meet Maurice. He stood at the entrance to the plaza onto which the museum fronted and wondered why he had chosen to make the rendezvous here, at the museum dedicated to the extermination of the undesirable races of Germany and conquered Europe.

The museum was a hulking neoclassical structure that, like most of the architecture of the Reich, attempted to combine power with a sweeping grace and beauty, but only succeeded in conveying clumsy, depressing, monotonous brute force. Directly above its main entrance, a four-meter high marble swastika superimposed over the Star of David dominated its façade. In the center of the plaza stood a trio of three-meter statues in military-looking uniforms, staring nobly into the distance. Quinn walked forward to the raised pedestal on which they stood and read the plaque at their feet.

From left to right: SS-Obersturmbannführer Karl Adolf Eichmann (1906–), SS-Oberstgruppenführer Reinhard Heydrich (1904–) and Governor-General Hans Frank (1900–1968). And then, in a smaller font beneath: *Three German heroes who were instrumental in cleansing the German people of the racial filth that had defiled us for a millennium. Learn more about these great Germans and more like them in the Hall of Heroes inside the museum.*

Quinn stared up at their faces. The one in the center, Heydrich—now Reich Commissar-General of the East—dominated the three, standing slightly in front of the other two, with his arms akimbo, for it had been Heydrich who bore overall responsibility for the purification program that had eradicated the Jews and other undesirables during and after the war.

Quinn skirted the perimeter of the statues and headed up the museum's steps toward its entrance. A wrought-iron archway set into the wall framed the entrance; across its crest was emblazoned the legend "Arbeit macht frei." Work makes you free. A plaque by the door informed him that the arch had originally been the frame for the entrance gates at the Auschwitz Purification center.

The museum's expansive entrance lobby, kept bright and airy by its glass roof, was deserted save for a pair of elderly docents talking quietly at a reception desk off to one side and a family of

Japanese tourists snapping photographs and chatting amongst themselves. Quinn wandered over to the large gilt dedication set into the floor at the lobby's center.

When National Socialism took power in 1933, it read, *our Führer had two principal, intertwined goals: the restoration of Germany to her proper place at the forefront of Europe, and the purification of the base elements that had polluted the German race for too long. This museum is dedicated to the second of those aims.*

Quinn broke off from his reading and looked up as he felt a presence: one of the docents, a small, friendly-looking man in his seventies, was standing at his shoulder. The docent cast a slightly disapproving glance at the Japanese tourists and smiled at Quinn.

"You are German, mein Herr?" He nodded, and the old man's smile widened. "It is good to see a young German taking an interest in his heritage." His expression became more solemn, but he remained just as friendly. "You have picked a very appropriate day to visit us—what better way to honor the Führer on this day of days than to contemplate the greatest gift he gave us?"

He paused, clearly waiting for Quinn to say something. When nothing was forthcoming, he cleared his throat and continued, gesturing toward a large archway off to one side of the lobby. "The museum is arranged roughly in a circle; beginning your tour through that entrance will take you along the full path of the purification, beginning with an overview of the full extent of the infiltration of German culture by the undesirable races prior to 1933. Giving every section of the museum the attention it deserves can be a daunting task, however, so each section is also accessible individually via the Garden of Purification at the museum's center."

He paused again expectantly. Quinn broke eye contact with

him, not sure what to say. The docent's uniform had a distinctly militaristic tinge, accentuated by the row of ribbons on his jacket's left breast. He nodded at them. "That's a lot of ribbons." His throat felt thick and rough.

The docent nodded and brushed his fingers over them. "These are service decorations," he explained. "I was a camp guard."

"Which camp?"

"At Sobibor," the old man said proudly.

Quinn nodded, turned and simply walked away, leaving the docent standing there. His throat suddenly felt very uncomfortable, and he did not think he would be able to speak. With nowhere else to go, he headed through the archway the docent had indicated.

The images and exhibits along the walls of this first hall were divided into the various groups targeted during the Purification: Communists, homosexuals, the genetically criminal, the mentally retarded or physically deformed, gypsies, and, last of all, the Jews. Quinn walked slowly down the hall, stopping at the Jewish exhibit.

A large photograph taken in the 1920s or early '30s showed a dark-complexioned family sitting down for a meal in an opulent dining room; the butler and maid serving them were both blond and fair skinned. A caption informed him that the photograph was of the family of a Jewish factory owner in Mecklenburg. A few feet away, a photograph of a rich Jewish banker, in top hat and a tuxedo, was juxtaposed with a photograph of a German worker, his face covered in grime, with his wife, both of them in ragged clothing.

At the very end of the hall, a large glass case contained a row of human skeletons. Its caption informed Quinn that each skeleton came from a member of a different one of the purified races, while the skeleton at the very end was actually a plaster cast of the skeleton of a Nordic soldier from the Waffen-SS, killed during the conquest of Stalingrad. Quinn stared at them. The Nordic skeleton, a purer white than the others because it was made of plaster, stood ramrod straight, towering over the others, which the museum's curators had arranged to stand crooked and hunchback—and, no doubt, had selected in the first place because of their small stature. Signs next to the skulls, the ribcages and the thighs compared the physiognomy of the purified peoples unfavorably to that of the Nordic race. A gypsy; a dwarf; a Jew. He stared at the Jew. In the reflection from the glass case he could see his own dark hair and beaked nose. He raised his hand before his face, staring first at its back, then at its palm.

Abruptly he turned and walked out the exit. Rather than continuing into the next hall, he instead went through a door through the cracks of which he could see daylight. He emerged into an idyllic garden, its winding brick paths lined with pleasant, shady trees and intermittent benches.

"The Purification Garden," a sign informed him. *This garden marks the center of the museum. The tree is an ancient symbol of the renewal of life. The trees planted in this garden symbolize the renewal of the German and Aryan races that the purification of the pollutants has made possible. Each tree is dedicated to an individual German hero who played an especially significant role in the Purification, or to an Aryan colony in the East founded on lands freed from subhuman infestation during the Purification.*

Quinn passed quickly through the garden, for its serenity did nothing to dispel the growing sickness he felt rising in his throat. He picked a door at random on its far side and exited the garden into another exhibition hall.

Another sign greeted him at the hall's entrance: *The purification proceeds. As Wehrmacht forces completed the pacification of the Soviet Union, the SS constructed several more camps dedicated solely to purification in the newly conquered territories and accelerated the deportation of subhumans to the Eastern Territories, concentrating especially on Jews.*

Large black and white photographs of emaciated inmates arriving at the camps in cattle cars, being sorted into male and female, healthy and unhealthy groups by SS doctors, dominated the walls. The inmates' uniforms bore triangles whose different colors would have indicated what class of prisoner they were; the Jews bore the Star of David in place of a triangle. Prisoners classed as troublesome had large targets sewn onto their backs. Quinn's eyes searched the inmates, staring at their gaunt, emaciated faces, shaven heads, and sunken eyes.

A sudden peal of laughter jerked him out of his reverie, and a young girl—four or five years old—ran past him, clutching something black in her hand. A moment later another child—a boy, a year or two older—followed, carrying something grey. He turned to follow them with his eyes. The boy caught up with the girl and grabbed her by the upper arm, reaching for the object in her hand, and Quinn realized it was a Waffen-SS figurine, possibly from the museum's gift shop; the grey toy the boy clutched—it took Quinn a moment longer to tell what it was—was a figurine of a partisan fighter, one of the groups of Slavs or Jews who had taken to the hills and fought the German conquest. The Propaganda Ministry represented them as pests, a minor irritation who struggled futilely against their inevitable cleansing. They were less than the German soldiers they opposed: smaller, toothless, in ragged clothing. The girl was managing to keep the Waffen-SS figurine just out of the boy's reach, and giggling uncontrollably.

"Hans, Frida," a voice said, firmly but not angrily, and Quinn turned to see a couple standing next to one of the exhibits, the father facing the children while the mother examined the display. "Come here," the father said. "Don't stray so far from us."

Obediently the children returned to their parents, the girl still giggling as she successfully kept the Waffen-SS trooper away from the boy. Quinn turned away and focused his attention once more on the exhibits.

In the center of the hall was a sunken pit. Quinn stood over it and peered down. It contained three piles: what looked like a mass of rubber, a glittering pile of tiny gold pebbles, and a mass of sheared animal hair. *Recovered from incoming inmates*, a sign set into the floor informed him. *Every effort was made to reap as many resources as possible from the purified. Their shoes were kept for the rubber soles, and their hair was shaven to provide raw material for woolen garments. After incineration, gold tooth fillings were recovered from the ashes.*

The bile rising in Quinn's throat threatened to overpower him now. He stepped back and checked his watch. Twenty-five past one; five minutes until he met Maurice. He turned and hurried from the hall. He crossed through the garden once more, then through the lobby, ignoring the docent he'd met before when the old man called out to him. Half stumbling in his haste, he passed through the front entrance and out into the plaza beyond.

He saw Maurice Beauchamp immediately, sitting on one of the public benches ringing the plaza. The Frenchman was expecting him to come from the direction of the street, not the museum, so Quinn was able to come upon him from behind. As Quinn approached, he paused to collect himself and took the opportunity to study any changes in the man he had once known so well.

Maurice was of medium height and rather thin, with a thin mustache. He had bad eyes and, to correct them, wore a pair of wire-rimmed spectacles with circular frames. A shock of bright red hair had already gone half grey after only forty-two years. Quinn regretted the grey; he knew that it came, like his nervous tic and stammer, from the immense stress under which Maurice lived every second of his life, and to which Quinn had been a great contributing factor; for it was he who had discovered Maurice's secret.

Quinn walked over to the bench and sat down next to Beauchamp. The Frenchman looked up at Quinn with a start. He had been feeding pigeons with breadcrumbs from a paper bag.

"S-so you're r-really here," he stammered. He spoke French, as the two of them always did together. There was less chance of an eavesdropper overhearing them this way, and Maurice spoke almost no German anyway. "I don't think I've really b-believed it until now I've actually s-seen you."

"Believe me," Quinn said, "I wouldn't ever again set foot in Germany of my own free will." He paused. "It's good to see you, Maurice."

Beauchamp went back to feeding the pigeons. "I w-wish I could say the same. I'm risking my life just sitting n-next to you. Himmler's eyes are everywhere." Reflexively, his eyes darted around his surroundings, searching the passersby for any who might be clandestine agents of Heinrich Himmler's Gestapo. "Why are you here?"

"What do you know about Richard Garner?"

Beauchamp did not look up from his pigeons. "I know he's

part of the MI6 contingent at the British embassy. Liaison with the local Resistance, I believe. Rumor has it that he's gone to ground. Preparing to defect."

"I see the intelligence agencies in Berlin are still just as good at keeping each other in the dark about their affairs," Quinn said dryly.

"Sent you after G-Garner, have they?" Beauchamp asked, bitterness creeping into his voice. "You always were the best at ferreting out whatever it was anyone had to hide."

Quinn was instantly defensive. "Hey! Karl was my friend too. I didn't want him killed anymore than you did."

"Yes," Beauchamp said. "B-but it wasn't *my* people that killed him."

Quinn frowned and opened his mouth to ask what Beauchamp meant; the *Germans* killed Karl. But now he did not have the time. With a strong effort of will, he pushed these thoughts to a back corner of his mind and returned to the more pressing matter. "Can you help me with Garner?" he asked. "You said he works with the Resistance. Do you know any of his contacts?"

Beauchamp stared at him for a moment, obviously noticing the reaction his words about Karl had produced, before he answered. "Yes," he said. "One. Jürgen Denlinger, a student at Friedrich Wilhelm. He's the leader of a local *Weisse Rose* cell."

Weisse Rose, the White Rose. There were several civilian anti-Nazi organizations in Germany, most of them student-based, and they loved to name themselves after the ring of Munich students who had been beheaded by the Gestapo in 1943 for distributing anti-Nazi literature. In reality, none of the various small meetings that used the name had anything to do with each other. The Gestapo and the dissidents they tried to suppress both liked to talk of "the White Rose" like some monolithic institution with conspirators at every German university, but really it was simply dozens of disparate, isolated groups.

"Where would he be right now?" Quinn asked.

"At home, probably. The university probably canceled classes for the day."

"Do you know where he lives?"

Beauchamp hesitated. "Yes," he said reluctantly.

Quinn rose. "I can't just walk in and ask him about the White Rose. You'll have to introduce us."

"What? Right now?"

Quinn nodded. "I'm in a hurry."

"B-but I can't right now. I have things to—"

"I don't have time to argue, Maurice. Come on."

He turned and headed towards the museum. With a sigh, Beauchamp got up and followed.

There was a bank of payphones in the museum lobby. Quinn waited while Beauchamp looked up Denlinger's number and called him.

"Hello?" Beauchamp said into the receiver. "Jürgen Denlinger? We have met before. My name is Maurice Beauchamp, from the Fren— yes, well, I'd like to meet with you please. Immediately..." His German was halting, broken. "There is someone who would like to meet you.... No, no, I assure you, you are in no danger. There is no deception here... Herr Denlinger, if the Gestapo r-really wanted to take you into custody, don't you think they could come up with a better and l-less complicated method than having a French diplomat lure you to a meeting with a mysterious stranger?... His name is—" He faltered, looking at Quinn.

"Matthias Kaufholz," Quinn supplied quickly.

"—Matthias Kaufholz," Beauchamp finished. "He—is interested in a mutual friend.... What? Yes, I know the place.... Yes, we'll be there. Half an hour?... Excellent. See you soon, Herr Denlinger."

Beauchamp hung up the phone and started walking towards the museum exit. Quinn fell into step beside him.

"He wants us to meet him at a small corner café in the student district," Beauchamp said. "In half an hour."

Quinn nodded. "Good job, Maurice. I appreciate it." Maurice just shot him a dirty look.

"So," Quinn asked, once they were in the car and on the way to their rendezvous, "is there anything else you can tell me about Garner?"

Beauchamp thought for a moment. "I think I may have heard that he's been at some of the meetings."

"Meetings?"

"The meetings. At Prinz Albrechstrasse."

Quinn stared at him. Gestapo headquarters? "What meetings?"

"You haven't heard about them?"

"I landed in Berlin less than two hours ago."

"But if they didn't include them in your briefing, perhaps he hasn't been to them after all."

"What meetings?" Quinn asked.

"There have been meetings going on at Prinz Albrechstrasse for almost a year now," Beauchamp explained. "Between British embassy staff and representatives from the RSHA."

RSHA—*Reichssicherheitshauptamt*—State Central Security Office. The parent body of the SS, the SD, and the Gestapo, and the most feared intelligence agency in the world.

"Why would British embassy staff be at Prinz Albrechstrasse?"

Quinn asked. "What were these meetings about?"

Beauchamp shrugged. "I've no idea. They're supposed to be very secret. Very few people know about them, but I have my sources."

"How high-ranking was the British staff?"

"I really don't know. The embassy first secretary was at a few, I believe."

"And from the RSHA?"

"Just aides. But aides to powerful men—Skorzeny, Kaltenbrunner. Even Himmler maybe."

Quinn frowned, considering. Otto Skorzeny, the SS's greatest wartime adventurer, and Ernst Kaltenbrunner, head of the RSHA under Himmler's supervision. And Heinrich Himmler, Reichsführer, the man who had built the SS and RSHA into the most feared secret police the world had ever seen; after Adolf Hitler, the most powerful man in Germany. And now Hitler was dead.

What could these meetings have been about?

And why had Talleyrand not mentioned them?

Quinn decided not to voice these questions, but brooded on them the rest of the way to their rendezvous.

The café stood in a run-down area full of low apartment buildings a few blocks from Friedrich Wilhelm University. There were few people about. The café's only customer sat nursing a cup of coffee at one of a handful of tables lining the pavement just outside the café door. He was tall and gaunt, with stringy, shoulder-length blond hair and an unimpressive scraggle of stubble. He wore a grey coat and a pair of jeans, and in his hand he held of beer bottle bearing the distinctive Heineken logo of a red star clutched in the claws of the National Socialist eagle.

He looked up and fastened his gaze on Maurice as he and Quinn approached. "Beauchamp," he said when the two men reached his table. His voice was thin and reedy. He cocked his head slightly, shifting his gaze to Quinn. "You must be Herr—Kauffmann?"

Quinn nodded, aware of the trap to see if he really responded to the name. Only the very inexperienced would fall for it, but it was still worth paying attention to the basics. "Kaufholz," he corrected. "A friend of Richard Garner." His German, he knew, was flawless, with the slightest hint of a Bavarian accent.

Denlinger's eyes widened slightly at Garner's name, then darted about as if to check that no SS man had craftily hidden himself behind one of the café's small wire-framed chairs. Finally he nodded for the two men to sit down. "How do you know Garner?" he asked.

"We work for the same people," Quinn said. "I assume you know he's disappeared?"

"I'd heard something along those lines."

"I've been sent to find him."

"Sorry, can't help you," Denlinger said quickly. "I have no idea where he is."

"Maurice tells me you're his contact with the White Rose. Are there any other members of your cell that Garner knows?"

Denlinger paused and stared at Quinn. Quinn could see the thoughts running through his mind: was he really who he said he was, or was he Gestapo? But if he was Gestapo, then why was he here? Denlinger was, after all, a known associate of Richard Garner, so he would already be under surveillance. And, at the moment, he was not enough of a threat to do anything more than simply keep an eye on. There had not been any strong resistance movements in Germany outside the military for over twenty years. At best, all the White Rose did nowadays was spray seditious graffiti on alley walls. The SS was always trying to stamp them out on general principle, but they were not willing to put any effort into it.

At last, Denlinger said, "Yeah, he came to a few of our meetings. I don't know which of the group he might know."

"I'll need to speak to them," Quinn said.

Denlinger looked at him in horror. "*All* of them? That's not possible."

"I'm afraid it has to be, Herr Denlinger. I'll need their names and phone numbers from you. And addresses, if you have them."

Denlinger shook his head, but Quinn stared at him implacably. "No, no," he said, trying to draw strength from the repetition of the word. "No, I can't." He tried to meet Quinn's gaze but couldn't. He hesitated, then conceded, "But we're having a meeting tonight. You can come, if you want."

Quinn nodded. "All right. Where is it?"

"At my flat, a couple of blocks from here." He looked down and patted the pockets of his coat, then looked up. "Do you have a pen and paper?"

"I do," Beauchamp said. He reached into the inside pocket of his coat, pulled out a small notepad with a pen clipped to it and handed them to Denlinger.

Denlinger took them, flipped the pad open, and scrawled something across the top sheet. He ripped it off the pad and handed it to Quinn.

"That's my address," he said to Quinn. "Be there at seven this evening."

Quinn nodded. "I will."

CHAPTER IV

"SO, WHAT did you do?"

Ellie Voss looked up from the memorandum she was typing. Her eyes twinkled mischievously. "Exactly what he deserved," she said. "I threw my wine in his face and took the U-bahn home."

Katerina giggled. "Oh, I wish I could have seen his face. I've always thought Herr Department's Youngest Investigator needed to be taken down a peg."

Ellie allowed herself a small smile but said nothing further, instead brushing a lock of golden blonde hair from her forehead and going back to her memorandum. It had been a very satisfying moment, it was true, but she knew that her mother would be mortified that she had so treated one of the rising young stars of the Gestapo's Department A. She could just hear the reproving voice now: *Elspeth, by the age of twenty-four, a dutiful Aryan daughter of the Reich should have already presented the Führer with her first future soldier or matron. Why, by the time I was your age, your father had spent most of our marriage at the Eastern Front, but we already had a son* and *a daughter. And to treat* such *a distinguished young officer that way!*

Down the corridor, the door to one of the investigators' offices opened, then closed again, followed by the approaching click of boot heels on the linoleum. *Sturmbannführer* von Hart appeared in the entranceway, half a dozen thick brown folders under one arm. He placed the folders on Ellie's desk. Paperclipped to the top folder was a scrap of paper bearing a handwritten list of six names.

Hart smiled at her without any warmth. "You can return these files to Central Records, Ellie." He tapped the scrap of paper. "And if you would be so good as to fetch these others while you're down there? Thank you."

"Of course, Herr Sturmbannführer." Gracefully, Ellie rose, skirted her desk and picked up the files. Hart did not step out of her way, and she had to lean in close against him as she reached for them. She could feel his eyes on her as she walked over to the door and opened it. She paused in the doorway and looked back over her shoulder; Hart did not exhibit the slightest embarrassment at being caught staring at her rear. "I'll just be a few moments, Herr Sturmbannführer," she said. "I'll bring the files to your office when I get back."

———————

FORTY-FIVE MINUTES later, having dropped Beauchamp off back at the Purification Museum, Quinn found a quiet alley where he could change into his black SS uniform. He stood across the street from the mammoth building before him and stared up at it: No. 8 Prinz Albrechstrasse, inner lair of the Gestapo.

He was curious about these meetings Beauchamp had mentioned, between the SS and the British embassy staff, and at the moment he had no better leads. Gnawing at the back of his mind was a desire to know why he had not been told of them. If Garner had attended, it could only have been as the representative of MI6, which meant the old man had to know about them. Even if they really were unimportant, their attendees were important men. It just did not feel quite right.

He headed across the street. Two Waffen-SS troopers were posted at the main entrance. They snapped to attention when they saw Quinn approach in his black lieutenant colonel's uniform. Quinn checked their insignia: one was a sergeant, the other a private. He addressed the sergeant.

"Good day, *Unterscharführer*," he said with a polite, if superior, nod.

The sergeant saluted in the Nazi style, his right arm held stiffly before him, with elbow, wrist, and fingers all ramrod straight.

"Herr *Obersturmbannführer*, sir," he said.

Quinn gestured to the Amt III insignia on his uniform. "You see this?"

The sergeant glanced at it and became even stiffer and straighter, if such was possible. "Yes, Herr Obersturmbannführer."

Quinn reached into the inside pocket of his greatcoat and pulled out the photograph of Richard Garner. "This man is a known British secret agent working at the Berlin embassy. Have you seen him before?"

The sergeant peered dutifully at the picture, obviously not understanding why he was being asked this question, then shook his head. Quinn showed the picture to the private but got the same response.

"I have reason to believe," he said, "that this man attended several meetings between members of the RSHA chain of command and officials from the British embassy. Do you know of such meetings?"

The sergeant faltered, his ingrained German fear of drawing attention to himself warring with his ingrained German fear of authority. The meetings were classified, and for a lowly soldier whose only knowledge of them came from whispered rumor, discussing them on the record was obviously something that caution dictated as unwise. Quinn could see this fear on his face, struggling with what would surely be an almost reflexive fear of Amt III.

Amt III won out. "I... have heard, Herr Obersturmbannführer," he said at last.

"Heard what?"

"About these meetings, Herr Obersturmbannführer."

"What about them?" Quinn pressed.

"Simply that they occur," the sergeant said. He fell silent, obviously not wanting to volunteer more than he had to. Wise, under the circumstances. Quinn simply stared at the man, and finally he conceded, "They happen, I am led to believe, about once a month. Have done so for the past year or more. The British officials arrive unobtrusively, through the entrance to the parking bay in the basement, in cars with darkened windows."

"And who attends these meetings?" Quinn asked.

Finally, though, the other fear had asserted itself. The sergeant hesitated, then said, "Men, Herr Obersturmbannführer, whom I would prefer not to name, if it is all the same to you. Men whose names I am sure you already know, if you already know of these meetings. One never knows who might be listening when one speaks of such matters."

Quinn nodded, not wanting to press the point. "Quite right, Unterscharführer. You are a very judicious man." He turned to the private. "Is there anything you have to add?"

The private shook his head. "No, sir."

"Very well, then," Quinn said, putting Garner's photo back in his pocket and turning back to the sergeant. "You have been very helpful. Thank you."

"You're welcome, sir," the sergeant said, visibly relieved that the interview now appeared to be over.

Quinn entered the building and emerged into the main lobby. It was a large, imposing, impersonal room, intended to make any newcomer to the inner sanctum of the world's most feared secret police feel suitably puny. The floor, a sea of green linoleum tiles, stretched away from him, combining with the whitewashed plaster walls to provide the room with a distinctly antiseptic, dehumanized flavor. At the opposite end of the lobby, a wide staircase led up to an archway leading to Prinz Albrechtsrasse's upper levels. There were similar archways leading into the labyrinthine innards at the ground level, two framing the staircase and one set into each side wall.

Quinn looked around, taking in the place in all its linoleum and plaster glory. He watched the people who would emerge from one of the archways, generally with manila or brown files under their arms, and walk purposefully to disappear through another, heels clicking smartly on the tile: male Gestapo officers in their feared all-black uniforms, female clerks in black skirts and white blouses.

There was an information desk to Quinn's right, with a female clerk seated behind it. Quinn walked up to it. "Where is the records office?" he asked.

The young woman flicked a glance at his Amt III insignia and pointed to one of the archways that framed the staircase. "Down that corridor, third door on the right, Herr Obersturmbannführer."

Quinn nodded. "Thank you, mein Fraulein."

He took the archway she indicated and soon came to a doorway over which hung a cream colored sign with "Central Records" stenciled on it in businesslike black letters. He turned into the doorway—and collided with a young female clerk carrying a stack of files against her chest.

The clerk stumbled backwards, and her files went flying. They hit the floor and slid along the linoleum tile with a hiss, their contents scattering down the corridor. The clerk was on her knees instantly, collecting folders and papers.

"I'm terribly sorry," Quinn said. He crouched down to help her gather them up. "I apologize, Fraulein—"

She glanced at him briefly, then returned her attention to the floor. She was startlingly beautiful—short blonde hair reaching to the bottom of her ears, cut in long bangs to frame her face; piercing blue eyes and fair skin. A poster girl for the Master Race.

"Think nothing of it, sir," she said brusquely, obviously intending to put an end both to his apology and to any further conversation.

She got smoothly to her feet, her files cradled in her arms, and

Quinn rose too and handed her the papers he had gathered up. He glanced at the nametag clipped to her collar—"E Voss"—and at the departmental badge beside it: IV-A2. Amt IV was the Gestapo, and Department A, Section 2 was—

"You work in Counter-Sabotage," Quinn said.

She had taken a step forward as if to leave, but Quinn was blocking her exit into the corridor. She gave the slightest of sighs and reluctantly nodded.

Counter-Sabotage was one of the sections that would deal with student resistance movements. Quinn fished Garner's picture out of his pocket. "Have you ever seen this man, mein Fraulein?"

———

ELLIE RECOGNIZED Garner's face immediately, of course. Nevertheless she studied it dutifully for several seconds, then shook her head. "No—" she glanced at the officer's rank insignia "—Herr Obersturmbannführer."

"You're sure?" he asked. "He's a British diplomat with contacts in the White Rose," his voice took on the slightest tinge of disgust, "and other such groups. You might have seen his photograph in a surveillance file." He was in his middle thirties, athletic and well-built, but there the resemblance ended between this Amt III Lieutenant Colonel and what one would expect of a senior investigator from one of the RSHA's elite divisions. He was dark-haired, dark-eyed, and dark-complexioned, with a prominent hook nose that a Propaganda Ministry missive would have to describe as patrician, while particularly unkind professional rivals might even resort to calling it Jewish. His hair was unkempt, and his face was unshaven.

She looked at the photograph again with an expression intended to convey that there was no possibility of her changing her answer. "No, Herr Obersturmbannführer," she said. "I have never seen this man, either in person or in a photograph." She affected an air of boredom and condescension. "With all due respect, sir, I am a clerical worker, not a Department Investigator. Rarely do my duties entail the study of surveillance photos of Reich undesirables. Herr Obersturmbannführer."

"I see," he said, the hint of an amused smirk at the corners of his mouth, and returned the picture to his pocket. He opened his mouth, apparently about to ask her something else, but thought better of it. "My thanks, mein Fraulein, and again, my apologies." He shifted his body slightly to the side, moving out of her way.

She nodded curtly, brushed past him and headed down the hall, her heels clicking smartly on the tile. She had seen him notice her when they were both crouched on the floor and she glanced back over her shoulder, expecting to find him staring after her as she retreated down the corridor, but he was not. He had disappeared inside the Central Records office. She frowned, surprised and vaguely disgusted with the slight twinge of disappointment she felt, then shuffled all that aside and continued on her way.

CHAPTER V

DENLINGER'S APARTMENT was not difficult to find, and his wristwatch had reached only five to six when Quinn rapped authoritatively on the door, now dressed once more in civilian clothing. The flat was located on the second floor of a decaying tenement nestled amongst a colony of decaying tenements a few blocks from the university.

Quinn had spent the afternoon at Prinz Albrechtstrasse, most of that time in Central Records, but had been able to unearth almost nothing about Beauchamp's meetings. What he had managed to turn up consisted only of oblique references—room reservations and a missive regarding the need for a "trustworthy" English interpreter to be made available. Only one document had caught his attention: a memo regarding the urgent need—Quinn suspected that haste had been the reason it was missed by whoever was being so careful that no other evidence of these meetings ended up in Central Records—to set up a meeting with a British representative to discuss the implementation of certain problematic aspects of the "Columbia-Haus protocol." Quinn had no idea what the Columbia-Haus protocol might be, but he was sure it was something he should find out. He was almost positive the phrase was a codeword of some kind. Columbia-Haus had been a Gestapo prison in the Reich's early days, but it had been abandoned as such, even before the invasion of Poland, and now stood derelict on the outskirts of Berlin.

Nor had anyone Quinn spoke to seemed to know anything, at least nothing anyone had been prepared to reveal under his cautious questioning. Quinn had his Amt III ID to protect him, and every German's natural reticence to draw attention by asking questions, but such safeguards would only go so far. If he asked too many people too many questions, someone was likely to start poking around to see where his authorization came from.

He knocked again on Denlinger's door. After a few moments it opened a crack, and Denlinger's gaunt, sallow face peered out suspiciously at him. After seeing that it was Quinn, he shut the door, and there was the sound of the chain being unfastened. Quinn couldn't help but be mildly amused at the caution. What would Denlinger do if he had opened the door to find the Gestapo waiting for him? Shut it tight and not let them in?

The door swung open, all the way this time, and Denlinger stepped aside to give Quinn just enough room to enter. He stepped through the doorway, but Denlinger, shutting the door behind him, stepped quickly in front of him to bar his way any further.

Quinn understood the gesture: the German did not want him in his flat, but neither did he want him out in the hall in public view while he told him as much.

"I've already asked around," Denlinger said. Quinn was not sure whether to read the hushed tone of his voice as conspiratorial or simply sullen. "No one here knows anything about Garner." *You're not wanted here. Leave.*

Quinn nodded, deliberately taking the words at face value. The flat was tiny and cramped. Quinn could see the gathered Resistance members over Denlinger's shoulder looking suspiciously at him. "I see. That is unfortunate. Well then, I'll just be needing to speak briefly with your associates, and then I'll be on my way." He held up his hand as Denlinger opened his mouth to object. "It's not that I don't trust you, Herr Denlinger. Of course not. But I still need to speak with people from your cell who have had contact with Garner, even if they don't know his current whereabouts." He smiled. "Don't worry, I don't want to disrupt. After you have finished your other business, of course."

Denlinger glanced uncertainly over his shoulder, to see if anyone else would come to his aid. The motion confirmed the opinion Quinn had formed when he first met the German student this afternoon: a coward, an intellectual who fancied himself a revolutionary. He would attend these meetings, tell people that he already knew agreed with him about the need for change, but he would never take action, never put himself in harm's way.

No one else spoke, and reluctantly Denlinger stepped back out of his way. "We were just about to start, Herr Kaufholz," he said, and paused, waiting for Quinn to ask his questions now, before the meeting started. Quinn simply waited, patiently staring at the Resistance leader. Denlinger shifted uncomfortably.

At last the young man said, "Go ahead. What is it you wanted to ask?"

"Nonsense, Herr Denlinger," Quinn said. "Please, I wouldn't want to delay your meeting any more than I already have. I can ask my questions after you're finished."

Denlinger looked around at the others in the room again, but still no one came to his aid. Reluctantly, he stepped across the room and resumed his seat, then began talking to the group, now obstinately ignoring Quinn. Quinn understood his reservations; being part of a Resistance cell, even one that just met and talked like this, had always been dangerous in Nazi Germany, but it must have gotten considerably more so since the student riots in Prague a few summers ago had brought a wave of government repression.

Quinn hung back in the shadows by the door, studying the room. It was sparsely furnished, almost bare. There were eight others besides Denlinger, five men and three women, some of them still watching him suspiciously, some now giving their attention to the meeting. None of them looked older than early twenties; they would all be university students. They had already taken up anything in the room that could serve as a seat: a couple of wooden chairs, a rickety stool, the kitchen counter. One woman was standing, off in the corner, out of the way.

Quinn's eyes paused on her; he smiled slightly when he realized who she was. She was staring at him, and a slight frown creased her forehead; she had recognized him, too, but she was unable to place him. That was only natural; even with the name of Richard Garner to make the association, this afternoon she would have seen only his uniform, not his face. Unobtrusively, he made his way over to stand next to her.

He nodded in greeting, facing the center of the room and the gathering but turning his head slightly so as to make eye contact with her. "Fraulein—Voss, isn't it?" he said, low enough for only her to hear. "You've changed out of your uniform. Probably appropriate in these surroundings."

Her eyes widened slightly as she realized who he was. He held up his hand to forestall whatever she was about to say. He nodded over her shoulder, at a door ajar next to which she stood, leading to the flat's only other room. She followed his look, then turned to him and nodded. As the two of them stepped through the doorway into a bedroom even smaller than the main room, Quinn shot a look back over his shoulder at the men and women in the room. Denlinger was still talking to the group, but was once again staring at him, an inscrutable look on his face.

Fraulein Voss wheeled on him as he closed the door silently behind them. "Who are you?" she demanded in a hushed, angry hiss.

"Peace, mein Fraulein, peace," Quinn said. "I am not an enemy. I am on your side."

She looked at him suspiciously. "And you expect me to just believe that? I'm not supposed to tell those people out there that you're from Amt III?"

"I am not from Amt III," he said. "Mein Fraulein, if I were trying to infiltrate the *Weisse Rose*—to what end? Just exactly what threat do you suppose those talkers and intellectuals out there pose to Germany? But if I *were* trying to infiltrate them, don't you think there are subtler ways of going about it?"

She stared at him, obviously conflicted. There was logic to what he said—but the German Reich was not a state where trust came naturally.

"Then what *are* you doing here?" she hissed. "And what are you? Why were you at Prinz Albrechtstrasse this afternoon?"

"The man I was asking about this afternoon—Richard Garner. Herr Denlinger informs me he has already asked your group here about him?" He waited until she had nodded in confirmation. "I am an associate of Herr Garner, mein Fraulein. A friend, perhaps. He has disappeared. I am trying to help him. Germans who believe as we do are all forced to engage in small deceptions for our safety, especially when we are as close to certain arms of the government as you or I." He paused. "For instance, I suspect that you were not being entirely truthful this afternoon when you told me you had never met Garner. Yes?"

She hesitated, then nodded again.

"Excellent," Quinn said. "Then perhaps you can help me, and, I hope, at the same time help Herr Garner and," he nodded in the direction of the meeting, the low voices of which were still reaching them through the partly open door, "the cause in which you believe?"

There was still hostility in her eyes. At last she shook her head. "No, no. I'm sorry, but I can't accept that. You were in an Amt III uniform this afternoon. If nothing else, even if you're not Gestapo, the others deserve to know that you're not what you say you are."

She took to a step toward the door, but reflexively Quinn reached up and grasped her upper arm. "Mein Fraulein, please—"

She twisted in his grip. "No," she said, her voice rising. "Let go of—"

She was silenced by a sudden, authoritative knocking at Denlinger's front door. The low voices in the other room were instantly silent as well.

For a few moments, no one in the flat moved, or even breathed. Those with their backs to the front door were not even willing to turn and face it.

The knocking came again. "Open up," a male voice demanded.

Quinn and Fraulein Voss stepped through the doorway into the main room, but went no further. Voss pulled the door closed behind them. Denlinger looked at each of them in turn, then around at the other faces in the room, as if willing any one of them to take the lead. At last he got uncertainly to his feet. He licked his lips and called, "Who is it?" His voice trembled.

"Open up on the authority of the Reich," the voice demanded. "We are here on state business. This residence has been selected for random inspection."

In four quick strides Quinn had crossed the room and grasped Denlinger by the shoulder. No one else moved.

"You have to get me out of here," he hissed in the other's ear.

Denlinger merely stared at him uncomprehendingly.

Quinn's grip on his shoulder tightened. "This is no random inspection, and you know it. They're looking for me. They're looking for a foreign agent. If they find a half dozen student dissidents in here, you'll be detained for a few days and placed under surveillance. But if they find me with you, you'll end up in a work camp." A work camp was a virtual death sentence.

This was far closer to active resistance than Denlinger would have ever willingly brought himself of his own volition. His jaw worked soundlessly for several moments. "For... foreign agent..."

The knock came again. "This is your last warning," the voice said. "Open up or you will be detained."

"A back door," Quinn pressed. "A fire escape."

At last Denlinger broke eye contact with him and moved, hesitantly at first, in the direction of the closed bedroom door behind Fraulein Voss. "Fire escape," he mumbled.

There was a much louder thud and the front door rattled in its frame as someone tried to break it down. It would not hold long—one more blow, maybe two. Denlinger reached past Voss and pushed the bedroom door open, then stepped through. Quinn followed, pulling the woman by the elbow after him.

Denlinger had stopped so abruptly that Quinn stumbled into him as he came through the doorway. He stepped back, ready to let out a mild curse, but the word died on his lips. The bedroom window was open, the iron bars of the fire escape visible beyond it. Blocking the window were five men who must have come up through the fire escape: a Gestapo officer in his forbidding black cap and gloves, black uniform and greatcoat, flanked on either side by two coalscuttle-helmeted Waffen-SS stormtroopers bearing submachine guns.

The officer's eyes had fastened on Quinn. He held what looked to be a small photograph by the thumb and forefinger of his left hand. He glanced down at the photograph, then back at Quinn. After a moment, he flicked the photograph round and held it out for Quinn to see.

Quinn broke the officer's gaze unwillingly, knowing all too well what the picture must be. He stared at it; it was an image of a man's face.

His own.

CHAPTER VI

DENLINGER SEEMED to have discarded his paralyzing indecision of a few moments before for pure, unthinking self-preservation. At the sight of the photograph, he turned round, pushed Quinn aside and went tearing back through the doorway into the main room.

For several agonizing seconds, no one else moved or said anything. At last, the Gestapo officer spoke. "Mr. Quinn?"

Quinn blinked; it took him a beat to register what the officer had said—and that he had spoken in English. "I'm sorry?" he said, in German.

The officer slipped the photograph into his greatcoat pocket and took a step forward, holding out a calming hand to reassure

Quinn and Fraulein Voss. He was probably just under thirty, with short fair hair and hazel eyes. "You are Simon Quinn, sir?" he asked. He spoke with a perfect upper middle class accent.

Quinn nodded, not sure what was going on.

"Captain James Barnes, sir," the officer introduced himself. "Royal Marines. We understood you might be in a spot of bother." He smiled and extended his hand.

Through the bedroom doorway came the loud crack of the front door splintering. Quinn stared at the proffered hand. The politeness was almost surreal; only a British officer could shake hands in such a situation. Tentatively, he clasped it.

Barnes stepped aside and nodded to the open window. "We should probably be getting a move on, sir."

Quinn nodded and stepped toward the window, but Fraulein Voss stayed where she was. He turned towards her. "You should come too," he said in German. "You work for the Gestapo. They can't find you at a *Weisse Rose* meeting."

"What's going on?" she demanded. "Who are you? Who are *they?*"

"We can sort all that out later," he said. "Whatever's going on, it's better than what's going to happen if you stay here."

She still did not move forward on her own, but she did not resist when he pulled her with him.

Two of the stormtroopers were first through the window, then Quinn. He poked his head tentatively over the fire escape rail to survey the alley below in the dim twilight, half expecting to see a squad of a dozen stormtroopers with submachine guns raised, waiting to arrest him—in which case he still could not say with confidence which side his apparent rescuers would be on. But there was only a nondescript, unmarked van, its engine running but its lights off, with two men dressed as stormtroopers—presumably two more Royal Marines—standing by its open back doors, watching the entrance to the alley intently.

Satisfied, Quinn turned and held out a helping hand for the woman. She ignored it, but still allowed Captain Barnes to support her by the elbow as she climbed through. By the time Barnes and the last two stormtroopers had followed, Quinn was already clambering down the metal ladder after the first two men.

He dropped the last few feet from the ladder to the ground, then reached up to grasp Fraulein Voss round the waist and lift her down. He felt her stiffen in his arms.

They were heading for the van when they heard the crunch of quick-marching feet approaching. An SS officer, Luger in hand, came round the alley corner at the head of a dozen armed stormtroopers. "Stop!" he cried when he saw the group at the van.

He came running toward Barnes, his eyes flicking between the captain, Quinn, and the woman. Quinn caught sight of the rank emblem on his greatcoat's lapel: *SS-Sturmbannführer,* a major. Barnes's emblem was that of an *SS-Hauptsturmführer,* a captain. The other officer outranked him.

"What are you doing back here?" the sturmbannführer demanded. "We're supposed to be the only ones back here. Who are these prisoners?"

Barnes opened his mouth, obviously searching for something to stay. Quinn stepped forward, reaching into his inside pocket. The sturmbannführer stepped back quickly, raising his automatic pistol, but hesitated when he realized that Barnes's stormtroopers were not doing anything to restrain their supposed prisoner.

"These men are under my command," Quinn said as he pulled his ID from his pocket and flipped it open. "Herr Sturmbannführer," he added significantly.

The officer snapped to attention when he saw the lieutenant colonel's badge on Quinn's ID and hastily holstered his pistol. "Yes, Herr Obersturmbannführer," he said. He hesitated, then pressed on, "But if I may say, sir, there is still supposed to be no one else back here. I am under orders."

Quinn waved his ID dismissively, then slid it back into his pocket. "The incompetence of the other branches of the RSHA does not concern me, Herr Sturmbannführer—at least, not today." The sturmbannführer blanched; clearly he had also seen the ID's Amt III badge. Quinn gestured toward Fraulein Voss. "This woman is the true target of this operation. Your raid has been ordered as a cover to ensure that my men were able to get her into custody safely and with a minimum of commotion. To be quite frank, I couldn't care less whether your superiors notified you of this. Now you will stand aside and allow me to continue with my duty."

The sturmbannführer was clearly unsure, but after only a beat his natural German fear of authority won out. He clicked his heels together and snapped off a crisp Nazi salute, right arm extended straight forward, fingers extended and palm down. Quinn returned the salute with an air of practiced superiority; Barnes saluted also—though slightly awkwardly, Quinn noticed—then turned and nodded to his men.

The first two "stormtroopers" climbed into the back of the van, the woman between them. Quinn and Barnes followed. Then came the rest of the troopers. When the last two had slammed the van doors shut behind them and everyone was seated on one of the two benches that ran down either side of the van's length, Barnes turned and called to the stormtrooper who had been waiting for them in the driver's seat, "All aboard, Gunning."

"Right, sir," the trooper responded. He flicked the headlights on and put the van into gear.

Barnes turned back to Quinn, sitting opposite him, as the van started to move. The Royal Marines captain smiled affably. "Thank you, Mr. Quinn," he said. "Might have been a bit of a sticky situation you got us out of back there."

Quinn nodded to acknowledge the thanks. "I think, Captain," he responded, "not so sticky as the one out of which you just got me."

Barnes touched the brim of his cap with two fingers of his right hand in desultory salute. Quinn smiled at the gesture—the salute had been Western, not German. "Not quite comfortable with the German salute, are you, Captain?" he asked.

Barnes shrugged and returned the smile, a touch ruefully. "We try to discourage saluting except where absolutely necessary when we're out like this," he said. "Never know when one of the lads might forget himself and snap off a good British salute without thinking about it."

"Or a German salute by accident when he's in a British uniform," Quinn added.

Barnes looked genuinely horrified. "Oh no, Mr. Quinn," he said. "Not one of our lads. Never."

Quinn chuckled and leaned back against the van wall, expelling a great breath of air. It was only now that he was becoming aware of just how fast his heart was pounding.

Fraulein Voss was seated next to him, staring straight ahead at the opposite wall. "Are you all right?" he asked her.

She didn't respond, so he touched her forearm. She jerked it away and shot him a venomous glance. "You're a spy," she hissed.

He nodded. "I am."

She made a curt gesture around the van. "These men are all American spies."

"British, actually," he said.

She looked at his hand, which he had not moved since she pulled away from it. "Do not touch me," she said.

Quinn shrugged to show acceptance. They lapsed into silence.

After a few moments, Quinn spoke to Barnes. "How did you know where I was?" he asked. "How did you know there'd be trouble?"

"Your chaps got word through one of their usual sources that a raid was planned," Barnes said. That would be MI6. "So the embassy sent us out to look after you." Before Quinn could press him further, he said, "We'll be headed back there now, Mr. Quinn. To the British embassy. Where would you like us to drop you off?"

"Where would you like to be dropped off?" Quinn asked Fraulein Voss in German.

"Any U-bahn station will be fine," she said. "Preferably on the southern line."

"Are you sure?" Quinn said. "They can get you closer to home than that."

"The U-bahn will be more than sufficient, thank you," she said tartly.

Barnes called to the driver, "Gunning, how close are we to a subway station on the southern line?"

"Um—I think there should be one just over the Stalingrad Bridge, sir. Another five minutes or so."

They rode the rest of the way in silence. It was actually closer to ten minutes when the van eventually pulled up to the curb and stopped. Barnes nodded to the two troopers at the end of either bench, and they swung the back doors open. Quinn went first, followed by Fraulein Voss. Again she ignored his proffered hand and climbed down herself.

Quinn nodded to Barnes. "My thanks, Captain."

Barnes smiled. "Just doing my duty, Mr. Quinn." He nodded to the troopers and obediently they pulled the doors shut. A moment later the van pulled away from the curb and back into the evening traffic.

They were next to the entrance to a U-bahn station, but Fraulein Voss had not yet descended the steps. She was watching him.

After a few moments of this, Quinn extended his arm toward the U-bahn entrance. "Aren't you going to go?" he asked.

"I'm waiting to see which way you go first," she said. He arched his eyebrows, and she added, "I want to make sure you don't have any ideas about accompanying me."

He smiled and made a gesture of concession. "That was indeed my intent, I'm afraid."

"Don't bother," she said. "I'll be fine on my own."

"I'd rather satisfy myself of that," he said. "But that's not why I was going to follow you. I still need to speak with you about Richard Garner."

She looked at him with disgust. "I have nothing to say to a spy," she said and brushed past him, descending the steps.

"I thought we were supposed to be on the same side," he called after her. "You *are* in the Resistance, are you not?"

She paused, turned back and looked up at him. "I do what I do for Germany," she said. "I want what I believe is best for Germany, and that is not the National Socialist Regime. But I am not a spy. I am not a traitor. I would never betray Germany."

"The men you work for at Prinz Albrechtstrasse would take a different view of your activities."

"The men I work for at Prinz Albrechtstrasse are the evil from which I wish to save Germany," she said. "But I wish to remove them and the regime they support for Germany's good. I do not wish to betray Germany altogether. I am a member of the *Weisse Rose*, not an American or an *English* spy."

"But you work with an English spy," Quinn countered. "Richard Garner works with the *Weisse Rose*. Isn't that treachery to Germany?"

She let out a frustrated sigh. "I will not stand here in the cold playing word games with you. Yes, Richard Garner has attended meetings of our cell. Yes, there may be times when we in the Resistance can sometimes help Germany by working with a foreign power. But Richard Garner has never incited me or anyone else that I know of to treachery against the Fatherland, and if he did I would refuse. I would not betray Germany for him or anyone else." She stared pointedly at Quinn, then started to turn away again.

"Spy or no," he called after her, "I am trying to help Germany now." She paused but did not turn toward him. "Richard Garner has disappeared, mein Fraulein. We think he may have gone over to the Ger— to the National Socialists. I want to find him and find out if that is true, before events spiral out of control and damage is done, to both sides, that cannot be undone." He looked up, scanned the shop fronts on the other side of the street. "There's a café over there that's still open. Let me buy you a cup of coffee, and you can hear me out. Then you can decide if you wish to help me, mein Fraulein. And if you do not, I shall leave you alone. I give you my word."

She was silent awhile, considering. At last, she turned and walked back up the steps. She stopped in front of him and stared up at him, absently brushing a strand of golden hair from her face. "I will listen to what you have to say," she said, still no friendliness in her crystal blue eyes. "But only," she held up a cautionary finger, "so long as I believe you are not asking me to betray Germany." The street was empty; she looked around, saw the café he was indicating and headed across to it. He stood at the U-bahn entrance and stared after her retreating figure.

CHAPTER VII

WHEN MI6 had first recruited him out of Army Intelligence in 1956, Quinn and a half dozen other recruits had been transported by plane during the night to an RAF base whose location they were not told—Quinn suspected it was in Gibraltar—there to undergo their training program's first phase, the primary purpose of which was to disabuse them thoroughly of any notions they might possess about glamour and adventure in Her Majesty's Secret Intelligence Service. The program had begun with a lecture from a grizzled veteran who had lost an eye, two fingers, and several teeth to SS questioning when he had been captured in the Channel Isles during the war.

"After all the millions and millions of bombs dropped in Europe and

the Pacific over six years," he had said with his odd Guernsey accent, *"it took only three to change the world. The Americans dropped two, on Hiroshima and Nagasaki, and the Jerries dropped one in reply, on London. With those three bombs we stepped into a new age. For now, if we continue to allow ourselves free rein in our warfare, to give vent to our hatreds with all the weapons at our disposal, we could very easily blow the entire human race into extinction. We now have to limit ourselves in how we fight each other, to move our warfare into different spheres.*

"The threat of the atomic bomb has forced us to limit our wars waged with traditional methods—in Siberia and Algeria, and now our conflict with Egypt and Italy over the Suez Canal—to small-scale sideshows. Now, men like us fight the battles that truly determine the fate of humanity. We wage wars of secrets, silence, and deception.

"Never delude yourselves into thinking that our ultimate goal is the demise of Nazi Germany and her European satellites. That's what the men in London, in Washington and Berlin, tell their peoples, and probably even what they believe themselves. But they're wrong. Quite the contrary, victory in this 'cold' war—for either side—is exactly what we want to avoid. The fall of one side will mean massive upheaval, and with such upheaval our enemies, and even our friends, become scared and unpredictable. Our goal is the prevention of atomic war, and we can only achieve this through the preservation of stability. Today you take the first step into a world where deception marks every aspect of your life, and this is the first deception you must learn. Pray learn it well."

Quinn had taken easily to a life of casual deception, as deception had been a part of his life since the day he ran away from home to join the Army. Now, as he sat down in the iron chair and slid the girl's coffee across the table to her, he considered how much of what he might be about to tell her would be truth, and how much deception. It would not *all* be a lie, of that he could already be certain—that was the mistake of the amateur. No, the truth was always mixed in to a degree. When done correctly, it should no longer be possible to tell where the truth ended and the deception began.

For a while they sat in silence. Quinn checked his watch: a quarter past nine. His eye wandered along the shop fronts he could see over the Fraulein's shoulder: a bookshop and a travel agent's. The bookshop had replaced whatever bestsellers it might have been displaying in its window with stacks of *Mein Kampf*, the Führer's National Socialist manifesto written in the 1920s, and its sequel *Mein Sieg*, his memoir of the National Socialist triumph, published in the 1960s. The travel agent's had hung black draperies in its window, but not so as to obscure its large color photographs of a Norwegian fjord at high summer or a smiling German family assembled in front of the Eiffel Tower, a swastika flag visible, flapping from its peak.

"So," he said at last, "what do you want to know?"

She set her coffee down and pursed her lips. "Who are you? You work for the English government?"

Quinn nodded. "As long as I'm in Germany. My association with the British government ends when I leave the Reich." Truth.

"And you're not a German? You're an Englishman?"

After a pause he said, "I'm a British subject, yes." True enough, though he deliberately sidestepped the question.

She leaned forward. "What's your name?"

"Matthias Kaufholz. Have I earned a question of my own?"

"No. What's your real name?"

"Simon Quinn." Deception. Before she could ask anything

further he pushed on, "But it seems to me only fair, Fraulein Voss, that now that you have my name, I have yours in return."

She sat back, crossing her arms across her chest and studying him. "Elspeth," she said at last. "I prefer Ellie."

He smiled. "Ellie," he repeated. "A very pretty name."

She ignored him. "How do you know Richard Garner?"

"I don't. I've been sent to find him." Truth.

"He's defected?"

He spread his hands, which had been cradling his coffee cup, on the table, palms upward. "We don't know. He's disappeared. He's taken some very sensitive information with him. It's what I'm here to find out." Truth.

"What do *you* think has happened to him?"

"I don't know, mein Fraulein. If he *has* defected, he's in a position to greatly compromise British security. I need to prevent that from happening." Truth. "If he hasn't, I need to find out what has happened, and help him if I can." Deception. "How well do you know him?"

She shook her head. "Not well at all. I fear there's nothing I can do for you. What do you mean, you're only working for the English as long as you're in Germany? Are you planning on leaving soon? What kind of spy are you?"

"A retired one, by preference. I parted ways with the Secret Intelligence Service four years ago. I am here—as a favor, you could say."

"Why? Why did you come back? Why did they want you to?"

"To find Garner. They need to find him, to know what happened to him. In this business, instability is the greatest enemy. The situation is very unstable right now." Truth.

"Because of the Führer's death."

Quinn nodded. She was perceptive for someone who had never done this. Ellie was silent for a moment, considering this, and he took advantage. "Have you ever spoken with Garner? Outside of a *Weisse Rose* meeting, perhaps?"

She shook her head.

"Come across him in your work?"

Another shake of the head. "I don't deal with spies. That's another department. Besides, I'm only a clerical worker. Why did you leave in the first place?" she asked.

He considered. "A traumatic experience," he said at last. Truth.

"What do you mean?" He hesitated, and she said, "I can get up and leave now if I don't trust you."

He nodded. "I ran an operation to get copies of some crucial Wehrmacht documents into British hands. The Germans killed one of my principal operatives." Karl. Quinn hesitated.

Quinn spun around to see what was happening, but the headlights glared so brightly that he had to throw his hands up in front of his eyes to shield them. All he managed to catch was a glimpse of Karl, standing transfixed in the headlights' beam.

He forced himself to put the memory away. "They killed him," he said again. He swallowed and continued more firmly, "And I was shot and almost died, but we got the documents out. Because we did, a lot of people died who wouldn't have otherwise. I had a... disagreement with my superiors over the relative success of the operation."

She frowned. "What do you mean?"

He took a deep breath. "The documents contained the initial plans for the Croat invasion of Greece. Because British intelligence gained access to them, the British and American garrisons in Greece were prepared for the invasion and were able to prevent themselves from being overrun long enough for the Greek forces to mount a resistance. My superiors therefore considered the operation a success."

For a moment Ellie said nothing. Then, hesitantly, "You—you started the war in Greece?"

Quinn felt defensive. "I allowed Greece to defend itself."

"But without what you did, we would have overrun the country—it would all have been over within days, maybe weeks."

He couldn't tell what was going on behind her eyes, but he held her gaze nonetheless. "You can choose to hate me if you want, mein Fraulein. You may have brothers in Greece, or a fiancé. They may have *died* in Greece, I don't know. But I have borne this cross every day for four years. I must bear it in my own way."

She did not respond. She was no longer looking at him, just staring at an indeterminate point over his shoulder. When at last she refocused on him and opened her mouth to speak, he expected either a condemnation or a refusal to work with him any further. Instead she said only, "It must be very hard."

Quinn met her gaze. Then he drained the last of his coffee and set the empty cup on the table. "I think, mein Fraulein, that we have accomplished all here that we can. I thank you for taking the time to speak with me and apologize for detaining you unnecessarily." He rose to leave.

"Wait." She reached out a hand to his wrist to stop him. She looked up at him. "What time is it?"

He checked his wristwatch. "A little before ten."

"You have a place to stay?"

He shook his head. "I haven't had time to find one. I only arrived in Berlin this afternoon."

"You'll never find a hotel now," she said. "The city will be packed with mourners for the Führer." She hesitated, then went on, "You may stay at my flat. You can sleep on the settee."

"Are you sure that's a good idea?"

Her eyebrow arched. "I have my reservations, but I have made the offer."

He thought, then finally inclined his head. "Very well then, mein Fraulein. I thank you for your generosity."

She rose, and they walked across the street and descended the U-bahn station steps. He paid her fare. They waited ten minutes for the next train to arrive. All this occurred in silence. Only after they were seated and settled on the U-bahn did Ellie say, rather distantly, "Two." She was not looking at him.

Quinn frowned. "Mein Fraulein?"

"I have two brothers in Greece. Both junior officers with the *Panzerkorps.*" She smiled ever so slightly. "No fiancé." The smile faded, and she went on, "Hans was injured last year in the action at Thessalonika. He won the German Cross for it. Neither of them are dead, though. Not yet." She considered a moment. "They would not be proud if they knew I was in the *Weisse Rose.*"

He hesitated, unsure of how to respond. In the end he elected on silence.

After a while she asked, "How long were you a spy?"

"Eleven years. And five in the army before that."

"That's where they found you? The English spy service? In the army?"

"Yes."

"What did you do there?"

"I was a tank driver at first. With the 8th King's Royal Irish Hussars in Siberia." He paused. "I have something of a way with languages. I learned Russian fairly easily while I was there. Then I was captured by the Germans, but escaped after three weeks, and when I made it back behind the British lines I'd picked up a fair amount of German. So I ended up in the Intelligence Corps. That's where MI6 found me."

She said nothing for a long time, and Quinn assumed the conversation had ended. But then she murmured, "We each serve our country in the best way we can." He wasn't entirely sure whether she was talking to him or to herself.

After that they rode on in silence.

PART 2

CONFLICT

All nations want peace, but they
want a peace that suits them.

—ADMIRAL LORD FISHER
OF KILVERSTONE

CHAPTER VIII

ELLIE'S SETTEE was old and threadbare, but Quinn slept comfortably nonetheless; four years in Siberia with, frequently, his tank as his only shelter had taught his body to take its sleep whenever it was offered. He awoke automatically at seven and was surprised to find Ellie already up and about.

She was in the kitchen; he could hear her footsteps and the quiet opening and closing of cupboards. He could also hear the tinny sounds of martial music—Wagner, he imagined, though he did not know the piece—issuing from a cheap radio in another room. He had no doubt that that would be all that was playing on any of the radio stations, in memoriam of the late Führer.

He yawned and stretched, then sat up. Like Denlinger's flat—like most urban flats for the unmarried in Germany—Ellie's was state-owned, small, and cramped. The main room, where he had spent the night, was about five meters by three. Two doors along one wall led, respectively, to the kitchen and the only bedroom.

Quinn folded up the blanket Ellie had given him, then stepped across the room to its small single window and peeked through the blinds. The uniform, impersonal concrete face of another block of state flats stared back at him. The sky was overcast and forbidding, the clouds hanging very low. There was very little car or foot traffic in the street below. A public bus trundled by, but the bus stop was deserted and the bus did not stop.

He heard Ellie's footsteps stop in the kitchen doorway, but did not turn to see her.

"Spies rise early, it seems," she said at last.

"Apparently not as early as some," he responded, and only then turned round to her. She was wearing a pink cardigan and long, pale brown skirt that might have been fashionable in the States fifteen years ago, or in Britain five years after that. Her low-heeled cream pumps looked to be made of some sort of faux leather and had probably been manufactured in one of the Eastern Reich Commissariats like Kiev or Moscow, on an assembly line staffed by emaciated, toothless Slavic slave laborers. She had already washed, and her short, straight, shiny gold hair was brushed in bangs that left her forehead exposed and ran along her cheeks, neatly framing her face in soft, shallow curves.

She held a tray with two empty glasses, two plates each bearing a pair of French pastries and a couple of slices of orange. She set the tray down on the small dining table near the kitchen entrance, then walked over to the front door, unbolted it, and opened it. She brought inside a single bottle of milk that was waiting there for her, closed the door, and bolted it again.

"I hope milk is all right," she said, crossing the room back over to the table.

Quinn waved his hand airily. "More than I could ask, mein Fraulein."

"You've spent the night in my home," she said matter-of-factly as she poured two glasses of milk. "It's probably all right for you to call me by my name."

He smiled. "Ellie."

Two glasses poured, she sat down, took one of the plates from the tray and began eating one of the orange slices. Quinn stood at the window, watching her.

She glanced up at him. "Is there something I should know about the table I set, mein Herr? Probably not quite so glamorous as you're used to in your world, I'm sure, but it's the best I could do on such notice."

"I've spent the night in your home," he said. "Call me Simon."

She glanced up. "For now, I'm happy with mein Herr."

He crossed the room, sat down at the table and picked up a pastry. "Is today your day off?" he asked, nodding at her clothing.

"It's everybody's day off," she explained. "It was on the radio. Days of National Remembrance, today and tomorrow. And of course for the Führer's funeral on Friday."

Quinn nodded. It was a logical step; evidently someone in the Reich bureaucracy had finally been willing to assert himself sufficiently to take it.

They ate in silence. Quinn studied the cover of a celebrity

magazine lying on the table. It bore a photo of Gustav Gründgens, the elder statesman of German cinema who, according to the caption, played the Pope in Riefenstahl's latest film, *Charlemagne.*

After a few minutes Ellie asked, "What will you do now?"

"I don't know," Quinn admitted. "I seem to be out of leads at the moment. All I have is that Garner was participating in clandestine meetings at Prinz Albrechtstrasse between officials of the British embassy and the RSHA."

She frowned. "Really?"

He nodded. "But that's come to naught. The only thing I've been able to find is a reference to something called the 'Columbia-Haus protocol.'" He noticed the look on her face. "Why? Do you know something about this?"

She opened her mouth to say something, then evidently changed her mind. "No," she said instead. She shook her head but was unable to meet his gaze. "No, this is the first I've heard of anything like that." She busied herself, putting their empty plates and glasses back on the tray, then gathering it up and carrying it through to the kitchen.

Quinn turned in his seat to follow her. "Ellie," he said, "if there's something you know, I need you to tell me."

She tossed the orange rinds into the dustbin, deposited the tray's contents into the kitchen sink, and turned on the tap, moving her hand back and forth through the flow of water to check that it was heating. She glanced up at him. "You forget," she said, "that I haven't yet decided that I'm helping you." After a moment, she added, "Besides, it's not like I really know anything. I've just heard of Columbia-Haus, nothing more. No more than you've already learnt, and probably far less."

Quinn remained silent, knowing when it was time to back off.

Satisfied with the water temperature, Ellie took some soap and a rag from beside the sink and set to scrubbing the dishes.

After a while she asked, "What will happen if you don't find Garner?" Her attitude was affectedly offhand, but Quinn was fairly sure it was an act. "I mean, spies have defected before. It's not like there'll be an atomic war."

Quinn shrugged. "If we knew what the consequences could be, we probably wouldn't need to find him so desperately. Atomic war? I doubt it. But even among the mildest of possible consequences, he could divulge to the SS the identities and locations of every British agent in West Prussia. If that happens, those men and women are dead—if they're lucky, before they're subjected to days or even weeks and months of Gestapo custody." He rose and stepped into the kitchen doorway. "Ellie, I understand this is hard for you, but if there's anything you can tell me, I beg you to do so. Nuclear war? I pray not. But regardless, lives *do* hang in the balance."

"Lives of English spies and *Germans* they have incited or blackmailed into treachery," she countered, but there was no venom behind the words and she couldn't bring herself to meet his eyes as she said them.

Several minutes of silence followed. She finished washing the dishes and turned off the tap. She was a fairly small woman, and Quinn watched as she had to stand on her tiptoes and reach up, stretching, to place the clean dishes comfortably in the cupboard above the sink. When she had finished, she turned to face him, crossing her arms and leaning against the kitchen counter.

At first she only looked at him. He waited silently. "Garner has a—a girlfriend, I suppose," she said at last. "Gertrud. She's a professor of medieval literature at Friedrich Wilhelm. Every once in a while she comes to a *Weisse Rose* meeting. That's where they met. She wasn't at the meeting last night. I don't think they're much more than good friends, but if anyone knows where he's gone, my guess—and I don't know either of them very well—is that she does."

"Do you know where she lives?"

She shook her head, but not in answer to his question. "She won't talk to you. But she *will* talk to me."

"No," Quinn said. "You shouldn't be involved in something like this. This could very quickly get very dangerous."

She held up a cautionary finger. "I'm afraid I *am* involved. I have no choice, at least not till I've satisfied myself that you really aren't betraying Germany." Her expression as she gazed at him was not defiant or challenging, but neither did it look open to argument.

Quinn sighed and nodded. "All right."

"Good." She flashed a smile. "She lives on the other side of the river. We can leave in just a few minutes if you'd like." Her forehead creased slightly in the mildest of frowns as she looked him up and down. "But first," she decided, "you should shower. And shave."

———

ELLIE WAS half listening to the solemn voices intoning the Roman Catholic mass on Gertrud's television, instead gazing out at the peaceful suburban street. Ellie herself lived in the city, where the residents were unmarried; there the flats were tiny, as were the windows, forcing the occupants to rely on electric lighting to provide illumination, and the walls were made of plain concrete. It was all designed to encourage the inhabitants to do their duty to the Reich, find a mate and receive a nice home like this, in the suburbs.

For in the suburban communities public housing projects could be quite imaginative and inviting; a newlywed couple, young and ready to start providing the Führer with the litter of strong, healthy Aryans he expected of them, applying to the Reich for a home might expect to be assigned a thatched, whitewashed Tyrolese cottage like this one, straight out of Hansel and Gretel, situated in a pleasant, tree-lined avenue of two dozen identical such cottages.

The street of happy little cottages was deserted, a combination of the Day of National Remembrance and the unpleasant look to the overcast sky, which, just for good measure, rumbled threateningly every quarter of an hour or so. Quinn's Focke-Wulf was parked by the opposite curb; its windows were tinted and she couldn't see him waiting in the driver's seat. The two of them had taken the U-bahn to retrieve it from where he had left it, a few streets over from Jürgen Denlinger's flat, before they came here. She had wanted to go knock on Jürgen's door, but he had said that it was too dangerous. She thought about insisting, but decided not to. In the first place, he was right; the flat was sure to be under surveillance, and if the Gestapo really had been there looking for Quinn last night, they probably still had a man or two they had left behind to detain anyone who showed up subsequently. And in the second place, even if they were just detaining Jürgen and releasing him, they probably still wouldn't have finished processing him yet, and would still have him in custody.

Ellie turned away from the window and back toward Gertrud's living room. The room was furnished with some of the finer things the Reich government had made available to its middle class:

Italian furniture, Persian rugs, Spanish oranges in a bowl on the coffee table. Photographs of Gertrud and her late husband—who, as Ellie understood it, had also taught at the university—crowded the ornate mahogany mantelpiece. The Reich strongly encouraged all its citizens to spend their leisure time in travel, and the pictures had been taken at sites throughout Germany—Saint Stephen's in Vienna, the Old Town Clock Tower in Prague, and the Kremlin in Moscow—and in several of the major cities of the European satellite states. Ellie recognized Paris, Rome, Budapest, and one or two others.

She returned her gaze to the screen just as the remembrance mass for the Führer was concluding. "This mass is ended," the cardinal archbishop intoned solemnly. "Go in peace to love and serve the Lord."

"Thanks be to God," the congregation responded ritually, and then, as the Reich required all religious ceremonies to conclude, added, "and God bless our Führer, Adolf Hitler."

Tinny organ music replaced the sound of voices, and the assembly of attendants surrounding the cardinal archbishop at the altar began to proceed down the cathedral's aisle. Gertrud, about forty years old with dark hair that was just beginning to grey, sighed, rose from her chair, and turned off the television.

"I didn't know you were Catholic," Ellie said.

Gertrud nodded. "For those of us who reject the German Faith and still cling to the old churches, National Socialism doesn't encourage us to make too public our religion." She shrugged and changed the subject, forcibly brightening her tone. "I thank you for letting me finish watching the mass, but you've allowed me to be a poor hostess. Would you like something to eat?"

Ellie shook her head, indicating the teacup sitting before her on the coffee table with a nod of her head. "No, but thank you. The tea is fine."

"Are you sure?" Gertrud pressed.

"I'm sure."

Gertrud nodded in acceptance and sat back down again, taking her own teacup up from the table and sipping at it, then holding it in her lap. An awkward silence followed. Suddenly, her look turned wistful once more and she glanced at the television again. "You know," she said, "I'm surprised. I've spent most of my life disagreeing with the Führer, wanting the National Socialist government removed and an end to the constant war he has brought on our borders. But still—he's *dead*. It feels so strange, no?"

Ellie nodded. She understood just what the other woman meant. She asked, "Are you old enough to remember before he was in office?"

Gertrud chuckled. "Bless you, dear, I may look it to someone of your age, but I'm not *that* old. I was eighteen months old when President von Hindenburg appointed the Führer Chancellor, far too young to remember." She considered Ellie. "But then again, *you're* not even old enough to remember the war itself, are you?"

Ellie blushed and shook her head.

"How old are you, my dear?" Gertrud asked.

She hesitated, then admitted, "I'm twenty-four."

"Why bless!" Gertrud said. "I bet you've never even seen a Jew, have you? A *real* Jew, I mean, not just pictures."

"Once," Ellie said. "When I was very young, and my father was stationed in the East."

Gertrud nodded. "The East. Of course. I would imagine they were around for longer there." She set her empty teacup down.

"But talking like this makes me feel old, and I'd like to think I'm still young enough not to feel that way."

Ellie understood the subtext: *Obviously you haven't come here to talk about this. So what* have *you come to discuss?*

She took a breath and said, "I'd like to ask you about Richard Garner."

Gertrud's face had been open, friendly; now all of a sudden, it became a closed, blank mask. "What about Richard?" she asked.

"You know he's disappeared?"

"No," Gertrud said, quickly. "No, I hadn't heard that." She rose and turned, about to step away, then seemed to be unable to think of anywhere to go, and stopped. Instead she turned back around and bent over the coffee table, gathering the teacups and teapot onto the tray to take them back into the kitchen. But Ellie's cup, sitting on the table, was still half full. Gertrud's hand hovered over it, as if she was unsure how to proceed.

Ellie leaned forward and gently placed the teacup in her hand. Gertrud glanced up at her, smiled gratefully, and deposited the cup on the tray. Then she straightened, leaving the tray where it was on the table.

"I—I understood something was wrong," she conceded, "though I didn't know that it was anything drastic. What do you mean, 'disappeared'? Ellie," she leaned forward, her eyes narrowing, "you don't know Richard. He's not a concern of yours. Who are you here for? There have been some in the group who've said that a Gestapo worker shouldn't be allowed among us, that it's too dangerous, but I've always believed you when you've told us that your employers don't know where your sympathies lie. But if you're here for them—"

"No, no. Gertrud, no." Ellie shook her head, leaning earnestly forward in her chair. "Gertrud, this has nothing to do with the Gestapo."

"Then who *does* it have to do with, Ellie?"

Ellie sighed. "I'm going to have to tell you." She pursed her lips, then went on, "Honestly, Gertrud? It's the English."

"The English?"

She nodded. "He's vanished. They're trying to find him."

"And what does that have to do with you?" Gertrud asked.

"It's a long story. I'm—I have a friend who's trying to find him. For the English. Not for the Gestapo, Gertrud. They have no idea I'm here, or that I even know who Richard Garner is. They're not going to come looking for you about him, at least not from me. I swear it."

Gertrud regarded her suspiciously for several long moments. At last she sat down. "What do they think has happened to him? The English? Do they think the Gestapo have got him?"

Ellie shook her head. "I don't know. But I *do* know that they have no idea where to look. At the moment, you're our—you're *their* only hope."

Gertrud looked at her uncertainly. "If it's the English who are looking for Richard, then they wouldn't hurt him, would they? He's one of theirs, after all."

Ellie shook her head. *No, they wouldn't hurt him.* She couldn't bring herself to agree aloud.

Gertrud took a deep breath, then admitted, "There had been something wrong for a while. We only see each other once every two or three weeks, but the last couple of times I could tell there was something bothering him. I never asked him about it. We didn't talk about... about his work. Then, a few days ago—" She hesitated.

Ellie leaned forward and laid a comforting hand on her knee. Gertrud smiled.

"A few days ago," she continued, "I got a call from him. He said—he said that we weren't terribly close, and I probably wouldn't be in any danger. He said he thought they would leave me alone. But he said that there was a chance they wouldn't, and that if anything happened I should—he gave me a number I should call."

"Can I have the number?" Ellie asked.

Gertrud pressed her lips together, but, after the briefest of moments, nodded.

———

QUINN SAT drumming his fingers against the top of the steering wheel and staring out the window at Gertrud's quaint little house across the street. He had turned the car radio off some time ago; he was on edge quite enough as it was, and the constant stream of Wagnerian opera and Bruckner concertos only exacerbated his tension.

The girl's—Ellie's—involvement had come as a surprise, and he didn't think it was a good idea. He had now more than satisfied himself that she knew nothing about Garner or the elusive Columbia-Haus protocol beyond scraps of rumor that might make their way around Prinz Albrechtstrasse. It was true that she was both Gestapo and *Weisse Rose,* either one of which would be enough to turn her into a potentially useful source, but on further analysis, all she really amounted to was a minor clerical worker who attended meetings of a student Resistance group that sat around and expressed intellectual dissatisfaction with the Nazi Regime while doing absolutely nothing to change it. She would have made a useful investment, well worth his time and energy, when he had been working long-term in British service. But not now. Now he just needed to find Garner, complete his mission and get back to the Med.

But she was troublesome. He had been too open with her last night, told her more than he should. He still had not won her over, and he was well aware of it. By speaking so freely with her, by trusting her now to talk with Garner's girlfriend, he was placing himself in her power, and she could turn around at any second and betray him to the Gestapo. She had evidenced an obvious distaste for him and his work. He suspected that, at least initially, the only thing that had stopped her from notifying the authorities about him would be that then she would have had to explain that she was a member of the *Weisse Rose*. Yet the more time he spent with her, the more sure he became that, even if she decided to turn him away, she would tell no one else of him.

He was rusty; he hadn't been a spy in a long time. He knew what Isaac would have said. He would have tutted, just as he had during the long and painful hours he had spent teaching Quinn football, or how to ride his bicycle, and said, *"You need practice, little one. Take your time, think about what you are doing. You're letting yourself get in over your head."* Quinn hated being called *little one;* that was why Isaac did it.

Unbidden, his older brother's image came into his mind, the way he had appeared the last time they had seen each other: Quinn had been nine, Isaac had been seventeen, dressed in his new private's uniform, standing at the garden gate, ready to march off to North Africa. Their mother had been crying; their father had somberly shook Isaac's hand and clasped him on the shoulder without saying a word. Sarah, only four years old, had been clutching her Peter Rabbit doll and crying, nominally over a bruised knee but, Quinn suspected, in reality because it was Isaac who was getting the attention rather than she. Quinn, wanting to be accepted by the grownups, had aped his father's solemnity, but inside had been seething with excitement because his brother was going off to be a *soldier.* The possibility that he might not come back had never crossed his mind.

Motion glimpsed in his side-view mirror brought him back from his reverie with a start. Ellie had just exited Gertrud's front door and was hurrying across the street. A middle aged woman with dark hair that had started to turn the color of iron—Gertrud, he presumed—had seen her to the door, but did not wait to watch her cross the street. He watched through the mirror as she came around the back of the car, opened the door, and climbed into the passenger seat.

He looked at her expectantly.

"He's been in touch with her," she said. There was a slightly breathless quality to her tone, but it wasn't because she was winded—she was beginning to get caught up in the excitement of the chase. "Just once. Gave her a number to call in case she has any trouble."

"Do you have it?" he asked.

She nodded, pulled a folded slip of paper from her handbag and handed it to him. "Here. She's supposed to ask for Reinhardt Grubbs."

Quinn studied the number.

"What are you going to do?" she asked. "Are you going to call it?"

He shook his head and glanced up at her. "No." He saw her bristle at the dismissal and explained, "Calling would just give whoever's at the other end a chance to run away. No, I need to find out where the number connects to and pay them a visit."

"Do you recognize the prefix? I don't."

Quinn nodded. "Bavaria. It's a Bavarian number." He folded the paper and slipped it into his jacket pocket. "Looks like I'm going to have to get back into uniform," he said, turning the ignition key. The car coughed into life.

"No, I should do it," she said. He opened his mouth to object but she pressed on before he could. "I'm a clerical worker at Prinz Albrechtstrasse. If, for some reason, they decide to check up on *me*, they'll find I'm authentic. Besides, it won't even get that far. It'll just be a routine call to the Munich SS office. They'll have every phone number on file for all of Bavaria. It won't even take me five minutes."

Quinn didn't say anything for several moments, trying to find an excuse to reject her offer. Then, reluctantly, he nodded his head. "All right. Where do we need to go?"

"Albrechtstrasse. I can get the Munich office's number there."

He put the car into gear and pulled out into the street.

———

GERTRUD WATCHED from her window as Ellie hurried across the street and got into the passenger side of the Focke-Wulf parked there. The car's windows were tinted, so Gertrud couldn't see the features of whoever was waiting for her, but she could make out the motion of the two of them talking. She thought about Ellie and how young she was—so young that Jews were really just fairy stories to her. Gertrud remembered when she had been a young girl in the years before the war, when Jewry had still been a fact of life in Germany.

She remembered the friendly, plump woman who had owned the sweets shop at the end of the road, and how one day the woman had simply not been there anymore. Three of the teachers at school had similarly vanished a few months later— two Jews, it was whispered, and a homosexual. Two of them had been very friendly, the sort of teachers that children liked, and Gertrud and the other students had never suspected they were in fact indoctrinating them against the truths of the Master Race, and polluting Germany's racial heritage by their very presence in society.

By the end of the war almost all the Jews and other undesirables in Germany and occupied Europe had been deported East, to the labor camps. Over time they had been replaced by the East's dwindling population of Slavs as the Reich's source of slave labor. The Führer had built the Purification Museum as a monument to what had happened to them then, and a good German, even one who opposed the policies of National Socialism and longed for democracy for the German race, did not question the *rightness* of their fate. Such questions were probably the most dangerous that a German could ask.

After a few minutes, the car pulled into the street and drove off. Gertrud picked up her telephone receiver and dialed the number she had written down for Ellie. After several rings there was an answering click.

"*Hotel Udet,*" said a disinterested feminine voice.

"Reinhardt Grubbs," she said.

Another click, then a ring. This time the phone was answered almost immediately.

"*Hello?*" The voice was male, tense.

"It's me."

"*Are you all right?*"

"Yes, yes," Gertrud said. "Don't worry, I'm fine." A pause. "Someone came. Just as you said."

"*Who?*"

"Ellie Voss. I don't know if you know her. She comes to the group meetings. Young, short blonde hair. Very pretty."

"*The one who works for the Gestapo? She was asking about me?*"

"She was. But she insisted she wasn't here for the Gestapo."

"*Then for whom?*"

"She said she was working for the English. She was with someone, but I didn't see him. He waited across the street in a car."

There was a long pause at the other end of the line. Finally the voice said, "*Something's wrong. If she was a British agent, I'd know about her.*"

"I gave her the number like you said. Should I not have?"

"*No, no. You did the right thing. Thank you. God only knows how much danger you've put yourself in for me.*"

"I care about you. And I care about what we both believe in."

"*I should go now. It's not safe to talk for too long.*"

"I understand." The words caught in her throat as she said them.

"*It seems that things are in motion. I hope we get to speak again. If we don't—if we don't, I care about you too. A great deal.*"

"Ric—Reinhardt?"

"*Yes?*"

"Be careful."

"*I'll try.*"

The line went dead with a click.

CHAPTER IX

PRINZ ALBRECHTSTRASSE was eerily empty; the only person Quinn and Ellie saw was the desk clerk, who flicked a disinterested glance at each of their IDs before nodding them inside, though the echoing *ratta tat tat* of someone punching at a typewriter reached them through the deserted, labyrinthine halls. Apparently even those charged with maintaining the political and racial integrity of the German people could afford to take a day off in light of such a momentous tragedy.

The Department A office, where Ellie worked, was locked and deserted, but she had a key. It was indeed a matter of only a few minutes on the phone before she was scribbling down an address onto a pad of paper on her desk. She thanked the person to whom she had spoken and hung up.

"Munich," she confirmed. "Somewhere called the Hotel Udet."

Quinn held out his hand for the pad. "Thank you," he said. "Your help has been priceless."

She frowned, looking down at his hand then back up to meet his eyes again. "What do you mean?"

He had of course guessed she would be resistant but he pressed on nonetheless. "I'll take you back to your flat if you like."

Her eyes narrowed. "You know I'm not going to let you do that. I've come this far. I'm going further."

"No," he said. "There's no telling what can happen from here on out. This isn't your fight. I should do this alone." He still had his hand held out.

She slipped the pad into her purse. "We go to Munich," she said. "Once we've reached the Bavarian border, I'll let you see the address."

He should just take it from her, he knew that. He was positive now that, even if he did so and left her, she wouldn't report him to the Gestapo.

He let his hand drop to his side. "Very well. But if you're to come with me, you must do exactly as I say. *When* I say it. *I'm* the spy, remember?"

She nodded solemnly. "Of that I remain very much aware."

THE AUTOBAHN heading south out of Berlin was almost empty, and they made good time through Brandenburg and northern Saxony. In the opposite direction, though, the traffic heading north into the capital was extremely heavy and slow. During breaks in the interminable Wagner and other favored composers, now being interspersed with recordings of the Führer's speeches from the past forty years, the radio announcer explained why: the Führer's body was lying in state today in the Grand Plaza in Berlin, at the foot of the steps of Speer's Great Hall. The cars entering the city were mourners wishing to pay their last respects before the Führer left his capital for the last time.

Tomorrow morning an honor guard would transport the body to Linz, leaving at dawn and arriving late in the evening, in preparation for the state funeral on Friday. The funeral procession would take the same autobahn Quinn and Ellie were driving now, directly south out of Berlin. It was the massive highway that bisected the Reich from north to south, one of two great axes linking the four corners of the Germanic empire. Its northern terminus was in Scandinavia, at Nordstern, a German colony the Führer had built with the intention of overshadowing the nearby city of Trondheim, though he had managed only to turn it into a Kriegsmarine submarine base on the Norwegian Sea. From Nordstern it traveled south to Oslo, then was forced to pass out of the Reich so it could run along the Swedish coast through Gothenburg and Helsingborg. At Helsingborg it crossed the Sound, re-entering the Reich, and linked Copenhagen and Odense before turning south again to pass through Hamburg, Berlin, Dresden, Prague, and Linz, terminating at Klagenfurt near the Italian and Croatian borders. Another massive autobahn linked the Reich from east to west, from Volgaburg, once called Stalingrad, on the banks of the Volga to Amsterdam on the North Sea coast.

Quinn and Ellie drove in silence for a long time. The Führer's death was the only news the radio reported: even Greece was mentioned only to note the spontaneous outpourings of grief not only from the soldiers of Germany, but also of Italy and the Independent State of Croatia.

After they left the Berlin suburbs, the parkland that ringed the city rolled by on either side of them, broad expanses of woodland and meadow preserved by the State. Here Aryan parents could bring their Aryan children to teach them of their natural heritage; the Hitler *Jugend* could bring its young members for the nature walks and camping trips it used to instill fellowship, fraternity, and complete devotion to the Reich; and the Party and government leadership could build their villas and estates in quiet seclusion, away from the dreariness and stress of government life in the capital and, indeed, from the oppressiveness of the giant, imposing architecture with which Speer, with the Führer's enthusiastic approval, had rebuilt Berlin into a monument to the National Socialist Triumph in the years after the war.

From the time it got underway in earnest in 1942, the Allied bombing campaign had continued without interruption—the bombers of the U.S. Army Air Forces flying during the day and the Royal Air Force at night—until the representatives of America, Britain, Germany, and Italy signed the hasty Corunna Armistice in Spain in the aftermath of the atomic bombings in Japan and England. For almost four years the Allied bombs had rained inexorably down on Germany. They eradicated German industry and, in the process, gutted the Reich's major cities: the urban centers of Berlin, Hamburg, Dresden, Munich, and Frankfurt, among many others, were all flattened. Germany had to rebuild her industrial capacity from the ground up after the war.

This had fit the Führer's grand design perfectly, for he had always envisioned removing the Reich's manufacturing base to the territories of the East annexed during the war—Poland, the Ukraine, European Russia. These regions, mostly empty after the native population was culled, he planned to open up for colonization by the Reich's rapidly growing Aryan population, which had heretofore been confined within Germany's traditional borders, while their conquered Slavic native populations would serve as a pool of slave labor, provided with only the minimum means needed to keep them barely alive and sufficiently able to service the assembly lines and massive plantations that would support the Aryan population.

That left the question, of course, of what to do with the shells of Germany's great cities destroyed by the Allies. But the grand design had an answer for this as well. After the fire of A.D. 64, Nero had been able to rebuild Rome as a monument to himself; Charles II had rebuilt London following the Great Fire of 1666. But now the Führer had the opportunity to rebuild an entire nation in his own image, and he embraced the task passionately. Rising from the ashes of the war, each of Germany's great cities would now become a tribute to National Socialism, and to the Führer. There was Nuremberg, the Party's spiritual home, with its incredible arena where the Party held its annual rallies; Munich, birthplace of National Socialism and site of the famous Beer Hall Putsch; Linz, near the Führer's birthplace of Braunau, where he had spent the twenty-five years since the war constructing a palace intended to serve as his mausoleum in the tradition of the Egyptian Pharaohs; and of course Berlin, where Speer's Grand Avenue linked the Führer's Palace at one end with the Grand Plaza at the other, overlooked by the Great Hall and the new Reichstag.

To their left Quinn and Ellie passed the grounds of the Baldur von Schirach Youth Academy, whose medieval spires rose above the treetops about a kilometer away. It was one of half a dozen youth academies throughout the Reich, where promising young boys of suitable racial heritage, their aptitude established through national testing, were admitted between the ages of eleven and thirteen to be prepared for careers as officers in the SS, Wehrmacht, Luftwaffe, or Kriegsmarine. The student body hailed both from Germany and from the suitably Nordic satellites whence the Reich was also willing to draw its elite class: Sweden, Belgium, France, or Switzerland—if the prospective student could prove his satisfactory ancestry. Not far after the youth academy, the parkland gave way to grazing and farmland, punctuated by the occasional town or village visible from the autobahn.

This is Germany, the Propaganda Ministry wished to say. The great stone and concrete modern monuments of the cities and the verdant, picturesque countryside with its idyllic, medieval hamlets existed side by side as twin testaments. *This is the Triumph of the Master Race.*

The reality, of course, was that this was only the western end of Germany, where the life the Master Race enjoyed was made possible by the sweat and blood of the Slavs in the East. Quinn had lived in the East; he had spent three years based in the Crimea maintaining intelligence on the Kriegsmarine's Black Sea Fleet. He remembered the vast expanses of forest and uncultivated steppe stretching to the horizon without interruption, and the ruined, abandoned husks of farmhouses and villages from the days when what were now the five Reich Commissariats of the East—St. Petersburg, Moscow, Kiev, the Crimea, and the Volga—had been the European territories of the Russian Empire or the Soviet Union.

One could drive for hundreds of kilometers along the East's marginal autobahn network without seeing another human being or, indeed, any sign of recent human habitation. Occasionally the barbed wire, stone walls and guard towers of a work camp, or—very rarely—a colonist's homestead would break the monotony. The Propaganda Ministry was constantly trying to attract colonists with its tales of the paradise awaiting them in the East, but few had taken them up on their offer. Those who did had generally been forced to abandon their homesteads after a very short time and now clustered together, dreaming of being able to afford to move back west, in walled settlements surrounding Wehrmacht and Luftwaffe bases in defense against the small bands of Slavic terrorists, supported by the Siberian government to the east, who roamed the countryside. The whole region was kept in a constant state of martial law as the personal kingdom of Reinhard Heydrich, the Reich Commissar-General of the East, Heinrich Himmler's former protégé and the wartime leader of the SS.

Quinn thought about those vast, endless wastes, about the derelict ruins of farms and towns that millions of Polish, Russian, and Ruthenian Slavs had inhabited thirty years ago. In his mind's eye he saw again the images of the inmates at the Purification Museum, the millions of Jews and others who had died in the death camps in those trackless wastes: emaciated, broken creatures with their heads shaven, their eyes sunken into their heads, and the skin sagging from their bones.

"Have you ever been to the East?" he asked abruptly.

Ellie started; she had been staring out the window at the passing farmland. "I was born there," she said. "Novgorod. My father was stationed there for the last of the fighting."

"How long did you live there?"

"Not long. My mother sent me to a BDM school in Heidelberg

when I was four. I haven't been back since." After a moment she added, "I have no memory of it. Is that why you're asking?"

He shrugged, deliberately nonchalant. "Yes. It was just something that was on my mind."

"Why?"

He did not answer. "Your father was in the Wehrmacht?"

Ellie did not press him, though he could tell she was wondering. She nodded. "He still is. He was a lieutenant when we invaded Poland in 1939. He fought in Poland, France, Russia, and Greece. By the time I was born he was colonel of his own Panzer regiment. He was transferred to Novgorod after we made peace with England and America."

Quinn understood why her father had had to return to Russia. When the Germans had made their breakthrough at Moscow in early 1943, then at Leningrad and Stalingrad a few months after that, the Red Army had simply collapsed and the German Panzer divisions had rolled forward unopposed onto the Russian steppe, eventually coming to a halt at the Ural ridge, more because of overextended supply lines and a general lack of interest than because they had finally met some resistance.

The startling rapidity of the German advance had meant that a number of Soviet divisions had been left, scattered and beaten, in their wake. While the bulk of the German forces in Russia had shifted to Italy and Greece, to combat the Allied invasion coming up from North Africa, the few remaining Soviet senior officers had tried to organize the remnants of their army into a fighting force.

These last Red Army divisions, who had to pillage outlying Wehrmacht camps for munitions and supplies, had never been more than a nuisance to the occupying German forces, but it was not until after Germany had signed the Corunna Armistice and was at peace with the Western Powers that the Reich had finally had the forces necessary to divert to the East to stamp out that resistance once and for all. The Germans referred to this period as "the last of the fighting."

The last of the Soviet units had retreated beyond the Urals in the late 1940s, taking refuge with the nascent, strife-ridden Siberian People's Republic that had emerged out of the chaos of the Soviet collapse. Neither the People's Republic nor the Reich had ever taken the trouble to attempt diplomatic relations with the other, and sporadic border clashes continued to this day.

Britain and the United States sent supplies to the Siberians and, in the 1950s, had even sent troops. Quinn had been one of them, when he first enlisted; he had spent three long, cold winters with a British tank battalion in the Siberian wilderness. But they had withdrawn the troops after a few years, when it became clear that neither side really had any interest in achieving any sort of goal that would end the conflict and bring about a settlement: the Germans liked having a theater where they could keep their young troops blooded, and the Siberians kept fighting merely out of hatred for Germany.

Thinking about that made him think of his brother again, in his olive private's uniform.

"My brother fought in Greece as well," he said. "During the last war."

"Really?"

He nodded. "He was killed in the invasion of Istria in 1944."

"Was he your only brother?"

"Yes."

"He was older than you?" He nodded. "You joined the army because of him?"

"I suppose."

Something in his voice made her look at him. "I'm sorry," she said softly, and they lapsed into silence once more.

They passed through Dresden and into the Protectorate of Bohemia and Moravia, which the Reich had created from the half of Czechoslovakia it had annexed to itself; the Führer had turned the other half into the puppet state of Slovakia. North of Prague they stopped for lunch then left the great north-south autobahn, heading west toward Nuremberg and Munich. By half past two they were passing through the outlying Munich suburbs, and an hour later they had reached the city proper. Just as in Berlin, the ominous, low-hanging overcast sky cast a dispiriting pall over the day.

Munich's major industry was tourism, built around its ancient role as capital of the Kingdom of Bavaria and its hallowed place in the history of the National Socialist Party. Here, in 1923, a young Adolf Hitler, alongside the war hero Erich Ludendorff, had staged his so-called Beer Hall Putsch, when he had led six hundred armed Nazis as they stormed the Bürgerbräu Keller beer-hall while the State Commissioner for Bavaria was giving a speech there. Over the course of the night the insurrectionists had grown in number to three thousand, but when they had attempted to march on the city center a hundred armed policemen had met them at the Odeonplatz near Feldherrn Halle and blocked their path in a brief encounter that had claimed nineteen lives. The future Führer had served nine months for leading the Putsch, but had been catapulted overnight from the farcical leader of an obscure fringe group to national celebrity.

The site of such a seminal event in the Führer's life was evidently a significant destination for those mourners unable to make it all the way north to Berlin or south to Linz, and heavy traffic clogged the city streets. The Hotel Udet was on the city's far side, and Quinn and Ellie had plenty of time to admire the sights from their car as they inched their way across the city.

They crossed the Glory Way, as the route of the march from the Bürgerbräu Keller to Feldherrn Halle had been named. The Führer's expansive building program had expanded it into a broad, majestic avenue, scattered with monuments to the nineteen who had died that day and statues re-creating the events of the march, culminating in the Odeonplatz with the famous statues of the Führer, General Ludendorff, Göring, and Himmler facing down the Bavarian state police.

Ellie stared down the avenue at a statue they passed by, depicting a man in a military cap, soldier's smock, and spectacles standing before a barricade with some comrades and holding aloft a military ensign emblazoned with a swastika.

"Every summer my mother would choose where we would go for our holidays," she said. "Invariably somewhere of great historical significance to the Reich and the Aryan nation. We visited Munich when I was eleven—I think. Maybe twelve."

Quinn was also looking out the window, but not focusing on anything in particular. "I was born here," he murmured.

She looked at him sharply, a frown creasing her delicate features. "You were born in Munich?"

He glanced at her, nodded. "By the time of my second birthday we had moved to London. But I was born here. The thirtieth of January, 1933."

A date every German schoolchild knew. "That's the Day of the Seizure of Power. The day the Führer took office as Chancellor."

He nodded again.

"Your parents were English, though?"

He half-smiled. "My mother's family is from Krakow. My father's family had lived in Munich since the seventeenth century. My father fought in the Bavarian Army during the first war. Served in the same regiment as the Führer, as it happens, though so far as I know they never met."

"Why did you leave?"

Only now did he finally make direct eye contact with her. "National Socialism," he said simply.

CHAPTER X

THE HOTEL Udet stood a few blocks beyond Glory Way; it looked affordable without being run down. The sign by the entrance to the small car park bore a painted image of the hotel's namesake, Ernst Udet, the native son of Munich who had flown alongside Hermann Göring and the famous Red Baron Manfred von Richthofen in the first war, then gone on to serve as a Luftwaffe general during the first decade of the Third Reich.

A light rain had started falling as Quinn and Ellie sat in the hotel's car park, studying the building. "Wait here for me," Quinn said finally.

"Now, this is getting—" The protest died on Ellie's lips as Quinn pulled his Luger from its shoulder holster and checked that it was loaded and cocked, the safety on. He replaced the gun and looked at Ellie.

"You're staying here," he said. "We've no idea what I'm going to find in there." She nodded. "Come round to the driver's side. Keep the car running, keep the doors locked and keep an eye on what's going on around you. If someone approaches the car, leave. If an hour goes by and I haven't come out, leave." She nodded again.

He opened his door and climbed out, then waited while she got out too and came round to him. She climbed into the driver's seat and he bent over to speak to her. "I'll try to be as quick as possible," he said by way of reassurance. He straightened, closed the door and headed inside.

The ground floor of the hotel was a small reception area and bar. Just inside the doorway was the reception counter, two dozen room keys hanging from pegs on the wall behind it. Beyond the reception area, half a dozen round wooden tables were scattered around the room, each with four chairs, and the bar stood along the opposite wall. A narrow staircase led upstairs, presumably to the rooms. The electric ceiling light was turned off and the room was gloomy, as the only illumination was provided by the dismal, rainy daylight coming in through the windows.

A solid middle-aged woman who looked like she could probably hold her own in a brawl with several Waffen-SS boxing champions sat behind the counter reading a newspaper. All the pictures in the paper were of the Führer, from various points in his life. The woman glanced up disinterestedly at Quinn as he came through the open doorway, said, "No rooms left," then went back to her paper. He walked up to the counter and waited, fishing his ID from his pocket as he did so.

After a few moments the woman found his silent presence sufficiently irritating to look up at him. "Can I help you?" she said resentfully.

"I'm looking for Reinhardt Grubbs," he said.

"And I'm looking for my Nordic prince who'll—"

Her voice trailed off as he flipped his ID open and held it in front of her. She straightened and looked up at him more respectfully. "Room seven," she said. She nodded to the staircase on the other side of the room. "Upstairs."

"Is he in there now?"

"I—I don't know. I don't think he's left his room since he checked in, except for maybe an hour every morning when he goes to buy food."

"And how long ago did he check in?"

"Um, about a week, I think. I'm not sure." When Quinn continued to stare silently at her, she said, "Here, mein Herr, let me check." The ledger was spread out on the table before her, facing toward Quinn and away from her, so that it could easily be lifted up onto the counter for new guests to sign in. She turned it round and flipped back through several pages. "Here he is. Since Saturday, mein Herr."

That was the day Garner disappeared. "And how is he paying?"

"He paid in advance, mein Herr," the woman said. "In cash. For ten days."

"Have you spoken to him at all? Has he talked to anyone about himself?"

The woman shook her head vigorously. The last thing she wanted was for her or any of her employees to be connected with a man evidently under SS surveillance. "I haven't, mein Herr, beyond the strictest pleasantries, and neither to my knowledge has any of the staff."

Quinn returned his ID to his pocket and pulled out the photograph of Richard Garner. He held it in front of the woman. "Is this Reinhardt Grubbs?"

She peered at it, then nodded her head. "Yes, yes, mein Herr, that is definitely him."

He was not entirely sure that he could not have shown her a picture of the Führer, or even of Ellie, and got her to swear that it was a photo of the man he was looking for, but the identification was enough to satisfy him. He replaced the picture in his pocket.

"The key," he said.

She looked puzzled. "Mein Herr?"

"Herr Grubbs's room key. Room seven."

"Ah, yes, of course, mein Herr. How foolish. Please excuse me." She turned and fumbled one of the keys on the wall behind her off its hook and handed it to him.

"My thanks for your assistance, Frau *Kamerad*," he said.

"I am but a loyal servant of the Reich," she said, but he had already turned away and started for the stairs. *"Heil Hitler!"* she called dutifully at his retreating back.

The upstairs hallway was even gloomier than downstairs; the only illumination came from an ancient wall lamp above the landing. Room seven was at the far end of the hall. Quinn knocked loudly on the door.

There was no answer, but he had expected none. He knocked again and said, "Reinhardt Grubbs, I'm here on state authority."

Still no answer. Quinn drew his pistol with his right hand and inserted and turned the room key with his left. The old lock clicked loudly. He pushed the door open less than a centimeter, just enough to free it from the doorframe but not nearly enough to allow any light to appear through a crack. Then he released his hand from the key and gently nudged the door with his left foot. It swung open away from him.

The room beyond appeared deserted. He could see a chest of drawers with a mirror above it, a wooden chair, a window with the blinds up and the rain spattering against it outside, and the foot of the bed. The wallpaper and the bedspread were faded; the carpet looked old.

He took one cautious step inside, then another. Unfortunately the mirror was at too acute an angle to offer him a view of the room.

He froze instantly when he felt the metal muzzle of the gun against the back of his neck at the base of his skull.

"Don't move." The command was entirely unnecessary. The voice was masculine; its German was marked by a slight northern accent, Hanoverian or Holsteiner.

The man's left hand reached from behind him and plucked Quinn's pistol from his grasp.

"Hands up."

Quinn obeyed. He heard the door being closed quietly behind him, then felt himself getting patted down. His captor found his ID and his passport and fished them from his pockets. The gun muzzle was removed from the back of his neck, and he felt the other man moving round. The man stepped into Quinn's field of vision, his gun still kept carefully trained on him, and Quinn saw the face from Garner's photograph: dark hair, receding hairline, cheeks starting to get jowly with age, thick-rimmed glasses.

Garner held Quinn's passport, ID and pistol all in his left hand.

He deposited the pistol on the dresser so he could examine the ID. His eyes flicked from the ID to Quinn's face and back again, comparing Quinn with the photograph. When he was satisfied he tossed the ID aside and flipped through the passport.

Discarding the passport as well, Garner settled himself in the chair. All the while his pistol remained pointedly trained on Quinn. For a while the two men regarded each other silently.

At last Garner broke the silence. "I'm surprised," he said, "that the SS bothered to send someone in plainclothes after me. Not really your lot's typical style, eh, Herr Obersturmbannführer? Though I must add, I'm rather flattered that I merited Amt III over simply the Gestapo."

"Actually, Mr. Garner," Quinn said in English, "I'm not here from the SS at all."

A flicker of surprise crossed Garner's face, but the gun did not waver. "You're with the Service?"

Quinn nodded.

"Then you're here to kill me." It was not a question.

"Those are indeed my orders, Mr. Garner."

"You're not out of the Berlin Station," Garner said. "I'd know you. Are you local? With the Munich consulate, maybe?"

"No. I'm not local."

"What's your call sign?"

"I was called Lancelot."

Garner frowned, then his eyes widened. "My God," he said. "I thought you were dead. That's what we assumed, anyway. Lancelot. Christ. *The* Lancelot?"

"I should think so. I'd hope that I wasn't so unmemorable that they assigned my codename to another operative."

"Lancelot," Garner murmured to himself. "They've pulled the big guns out for me." He frowned and peered at Quinn. "What happened to you? Where have you been?"

"How much of my operational history do you know?"

"You were deep cover and run direct through London. The Berlin Station is the best-run MI6 post in the world, and for five years you put us to shame. Every solid piece of intelligence that came through our hands from London was listed as being sourced through Lancelot. Then there was the big one—the last operation. That was, oh, I don't know—"

"Four years ago," Quinn supplied.

Garner nodded in acknowledgment. "'Be ready to accept native operative for asylum,' we were told. 'Target may or may not be in immediate jeopardy of apprehension by SS. Target may or may not be carrying vital information. Target's contact is Lancelot.'"

He paused, remembering. The memories were boiling in Quinn's head as well.

Garner went on, "I don't know what went wrong, how Jerry figured it out. But it went bad. Your target was killed. We were given to understand that the 'vital information' was gotten out by someone, and that it was what kept us in Greece through the first Croat assault. But we were never notified what happened to Lancelot. We just never heard of him again from that point on." He leaned forward. "So what *did* happen to you?"

"Can I put my hands down?" Garner waved his assent with his pistol, and Quinn slowly and deliberately lowered his hands. He took a slight step to the side, repositioning his feet. He moved cautiously, but Garner did not react, just kept his eyes on him. Quinn realized he could now see himself in the hotel room mirror:

dark hair, dark eyes, hawk-like nose. He stared into his own eyes for a moment, then he went on, "It was that last operation. Everything went sour. Left a bad taste. I was sick of it. I wanted out."

Garner pondered this. "The man who was killed," he said. "He was your friend?"

Quinn hesitated, then nodded.

"Mm," Garner murmured, nodding to himself and looking away. "Always bad, getting close with your operatives." He looked up, meeting Quinn's eyes. "I'm sorry."

The ensuing silence felt uncomfortable and Quinn spoke to break it. "I'm given to understand that you were part of that operation."

Garner nodded reluctantly. "I was."

"How so?"

He considered. "I'm not terribly proud to admit this, considering that I'm probably about to have to kill you." He took a deep breath. "I gave the order to fire."

Quinn frowned. "What do you mean?"

"I was the spotter on the embassy rooftop. I gave the order to shoot when your man's apprehension became imminent."

"Karl? Karl Mundt?"

Garner clearly felt discomfited at having to prolong the discussion on the topic. "If that was his name. Look, I'm sorry."

Quinn didn't say anything for several moments, merely stared off into space, a deep frown creasing his brow. "Mundt wasn't shot by ours," he said at last. "He was shot by the Gestapo. He made a run for the British embassy gate, and he was shot by the Gestapo."

Garner's eyes widened, and he lowered his gun. "Is that what they told you?"

Quinn looked at him and nodded. "When I was being debriefed at the Lisbon consulate. Why? What really happened?"

Garner hesitated. "The Gestapo shot him," he said, "but they hit him in the leg. He was wounded and couldn't make it to the embassy gate. I gave the order to shoot, or the Gestapo would have got him alive."

Quinn felt the floor shift beneath his feet. Truth and deception. The bastards had lied to him. No, they hadn't lied. His debriefer's words came back to him now, giving him the news. *"Shot by the Gestapo and killed while attempting to reach the British embassy."* The Gestapo *had* shot Karl. But they hadn't told him the rest. Truth and deception mixed, till the two were indistinguishable.

"My God," Garner said, "you had no idea. Terribly sorry. Wouldn't have wanted to be the one to tell you."

They lapsed into another uncomfortable silence as Quinn tried to assimilate what he had just been told. This time it was Garner that broke it. "It seems to me, however, that we still have quite a problem." He held up his pistol to illustrate his point. "You see, one of us still has to kill the other."

"And I have to recover the file," Quinn said. "The information you removed with you from the embassy."

"Ah," Garner said. "Yes, forgetful of me. You know what it contains, I suppose?"

"Actually I don't," Quinn admitted. "I was rather hoping it would have something about Columbia-Haus."

Garner's eyes narrowed. "They didn't brief you on Columbia-Haus?"

"No."

"Then how do you know of it?"

"I've come across it while searching for you. You attended those meetings at Prinz Albrechtstrasse." He hesitated; this was not how the encounter was supposed to go. He continued. "What were they about?"

Garner seemed to mull something over for several minutes. Quinn dared not interrupt him for fear of upsetting whatever conclusion he was, evidently reluctantly, bringing himself to. At last, Garner rose. Quinn tensed, but the other man merely placed his gun on the dresser, opened one of the drawers and pulled out a large manila envelope. He turned to Quinn.

"I think we're on the same side," he said. "I don't think I have anything to fear from you. In fact," he continued, holding out the envelope, "I rather get the feeling that this would probably be safer in your possession than in mine. You *are* Lancelot, after all."

Quinn hesitated, then accepted the envelope. "This is the file you took from the embassy?"

"It's all there," Garner confirmed. "What you hold in your hand *is* Columbia-Haus."

Quinn stared at the envelope. Garner picked up Quinn's ID and passport, then handed both documents back to him. When Quinn had slipped them into his pocket, he also handed back his Luger, which Quinn replaced in its holster.

"I don't know what the next step is," Garner said. "If I did, you wouldn't have found me still sitting around in a second-rate hostel in Munich. But whatever that step is, you have a decision to make before we take it. I should remember, though, that we don't have terribly much time. I'll be here when you're ready."

Quinn nodded, not quite sure what had just happened. He slid the envelope under one arm, turned round and opened the door. He stepped back out into the hallway. His hand was on the doorknob, ready to pull the door shut, when Garner spoke again.

"It must have been the old man who brought you back for this. There's no one else it could have been."

Quinn looked back at the other man over his shoulder and nodded. "Talleyrand. Yes."

"I wonder. Why you? I mean, if he wasn't going to even brief you on Columbia-Haus. That man has a reason for every choice he makes."

Quinn pondered, then shook his head. "I don't know. But you're right. He does."

He pulled the door shut behind him.

CHAPTER XI

IT WAS still raining, a little more heavily than before, as Quinn emerged from the Hotel Udet into the car park. He paused in the rain, turned, looked up and counted the windows over to Garner's room. Garner was sitting at his window, staring down at him.

After a long moment Quinn turned away and headed towards the car. Ellie leaned over and unlocked the passenger door at his approach.

"What happened?" she asked as he climbed into the passenger seat.

He slammed the door shut. "I'm not sure," he said. He held the envelope in his hands and stared at it.

Ellie glanced down at the envelope and frowned. "Did you find

Garner?" He nodded. "And? Where is he?" Her eyes widened. "Is he dead?"

He looked up at her. "No. Nothing like that. He's fine. He's still in his room." He ran his thumb contemplatively along the envelope's seal.

"You just left him?" He nodded again. "Is he defecting?"

"No. I don't think so."

She gestured to the envelope. "*What* is in there?"

"I think... I think answers. But I'm not sure I want to know them." This was not why he was here. He was here to do a job. Neutralize Garner, destroy the file. He did not want to know what was in the envelope, because he knew it would change everything. Whatever was in this envelope had made Garner turn, and Garner believed it would make Quinn turn too. The look on Garner's face had unsettled him. If he opened the envelope, everything would change, and he would not be able to change it back.

He blinked, trying to clear his mind, and stuffed the envelope into his coat's inside pocket. "We should get going."

"To where?"

"I don't know. But we should get going."

She frowned at him, but nevertheless put the car in gear and pulled out of the parking space and into the street.

Quinn checked his watch. Five to six. "Are you hungry? We should probably get something to eat."

She shrugged. "I'm all right. But we can eat."

They stopped at a tavern a few blocks from the Hotel Udet. They ate in silence. Quinn brooded. Ellie was confused as to what was going on, and that made her angry and a little sullen. For the first time Quinn regretted that she had become involved. He deliberately ordered himself a large meal so that he could delay dinner as long as possible. The longer he spent here, the longer it would be before he had to decide what do next. They both drank several tankards of beer during the meal.

"Did you leave the documents in the car?" Ellie asked.

Quinn shook his head and patted his coat, feeling the outline of the envelope underneath. "I have them here."

"And you haven't read them?"

His throat went dry at the thought. "Not right now," he said. "In so public a place." It was a perfectly valid objection—it just wasn't the real reason he hadn't opened the envelope.

At the next table a pair of tourists, a middle aged American couple, were arguing; their voices grew steadily louder as the argument progressed. "Well it's not *my* fault," the man declared. "What do you want *me* to do about the weather?"

"Oh, it's not just the weather," the woman said. "The whole damn country's shut down because of their dead goddamn Führer. Only thing left to do is take pictures of the sights. And even *those* are packed now with Germans. Goddamn Jew-killing Germans."

"Would you keep your voice down?" the man demanded. "A lotta these Fritzes can understand English, you know."

"What do I care if they understand me? They know they killed the Jews. They're goddamn proud of it, for God's sake! I can't believe you dragged me round that *disgusting* museum in Berlin."

"What are they arguing about?" Ellie whispered.

Quinn turned back to her reluctantly; the woman's mention of the Purification museum had reminded him of his own visit there yesterday. "The weather," he said after a moment.

"They're this upset with each over the weather?"

He hesitated, then confessed, "They're arguing over the Purification."

She frowned, confused. "The Purification? What do they disagree about over the Purification?"

"It's not that," Quinn said awkwardly. "It's—they're ascribing guilt."

"Guilt?"

Quinn nodded. "To the German people."

Ellie's frown deepened, then, suddenly, her eyes widened and she looked at the tourists, then back to Quinn. "Are they Jewish?"

"I don't think so," Quinn said. "Well, they've given no indication either way."

Her frown returned. "Then why are they so upset?"

To change the subject, Quinn said, "We have to decide whether or not we're going to drive back to Berlin tonight."

Ellie shrugged, accepting the change of topic without further comment. "I think that's more up to you than me." She gave him a pointed look. "*I* can't contribute without knowing what's going on."

Quinn stared out the window next to their table. The rain continued to come down in a light but steady drizzle. "I don't like the idea of driving in this weather," he said. "Besides, it's getting a little late to be setting out for Berlin." The weather was a valid, if not insurmountable, objection, but they both knew that the time really was not. The real reason they had to stay the night was that Quinn could not leave until he had decided what to do about Garner.

They left the tavern at half past seven. Quinn could feel the beer manifesting itself in his overly delicate sense of balance as he followed Ellie across the room. She was a very small woman and had drunk as much as he had, so he imagined she must be feeling the effects of the alcohol as well. He found himself studying the sway of her hips as she walked, admiring the perfect curve of her waist and buttocks.

Stop it. That was the beer thinking.

It was too early for sunset at this time of year, but the overcast sky had brought on a premature dusk and they emerged from the tavern into a city under the blanket of an early night. They hurried quickly across the car park in the rain. They were halfway to the car when the street was suddenly illuminated by a flash of lighting, and simultaneously they were assaulted by a clap of thunder powerful enough to rattle the windows of the tavern behind them. Ellie yelped and jumped; instinctively, Quinn reached out and wrapped a protective arm around her.

Released by the lightning and the thunder, the rain was all of a sudden coming down in sheets. Ellie pressed herself against him, nestling her face against his chest. Quinn found himself willing to stand there as protection against the sudden downpour for a long time. She was indeed very small-framed; it only heightened her femininity.

But the contact was frustratingly fleeting. Abruptly she turned and dashed the last few yards to the car. Her pumps forced her to take short, mincing steps. Quinn followed, less hurriedly. He bent forward to unlock the passenger door for Ellie. As he did so, he felt the stiff bulk of Garner's envelope in his inside pocket, and it sobered him a little. He opened the door for her and closed it behind her, then walked round and got in the driver's side.

They were both soaked to the bone. Quinn nodded towards a hotel across the street. It looked like the Hotel Udet, affordable without being ratty. "How does over there look?"

She followed his gesture, nodded in agreement. "Fine."

The hotel had only a single vacancy, so they had to share a

room. It had one bed, a small bathroom and no television, but it did have a radio. They took off their coats and hung them over the radiator to dry; Ellie showered to wash the cold, soaking rain off herself and emerged from the bathroom in the hotel's bathrobe. Quinn sat on the bed and brooded. He would have preferred silence, but Ellie turned on the radio and filled the room with the sound of one of the Führer's speeches.

Quinn recognized it after a few moments: it was his closing speech from the treason trial after the Munich Putsch—though it had not been recorded at that time. Rather, the recording that was playing now was part of a series made in the 1950s and 60s, when the Führer had recorded a number of his great speeches from his early career. The Munich Putsch speech, when the fringe Nazi Party had attempted to seize control of the Bavarian state government, was chief among them. The incident had catapulted Adolf Hitler overnight from the slightly comical leader of an obscure neoconservative group to national attention. During his consequent prison sentence, he had composed *Mein Kampf,* the Party's testament.

"I have hopes that the old cockade will be lifted from the dirt, that the old colors will be unfurled to flutter again, that expiation will come before the tribunal of God. Then from our bones and from our graves will speak the voice of the only tribunal which has the right to sit in judgment over us. Then, gentlemen, not you will be the ones to deliver the verdict over us, but that verdict will be given by the eternal judgment of history, which will speak out against the accusation that has been made against us. I know what your judgment will be. But that other court will not ask us: Have you committed high treason?"

The voice went on and on. Quinn watched Ellie as she moved around the room. She bent over to open a drawer, and he admired the curve of her backside through the robe. She sat on a chair and rubbed her feet; she had been wearing her pumps all day. She got up again and reached up to turn on the wall lamp. He ran his eyes along the silhouette of her profile underneath her robe.

"That court will judge the quartermaster-general of the old army, its officers and soldiers, who as Germans wanted only the best for their people and Fatherland, who fought and who were willing to die. You might just as well find us guilty a thousand times, but the goddess of the eternal court of history will smile and tear up the motions of the state's attorney and the judgment of this court: for she finds us not guilty."

The speech ended and gave way to the news report, detailing the ongoing preparations for the funeral the day after tomorrow. The Führer's body was still in the Grand Plaza, protected by a detachment from the *Leibstandarte*-SS Adolf Hitler, the Führer's personal bodyguard regiment of the Waffen-SS. Tomorrow the whole of the *Leibstandarte's* mechanized arm would escort the Führer's body on its public route from Berlin to Linz. Dignitaries were starting to arrive in the southern city for the funeral already. Ribbentrop, the former Foreign Minister, and Bormann, the Führer's longstanding private secretary, had both arrived today, as had several rulers from the European satellites: General Franco, the fascist ruler of Spain; Kekkonen, the Finnish President, who as his country's prime minister had negotiated the agreement whereby Germany returned the territories Finland had been forced to cede to the Soviet Union in 1940; and Count Ciano, son-in-law and successor to the late Mussolini.

Pope Lucius IV—who, the radio reminded the listener, was a German and the first non-Italian Pope to occupy the Papal See in four centuries—had issued a statement of condolence to the German people. The Führer's mysterious final testament, containing the identity of his successor, was being held in a secure vault in his palace in Linz, under guard by both the *Leibstandarte* and a Guards regiment of the Wehrmacht's Eastern Command.

This last confused Quinn when he heard it. Why would a unit from the Eastern Command be charged with guarding the Führer's will? Then he understood. The *Leibstandarte*, as part of the Waffen-SS, was under the command of Himmler. But the Eastern Command was under the control of Reinhard Heydrich, the Reich Commissar-General of the East. The presence of one of Heydrich's regiments kept the will from falling completely under Himmler's control.

Heydrich and Himmler had begun as political allies. Heydrich's rise to prominence had come through Himmler's patronage; as Chief of the RSHA, the SS's security service, he had been Himmler's right hand man. Young, charming, tall, athletic, blond-haired and blue-eyed, Heydrich possessed all the lauded Nordic physical virtues that were conspicuous by their absence in the Party's ruling clique: Hitler, Göring, Himmler, and Goebbels. It had been Heydrich's place in the Führer's good graces that had allowed Himmler to achieve the central position in Reich culture that he so coveted for his beloved SS.

When the Reich swallowed most of Czechoslovakia in two great bites in 1938 and 1939, Hitler had organized his new territory into the Protectorate of Bohemia and Moravia and given it as a fief to Reinhard Heydrich, who proceeded to rule it with an iron fist. In 1942 Czech nationalists, supported by the British government, had attempted to assassinate him. He had survived, but had been forced to retire to his estates for a time to convalesce. Himmler's new protégé, Kaltenbrunner, had replaced him as Chief of the RSHA.

Eighteen months later, when the Führer had needed to find someone to begin the work of turning the newly conquered East into the fertile seeding ground for Aryan colonization that he envisioned it, his eye had fallen on Heydrich, now fully recovered from the botched assassination. He had appointed Heydrich Reich Commissar-General; and as the Führer's health degenerated over the coming decades and he slowly retreated from public life, Himmler had gradually managed to tighten his hold on all aspects of life in western Germany, while Heydrich ruled as a military despot in the East. For several years the two former allies had been the principal rivals for the supreme power, and now that the Führer was dead that rivalry was coming to a head.

When the commentator concluded his report and announced that it would be followed by a selection of the Führer's favorite pieces from *The Ring of the Nibelungs*, Quinn reached over and turned the radio off. Ellie, kneeling on the floor and resting her head on the bedcovers, looked up expectantly, thinking that he must want to talk. But he merely continued to brood silently. The only noise was the continuing downpour outside.

"Look," she said after a minute, "if you don't want to talk, that's fine. But I don't like this quiet. Either you tell me what happened with Garner, or I'm going to listen to the radio."

He stared at her wordlessly.

"What did he say to you?" she asked. "Why did you just leave him there? Did he tell you why he defected?"

"No." Quinn shook his head. "He didn't tell me why. But he was so *sure*." Garner had been so *sure* that whatever was in that envelope would turn Quinn as well that he hadn't felt the need to justify himself; he had just handed the file over.

Ellie's eyes widened slightly. "My God," she said. "You're scared.

That's it. Whatever he said to you, you're terrified. And that's why you haven't looked at those documents."

He looked at her bleakly and did not respond. She got up and sat next to him on the bed, nestling herself against him. Reflexively, for the second time this evening, he put his arm around her. His nostrils were filled with the scent of her damp, golden hair.

"What is it you're scared of?" she asked.

"Of finding out what's going on," he murmured after a few moments. "Of understanding what he's trying to do."

"Why?"

Her question caught him short; he opened his mouth to respond but found that he was unsure of the answer.

Then he realized. "Because I think that once I do, I won't be able to pretend anymore."

"Pretend? What do you mean?"

He spoke slowly, choosing his words carefully. "As long as Garner is just a defector, all I have to do is take care of him, and I can go. But I think if I find out what's going on, I'm going to have to choose sides."

"You'll have to do what you think is best for England? Even if England turns against you for it?"

Her insight surprised him; he glanced down at her and smiled slightly, even though she could not see it. "Yes."

"Like joining the Resistance."

He made no reply. After a moment she raised her head and looked up at him. He stared back at her, into those piercingly sharp blue eyes. Tentatively she leaned forward and kissed him. He kissed back. He liked the taste of her mouth. He knew he should think about the beer, and the stress they were both under, but instead he pushed them from his mind.

He felt the gentle pressure of her hand on his chest, pushing him back onto the bed. He allowed himself to be pushed and lay back. Her robe was starting to come open at the front, and he could feel the heat of her body, half on top of him, pressing against his through his damp clothes. He ran his hands down her sides and over her hips, feeling her soft, supple firmness through the flimsy robe.

They were still kissing. Her hand teased its way up under his shirt and ran along his abdomen; the hairs on his stomach tingled and he quivered. She giggled, kissing now along the line of his jaw toward his ear. The caresses from her hand moved downward, out of his shirt. Gently but firmly, she rubbed her palm back and forth across his crotch. He moaned.

Her fingers started to fiddle at the buttons to his trousers, pulling the first one free. Nibbling on his ear, she giggled again.

"I wonder if those Americans from the tavern are doing this now," she whispered. "Or if they're still arguing about the Purification."

Suddenly he stiffened underneath, catching her by the wrist just as she reached inside his pants. He pulled his ear away from her tongue and looked her in the eye. "What does that mean?"

She stared at him, confused. "What? Well—nothing." She smiled hesitantly. "I mean—it was just a joke."

"Well, it wasn't very funny." He pulled out from underneath her and sat up on the edge of the bed.

He felt her get up onto her knees behind him and put her arms around his chest. "Come on," she whispered in his ear. He could hear frustration and confusion in her voice, but she was also trying to rescue the mood. "What's wrong all of a sudden?"

He broke free of her grasp and stood up, turning round to face her. The pleasant alcoholic mist he had allowed to fog his mind had suddenly cleared. "Perhaps this isn't such a good idea."

"Perhaps *what* isn't such a good idea?" she demanded. She thought she was being rejected now, and it was making her angry.

"At the tavern, you asked if the Americans were Jewish," he said, his voice cold. "I don't know if they were or not, but *I* am."

For several seconds she just stared blankly at him; her mouth worked without any sound coming out. Finally she managed, "You're *what?*" It was barely audible.

"I'm Jewish," he repeated. His heart was pounding, but he forced himself to sound calm, soothing. "My name is Mordechai Rosenhoch. I was born here, in Munich, but when the Nuremberg Laws stripped Jews of their German citizenship in 1935, my family moved to England. When my brother enlisted in 1942 he used the name Thomas Quinn—Tommy. So when I enlisted in 1951, I used the name Simon Quinn. But my name is Mordechai Rosenhoch." Truth.

She was looking off into space. "A Jew," she murmured. "You're a Jew." Her eyes fastened on his and she stared at him, her face inscrutable. He reached out slowly and gently touched her shoulder, but she jerked away from him as if he might be contagious. She realized her robe was still hanging open; she pulled it tight across her front and turned her back to him.

He reached out again, but his hand hovered uncertainly over her back, then pulled itself away. He stood up and fastened his trousers, then took his jacket from over the radiator and opened the front door. He paused in the doorway, trying to think of something to say, but there was nothing. She had not responded at all to the sounds of him getting ready to leave. Wordlessly, he closed the door behind him and walked down the hall.

CHAPTER XII

HE STORMED out the hotel lobby's front door onto the pavement and stopped, letting the rain wash over him. It was coming down hard, harder than anything he had experienced living in the mild Mediterranean climate the past four years. In just a few moments it had completely soaked him again. He stared up into the night sky. Rainwater washed across his face, running into his eyes and blurring his vision, and down the back of his neck under his jacket. The smell of it filled his nostrils and ran into his mouth.

His jacket was open at the front and he could feel his shirt plastered against him, clinging heavily to his chest as he breathed. His trousers would feel the same way against his thighs when he walked. The only sound was the loud, omnipresent hiss of the rain striking pavement, tarmac, brick, and concrete. The rain filled every one of his senses; it was all he knew. The water felt cold against him, and he shivered. But it also felt good.

After a while he looked down again. The rain had washed away her scent, the taste of her in his mouth, and the feeling of her lips rubbing against his, the lingering sensation of her body pressing itself into his own. But much as he would like to believe otherwise, he knew that was not what he had wanted. What he was trying to wash away went much deeper than she did, and the rain could not get at it. Abruptly he turned and walked quickly away along the pavement. He did not care where he was going, so long as he was in motion.

"My name is Mordechai Rosenhoch." Was that even true anymore? The name had felt strange on his lips; it had been two decades since he had last spoken it aloud. He had left Mordechai Rosenhoch twenty years ago, in the small, decaying tenement flat in Wapping that the family had ended up in after the war. During their first few years in England, they'd lived in a nice house in Ealing. But then the German A-bomb had turned most of London into a single smoking ruin, a massive open wound on the banks of the Thames, and had turned the surviving Londoners into an army of refugees. And the Rosenhoch family had found themselves squeezed into a Wapping flat, which at first they'd had to share with two other families.

Those had been hard years, following the war. As aliens and German nationals, they had lived under the perpetual cloud, in that the government could deport them at any time under the harsh citizenship laws Lord Mountbatten had enacted after he became Regent. Only the fact that his father had been one of the few who managed to remain regularly employed had stopped that from happening.

His parents had been implacably set against the idea of his enlistment. His mother had objected nine years earlier when Isaac had signed up, so he had expected her sobbing and her hysterics. Their father, though, had told Isaac in his quiet, dignified way that he understood the decision and would pray for his safe return. So when young Mordechai had declared his intention to follow in Isaac's footsteps, he had at least expected his father to be supportive. But instead the old man had told him not to be a fool, that he would be throwing away his life for a hopeless, discredited cause.

He had been furious that his father could so repudiate the sacrifice Isaac had made for all their sakes; he had not understood that the older man spoke out of pain, grief, and a desperate desire not to lose his only remaining son. If his family wanted to reject what his brother had loved enough to die for, then he would reject his family. Mordechai Rosenhoch had stolen away out his bedroom window and down the fire escape in the middle of the night, and the following morning Simon Quinn had presented himself at the recruitment office.

But if not Mordechai Rosenhoch, then what *was* his name? He wandered aimlessly through the Munich streets, turning at random corners, neither noting nor caring which streets he was turning into.

To the Army he had been Simon Quinn for five years, and that was the name he had used more often than any other in the four years since he left MI6. But in the intervening decade, he had not encountered it once. For those years, when he had lived in Paris, the Crimea, and Berlin, MI6 had made him into Johann Kreuz. And now, according to the passport and SS ID he carried in his pocket, they had made him into Matthias Kaufholz. Those were just pieces of paper, of course—but then again, what legitimized the name Simon Quinn, except for a handful of pieces of paper? His enlistment papers, the gazette for the Military Medal he had won in Siberia, his British passport in his cabin aboard the cruiser in Greece. Lying in the drawer on top of that British passport was his Sicilian passport, listing his name as Simon Morlino. Truth and deception.

He emerged from a narrow street onto a broad, open boulevard, and he realized he had come to Glory Way. The storm and the late hour had driven away any lingering tourists, and the statues scattered along the length of the avenue formed eerie, motionless silhouettes emerging out of the rain as far as he could see, cast into curious relief by the bright white streetlights spaced every few hundred meters.

A cluster of statues loomed immediately before him, and he walked up to them and stared at them. They were the ones past which he and Ellie had driven earlier: four men in pseudo-military uniforms stood before a wood and barbed wire barricade, their mustachioed and bespectacled leader holding aloft a red, white and black military ensign that now hung, limp and heavy with water, molded to its staff. He stared at the face of the young man holding aloft the ensign and realized that he recognized him: he was staring at Heinrich Himmler. He peered at the young, but still chillingly familiar features, then moved on.

Of course, the name that had haunted him the most was Mordechai Rosenhoch. For the decade he had spent in fascist France and Nazi Germany, he had lived in fear of being discovered, of getting into a situation like he had tonight. He remembered the week in Siberia, separated from his company and trapped behind the German lines; the thought of capture then had been the greatest terror he had ever known in his life.

There had been other times since, of course. Stationed in Paris, posing as a German secondary-school instructor, his heart pounding every time he crossed the border into Germany that the frontier police would stop him for a random anti-terrorist check, would see him, would *know* just from looking at him. Once he had been moved on to his assignments in Germany, his cover had become more official—a Kriegsmarine intelligence analyst in the Crimea and a Gestapo investigator in Berlin—and he had therefore become more immune from the idle and arbitrary attention of the German security services to which the rest of the Reich's citizens were subject. But there were times when he was trapped, as at Denlinger's the night before, and then survival and escape crowded everything else out of his mind. He must maintain his secret—he must not be found out. Truth and deception.

Glory Way ended and opened onto the Odeonplatz, where the hundred Bavarian policemen had confronted Hitler's disorganized mob almost fifty years before. It was dominated on one side by the Feldherrn Halle, the Hall of Fallen Heroes. At the time of the Putsch the Feldherrn Halle had been dedicated to the soldiers of the Bavarian Army who had died fighting for Germany in the first war; in the 1950s, though, the Führer had demolished it and replaced it with a larger, more grandiose edifice, a monument now also to Bavarians who had died in the second war, and, of course, to the sixteen Nazis and three state policemen who had died in 1923.

From his position at the edge of the square's broad, open space, with the view obscured by the rain, he could make out the famous statues at its center only as obscure, hazy shapes. He walked forward, and they began to resolve themselves: the Führer, Ludendorff, Göring, and Himmler, faced by six policemen with rifles raised.

He stopped before the four Nazi leaders. Ludendorff stood a few steps in front of the others, his right arm half-raised in a gesture of supplication towards the policemen. The scene was a fabrication, of course: the Bavarian police had deliberately avoided putting themselves in a position where they might have to fire upon Ludendorff, venerated hero of the first war, and Himmler had been a minor Party functionary at the time, not a member of its ruling echelon up here alongside the Führer and Göring—he would have been with the rank and file. Truth and deception.

The rain bouncing off the copper statues gave them an eerie, translucent white halo. He peered at the Führer, unflinching and upright in the face of the raised rifles, nobly staring down the Bavarian police in the unshakeable knowledge that only he could achieve Germany's true and rightful destiny.

"You took my name away," he said, and turned and walked away, wanting only to be in motion once more.

He took one of the smaller side streets leading off the square, turned one way at the first intersection to which he came, then the opposite way at the next. After a block or two he once again no longer had any idea where he was. Ellie's face floated before his eyes, the unreadable expression she had had when he had told her his secret, how she had jerked away from him when he touched her.

In his mind, her face changed. The skin shriveled and tightened, lost its softness and femininity; the color drained from her cheeks and lips. Her mouth puckered, a telltale sign that it no longer contained any teeth. Her hair fell away and her eyes sunk back into her head, darkening and losing their spark, their *life*, and before him once again he saw one of those gaunt, broken faces in the pictures at the Purification Museum, so emaciated he could no longer guess age or even gender—it could have been his own grandmother or uncle or cousin for all he knew.

And he wept, though he could not distinguish his tears from the rain pouring down his face. He had been East, to where the Reich had deported Europe's Jewish population to a network of Purification centers where they had been gassed and fed into furnaces—he was probably the only free Jew who had been there in thirty years. He had found an empty land there, just the occasional scattered German colony or Slavic slave labor camp. But of the death camps, and of the millions and millions of Jews who had met their ends there, nothing remained. And what had he done for them? What simple act of vengeance, or even of memorial?

Nothing. Jews who had emigrated abroad when the Nazis came to power had tried to drum up international concern about the relatives they had left behind, but over the years they had grown older and passed on. The younger generation growing up in England and America, concerned with the Cold War and the threat of mutual nuclear annihilation, simply did not want to hear about a problem they could do nothing to solve. It amounted merely to another reminder of a painful, horrific, destructive war that their parents and older siblings had lost. They wanted to put the war, and their families' pasts, behind them, and build their new lives in Birmingham, Liverpool, or New York.

But Quinn, though—Quinn had been East. His mother's family, his father's family—grandparents he had no memory of ever meeting, uncles and aunts, cousins; all had died—*been murdered*—in that land. But he had ignored that inconvenient fact, had dutifully filed reports with London on fleet movements in the Black Sea and the number of missile silos with nuclear warheads in the Kiev region, all the while trying to forget that he was Jewish, shoving his Jewishness aside as something shameful, something that—when he allowed himself to think of it at all— he only wished he could wave away into nonexistence.

HE TURNED a corner out an alleyway and found himself in a larger street. He recognized it immediately: a dozen meters up on the other side of the road stood the Hotel Udet. He hesitated, about to turn in the other direction, but instead he headed toward the hotel. He took up a position directly across the street, standing concealed in the shadows at the mouth of another alleyway, shielded from the rain by the protective lee of a building.

He counted across and found Garner's window once more. The light was on and the blinds were up, allowing him to see into the room. He began to think the room was empty or Garner was asleep, but then he saw his quarry in his horn-rimmed glasses move across his field of vision, from one side of the room to the other. A few moments later he crossed back again.

Quinn stood there for a long time, watching, and also wondering, in the back of his mind, what was in that envelope Garner had given him. He reached inside his jacket and fingered its creased outside. It felt slightly damp at the edges but had stayed mostly dry. He did not see Garner again after that first time, though the light stayed on and he assumed the man must still be awake.

Periodically vehicles would pass, going in either direction. There were not many of them, but there were enough that he did not take any special notice when the van came around a corner a hundred meters up the road and headed in his direction. He did not notice it until it turned into the car park of the Hotel Udet and pulled up in front of the main entrance.

The van's back doors flew open and disgorged six Waffen-SS stormtroopers armed with automatic rifles, their coalscuttle helmets wrapped in plastic covers to protect them from the rain, followed by a black-uniformed SS officer carrying a pistol. The officer banged on the hotel's front door and shouted something; he could not hear what, as the sound did not carry across the street through the rain's hiss.

When no one had opened the door after a few moments, the officer nodded to one of the stormtroopers, who stepped forward and smashed at the lock with the butt of his rifle. It took only five strokes for the lock to shatter and the door to swing open. The officer headed inside, followed by four of the stormtroopers; the other two remained behind and took up guard stations at the entrance.

He watched Garner's window, sickeningly certain of what was about to happen but unable to think of anything he could do to affect it. There was no way he could warn Garner; the stormtroopers at the front entrance would see him if he tried throwing stones at his windowpane, and at any rate, the other troopers would be at the room door before Garner could climb out the window.

It actually took a good two or three minutes, much longer than he would have expected; he supposed that whatever intelligence had led the SS to Garner had not given them his room number, and they still had to find it once they had gotten inside the hotel. If they knocked at Garner's door, Garner ignored them; all that was visible to him through the window was the door suddenly swinging freely open on its hinge as its lock was smashed from the other side.

Two of the stormtroopers came first, training their rifles on something he couldn't see. Then came the officer, who strode past his field of vision, followed by the last two stormtroopers, who appeared to start immediately searching the room's closet and chest of drawers. The officer reappeared a moment later, dragging Garner after him. He threw Garner to his knees and said something to him. Garner responded, seemingly calm, and the officer snapped back an angry response.

This time Garner did not respond. The officer spoke again, still to no response. Suddenly he struck Garner across the temple with the butt of his pistol, and Garner went sprawling. The two stormtroopers calmly continued their methodical search. The officer bent over and hauled Garner back up to his knees, then spoke once more. Now Garner responded, but his words were few and probably glib.

The officer said something; no response. He shook his head and raised his pistol, setting it against Garner's temple where he had just struck him. He spoke again, very briefly; Garner simply turned and stared up into his eyes. The officer pulled the trigger.

There was a flash, though even the sound of the gunshot could not penetrate through the window and carry across the street over the white noise of the rain. Blood spattered across the windowpane. The officer stared down at Garner's body, then turned and spoke to the stormtroopers guarding the doorway. One of them stepped forward and saluted crisply, bent elbow snapping at a crisp military angle, fingers perfectly straight as they touched the brim of his helmet, then turned and headed out the room.

He did not wait around to see what would happen next. Since the officer had pulled the trigger he had been slowly backing further into the alley at whose mouth he stood. As soon as he was sure he was deep enough that there was no possibility of the stormtroopers at the hotel entrance seeing him, he turned and ran for his life away from the Hotel Udet.

CHAPTER XIII

ELLIE LAY curled up on the bed, her face buried in the pillow, but she did not cry. She refused to cry. A Jew. He was a Jew. She almost could not believe it. He did not look or act like a member of a lesser race. He certainly had not felt different from a real human being when he pressed his body against hers—surely she would have been able to tell that she was about to give herself to a sub-human.

She knew she was somewhat unusual amongst Germans of her age in that she had actually seen a real Jew before. She had been very young at the time, three or four, still living in Novgorod where her father was stationed, northwest of Moscow. She had been walking through the town square with her mother one cold autumn morning when a trio of Waffen-SS stormtroopers had shepherded a half dozen hunched, broken-looking men through the square in the direction of the work camp outside of town. Their clothing, coarse fabric with faded black and white vertical stripes, had hung limply from their gaunt, malnourished frames. Their heads had been shaved, their skin sallow and loose. Some of them might have been in their twenties, or even their late teens, but their shriveled faces, sunken eyes, and hollow cheeks made them all look like old men.

They had shuffled despondently across the square and Ellie had stared at them curiously, even when her mother had herded her back and told her to keep her distance. The most chilling thing about them was their complete lack of reaction, their seeming inability to summon the energy to *care* about anything—the onlookers in the square, the biting cold through their thin fatigues, even when one of the SS stormtroopers had suddenly slammed the butt of his rifle into one of the prisoners' backs and laughed with his fellows to see the prisoner lurch and fall flat on his face. The prisoner had merely gotten back to his feet and rejoined the line. The troopers had not even bothered to bind their charges' wrists. The young Ellie had watched them, wide-eyed, and known that these could not be *real* people.

A year or two later Ellie's parents had dispatched her to the West, when her mother found her a place at a school in Heidelberg run by the *Bund Deutscher Madel*, the League of German Girls, and she had never again seen a Jew. Until tonight.

She tried in vain to reconcile Quinn—tall, athletic, intelligent, confident, quietly superior without being condescending—with the godforsaken wretches she had seen that day so long ago in

Novgorod town square, no flicker of activity behind their glassy, lifeless eyes. How could he come from the same racial stock as they?

She lay on the bed for a long time, unmoving. After a while, feeling cold, she rose and examined her clothes, which she had hung over the radiator when she showered. Judging them dry enough, she changed out of the robe and back into her original clothing. She sat back on the bed and tucked her legs up underneath her.

She was an opponent, albeit secretly, of the National Socialist state. As the daughter of a Wehrmacht brigadier and an exemplary member of the BDM, the girls' counterpart to the Hitler Youth, she had as an adolescent been selected for the trips abroad open only to the BDM elite. She had been exposed firsthand to life in Italy and Spain, fascist countries where the government had never managed to achieve the invasive dominance over every aspect of everyday life and thought that the regime in Germany had. She wanted political dissidence to be legalized in Germany, she wanted Germans to have a voice in their government, she wanted nuclear disarmament, and she wanted the Slavic population in the East to receive their own autonomous government, rather than serving as the slave labor that fed the Reich's industrial base. But Jews? She had never considered that what her parents, her teachers, and her government had told her all her life of Jews, that they were a parasitic people who sucked on the vibrancy of European civilization while contributing nothing of their own, might not be true. It had simply never been an issue. A few isolated Jewish communities clung to life in some of the countries on the fringe of fascist Europe, like Spain, Sweden, or Finland, where they had managed to maintain a degree of independence by not openly flouting it in the Führer's face; but within the Reich and the directly occupied states, the Reich had purified the last Jew decades ago.

Yet she knew she could not simply dismiss Quinn that way. He was not the lecherous, deformed, grasping monster of her school history and racial biology textbooks, preying on her virginal— hmph, the look on her mother's face if she ever learnt the truth about *that* little myth—Nordic virtue. She had been attracted to Quinn longer than she would have liked to admit; the beer tonight had simply diminished her inhibitions against acting upon that attraction. And more than that, she *liked* him—admired him, even. There was something noble to him: as much as she knew he would deny it if confronted, he was not the moral cynic he pretended to be. He fought for an ideal, though she was not sure what that ideal was. At first she had thought it was England; now that she knew his origin, she suspected it was simply the end of National Socialism. Just like her.

———

HE BOUNDED up the stairs and along the hallway, room key already in hand. He tried too hurriedly to force it into the lock and fumbled with it slightly, but after a moment he was able to slide it home and felt the lock click when he turned the key. He opened the door and went inside.

Ellie was sitting on the bed. She was already dressed. Good. He wondered idly if she had gotten dressed to leave before he returned, then he dismissed the thought; there were more important things to attend to now.

She looked up at him, her eyes wide, startled.

"Come on," he said. "We have to leave. Now." He bent down and picked up her pumps from beside the radiator, tossed them to her. They were still wet.

"What's going on?" she asked.

He hesitated, then decided to tell her. "The Gestapo. They've found Garner. He's dead. They could be coming after us next."

She stared at him for a long moment without any visible reaction, then simply nodded and obediently slipped on her pumps. Once she had her coat on, he let her exit the room first, then followed her and closed the door behind them. He left the room key on the reception desk as they left the building.

It was all running through his mind, over and over.

The stormtroopers emerging from the back of the van.

Garner on his knees, refusing to let go of his dignity

He let her into the passenger side of the car, then went round to the driver's side.

The officer setting the muzzle of his pistol against Garner's temple, pausing, and then pulling the trigger; then calmly turning around and issuing orders to one of his stormtroopers.

They took the long way around the city center, so as to avoid passing the Hotel Udet. His soaked clothing clung to his body, chilling him, and at a red light he peeled off his jacket and tossed it on the back seat.

The stormtrooper stepping forward and acknowledging the order with a salute.

They drove in silence; he wondered what Ellie was thinking, whether she was still thinking about earlier tonight. He would have expected her to demand he tell her more, tell her what he had been doing with Garner and how he had escaped the Gestapo.

The officer had been so businesslike, as had the stormtrooper to whom he spoke, saluting crisply, elbow bent at a perfect angle like he was on the parade ground, his eyes not even flicking down at the body at his feet.

The rain was coming down as fiercely as ever, making it hard for him to see the road, and he had to go slowly. Once they got on the autobahn they were the only car heading northeast, and he was able to speed up a little, though not too much. Heading in the opposite direction, though, southwest from Nuremberg and Berlin, was a different story. Traffic, even at this late hour, was heavy, the road busy with mourners in their Volkswagen Cabriolets and KdF-Wagens bound for the Führer's funeral in Linz, the day after tomorrow.

At last Ellie stirred. "Did they see you?" she asked. "The Gestapo?"

He shook his head. "No."

"What about Garner? Did you speak with him at all?"

"No."

"I wonder how they found him."

"Me too."

"He's definitely dead? He's not in custody?" *You saw his body? Or did you arrive after they had taken him?*

"He's definitely dead. I saw the whole thing from across the street."

The officer had been so businesslike, as had the stormtrooper to whom he spoke, saluting crisply, elbow bent at a perfect angle, his eyes not even flickering down at the body at his feet

He frowned. That couldn't be right. Could it?

—the stormtrooper saluting crisply, elbow bent at a perfect angle, eyes not even flickering—

—elbow bent—

He slammed on the brake and pulled over to the side of the road, throwing Ellie forward in her seat with a cry of surprise. If he had been driving one of the basic Volkswagens the Reich made so affordable to its working class citizens, like the cars passing them by in the opposite direction—the KdF-Wagen, or Strength-through-Joy car, or its slightly modified sibling, the Cabriolet—he would probably have left his transmission lying in the middle of the road behind them, but he was driving an SS Focke-Wulf. The mechanism gave a grating whine of protest and the stick fought back as he shifted gears, then all was well.

Ellie dusted herself off. Her eyes flashed angrily. "What the hell—"

Her exclamation died when she saw he was pointing his pistol at her.

"Are you working for the British?" he demanded.

She stared at him blankly, then managed, "What?"

He repeated himself more slowly. "Are you working for the British?"

She frowned. "What are you talking about? *You're* working for the British."

Her obvious confusion was already enough to satisfy him, but he still needed a denial. "And you're not working for them behind my back?"

"What? No. No, of course not. What the hell is going on?"

"Then how did they bloody well find Richard Garner?"

She blinked. "*What?*"

He put the gun away, reached over, and wrenched the glove compartment open. He pulled out the papers inside—car registry and his citizenship documentation, left there by MI6 when they provided him the car—and ran his hand along the compartment's inner wall. Nothing.

He bent over and searched underneath the driver's side dash in the same way, neatly and systematically running his fingertips along every surface, reaching up inside any opening and checking its interior as far as he could fit his fingers, running his hands along the underside of the accelerator, the brake and the clutch, then repeating the process beneath the dash on the Ellie's side. Beneath his seat. Beneath Ellie's seat.

Ellie watched him in confused, slightly alarmed fascination, remaining silent except to emit a slight yelp and jerk her feet up when he stuck his hand between her knees to check the underside of her seat. After he had checked there, he pulled up in turn both of the rubber mats on the floor beneath his own feet and Ellie's, but he found nothing under there either. Eventually he might have to check the gear box, but there were still other, easier places he could eliminate before he had to take *that* apart.

He pulled the lever to pop the car bonnet, got out of the car and went round to the front, leaving the car door open behind him. He lifted the bonnet and examined the engine. He held the bonnet to shield the engine parts from the rain, but it was coming down at an angle and a few drops of water still got in, sizzling against the hot metal and rubber. Three years as a tank driver in Siberia, where maintenance and replacement components were often hard to come by, had left him an expert on automotive engines, but he could see nothing wrong here. Damn.

He lowered the bonnet and went back round to the car door, leaning in, turning the car off and removing the key from the ignition.

"What's going on?" Ellie demanded, but he ignored her. He went round to the back of the car, unlocked the boot, and began to run his fingertips along its inside.

Ellie got out of the car and followed him round. She grabbed him by the shoulder and pulled him round to face her.

"*What* is going on?"

He ran a hand through his soaked black hair and wiped water from his eyes. He could feel the rain dripping off the tip of his beaked nose. "They were British," he said at last.

She stared at him. He was acutely aware of how beautiful she was in the eerie red glow of the car's taillights, already drenched after just a few seconds, water streaming off the end of her nose.

"What?"

"One of the SS troopers saluted." He demonstrated the Western salute perfunctorily, elbow bent, fingers of the right hand touched to the forehead. Not like the Nazi salute, right arm held straight out in front, open palm facing the ground and fingers rigidly straight. "He saluted. They were Westerners. They were bloody British disguised as Gestapo."

She blinked again. "You mean like the English soldiers at Jurgen's last night?"

"*Just* like the soldiers last night." Had Captain Barnes been the officer who shot Garner?

She did not respond. He bent back over the boot and began his search once more.

There. That strange bump under the upholstery. He probed at the fabric seam where it was glued down around the rim of the car boot, searching for a loose end. He tugged at it, hard, and it came free with a loud rip. He stuck his hand down inside the fabric and closed his fingers round the small, warm piece of metal he found there. Some sort of adhesive tape secured it to the inside of the Focke-Wulf's metal frame, and he had to pull twice at it before it came free. He removed his hand from inside the fabric, still clutching the device.

It was a small radio transmitter with a tiny red light blinking slowly at one end. He held it out to Ellie. She stared at it.

"What is it?" she asked.

"A shortwave transmitter. A beacon. They've been second guessing me the whole bloody time. They gave me the car. The British did, and it was bloody bugged. And then they've been following me since I got here."

He tossed it onto the ground and raised his foot, ready to smash it with his heel, but thought better of it. He picked it up again and instead threw it as hard as he could away from the road. That should confuse them for a few hours at least, thinking he was still sitting here by the side of the road a dozen kilometers north of Munich. They both stared after it.

What was going on? He needed to understand, and it was time he faced up to that. One man had already died tonight because of his own indecision.

He turned to Ellie. "Will you drive?" he asked.

She had not expected the question. "What?"

"Will you drive?"

She nodded. He closed the boot and tossed the keys to her, then went around to the passenger side and got in. He watched her get in on the other side, her soaked skirt clinging to her thighs, then reached into the back seat and grabbed Garner's envelope from his jacket as she turned the key in the ignition and the engine growled to life. As she put the car into gear and pulled back onto the road, he switched the car's dome light on and tore the file open.

CHAPTER XIV

HE EMPTIED the contents of the envelope onto his lap. There were three documents: two sets of papers, each maybe a dozen pages long and paperclipped together, and a loose, typewritten sheet. He examined the single sheet first. It was a letter from Garner.

Ellie glanced over at him intermittently as he sorted through the envelope's contents. "What is it?" she asked when he had still not said anything after the better part of a minute.

"I don't know," he said. He wanted her to be quiet for a bit while he studied the documents and came to some initial conclusions of his own.

I DO not take the decision I have reached lightly. For twenty-eight years I have served my Sovereign, my superiors, and my belief in right and wrong, and it has taken careful consideration of my present misgivings over an extended period to convince myself that the actions demanded by those three masters are no longer compatible. The path which my service has taken has, by its nature, occasionally demanded that I set aside qualms about what my country has required of me, and that I accept that conscience is not a luxury permitted to the men and women who fight the battles I fight. Previously, I have always found such a moral compromise bearable because I have known that the deeds I have done have been performed in the service of England, and that England remains a bastion of freedom in opposition to the world's greatest evil. Concepts such as patriotism, honor, and liberty are often considered out of date in the modern world, I know, especially in my line of work, but for me they are still the defining concepts of my life.

Yet now I find that my conscience has indeed discovered the act that it cannot countenance, the line it will not let me cross. My country demands of me an act of complaisance in direct opposition to what my belief in right and wrong tells me I should do. I am about to take the first step in a very drastic action, and for the first time in my life I will be betraying the oath I took to my Queen. I admit that, at the time I take this first step, I have no idea whether I will be able to take the second, or even what the second step will be. I only know that to refrain from taking action will be to serve the evil I have dedicated my life to trying to end, and that therefore action must be taken. I believe that now, in acting to fight against this evil, I am ultimately serving Great Britain and her people, even if I am committing treason against the British Government in so doing. I only hope that God—and perhaps one day my Queen and my country—can forgive me.

The documents accompanying this note are the final draft of the product of eight secret meetings between the elite echelon of the German SS hierarchy and senior officials at the British embassy in Berlin between February 1970 and April 1971. The principal negotiators were, for Germany, SS-Oberstgruppenfuehrer Ernst Kaltenbrunner, Chief of the RSHA German security service, and SS-Obergruppenfuehrer Hermann Fegelein, personal deputy to Reichsfuehrer-SS Heinrich Himmler; and for Great Britain, the British Ambassador to Germany and, representing Her Majesty's Secret Intelligence Service, myself. So as to remain away from watchful eyes, these substantive meetings were held at the abandoned Columbia-Haus SS prison in Berlin, though minor functionaries of both parties met several times at Gestapo headquarters at No. 8 Prinz Albrechtstrasse, Berlin, for the purpose of resolving minor procedural conflicts regarding the policies determined at Columbia-Haus.

Richard A. Garner
Berlin, 23 May 1971

HE SET the letter aside and turned to the two packets of papers. They appeared to be identical translations of the same text, one in English, one in German. Both documents were typewritten, though unlike Garner's letter, they had been typed on a typewriter capable of reproducing German characters. He studied the English document.

THE GREATER German Empire and the United Kingdom of Great Britain and Northern Ireland, hereinafter referred to jointly as the Parties and individually as, respectively, Germany and the United Kingdom,

Conscious that nuclear war would have devastating consequences for all mankind, and that their mutual policies regarding each other since the signing of the Armistice in January 1946 ending the previous hostilities have not been the most conducive towards preventing nuclear conflict, but to the contrary, have tended to escalate tensions between the Parties,

Declare hereby their intentions to take steps to promote the harmonising of relations between the Parties in the interest of the preservation of European and world peace, and in pursuance of such have agreed as follows:

"MY GOD," he said, unaware of whether he was speaking English or German. He leafed through the pages.

"What?" Ellie asked.

ARTICLE III. The British Zone of Occupation in Italy

The United Kingdom undertakes to withdraw completely from its Zone of Occupation in the Italian Social Republic within six months of the signing of this document, to turn over all facilities therein currently occupied by the British Armed Forces to agents of the Italian Government in said time frame, and to withdraw recognition of and sever all diplomatic ties with the government that it has established in the Zone of Occupation, namely the Republic of Sicily.

————

"IT'S A détente," he said.

"A what?"

"It's an agreement. A permanent treaty. Between Britain and Germany."

"You mean a peace treaty?"

"More like a bleeding surrender," he murmured.

"Speak German. I don't understand English."

He glanced at her. "I said it's more like a surrender than a peace treaty."

————

ARTICLE VI. The North Atlantic Treaty Organization

NATO being an offensive alliance constituted specifically to target Germany and Germany's Warsaw Pact Allies, and not, as its founding document maintains, a defensive alliance against any unspecified external threat, the United Kingdom undertakes to withdraw forthwith from NATO. The United Kingdom does not undertake to replace its NATO membership with membership in the Warsaw Pact, though neither Party construes this to prevent the United Kingdom's admittance to the Warsaw Pact at a future date. Once the United Kingdom has withdrawn from NATO, Germany undertakes, in the event of military invasion of the United Kingdom's integral territory in the British Isles, or of British territory in the Mediterranean Sea, to employ the full military force of the Warsaw Pact in defense of British sovereignty.

ARTICLE VII. Foreign military presence in the United Kingdom

In pursuance of the removal from the United Kingdom of offensive nuclear weapons targeted at Germany, as per Article I, and the United Kingdom's withdrawal from NATO, as per Article VI, the United Kingdom undertakes to re-establish sovereignty over all United States military and naval facilities within its borders in the British Isles and to expel all United States military and naval personnel stationed in the British Isles within twelve months of the signing of this document, excepting only those personnel expressly attached to United States diplomatic missions to the United Kingdom.

In the case of military and naval bases in the British Isles held by the United States as recompense for material assistance provided by the United States to the United Kingdom during the war of 1939–1946 under the provisions of the Anglo-American Agreement of 1940, Germany undertakes to compensate the United States monetarily for the proportion of such aid as those bases represent. This provision shall not apply to British facilities outside the British Isles leased by the United States under the 1940 agreement, such as the Royal Navy bases in Bermuda or the Caribbean Sea.

IN ELEVEN pages and nineteen articles, the document tied up every loose end left hanging for twenty-five years by the Corunna Armistice, neatly and succinctly—and, in almost every case, markedly in favor of the Germans. Occasionally a provision included a degree of reciprocity, as when Britain agreed no longer to fund Algerian freedom fighters against the French in exchange for an end to clandestine German support of nationalist terrorists in Northern Ireland. But clauses where it was Germany making concessions markedly in Britain's favor were hard to come by. He shuffled through the pages, searching for such provisions. They were few and, for the most part, minor.

ARTICLE XII. The Channel Isles

Germany undertakes to turn over possession of the German Luftwaffe base on the island of Jersey and the German Kriegsmarine submarine base on the island of Guernsey to the British Royal Air Force and Royal Navy, respectively, at a time chosen by the United Kingdom, and to withdraw wholly from the Channel Isles immediately upon receipt of notification from the United Kingdom that it is ready to re-establish its sovereignty there.

AND THEN, two pages later on,

ARTICLE XV. The Mediterranean Sea and the Suez Zone

The Parties agree that the Mediterranean Sea is a region of vital national interest to both the United Kingdom and Germany's Warsaw Pact Allies Spain, Italy, and Croatia. The Parties also agree that their interests in the area are not mutually contradictory and that the achievement of either Party's aims in the Mediterranean does not imply a concession of defeat by the other Party.

In pursuance of this, Germany undertakes to use its influence with its ally Italy to end Italian and Egyptian claims to sovereignty over the Suez Canal Zone.

EVEN THIS last was only half a victory; accepting that British interests in the Mediterranean were not "mutually contradictory" with Italian and Croatian interests would obviously entail the British Army's withdrawal from Greece. And with President Kennedy continuing to provide only air and naval support to the Greek war effort while refusing to send in American troops on the ground, that would mean the certain collapse of the Greek army.

He felt the anger rising in his throat. Karl had died because of the war in Greece—Karl, who had never wanted to spy against Germany or even work for the Gestapo in the first place, but whom Quinn had blackmailed into it. And so had hundreds, even thousands, of men and boys: Greeks, Britons, Italians, Croats. And now the British Government was going to back meekly away with its tail between its legs.

He came to the last page, saw the lines awaiting signatures: the Führer and Himmler for Germany, the Prime Minister and the Earl of Home for Britain. Then he saw the date: 2 June. Monday. The Führer's death had thrown everything into disarray with only another six days to go before the treaty would have been signed.

He went back to the beginning of the document and started to read it through, carefully. The car continued its way along the deserted autobahn through the storm and the night, and Simon Quinn's world teetered on its axis.

CHAPTER XV

THEY ARRIVED in Berlin shortly after dawn. It had rained in the capital, too, and the almost deserted city streets were damp and glistening in the bright sunlight of the early morning's cloudless sky. The SS had blocked off the processional route for the funeral carriage, due to depart in less than an hour, forcing Quinn and Ellie to take a detour across the River Spree in order to get to Ellie's flat. As they crossed the great stone expanse of the Josef Goebbels Bridge, Quinn glimpsed a rainbow floating over the water.

He was in the driver's seat once more. After he had finished examining every detail of the Columbia-Haus treaty, Ellie had insisted on switching back so that she could read the German version for herself. They had driven in silence as she pored over it intently, reading and rereading every clause, just as he had done. Even after she finished her examination and replaced all three documents in Garner's envelope, they still did not speak.

A man has already died for this.

Now he faced the same dilemma as Garner: what to do next?

He parked along the curb outside Ellie's building. He held out his hand and wordlessly, expressionlessly, she handed over the envelope. They got out of the car and headed inside. The decaying building's lift was broken, so they had to walk up the three flights of stairs to Ellie's flat. On the way, Quinn removed the two treaties and Garner's letter from the envelope and folded them so they would fit into the inside pocket of his coat.

When they got inside Ellie put some bread in the toaster for breakfast, then went into the bedroom to change. Quinn stood by the living room window and stared down at the street below. It was the same view he had seen yesterday morning—and yet, it was completely different.

Ellie came out of her room and got the toast and margarine. Still without a word of conversation, she set it out on the table, sat down and proceeded to start eating. Quinn was aware that breakfast was out, but remained at the window, staring at the German capital's rooftops.

Eventually he turned away from the view, crossed the room and joined Ellie at the table. He ate sparingly.

After a while she asked, "What will you do now?"

He thought for a moment, then reluctantly shook his head. "I don't know. I've been trying to figure that out all night."

They finished eating and he helped clean up, then went back to the window.

He became aware that she was sitting on her settee, staring

at the back of his head. He turned round to face her. For a long time they regarded each other silently. At last he said, "If there was something I *could* do, Richard Garner could have done it, too."

She nodded. "You're probably right." She continued to stare at him.

"Well?" he said after a few more moments of this. "What do *you* think I should do?"

She shrugged. "It's not up to me. You're the Englishman."

Now he turned fully towards her. "And if it *were* up to you?"

"It's not."

"But if it *were*."

She looked him directly in the eye. "If it were up to me, I wouldn't do anything at all."

He frowned and did not speak at first; the answer was so unexpected that it took him a moment to process it. At last he said only, "Pardon?"

She shrugged and looked away from him. "They sent you here to do something about Garner and to find that file. That's been done. You're finished."

He took a step toward her and leaned slightly forward; his sudden earnestness was in marked contrast to her deliberate nonchalance. "Didn't you read that bloody thing? Britain is *surrendering*. This isn't Germany winning. This is National Socialism winning. This is the Party you're supposed to oppose guaranteeing itself hegemony in Europe."

"I don't think so," she said. She was fiddling at a loose strand of fabric on the settee. It refused to come loose, and in a momentary instant of frustration she yanked at it, hard, ripping the cushion. In that moment he saw her offhand manner was just an act, a studied presentation for—what? To hide her nervousness? An excuse not to have to look Quinn in the eye as she said this?

He watched her consciously pull her hand away from the strand of fabric. "I don't think so," she repeated. "With this, the threat of nuclear war in Europe is over. The Cold War is over— the Americans have just lost their base of operations in Europe. Without the specter of the evil Jewish Western industrial democracies, the Party won't have a threat to divert attention from what's going on in Germany. People will be aware of their condition. They'll want changes and reform, and the Party won't be able to suppress it anymore. I think this treaty is good not just for the Party, but for Germany—and for England, too."

"You can't be serious," he said. "This is the National Socialist Party, Ellie. They're not going to just give in to a few dissatisfied student marches and dismantle forty years of totalitarian apparatus. And without an external threat any longer, they're going to be able to concentrate even more on transforming the German people into their Master Race. If you thought *this* was repression, you're in for a bloody surprise. You can't reason with them, and you can't capitulate to them. These are evil people."

"Well of course someone like *you* would say that."

She realized what she had said. Her hand flew to her mouth and she looked up at Quinn, wide-eyed. He simply gazed back at her. They were silent for several moments, then he spoke.

"Richard Garner knew this was wrong too," he said evenly, "enough to die to stop it, and *he* wasn't Jewish." He pointed at the city outside the flat's window. "*They* know it's wrong. The British government knows it's wrong. They know they need to hide it. They're ashamed of it. They negotiated the bloody thing in secret. They killed Richard Garner because he wouldn't keep their secret anymore. They knew that *I* would never accept it and

yet they couldn't find anyone else who would go along with them
to do their dirty work, so instead they've been second guessing me
since the moment I got here. They followed me to Munich and
murdered Garner. They were following me at Den—"

He broke off in mid-sentence. He broke eye contact with Ellie
and stared off at a point in space over her shoulder, his mind
working furiously.

"What?" she asked. "Following you where?"

He did not reply. *"How did you know where I was?"* he had asked.
"How did you know there'd be trouble?"

*"Your chaps got word through one of their usual sources that a raid
was planned,"* Barnes had answered. *"So the embassy sent us out to
look after you."* Then he had changed the bloody subject. He had
answered the second question, but never the first.

"Bloody hell," he swore. He grabbed his coat from over the
back of the settee, walked over to the front door, and opened it.

"Stop," Ellie said. "Where are you going?" She was up and
across the room in three steps. He had his hand on the outside
doorknob and was swinging the door shut when she caught him
by the forearm. "Stop," she repeated.

He turned his head to look at her. "I thank you for your
assistance thus far, mein Fraulein," he said, icily formal. "I could
not have accomplished what I have without you. But now our
loyalties seem to have diverged. Good bye, mein Fraulein. I will
probably be unsuccessful, but I am off to try to save Britain. And
Germany."

He shut the door firmly and, without hesitation, turned and
started down the stairs. There was no sound of the door opening
again behind him and her emerging in pursuit. He was unsure
whether he regretted that.

"*They followed me to Munich and murdered Garner,*" he had said, then had started to add, "*They were following me at Denlinger's flat.*"

He emerged into the street. There were a few more people about, though it was still very early. The U-bahn station was two blocks away. He started walking.

Barnes had neatly dodged the question—"*How did you know where I was?*"—and had then moved the conversation on to something else. Quinn's heart had still been pounding at the prospect of the Gestapo catching them a few moments earlier at Denlinger's. He had still been adjusting to the fact that he was here again, in Berlin, working for MI6; and, so soon after meeting Ellie, he had been acutely aware of her presence and was anxious to speak with her. Besides, after he had satisfied himself that Barnes really was who he claimed, he had trusted the man—they were supposed to be on the same side, after all. So the fact that Barnes had not answered the question had slipped his mind, and he had failed to return to it.

That had been a mistake. Worse, it had been an amateurish mistake, and he was cursing himself now for making it. Four years out of practice or not, missing such a basic point was an inexcusable blow to his professional pride, and Richard Garner might still be alive now if he had kept his wits about him for a few minutes.

Obviously, MI6 had known beforehand that he would be at Denlinger's flat for the meeting. A squad of Royal Marines could not just have been following him around disguised as Waffen-SS stormtroopers on the off chance he would get caught up in a Gestapo raid.

He paid the fare and entered the U-bahn platform. It was almost empty at this time of morning; all the crowds were already in the city or making their way back home after seeing the Führer's sarcophagus start its journey. A large movie poster advertised Leni Riefenstahl's new film, *Charlemagne:* Max von Sydow, dressed in medieval armor, face covered in mud and blood and contorted in a scream of rage or victory, raised his sword above his head over the tagline, *A thousand years ago, the first great German swore to civilize the barbarian Slavs to the East—with his sword.*

Only two men had known that Quinn would be at that meeting. Of the two, he was certain that Denlinger was not working for the British. He was a talented judge of character—in his line of work, he had to be—and Denlinger enjoyed making dissatisfied noises about the need for change in Germany, but would never voluntarily take the risk of actually doing anything about it. His abject terror when the Gestapo showed up at his front door had convinced Quinn of that.

That left only one.

It was about twenty minutes on the U-bahn to the Grand Avenue station, where he got off. He emerged from the U-bahn terminal into the Grand Avenue, in the shadow of the Führer's beloved Triumphal Arch, twice as large as Napoleon's Arc d'Triomphe in Paris. The Avenue stretched away from him on either side, the centerpiece of the city-sized testament to National Socialism that Speer had built from the ruins of Berlin after the war and the center of the National Socialist Party bureaucracy that ruled Germany and all of Continental Europe.

The Grand Avenue was busy, but not so crowded as it would have been less than an hour before, when the procession bearing the Führer's sarcophagus had left the Grand Plaza at the near terminus of the Avenue and passed solemnly beneath the Triumphal Arch and the Brandenburg Gate as it departed

Berlin for Linz. Now many of the hundreds of thousands who had gathered to watch the Führer leave his capital for the final time were taking time to gaze at Speer's magnificent monuments to National Socialism before returning to their homes, either in Berlin or in other cities in the western part of the Reich, in time for the funeral in Linz tomorrow.

The Grand Plaza and the Great Hall stood at one end of the Grand Avenue; the Führer's Palace stood at the opposite, over a kilometer away. The intervening distance was lined with government ministries, theaters and opera houses, museums, the European Assembly and the embassies of Germany's Warsaw Pact allies and satellites.

Quinn made his way through the bustling crowds towards the French embassy, a few hundred meters down the Avenue. It sat along the edge of a small square opening off the main Avenue, flanked on one side by the Public Works Ministry and on the other by one of Berlin's several art museums, filled with Europe's cultural treasures imported during and after the war. In the center of the square stood a two-meter-tall statue of Pierre Laval, who had served for fifteen years as French Chief-of-State following Pétain's retirement at the end of the war and had completed the transformation of France into essentially an external organ of the Reich.

A grey-uniformed Wehrmacht rifleman stood guard by the embassy's front entrance, a small blue, white, and red Tricolor sewn onto his upper sleeve indicating that he was a Frenchman. France, like most of Germany's fascist satellites, no longer had a military of its own. By the Warsaw Pact in 1955, the Führer had dissolved the satellites' independent armies and air forces and had absorbed them into the Wehrmacht. The new pan-European Wehrmacht drew its ranks and regimental officers from all the Warsaw Pact states, but the general officers were almost universally German.

Himmler, of course, had wanted to disband the Wehrmacht altogether and replace it with his Waffen-SS, which already had regiments recruited from every state of fascist Europe, thereby giving the Reich and its European empire a military that was as ideologically and racially focused as the National Socialist government. But he had been frustrated by Heydrich, who as Reich Commissar-General was commander of the massive Wehrmacht forces charged with keeping the East pacified and defending the Ural border against the Siberian raiding parties. Heydrich's victory in the dispute with Himmler over the fate of the Wehrmacht had marked the final, irrevocable rift between the two former political allies.

Quinn checked his watch. A quarter past eight. Still fairly early. He sat down near the bottom of the stone steps leading up to the embassy entrance, watched, and waited.

He did not have to wait long. It was just after twenty past when he saw Maurice Beauchamp enter the square from the Grand Avenue, wrapped in a long charcoal trench coat and a grey fedora and carrying a briefcase. He rose to his feet when he saw him.

After a few steps Beauchamp spotted Quinn too. Maybe the Frenchman already knew that Garner was dead and Quinn had read the Columbia-Haus file, or maybe he simply saw something in Quinn's eyes as their gazes locked briefly across the small square. Whichever it was, as soon as Beauchamp spotted him, he turned and ran as fast as he could back out towards the Grand Avenue.

Quinn took off after him, skirting past the statue of Laval as he darted across the square. He paused as he emerged into the Grand Avenue, scanning the vista before him for Beauchamp.

Momentarily he could not find him, but then he saw him: on the other side of the street, heading in the direction of the Führer's palace.

He followed, pushing his way past several sightseers who yelled after him in protest. He was much fitter than Maurice and gained on him quickly, but in such a crowded place the danger of losing him remained great.

Without warning the Frenchman cut inside the front gate of the Propaganda Ministry, his hat flying from his head with the sudden change of direction. A moment later Quinn followed. Maurice was charging across the Ministry's entry courtyard towards a small exit in the far corner. Quinn pursued him, vaulting over the edge of the fountain at the courtyard's center.

Beauchamp disappeared through the small archway in the brick wall, but Quinn was just a meter or two behind him now. The two men emerged onto the edge of the lawn separating the Propaganda Ministry from the Führer's Palace. Beauchamp had turned and was dashing along the side of the Ministry building, but in turning he had slowed sufficiently to allow Quinn into touching distance. Quinn reached out, stretching forward, and grabbed him by the shoulder.

Both men stumbled at the contact. Beauchamp turned about, arms flailing wildly, and his briefcase struck Quinn on the temple, hard. Quinn staggered back, putting out his hand against the Ministry wall to steady himself and dropping to one knee. The briefcase swung open, disgorging a flock of loose papers that were immediately caught up on the breeze and flurried around the two men.

Maurice, still off his balance, stumbled at the impact with Quinn's head and collapsed onto his back. He made to get up again, to continue running, but Quinn was faster. He caught the Frenchman by the leg and pulled him back down, then used the leverage provided by his grip to haul himself up on top of the older man and straddle him. With his left hand he pulled Maurice round by the shoulder, then drew back his right fist and punched him in the jaw. The Frenchman went limp beneath him and Quinn collapsed forward and rolled off him, lying on his back on the pavement and gasping for breath.

After a few moments he rolled onto his side and raised himself onto one elbow. Across the lawn a Waffen-SS guardsman was watching them apprehensively from his position amongst the columns of the colonnade along the side of the Führer's Palace. He had unslung his rifle and taken half a step forward, unsure of how he should react to the commotion twenty meters away.

Quinn dug into his inside coat pocket and worked his ID free from where it had lodged itself beneath the folded copy of the Columbia-Haus treaty. He flipped the ID open and held it up toward the guardsman, even though there was no possibility of the young man being able to make out anything of it from across the lawn.

"Amt III," he called reassuringly and waved the guardsman back. The young man took a cautious step backward but did not sling his rifle back over his shoulder.

Quinn looked around and spotted an alcove in the Ministry building's wall a few feet away. He got to one knee and grabbed Maurice by his coat lapels. The Frenchman was curled into a fetal ball and coughing as he tried to get his wind back. His spectacles lay a few meters away in the grass. Quinn hauled him up and half-dragged him across the pavement.

The alcove contained a small stone bench in a recess that

would be hidden from the prying eyes of the Waffen-SS guardsman or anyone else out on the lawn. Quinn hauled Beauchamp onto the bench and bent over him, hands firmly on the other man's shoulders to prevent him from making any sudden moves. Both men were breathing heavily and sweating in the chill morning air, which burned inside Quinn's chest every time he inhaled.

After a few moments Beauchamp looked up at him, blinking, trying unsuccessfully to focus on his face. Quinn straightened and walked over to the grass, clutching one arm across his abdomen as he bent over to retrieve Maurice's spectacles. One lens had completely shattered. Quinn stepped back into the alcove, took Maurice's hand and placed the spectacles in his palm.

The Frenchman closed his fingers around the bent wire frames, fumbled with them and managed to put them on. He frowned when he realized one of the lenses had broken. He looked around at his surroundings, blinking, one eye comically larger than the other. He looked at Quinn and blinked several times, trying to focus, then tried closing the eye behind the shattered lens. Evidently this was not sufficiently comfortable, for he shook his head and took off the spectacles, massaging the bridge of his nose with thumb and forefinger. After a moment he looked up but was unable to find Quinn and simply stared sightlessly off into space.

Quinn, satisfied that Beauchamp was not going to try to make a break for it, was sitting with his back against the opposite wall and his knees tucked up under his chin, watching the other man.

"What happened?" Maurice asked at last, in French. "What did you find out?"

"I think you know," Quinn said.

"Columbia-Haus," he said glumly. "You f-found out about Columbia-Haus."

Quinn nodded, then realized Maurice could not see the motion. "Yes."

"You've read it?"

"I have."

"Where did you find it? Garner?"

"Yes."

"You've found him then. Where is he?"

"He was in Munich. He's dead."

Beauchamp was silent for several moments. "You killed him?" he asked at last.

"No," said Quinn. "The British government did. They've been following me. But then, you already knew that."

"I had a fair idea they would be, yes."

Quinn shook his head. "You knew. You've been feeding them information on my whereabouts."

Maurice pursed his lips as if he wanted to say something but evidently thought better of it. Instead he said, "So why are you here? Wh-what do you want to know now?"

"Everything else you haven't told me." Quinn leaned forward. "How can I stop this, Maurice?"

Maurice laughed hollowly. "You can't, Johann—or whatever your name might b-be right now." Quinn was glad the Frenchman could not see him flinch at that. "It's done. Just waiting for the signatures. Just because the Führer is dead doesn't mean there won't be s-someone else to sign it in his place."

"There has to be something I can do," Quinn countered. "There has to be something in the balance. If there wasn't, there'd be no need for all this. They would never have brought me back if this whole thing wasn't absolutely desperate."

At first Beauchamp said nothing. Then, sounding slightly more earnest now, "Give it up, will you? You're beaten. You've r-read the damn thing. R-remember those names on the back page? Both countries are in too far to b-back out now."

The names on the last page. The Führer, Himmler, the Prime Minister, and Lord Home.

Quinn frowned. Prime Minister and Führer; Foreign Secretary and—Reichsführer-SS. Why not the Foreign Minister?

"Himmler," he said, and he saw Beauchamp start. "This isn't a Foreign Ministry treaty. This isn't a government treaty. It's an *SS* treaty. It's Himmler's." Beauchamp was becoming more agitated. Quinn frowned. "Maurice," he said warningly, "there's something you're still not telling me."

The Frenchman seemed about to object, then visibly wilted in resignation. "Yes," he agreed. "It's Himmler's. But the Führer had already approved it before he died. It's just as good as a Foreign Ministry treaty."

"Then why all the—" Quinn's eyes widened. "The will. There's something going on with the will. The treaty is due to be signed on Monday, but the will's going to be read tomorrow. So Himmler needs the treaty signed sooner. He doesn't think he's going to be named as the Führer's successor."

"He *knows* he's not the Führer's successor," Maurice corrected.

Quinn looked at him sharply. "What do you mean?"

"The will names Heydrich as successor," Beauchamp said. "Himmler knows this because B-Bormann told him; Bormann witnessed the will. Himmler has a draft copy of the treaty with the Führer's signature on it; Bormann had the old bastard sign it while he was delirious last week, after he collapsed and it became obvious he didn't have long left."

The Frenchman paused, taking in a long, shuddering breath,

then continued. "Himmler needs to get the English Prime Minister to sign the treaty before the funeral tomorrow so he can announce it during his eulogy before the will is read and create enough of a commotion to have the will overturned."

"So Himmler can seize power? Have himself made Führer?"

Beauchamp nodded. Quinn was leaning forward now. "How do you know this, Maurice?"

The Frenchman sighed. "Because I don't work for the English. I work for Himmler."

"What?"

"Well, Fegelein actually."

"You work for Heinrich Himmler's personal deputy?"

Beauchamp nodded.

"But how?" Quinn asked.

Beauchamp laughed again. It was not a pleasant sound. "I don't think you've ever appreciated, Johann, just what a thorn you were in the Gestapo's side. Lancelot was the bane of Berlin counterintelligence's existence. You were *good*. They would have done anything to stop you. Himmler placed Fegelein in personal charge of their efforts to discover your identity."

"And they found you?"

Maurice nodded. "About three months before you left Berlin. They'd figured out that you had an operative at the French embassy, and they fed different stories to each of the various department secretaries. It led them to me. They would have tortured me and killed me. I had no choice."

He stopped speaking, and Quinn looked up at him. He saw that Maurice's lips were trembling and his eyes were moist. He was about to ask what choice he was talking about, but then it dawned on him.

"It was you," he breathed. He sat back against the wall in surprise. He was no longer looking at Maurice. "You betrayed Karl and me to the Germans."

Maurice shook his head. "No," he said vehemently. "I betrayed *you* to the Germans. Not Karl. I thought—th-they told me—they told me Karl would be safe. They s-said once they had Lancelot they would let us go, leave us alone. They promised me a little cottage for the two of us in Corsica or the Côte d'Azur and a state pension from Paris. I believed them. What else could I do?"

The tears were running down his cheeks now. He was no longer speaking to Quinn, but to himself. "That was when I found out what your call name was. Lancelot. I hadn't even known before then that you were working for England; you could have been with the Americans, or Canada, or Australia. I knew nothing about you. But you knew everything about me. You'd known my secret, my one, fatal weakness, before the first time we even met. You bastard."

He was quiet for a few moments. Then, suddenly, he spoke again. "Afterward, though—after it was all over, and Karl was gone—they did leave me alone. Said I had to stay in Berlin, but they left me alone." The bitterness in his voice started to rise again. "Until I got a phone call at half past two in the morning three nights ago, and they told me I could expect you to get in touch with me sometime that day."

Once again he lapsed into silence. Quinn hesitated, unsure of whether Maurice was going to say something else, but the Frenchman gave no sign of preparing to speak again. Quinn said, "You told the Germans I would be at Denlinger's flat. And they told the British embassy."

Maurice shrugged. "If that's what they did. I had no idea what the Gestapo would do with the information. I just passed it on."

"But the *Germans*, Maurice," Quinn breathed.

Beauchamp chuckled again. The sound of it was beginning to make Quinn's skin crawl. The Frenchman's voice was very bitter now. "How could I work for Germany, you're thinking? I should hate Germany, you say, for what they have done to my country these thirty years. And I do, Johann, I do." He sneered. "But I hate *you* more. I hate you for what you did to me, and to Karl. I had to live with my secret every day, terrified someone would find me out. I decided I would have to bury it away, never ever act on it, never ever risk discovery. You don't know what it's like. You don't know how it is to live every day in fear of discovery of your one secret, because if they find out who you really are, they'll kill you." Quinn pressed his lips together and said nothing in response to this.

Maurice smiled sadly and shook his head. "But then I met Karl, when he was at the German embassy in Paris. And he—he understood, you bastard. He knew what I went through. He went through it too. And for a time—for the only time in my life—I was happy. And then you found us, and used it against us, and turned us into spies. We were just doing our national service. Three years and we were done, and we could try and find a way out of this hellish world the Nazis have created. But *you* made us stay. You made me stay with the foreign service, and you made Karl stay with the SS, and you used what we had together against us. So when the Germans said they could remove you from our lives and let us be together—damn you, you fucking bastard, of *course* I worked with them."

He collapsed into sobs and buried his face in his hands. After a few minutes he was quiet, and he sat up again, lowering his hands. "If I'd known what would happen to Karl," he said, "I wouldn't have cooperated. I would still have talked, of course. Eventually everyone talks when the Gestapo ask the questions. But by the time I finally did, I wouldn't have been human anymore. They would have turned me into a sniveling, broken lump of flesh with their 'questions,' and soon after that they would have killed me. And I wouldn't have to live like I do now. Without him. You bastard. You fucking, *fucking* bastard."

Another long silence. Quinn regarded him in the still morning air.

Suddenly Maurice said, "You have a gun, I assume?"

Quinn hesitated, then nodded. "I do."

"Shoot me."

"What?"

"Shoot me, you bastard. Right between the eyes. Put me out of this godless misery you created of my life."

Quinn said nothing. Maurice got hesitantly to his feet, then stood there uncertainly, unwilling to take a step forward without his spectacles. Quinn scrambled up to help him. The motion caught Maurice's eye, and the Frenchman stepped forward, arms outstretched. His fingers brushed against Quinn's sleeve and he grabbed hold, collapsing against Quinn pathetically. He fumbled around in his pocket and pulled out a penknife. His breathing was heavy in Quinn's ear. He flicked the knife open and pressed the blade against Quinn's throat.

"Shoot me in the head, you bastard, or I swear I'll slit your miserable fucking throat."

For a moment Quinn did nothing. Then he reached slowly up and closed his hand around the blade. He felt it bite painfully into his palm, and a thin rivulet of blood escaped from his fist and ran over the back of his thumb. He tugged the knife gently from Maurice's grasp, flicked it closed and tossed it aside. He lifted Maurice off of him and took a step backward.

"I'm sorry, Maurice," he said.

He turned and walked away, leaving the Frenchman standing in the cold.

CHAPTER XVI

HE REGRETTED taking the U-bahn to see Maurice rather than driving there, as it meant he had to return to Ellie's building to retrieve his car, but on this day of the Führer's funeral procession he would never have been able to get near the Grand Avenue if he had gone in the car.

As he approached where the car sat parked along the curb, he reflexively glanced up at the concrete face of Ellie's building. Her flat was round the far corner, so there was no possibility of seeing her watching for him from her window. The notion of her standing by the car, waiting for him, had flitted vaguely round the back of his mind, though, and he felt a mild pang when he saw that she was not there.

He hesitated as he approached, debating whether he should get in the car and drive off, or go upstairs instead. After only a brief moment he decided on the car. He stepped over to the door, unlocked it, opened it—and froze.

Both front seats had been slid back as far as they could go, so that someone could see if there was anything on the floor underneath them. The glove compartment door was hanging open, and the forged registrations from inside it were strewn on the front passenger seat.

The driver's door had definitely been locked. Quinn glanced at the other three locks: both backseat doors were locked, but the front passenger door was not. He closed the driver's door and went round to the other side of the car. The door was unlocked, but it had not been forced.

Someone had been in his car, and had had a key. It could only be MI6.

He locked both front doors and headed into Ellie's building, taking the stairs three at a time as he sprinted up to her flat. He slowed as he neared her floor's landing and drew his pistol.

Someone had forced her lock, and the door was hanging slightly ajar. He approached cautiously. It seemed quiet, and he could not see anyone in the slice of her living room visible through the half-open door. The place looked a mess, though.

He nudged the door open with his toe, just wide enough to let him slip through. It creaked, and he cringed, but no reaction came from inside. He took a few slow, catlike steps inside, pistol ready, being careful to check behind the front door as well.

The flat seemed deserted, but it was a tip. The intruders had pulled closets and drawers open, and their contents lay strewn across the floor in careless piles. They had overturned the furniture to check its undersides. The settee cushions had been slit open, their white, fibrous industrial stuffing lying in clumps on the floor.

He could hear the hiss of running water emanating from the bedroom. Slowly he picked his way across the living room to the bedroom doorway. The bedroom had received the same treatment: clothing from the closet and drawers scattered across the floor, the chest of drawers pulled away from the wall and lying on its face, the mattress and pillows torn open. But this room, too, was empty.

The water was coming from the bathroom, which opened off of the bedroom. The shower was running. He ran his hand under it: the water was ice cold, though the hot water was turned on. It must have been running for some time. He turned it off. The plastic shower curtain had been ripped from its rings. They had arrived and taken her while she had been in the shower. They had searched the medicine cabinet and the cupboard under the sink as thoroughly and as lovingly as the other rooms; pills from opened bottles lay scattered across the counter and the sink.

The phone started to ring, shrilly piercing the sudden silence in the wake of the shower being turned off. He put his gun away—clearly the place was empty—and hurried through the bedroom and living room to the kitchen. His hand hesitated over the phone, then he picked up.

"Hello?" he said.

"*Tegel, half an hour,*" the familiar voice said with its curious, almost imperceptibly faint hint of an unplaceable accent. Talleyrand. "*South airstrip. The girl for Garner's document. Agreed?*"

"If you lay a fin—"

The line went dead with a click. He listened to the silence momentarily, then hung up.

He stepped back into the living room and walked over to the window. He stared out, wondering from where they were watching him. He could see no one lurking across the street. Perhaps they were watching him through one of the windows of the building on the far side.

Abruptly he turned and walked quickly out of the flat, pulling the front door shut behind him but leaving it unlocked. On his way down the stairs he checked his watch to get a bearing on how long he had.

The roads were busier than they had been the past two days, but he found that, if he avoided routes leading away from the Grand Avenue and the city center, he made good time. While he sat waiting at a traffic light, he removed the two copies of the Columbia-Haus treaty and Garner's letter from his inside coat pocket. He set aside the German copy of the treaty and placed it in the glove compartment, then replaced the English copy and the letter in his coat.

He still had over five minutes to go when he pulled through the open south gate at the abandoned Tegel airfield. It had served as a military and experimental aerodrome for four decades, until the opening in the 1950s of the new, expansive Hanna Reitsch Airport just outside the city, named for the Reich's leading aviatrix, a Luftwaffe test pilot during the war who was the only woman ever to win the Iron Cross. Both Tegel and Berlin's old civil airport, Tempelhof, had shut down a few years later.

There were no signs of life outside the dilapidated terminal, but a grey Daimler was parked outside the entrance. Quinn pulled up next to it and turned off his car. The Daimler was empty. He got out and walked slowly in a semi-circle around it, examining it.

"Don't move. Hands on the car." The male voice came from the entrance to the terminal, to which he had his back.

Obediently he raised his hands and slowly placed them on top of the car. He heard the approaching footsteps, then felt a single hand patting him down. His pistol was found and removed from its shoulder holster.

He heard a step back, then the voice spoke again. "All right. Turn round."

Quinn turned slowly, holding his hands at shoulder height. Captain Barnes stood before him, automatic pistol leveled coolly at his head. The captain's manner had changed completely from when he rescued Quinn and Ellie from the SS raid two nights ago. His hazel eyes stared coldly down the gun barrel, devoid of any of the warmth or easy affability they had carried before. In place of his Gestapo uniform, he was dressed in a nondescript dark jacket and trousers; the wind blew furrows in his neatly brushed fair hair. Barnes glanced down the dirt airstrip that ran past the terminal and waved an all clear.

Quinn followed his look. A hundred meters away, three figures had emerged from the first of a row of five airplane hangars: Talleyrand, Ellie, and another man. Ellie wore her raincoat and had her arms wrapped protectively around herself. The other man had a firm hold on her upper arm.

Talleyrand waved in response. Barnes turned back to Quinn and jerked his head in the direction of the hangars. "Get moving."

"You first."

"I'm sorry. Do *you* have a gun?"

"I don't want you waiting here when she comes running over. I'll keep my end, but you're going to keep yours. You first."

For several seconds the two men held each other's gazes evenly, then with a grunt of disgust, Barnes lowered his pistol and started walking along the derelict cracked tarmac of the runway. Quinn followed four or five meters behind.

To his credit, Barnes did not glance over his shoulder every few moments to check either that Quinn was following or that he was keeping a safe distance.

"Did you kill Richard Garner?" Quinn asked.

"Shut up," Barnes tossed back over his shoulder.

"I saw it all," Quinn said. "Through his hotel room window. I was standing in the rain across the street, watching you murder him."

Abruptly Barnes spun on his heel to face him, raised his gun and pointed it at Quinn's head. "They don't tell me what's going on," he said, "because I don't need to know." He lowered his aim. "But somehow I don't think there'll quite be hell to pay if I put a bullet through your foot while we're out here."

Quinn raised his hands non-threateningly in a gesture of capitulation. Barnes turned back around and started walking again. Quinn followed.

As they approached, Ellie broke away from her captor and came running toward him. She stepped gingerly, and he saw that her feet were bare. With a pang he thought of her terror as Barnes and two or three of his goons burst in on her while she was in the shower. She came running up and he caught her, wrapping his arms protectively around her. She buried her face against his chest.

After a few moments he put his hands on her shoulders and gently guided her a step back. She looked up at him. Her eyes were red, and her cheeks were stained with tears. She brushed away a strand of blonde hair that the slight breeze had blown into her eyes, and she was the prettiest woman he had ever seen.

"Are you all right?" he asked.

She nodded. She looked terrified. He glanced back at where the two cars stood and nodded in their direction. "Get in the car," he said. "Wait for me."

She followed his gaze, then looked back up at him, obviously not wanting to leave him, but nodded in acquiescence. "All right."

He watched her go, picking her way carefully along the dirt track with her small, unshod feet, then turned back to the three men. Talleyrand had taken a few steps toward him; Barnes and the other stood a few feet behind him, expressionless.

"I've returned something of yours, Simon," the old man said. "I think now you have something of mine."

Quinn shook his head. "No."

For a long moment the old man stared at him, his face unreadable. Then, without glancing back at them, he indicated with a curt gesture of his hand that Barnes and his fellow should stay where they stood, and began walking slowly back up the airstrip. Quinn fell into step behind him.

"I had not thought you a stupid man," Talleyrand said, all trace of affability gone from his voice.

Quinn let out a brittle laugh. "I'd like to think I'm not. That's why you're not getting the treaty."

"So you opened it. You know what it contains."

"Of course I opened it. You knew I'd opened it when you discovered I'd slipped your leash."

"Indeed." He paused, then said, "What do you think you can accomplish here, Simon? Hand over the document. You know what I'll have to do otherwise. To you, and—" he nodded in the direction of Quinn's car, "—to that lovely young woman over there."

"Oh, I think quite the opposite," Quinn said. "She and I will only survive so long as you *don't* get your hands on that treaty."

Talleyrand stopped and turned to look into his eyes. The two of them had by now reached the halfway point, between the parked cars and where Barnes and the other man waited. Quinn removed the English copy of the treaty and handed it to the old man.

"That's one of Richard Garner's copies," he said. "He had two. The other one is in a safe place. And it will stay safe, so long as *Fraulein* Voss is permitted to return to her flat and resume her life, unmolested by you or your German allies. And so long as I'm on the next flight out of Berlin, back to Greece."

Talleyrand tapped the sheaf of paper contemplatively against his lower lip, staring off into space. Then his eyes settled once more upon Quinn's. "I think," he said slowly, "that whatever 'safe place' you've found for the other copy of this treaty, it will stay there, even if I kill you now."

Quinn shrugged. "Maybe. You have only my word that that's not true. But you tried that gamble last night, remember? You killed Richard Garner, and assumed that treaty would simply lie wherever he must have hidden it, undiscovered. And look where that's got you now."

For several long moments the old man continued to stare into his eyes, appraising him. Then at last he shrugged. "Very well." He sounded almost tired. "It seems you leave me no choice." He took a cigarette lighter from his pocket and struck it, then held the corner of the English copy of the treaty in the flame for a brief moment until the fire took. He watched the flames licking at the sheets of paper for several seconds before letting go of them. They fluttered slowly to the ground and came to rest on the tarmac. The two men watched them burn.

At last Talleyrand turned back to Quinn. His hand fluttered in the direction of Quinn's car. "Take the girl home, Simon. Then proceed directly to Hanna Reitsch Airport. I'll have a ticket waiting for you at the Lufthansa terminal for the next flight to Istanbul. When you arrive at Istanbul, you'll have a chartered flight waiting to return you to that little Greek city where I found you." He smiled in that maddeningly unflappable way of his. "I suppose our relationship has now of necessity reached its end, if not quite as amicably as I should have hoped." A hint of steel flashed in his eyes. "You'll be under constant observation, of course. I wouldn't recommend any sort of deviation from your course. Drop her off and get to the airport, my boy." He shrugged. "Besides, even if you *were* inclined to take some sort of action with your remaining copy of the treaty, it's not like there's anything you *could* do. The British government has committed itself; the German government has committed itself."

Quinn nodded. His bluff had worked—he had kept himself and Ellie alive. But he felt no relief, only anger. He wanted to say something, wanted to scream at the bastard for betraying Britain and her allies and the millions like his brother who had died fighting the Germans. Instead he only nodded impassively and turned to go.

Out of the corner of his eye he saw Talleyrand step quickly forward as he turned, and the old man touched him gently on the sleeve. He stopped and turned his head to look at him.

"You've lived up to every expectation I've had of you so far, Mordechai," Talleyrand said, softly but earnestly. "You're doing well."

Quinn said nothing, just stared at him bleakly, but inside his mind was reeling. The old man stepped back, and his face was once more inscrutable, save for the reappearance of that smug faint smile of his. "Oh, and do be a good lad," he said, "and leave the car unlocked and the keys in the glove compartment. Just one of those simplicities that makes life a little easier." Lost in thought, Quinn turned away and started walking towards the Focke-Wulf and Ellie.

She was waiting for him in the front passenger seat. He got in, started the car, put it into gear, and pulled away.

"What's going on?" she asked as they passed through the airfield's gate.

"I'm taking you home," he said. "Then I'm leaving for Greece."

"Just like that? *Now* you're just conceding defeat?"

"It's not like I have much of a choice," he said.

They lapsed into silence. He soon picked up their tail in the rear view mirror. He had expected the Daimler, but instead they were just using an unobtrusive, nondescript Volkswagen KdF-Wagen. It was definitely Barnes and the other man behind the wheel, though. They must have had it waiting for them in the hangar.

Eventually they reached her tenement. He pulled up to the curb outside the front entrance and put the car in park. He saw Barnes pass him, then pull up to the opposite curb ten or fifteen meters ahead of him. He turned to face Ellie.

"I'm sorry," she blurted out.

He shook his head. "Don't be. You followed your convictions. *I'm* sorry. I pushed you into this against your will, and I shouldn't have. You shouldn't have had to go through what you have, and there's no adequate apology I can give you."

"No," she said, "I'm sorry about last night. About the way I reacted. You're just—you're not what I would expect a Jew to be."

She realized that was not what she wanted to say and opened her mouth to try and rephrase it but hesitated, unsure of how to say it. He held up his hand to forestall her.

"It's all right," he said. "I understand."

She smiled gratefully at him, hesitated and then leaned forward, and they kissed. He was aware of her hand clutching desperately at the front of his shirt.

After a while the kiss ended and she stared at him with her soft blue eyes until he broke the gaze by glancing down at where her hand still tightly clasped his shirt. Her cheeks flushed as she realized, and she smiled shyly and released him. Without a word she turned and opened the car door, climbed out and shut it behind her.

He put the car into gear and pulled away. She stood on the curb, staring after him. He watched her in the rear view mirror till he also saw Barnes and his goon pulling into the street after him.

CHAPTER XVII

HIS CAR wound its way slowly through the Berlin streets. The old man's words rang in his ears. *"You've lived up to every expectation I've had of you so far, Mordechai. You're doing well."* Mordechai. He had never thought MI6 had any idea.

He brooded all the way through the city center and out to Reitsch, in the outer suburbs on the northeast side of the city. He was stopped for his first security clearance at the airport gate, a bored-looking SS corporal accompanied by a trooper in the blue uniform of the Luftwaffe, toting a rifle. He knew that procedure dictated they open his boot and briefly check through all his luggage; the threat of terrorism in the Reich loomed especially large at transit centers such as airports. But at the sight of Quinn's Amt III ID the corporal straightened to attention and waved him through.

He was inspected again as he entered the parking garage adjoining the terminal. The Luftwaffe sergeant here was a little more alert and tried to insist on checking the Focke-Wulf even after Quinn had flashed his ID, as this was the last checkpoint a car had to pass before its driver left it for an indeterminate amount of time while he flew out to his destination; but a long, silent, disdainful stare sufficed to make him pale and convince him to simply let Quinn through. He noted with amusement that Barnes, who probably had a diplomatic pass, had considerably more difficulty getting the sergeant to let him through in a timely manner.

After he found a parking space and turned off the engine, he sat with his hands resting on the wheel for several minutes, staring at the concrete wall in front of him. He did not know what to do. He was still unsure how he could stop the Columbia-Haus treaty, though Beauchamp had given him the beginnings of an idea. But more immediately, he had to avoid getting on the plane that was waiting for him. He glanced over his shoulder at where he had seen Barnes when Barnes had followed him in, wondering how he was going to get past the Royal Marines captain and his companion and get back into the city.

The thought of his two minders made him realize that they would probably be getting antsy by now, waiting for him to get out of his car. He removed the German copy of the treaty from the glove compartment and slipped it into his coat pocket, then, leaving the car keys in the glove compartment as promised, he got out.

Barnes and his crony were leaning against their car on the other side of the car park, staring in his direction with an entirely unconvincing impersonation of nonchalance. He gave them an ironic salute and headed for the nearest stairwell.

At the entrance to the terminal he had to undergo another check. Here was the largest checkpoint he had encountered so far: an SS lieutenant with four Waffen-SS stormtroopers, all uniformed in black, attended by a sergeant and two privates in Luftwaffe blue, each of the privates with a German shepherd on a leash, sniffing luggage. There were similar checkpoints throughout all the airports in the Reich, always SS and Luftwaffe together: the Luftwaffe to provide physical security, against bombs or other forms of terrorism, and the SS to provide political security, checking the identity of every passenger who passed through a German airport.

The four SS troopers sat along one side of a long table, checking the name and passport number of everyone entering the terminal against a typed list of all of today's passengers and their destinations, and against another list, this one of the few thousand most wanted political fugitives at large in the Reich today. The trooper Quinn ended up with blanched when he saw the Amt III ID and immediately waved over his lieutenant.

The lieutenant was extremely apologetic but implacably insistent that *all* entering passengers must undergo the passport check. Quinn nodded his acquiescence, but made it clear that he thought his time was being wasted by an extremely junior officer.

While he waited for the trooper to check his name against the list, Quinn gazed idly at the Luftwaffe sergeant and privates standing a couple of meters away with their rifles slung over their shoulders. After being cleared by the SS, arriving passengers had to submit to having their luggage sniffed by the privates' German shepherds.

At first glance Quinn thought the sergeant was the same as the one who had halted him as he entered the parking garage, but then decided he was not. The resemblance was caused purely by the uniform—one did not look at the face of a man in military in National Socialist Germany, only the uniform below it.

"Herr Obersturmbannführer?"

The voice penetrated his reverie, and he came back to the here and now with a slight start. He realized the lieutenant had been speaking to him: nervous, trying to appease Quinn's air of dissatisfaction at this unnecessary inconvenience.

"Your pardon, *Untersturmführer?*" he said.

Apparently Talleyrand had done his work quickly—Quinn's name had already appeared on the passenger list. "I was remarking that your destination is listed as Istanbul, Herr Obersturmbannführer," the lieutenant repeated himself timidly, regretting now having spoken at all. "You travel as a tourist, or on state business?"

"As a tourist."

"Ah yes. To admire the architecture, no doubt?"

Quinn nodded absently. "Yes," he said, preferring to agree rather than engage in conversation. The uniforms. The anonymity of the uniforms.

"Magnificent architecture," said the lieutenant. "I was there as a child." They lapsed into silence. The lieutenant looked awkward. As if worried that he had somehow said the wrong thing, he blurted, "But decadent. An excellent example of what decadence can do to a culture. Twice, Herr Obersturmbannführer. The Ottomans should have known better. After all, it was they who had overrun the decadent Byzantines. A lesson in the necessity of keeping a culture trim and strong, is it not?"

"Indeed," Quinn said. He was still staring at the Luftwaffe uniforms, and also at the SS uniforms. No one ever saw a soldier of the Wehrmacht or SS as a man, only as a uniform.

The rest of his identity check proceeded without incident. He carried no luggage and therefore was able to bypass the Luftwaffe riflemen and their dogs. Morbidly the notion flashed across his mind that perhaps Nazi dogs would be able to smell his Judaism. He walked calmly away from the checkpoint and into the terminal, but glanced back over his shoulder two or three times at the men in uniform.

The airport bustled with people leaving the city following the departure of the Führer's sarcophagus. It was also thick with security, even more so than would usually be the case: Luftwaffe privates strolled around the terminal in pairs, rifles slung over their shoulders, one of each pair typically holding a German shepherd by a leash.

First Quinn went to the Lufthansa check-in desk, where his ticket waited for him. Then he stopped at the cafeteria and bought himself a bratwurst, a paper cup of beer, and a copy of this morning's *Berliner Tageblatt*. Instead of finding a seat inside the cafeteria, though, he settled himself on a bench in the terminal's main area, facing the entrance to the men's lavatory.

Out of the corner of his eye he saw Barnes and the other man take up their own positions, watching him from next to a public phone ten or fifteen meters away. Barnes had picked up a newspaper of his own somewhere along the way. Quinn ignored them, pretending to read the *Tageblatt* while keeping an eye on the men entering the lavatory across the way, then emerging again a few minutes later.

The front page bore a huge, eerie black and white photograph of the Führer's sarcophagus at the foot of the steps of the Great Hall in the pre-dawn dark during the ceremony with which it had begun its journey to Linz, illuminated only by flickering torchlight. Half a dozen *Leibstandarte*-SS riflemen, their lower bodies shrouded in the darkness cast by the sarcophagus's shadow, stood at rigid attention along the length of the bottom step.

Himmler and Heydrich were both there, each carrying a torch: the foci of the Reich's two rival political poles, each about to accompany their late Führer on his final journey. They stood at opposite ends of the sarcophagus, staring solemnly at each other along its length, the Führer separating them. To Quinn it seemed appropriately symbolic.

He flipped idly through the paper. One page bore a roundup of the German publishing industry. The German language publisher of *The Day of the Jackal,* a bestseller in England and America about a minor SS officer's desperate race to stop an English mercenary from assassinating the Führer, had decided to postpone publication of the book's German edition indefinitely in light of the Führer's death. The same publisher was also trying desperately to bring forward by five weeks the publication of *Reichsminister* Albert Speer's memoir of the war, so as to release it within two weeks of the Führer's funeral.

The first boarding call for his flight sounded over the intercom. Quinn had already finished most of his bratwurst, and he was starting to worry that the opportunity he needed was not going to present itself. But then, there it was: a Luftwaffe sergeant—he did not see if it was the same man as either of the two he had already encountered—strolled into the lavatory.

Quinn calmly popped the last bite of his bratwurst into his mouth, then tucked the newspaper under his arm, rose, and nonchalantly walked over to the lavatory entrance, tossing his cup into the bin as he passed it. Out the corner of his eye he saw his watchers stir, then settle back again as they realized he was only heading for the toilet.

He was in luck; the Luftwaffe sergeant had chosen a quiet moment to relieve his bladder, and the lavatory was empty but for the two of them. The sergeant stood over a urinal with his back to the entrance; Quinn stopped a couple of meters away and stared at him.

After a moment the sergeant became aware of the scrutiny, and Quinn heard the liquid trickle falter. The sergeant looked over his shoulder and scowled. "What are you looking at?" he demanded.

Quinn held up his ID. "Obersturmbannführer Kaufholz, RSHA Amt III," he identified himself coldly.

The sergeant's eyes widened. He hastily shook off, buttoned his trousers, and turned round. "Err—yes, Herr Obersturmbannführer. What can I do for you?"

Quinn looked around conspiratorially, as if worried he might be overheard, then beckoned the sergeant over to the lavatory's far corner. "Over here, *Feldwebel.*" He took a step in the indicated direction, turning his back to the sergeant as he did so. He heard the sergeant behind him, following.

Without warning he halted and threw his right elbow back and up as hard as he could. It smashed into the sergeant's face, and he heard the satisfying crunch of cartilage. The sergeant's rifle clattered to the linoleum floor.

Quinn spun round. The sergeant had staggered back, stunned, and had both hands over his face; blood streamed from between his fingers. Quinn stepped forward, placed his hands on the sergeant's shoulders, and rammed his knee into the man's crotch. The sergeant doubled over, groaning. Expertly, Quinn found the sergeant's helmet strap with his fingers, unfastened it and pulled the helmet off. He grabbed a fistful of the sergeant's red hair and slammed his head against the tile wall with all his strength, then let go. The man crumpled to the ground. For a moment he struggled to get up, moaning, then he went limp, unconscious.

"Sorry, Feldwebel," Quinn murmured. "Just the wrong place at the wrong time."

He looped his arms under the sergeant's armpits and dragged him into a toilet stall, closing and locking the door behind them. Blood was flowing prodigiously from the sergeant's broken nose, and he also had a gash on his forehead from the impact with the wall. So far, though, all the blood was spilling onto his tunic; his greatcoat had escaped with no more than a few flecks on the lapel. Quinn quickly stripped the greatcoat from the limp form in order to keep it clean.

Next he pulled the sergeant's jackboots off, then unbuttoned his trousers and pulled them off. Then he removed his own jacket, shoes, and jeans. The sergeant's trousers fit Quinn comfortably, though the boots were a little loose and felt slightly awkward. He buttoned the greatcoat all the way up to hide the fact that he was not wearing a military tunic.

He emptied the pockets of his old coat and trousers and transferred everything in them—his passport and Gestapo ID, some money, and the Columbia-Haus treaty—to the inside pocket of the greatcoat. A quick search through the sergeant's tunic pockets produced fifty Reichsmarks and the sergeant's military ID and citizenship papers: Wilhelm Hamer, aged thirty-five, born in Metz, category 2 Nordic racial classification.

He hauled the sergeant up into a sitting position on the toilet seat, eliciting a groan of protest from the unconscious German. He pulled his old trousers on around Sergeant Hamer's ankles, then forced his old shoes, which were too small for the sergeant, onto his feet. Anyone looking under the door would see only the sergeant's feet with his trousers around his ankles.

Quinn left the stall by worming his way under the partition separating it from the next toilet, so that he could leave the stall door locked from the inside. The sergeant's helmet and rifle lay on the floor where he had fallen. He retrieved them, putting the helmet on and slinging the rifle over his shoulder, and headed for the exit.

He deliberately did not so much as glance in the direction of Barnes and the other man as he left the lavatory; he needed to ensure he did absolutely nothing to attract even their cursory attention. His plan depended on them not looking at him, on them simply seeing a uniform exit the lavatory, dismissing it, and returning their attention to the lavatory exit and waiting for Quinn to emerge.

He paused a few meters from the lavatory and scanned the overhead signs, then turned and headed in the direction indicated for the U-bahn entrance. He affected a disinterested, unhurried stroll, but his heart pounded against the inside of his chest. The helmet and the too-large jackboots felt awkward, and the unconscious berth of a meter or two that people now gave him disquieted him. *They* saw only the uniform, too.

As he passed the checkpoint at the entrance to the terminal one of the Luftwaffe privates' German shepherds growled at him, and he saw the SS lieutenant who had talked with him about Istanbul glance casually over in his direction, then return his attention to what he was doing. Quinn kept walking. He had spotted the U-bahn entrance now, just another ten meters ahead.

"Feldwebel!"

The voice came from behind him. He pretended not to hear it and kept walking.

"Feldwebel."

Closer now; he was reasonably sure it was the lieutenant's voice.

"*Feldwebel!*" A hand clasped his shoulder and pulled him around. He turned, desperately calm, ready to turn back around and run for it.

"Feldwebel," the lieutenant said, "you are out of uniform."

Quinn just blinked at him.

After a moment the lieutenant prompted, "Your helmet strap, Feldwebel."

Quinn managed, "Sir?" Then it dawned on him. "Oh. Yes, sir. Sorry, sir." Hastily he reached up and fumbled with his helmet's chinstrap, finally getting it fastened on the second try.

The lieutenant nodded, evidently mollified. He looked down at Quinn's buttoned up greatcoat. "Are you cold, Feldwebel?"

"Sir? Oh, that, sir. I—spilt a drop of tomato sauce on my tunic, sir."

The lieutenant pressed his lips together in an expression of disapproval. "You should take more care with your appearance, Feldwebel."

"Yes, sir. I'm sorry, sir. I'm not usually so careless."

"I should hope not." The lieutenant frowned, trying to place

Quinn's face, but he could not. More than likely he had simply seen the sergeant patrolling the airport, though he could not recall any specific instance when he had seen him before.

At last the lieutenant snapped his heels together and saluted. *"Heil Hitler!"*

Quinn returned the salute. *"Heil Hitler!"*

The lieutenant wheeled about and headed back to the checkpoint. Quinn also turned back around and started walking. In just a few meters, he was descending the steps to the airport's U-bahn station and safety. Safety being, of course, an entirely relative term.

CHAPTER XVIII

HE GOT a few odd looks on the U-bahn, but nobody felt like confronting the Luftwaffe sergeant with an automatic rifle over one shoulder and demanding to know his business. He sat on the hard plastic bench and brooded.

He had no idea where his destination should be. The British were probably already looking for him, and he imagined so would the Gestapo be shortly. He needed an ally, but there were no allies to be had.

Please God, let me get caught by the British. If I have to get caught, don't let it be the Gestapo.

He got off the U-bahn at one of the downtown stations, on the banks of the River Spree, a few blocks from the Grand Avenue.

For a while he leaned against the iron railing along the side of the pavement and stared down at the river's murky brown water.

He should find a place to get out of sight. Armed soldiers on the streets of the Reich were not an entirely unusual sight, but they typically moved in pairs and belonged either to the Wehrmacht or the Waffen-SS, not the Luftwaffe. Besides, once they found Sergeant Hamer in the airport lavatory, they would know to search for a man in a Luftwaffe sergeant's uniform. He thought about buying himself some trousers and shoes but decided against it; if he had to get himself to Linz, he would most likely need the money for something more essential.

Eventually he got up from the railing and strolled along the quiet street for a while until he came to a row of four or five decaying tenement buildings overlooking the river. He wandered across the street and entered the alley separating two of the buildings. Each had a rusty wrought iron fire escape running down its side.

Picking one of the buildings, he stood under its fire escape grille, reached up with the butt of his rifle and tugged at the bottom rung of the ladder till it came loose. The ladder came rattling down to the ground, clanging loudly as it struck the alley pavement.

He climbed up to the fire escape's lowest level and pulled the ladder up behind him, then started his climb upward. The tenement was five stories tall. He wondered if anyone saw the Luftwaffe rifleman climbing past their living room window, but doubted they would call the authorities if they did.

The tenement's roof was deserted. The surface was covered in gravel, except for where someone had a small vegetable garden in one corner. The rooftops of Berlin spread out around him, the huge dome of the Great Hall rising prominently from amongst them on the far side of the river. Quinn settled himself in the lee of the two-foot brick wall running round the roof's perimeter and closed his eyes. He could feel the warm sun on his eyelids and was glad it was no longer raining, though the gravel underneath his back still felt damp. His greatcoat kept out the chill breeze running over the city's rooftops.

He had been awake continuously since waking up on Ellie's couch yesterday morning before going to visit Gertrud, which seemed like years ago. Now, after less than half of a minute, he slept.

When he woke he knew that time had passed, but he was unsure of how much. Through his closed eyelids he could tell that nightfall was approaching, and the temperature had started to fall sharply. Quinn rubbed his eyes open and sat up, leaning his back against the roof's low brick wall. He stifled a yawn, then clambered slowly to his feet and gazed out across the river at the city spread out on the opposite bank.

The setting sun eerily silhouetted the dome of the Great Hall into stark, metallic, green relief and picked out the clouds and industrial smog that hung over the city as streaks of bloody red and orange against the pinks and purples of the evening sky. He was facing into the teeth of the brisk rooftop breeze, which the setting of the sun and the onset of the night-time chill had turned malicious and biting.

He checked his watch. A quarter to nine. He had slept for almost seven hours. He picked up his rifle and slung it over his shoulder, climbed out onto the fire escape's top landing, and began to clamber earthward.

He felt a bit dismayed that he had slept so long; he had expected to wake earlier and have a bit more time to prepare emotionally for the plan on which he had decided. But, he told himself, perhaps it was a good thing. Now he had time only for action; he did not have to sit and wait, and let the doubts start gnawing at the back of his mind.

He dropped the last eight feet from the fire escape's bottom landing, then walked slowly back along the alley's length, emerging cautiously onto the street running along the riverbank. A few blocks up the road was the U-bahn station from which he had come earlier this afternoon, but that line would not take him to Ellie's flat. Her building, though, was less than two or three kilometers away, in the opposite direction and on the other side of the river. He turned and started walking.

After a few blocks he came to a thick, low stone bridge, old enough that it had not been built to accommodate two-way car traffic, and started to make his way across it. He stared down at the brown, brackish waters as he walked, remembering in a quiet, detached way tipping over a railing and plunging into the river four years ago. The sensation of being shot came back to him: the momentary disbelief, followed by intense, agonizing pain, like nothing he had ever felt before. And then waking up in the alley on the riverbank hours later, the blinding pain now orders of magnitude greater than it had been when he had first been shot.

By the time he had crossed the bridge and started making his way through the Berlin streets towards Ellie's building, the memories of that last night in Berlin, the night Karl had died, had turned into disquieting doubts, which he was grateful had not had a chance to come to him earlier because he had been asleep. He would probably be shot and killed—indeed, his plan was sufficiently foolish that he *should* get killed.

A new, quietly fatalistic acceptance had settled over him; this was the only way he would be able to get to Heydrich, so this was the risk he must take. Even if he survived the next few hours, fate would probably catch up with him later tonight, or tomorrow, or within a few days. He would keep fighting them until they stopped him from fighting back. All he really hoped for now was that his newfound fatalism did not end up bringing Ellie down with him.

He stood on the corner opposite Ellie's building for a long time, staring up at its plain cement face, wondering if he would make it alive to her front door across the street. From here he could see both the front entrance on one side and Ellie's window on the other. Her light was on, and he thought the blinds were open, but from this angle he could not tell if there was any activity in her flat.

He took a deep breath and started across the street. His heart pounded in his chest, but he forced himself to move slowly and nonchalantly. He had no doubt that Ellie's building would be under surveillance: certainly by the British, since they had been there this morning, but probably by the Gestapo as well. Either one could decide to pick him off as he crossed the street.

It took years to cross the street, but somehow he made it to the other side alive. His hand shook as he closed his fingers around the handle to the building's front door and pulled it open. Only now did he give in to his nerves, hopping quickly inside and darting out of the doorway into the safety of the main stairwell. His knees trembled and he put out his hand, supporting himself against the cinderblock walls. He was suddenly aware that he was short of breath and his forehead had broken out in a cold sweat.

"'Newfound fatalism' my arse," he murmured.

When he had collected himself he started up the stairs. On

his way he removed his helmet so that Ellie would recognize him more easily.

He knocked on Ellie's front door, but there was no immediate answer. He knocked again. "Ellie," he called, "it's me. Simon."

After a few moments the door inched open a crack, and Ellie's suspicious face peered out at him over the chain. She tensed when she saw the blue Luftwaffe uniform, ready to slam the door shut again, but then she recognized his face and her eyes widened.

"Can I come in?" he asked.

Wordlessly she shut the door, then opened it again, this time wide, with the chain unfastened. She stepped aside, and he entered. He unslung his rifle and set it against the wall as she closed the door behind him.

She had made an attempt at clearing up, but the disarray in which her flat had been left this morning had been extremely thorough. She had righted the furniture, stuffed most of the padding back into her cushions and set the cushions back on the settee, with the torn seams facing downward. One of the legs on her dining table had been broken, making the table unusable, and it lay propped on its side against the wall by the kitchen entrance.

He turned to Ellie without saying a word. She regarded him, still suspicious, for a long time, then stepped forward and embraced him, pressing her face against his chest. He wrapped his arms protectively around her.

They stood like that for a long time. He let her choose when the embrace would end. At last she released him and stepped back.

"Have you eaten?" she asked. Her tone was emotionless and businesslike: take care of what needed to be done first.

He shook his head. "No. But I'm all right."

She nodded. "Something to drink, then?"

"Just coffee," he said.

He took off his greatcoat and sat on the settee while she made the coffee. When it was ready, she brought it out to him and sat down next to him.

"What happened?" she asked as he sipped gingerly at the hot liquid.

"They gave me airplane tickets and told me to get out of Berlin. They said they'd be watching me till I did." He gestured at his uniform. "I managed to disguise myself when they weren't looking, then I gave them the slip."

She nodded, absorbing it all expressionlessly. "They'll be out looking for you now."

"I know."

"They'll be watching my flat," she said matter-of-factly. "They'll know you're here."

He nodded. "I'll leave if that's what you want."

"No. That's not what I want at all."

They lapsed into silence while he finished his coffee. He set the empty cup down on the carpet by the settee, then rose and walked over to the window and studied the view. He saw no one he could be certain was watching. He reached up and drew the blinds.

He heard her get up and walk softly over to stand behind him, and he turned round to her. She was staring intently up at him.

"I'm sorry," he said. "I'm sorry about this morning. I'm sorry about whatever might happen tonight. I shouldn't have got you into this."

She shook her head. "You'd leave if I said that's what I wanted."

She rose on her tiptoes and kissed him. He kissed back. He felt her hands resting on his upper arms. He put his hands on her hips, then slid them up her sides, then ran them through her hair. The scent of her filled his nostrils, and he ran his tongue along hers, enjoying the taste of her. They pressed against each other. She felt wonderful, just like she had against him in the Munich hotel room last night.

Only this time, he did not have to stop. There was nothing to be afraid of.

He stepped back, breaking off their kiss. She looked at him quizzically, frowning, but he bent slightly, reached round her and lifted her easily in his arms. She gave a mild squeak of surprise as he lifted her, then giggled. She put her arms round his neck, linking her fingers, and kissed him. He smiled at her and carried her into the bedroom.

PART 3

RESOLUTION

In war, men are nothing. One man is everything.

—NAPOLEON BONAPARTE

CHAPTER XIX

AFTERWARDS THEY lay in the bed together, she sleeping soundly, her head nuzzled against his chest, he with his arm wrapped around her. Her hair tickled his chest in time with her soft, slowly rhythmic breathing. They were both slick with sweat, the sheets twisted around their legs; their clothes lay scattered around the bedroom floor. Quinn dozed fitfully, but was glad he had spent most of the afternoon asleep, as it prevented him now from falling into a deep slumber.

The moonlight came in through the cracks between the window blinds, casting bright white pinstripes across the bed and their bodies in the darkness. The angle of the light was changing almost imperceptibly as the moon made its slow pilgrimage across the night sky, and Quinn watched one stripe make its creeping way across Ellie's lower back and the curve of her backside over the course of most of an hour.

A creak from the other room brought him awake with a start and he listened tensely for several moments, but he heard no more. It must have just been the building settling. He glanced at the stripe he had watched cross down Ellie's back and saw that it had reached all the way down the back of her thighs and was approaching the back of her knees. He glanced at the clock on her bedside table: a quarter past one. He must have dozed off after all. He needed to find something to keep his mind alert.

Another sound. Instantly he was wide awake, all worries about sleep banished from his thoughts. He was sure that this time the sound had come from a human being—a rattling, the sound of a lock being tried.

There it was again. *Skeleton keys,* he thought. *Trying to get in quietly, without breaking down the door.*

Absently he kissed the top of Ellie's forehead, then gently slid himself out from under her and stood up. She murmured faintly in protest, then wrapped her arms around his empty pillow and resettled herself with it held against her breast. He was slipping his trousers on and buttoning them up, cursing himself for leaving his Luftwaffe rifle next to the door where he had propped it when he first came in. His heart was pounding inside his chest. Hurriedly he pulled his boots on. It always paid to be wearing footwear in a fight.

He was in the bedroom doorway, heading into the main room to make a grab for the rifle, when he heard the click from the lock on the front door. He froze. The door creaked loudly and eased open a crack. Quinn spun back into the bedroom and flattened himself against the wall. He held his breath and made a conscious effort to calm his pounding heart so that he could hear any sounds coming from the next room.

Luckily Ellie had fastened the catch chain after she let him in earlier, and whoever had unlocked the door could open it only a few centimeters. After a moment or two Quinn heard a dull thud, then a snap, as the door was smashed in, breaking the chain. Still, much quieter than having to break the door down without a key would have been.

Ellie stirred and let out a groan at the sound of the thud, reaching out a hand to where Quinn should have been lying next to her. When she did not find him she tried reaching out further, then, still not finding him, she raised her head and squinted groggily at his side of the bed. She frowned when she saw it was empty, propped herself up on one elbow and looked around for him.

When she saw him, tense and pressed against the wall, she froze. She opened her mouth as if about to ask what he was doing, but no sound emerged. Quinn raised his finger to his lips to indicate silence, then motioned that she should pull the bed sheets up and cover herself. Wide-eyed and awake now, she nodded and obeyed.

He could hear the quiet padding of feet in the main room. There were at least two of them, probably three. A man's shadow fell across the half-open bedroom door, then another man's as well. He could sense them now, just on the other side of the doorway. One took a step through—

Quinn pivoted round on one foot and neatly punched the intruder in the face. The man grunted, dropped the pistol he was carrying and staggered back, into a second man right behind him; both men were dressed all in black. Quinn grabbed the first man by the shirt while he was still stunned, hauled him through the bedroom door and shoved him aside, so that he could step forward and aim a blow at the second man.

The second intruder was ready for him, though, despite having been knocked momentarily off balance by his companion staggering into him, and he blocked Quinn's punch and countered with one of his own aimed at Quinn's jaw. Quinn blocked it reflexively, pivoted on his heel and kicked out at the man's leg. He felt the heel of his jackboot strike the man's kneecap and heard the satisfying pop of cartilage. The man crumpled silently to the ground, clutching his knee.

Quinn turned round, ready to face the first attacker whom he had left stunned just inside the bedroom.

"That's enough," a familiar voice said. "Hands on your head. Slowly now."

Quinn froze. The voice had come from over his shoulder, in the living room. Slowly he raised his hands and put them behind his head. The intruder he had left in the bedroom got shakily to his feet. Quinn recognized him as Barnes's companion who had trailed him to the airport earlier that day. Ellie, the bed sheets pulled up to her neck, was staring wide-eyed and silent at the scene unfolding before her.

The intruder let his eyes sweep down the length of Ellie's body, outlined under the sheets, then turned to Quinn and surveyed him with a look of distaste. His nose was bleeding. He took a step forward and belted him in the stomach. Quinn doubled over, expelling his breath in a grunt of pain, but kept his hands behind his head. "Dirty little Nazi traitor," the intruder grunted in English.

"All right, Gunning, that's enough," the voice said, and Quinn heard its owner approaching him from behind as he straightened up. A hand grasped his shoulder and spun him round. He found himself confronted with the barrel of a gun leveled an inch from his left eye, and beyond that, the unblinking, furious hazel eyes of Captain Barnes.

He returned Barnes's stare unflinchingly for several seconds before the captain's gaze flicked over his shoulder toward Gunning. Barnes jerked his head toward where the third man still writhed on the floor behind him. "See to Cokeroft," he said.

He shifted his gaze back to Quinn. He wore the same nondescript, black clothing as his companions. Still holding the gun on him with one hand, he grabbed him by the neck with the other and stepped backward, pulling Quinn out of the doorway. Next he pivoted slightly, changing direction, then took a step forward. Quinn stumbled backward and was slammed against the wall. He felt the muzzle of Barnes's gun jamming painfully into his jaw just below his ear.

"I want to know what the *fuck* is going on," Barnes hissed.

Quinn, Barnes's hand still clutched tightly round his throat, was gasping slightly for breath, but he blinked in surprise all the same. "Wh-what?" he said.

"First Garner," Barnes said. "Now you. I worked with Richard Garner for years. He was no Nazi. I never saw a finer agent." His voice was rising shrilly. "Then all of a sudden he bloody *defects* and I get the order to eliminate him. And now you—they send you in to hunt him down, but, as soon as you do that, you take his information and decide to run for the Nazis yourself." His eyes narrowed and he leaned closer in on Quinn and repeated in a deathly quiet snarl, "What the *fuck* is going on?"

His grip on Quinn's throat had tightened as he spoke, and now Quinn was making quiet choking noises. Reluctantly Barnes relaxed his fingers a touch. The chokes turned into rasping, constricted laughter.

Anger flared in Barnes's eyes. "What the bleeding hell is so funny, you Nazi bastard?"

"You—" Quinn broke off, gulping air, trying to breathe around the twin impediments of Barnes's grip on his throat and his own, slightly hysterical, laughter at the situation. "You mean," he tried again after a few moments, "you mean you—you don't even know?"

"Know what?"

"Oh, you stupid, stupid bastard," Quinn said. Barnes's eyes flashed, but he said nothing. "I'm not the one working with the Nazis, Barnes. *You* are."

This caught the captain off guard. He stepped back, releasing his hold on Quinn's neck but keeping his gun trained on him. Quinn slid down the wall to a crouch, massaging his neck, and coughed slightly.

"What are you talking about?" Barnes demanded.

Quinn glanced up at him. "Garner wasn't defecting. At least, not to the Nazis." He paused. This was it—the one element in his nascent plan over which he had no control. Even if he could persuade Barnes to believe him, that still did not mean that the captain would come over to Quinn's side.

He started to get his feet. He saw Barnes's finger tense on the trigger of his gun, and he stopped, holding out his hands placatingly.

"You stay right where you are," the captain said.

"Fine," Quinn acquiesced. He nodded to where his greatcoat had been left over the back of the settee. "It's in there. Right inside pocket."

"What is?"

"Garner's document."

"That's been destroyed. I was there, remember?"

Quinn said nothing, just stared up at him. At last Barnes stepped over to the settee, keeping his eyes and gun on Quinn. With his free hand he flipped the greatcoat open and began fishing in the pocket. As he did so he glanced over his shoulder at where Gunning was kneeling beside Cokeroft. "Will you live, Cokeroft?" he asked.

Cokeroft tried to match Barnes's bantering tone, but his voice cracked slightly with pain. "I should think so, sir." He had a heavy Scouse accent.

"All right to walk?"

"Ah—that one might be a bit tougher to manage, sir."

Barnes had now found the German copy of the Columbia-Haus treaty and pulled it from the greatcoat pocket. He unfolded it and began to read. After a few moments his eyes widened slightly, and slowly he lowered his gun so that it was no longer pointing at Quinn.

He looked up at Quinn without saying anything, then back down at the page, then at Quinn again. At last he said, "This isn't genuine."

"It bloody better be," Quinn said. "That's what Richard Garner died for."

Barnes was searching for a reason not to believe him. "This isn't Garner's document," he said, and repeated, "That was destroyed this morning. At the airstrip."

"Garner had two copies," Quinn said. "The other was in English. I kept the one and turned the other over this morning. I told the old man that's what I was doing."

Barnes swallowed and returned to his perusal of the treaty, leafing slowly through the pages.

Quinn could see Gunning looking uncertainly between him and Barnes, wondering if he could break into his commanding officer's reverie. At last he seemed to pluck up the courage. "Wh-what is it, sir?" he asked tentatively.

"It's... it's a—" Barnes, still staring at the document, broke off and shook his head, obviously unable to find the right word.

"It's a surrender," Quinn supplied.

Barnes nodded absently. "Yes. That's what it amounts to."

"Sir?" said Gunning uncertainly.

Barnes finally looked up from the treaty and turned his attention to his men. "It's a détente, Gunning. A treaty of reconciliation between Britain and Germany. It's—" He shook his head, once more leafing through the pages. "We capitulate, entirely. We blow off the Americans and NATO; we hand Sicily over to the Italians; we pull out of Greece. We relinquish all North Sea oil rights to the Jerries. We even have to remove all nuclear weapons from the British Isles." He shook his head again, then looked at Quinn. "This can't be."

Quinn let everything hang in the air for several moments as the reality of the situation sank in for Barnes, Gunning, and Cokeroft, then he spoke. "Looks like you have a decision to make, Captain Barnes."

Barnes frowned. "What do you mean?"

"You weren't supposed to speak to me tonight."

"No."

"You were simply supposed execute me."

"Yes." It was a simple statement of fact, not an admission of guilt; there was no embarrassment in Barnes's voice. Quinn had expected none.

"Just like I wasn't supposed to speak to Richard Garner. But of course I did. And consequently I had to make the same choice he did. The same choice he died for. I had to decide what I meant when I took an oath to serve my country." He took a breath. "The easy thing would be to kill me and let *that*—" he jabbed his finger at the treaty "—take its course. At least you'll be removing Britain from the threat of nuclear war with Germany—at the minor cost of making us a Nazi satellite state. Or you can choose like I did, and fight it. But whichever one you do, it will be *your* choice."

"But—" Barnes looked helplessly from the treaty to Quinn. "What can we possibly do to stop this?"

"Heydrich," Quinn said simply.

Barnes frowned. "The Reich Commissar-General?"

Quinn nodded. "Look at the names on the last page. Hitler— and Himmler. This isn't a Reich Foreign Ministry treaty. This is the SS. Himmler knows that Hitler has named Heydrich as his heir in his will. He's going to use this treaty—announce it at Hitler's funeral tomorrow before the will is read, and use it to overturn the will. We have to get that document to Heydrich. He's the only one who can stop this."

"What do you mean? Himmler gets prestige from this treaty, fine—but Heydrich's still a Nazi. He still wants Britain to capitulate, even if it's a victory for his rival. Why would he oppose it?"

"Heydrich and Himmler hate each other," Quinn said. "You know that. *Hate* each other. Whichever one is the next Führer, the other won't survive long in the new regime. Right now, it's Heydrich who will win that fight. But if Himmler can get this treaty in front of Germany at the funeral tomorrow, he can cause enough commotion to have the will swept aside and get himself made Führer. Once he knows the situation, Heydrich will do whatever it takes to stop that coming to pass. He'll have to repudiate the treaty to do that—paint it as treason, misrepresent it as favoring Britain over Germany. He won't be able to then turn round and sign it once he does that. Even if he does try to reconstruct it, all the furor will have made the British Government back out—or made them fall."

Barnes was silent for a while, thinking it all over. "But Heydrich is in Linz right now," he objected at last, "with the entire Nazi and European leadership. We'd never get to him." He paused, then added, "And what can he do anyway, with the city under an ironclad SS guard?"

Quinn nodded. "I agree. We'll probably fail. We'll probably die. The sensible thing for you to do would be to kill me."

Quinn could see the conflict playing across Barnes's face. At last the captain turned to Gunning and Cokeroft. "Sergeant Gunning," he said, "what do you think?"

Gunning looked at Quinn, uncertainty on his face, but when he spoke there was confidence in his answer. "I think you'll choose right, sir. I trust your decision."

"Cokeroft?"

Cokeroft had no hesitation. "You heard the sergeant, sir."

Barnes sighed, leafing through the treaty once more. "Not going to make this any easier on me, are you, lads?"

The silence lasted several moments. At last, Barnes looked up at Quinn, and Quinn could see the resolution on his face. "You'd better get dressed." He nodded at Ellie's bedroom door. "And get her dressed, too."

Quinn shook his head. "She stays here."

"She can't," Barnes said firmly; his voice left no room for argument. "We can't leave her here. The Germans will kill her." He paused. When he spoke again, his voice had taken on an odd tone. "Or the British."

They dressed in silence and left the flat. It was slow going down the stairs, as Cokeroft had to be supported between Quinn and Gunning. In the foyer they paused to catch their breath.

"Captain?" said Gunning. The sergeant was a large, dark-haired man with a mild Irish accent.

"Yes, Gunning?"

"What do we do about Holcombe and Massey?"

Barnes glanced reflexively toward the front door, as if trying to see out into the street, but did not answer immediately. "What's the problem?" Quinn asked.

"There are two more men in my squad," Barnes explained. "They have the building under surveillance from the rooftop across the street."

"Leave them," Quinn said.

Barnes frowned at him, then nodded reluctantly. He turned to Gunning and Cokeroft. "We make no signal," he said. "Just head straight for the car."

Gunning glared angrily at Quinn. "But Captain—"

"We are committing treason, Sergeant," Barnes cut him off. "I will not ask anymore of my men to collude with us."

Gunning clearly wanted to say more but refrained. Instead he nodded. "Yes, sir."

"You have the car keys?" Barnes asked. Gunning nodded. "You go first then. I'll help Cokeroft."

Gunning and Barnes switched places, and at Barnes's nod, Gunning opened the front door and headed out into the street.

"You next," Barnes said to Quinn. "I'll be fine."

Quinn slipped gently out from under Cokeroft's shoulder and made to follow Gunning. "Fraulein, you go too," Barnes ordered.

Quinn paused to allow Ellie to fall into step just behind him, then headed through the doorway. He had taken his first step down the stone steps when the whipcrack of a rifle being fired split the night silence, and a bullet bounced off the step a few inches from his foot in a shower of stone shards.

His reaction was instinctive and immediate. He twisted at the waist and dove back toward the doorway, barreling into Ellie's torso and wrapping his arms around her to carry her with him as a second gunshot split the night. She let out a scream, more of surprise than fright, and as he landed hard on top of her in the building's front doorway he heard the bullet that would have hit her in the chest strike the linoleum floor of the foyer beyond them, cracking tile.

He scrambled the rest of the way to safety inside the foyer, dragging Ellie with him. Cokeroft had been left slumped against the bottom of the staircase while Barnes, pistol drawn, had pressed himself against the wall next to the doorway. Gunning came hurtling back through the doorway, and Barnes slammed the door shut behind him.

For several moments the only sound was that of heavy breathing. At last Gunning broke the silence. "What the fuck was that?"

"It wasn't Holcombe and Massey," said Cokeroft.

"No," agreed Quinn.

Barnes looked at him sharply. "Then who?"

"Your watchers."

"What?"

Quinn raised his eyebrows as if to signal that Barnes should already have this figured out. "You really think this is something the Gestapo are just going to trust MI6 to do and leave it at that? First I turn, then you catch me and I escape you. They've sent someone along to make sure the job gets done this time."

Gunning cursed under his breath, and they lapsed back into silence. Ellie was sitting silently in a corner of the foyer with her back against the wall, and Quinn sat down next to her.

"Gunning," Barnes said. "Did you see where the shots came from?"

"Not precisely, sir," the sergeant answered. "Somewhere in the building right across the street."

"Damn," Barnes said.

"Is that the building your men are in?" Quinn asked.

Barnes nodded absently. "On the rooftop."

The conversation had all been in English, and Ellie had not understood it. Her eyes leapt nervously between Quinn and Barnes. Now, in the several moments of silence that followed, she whispered, "What's going on? Are the English shooting at us?"

Quinn shook his head. "The Gestapo. There are a couple of English sharpshooters out there, but they're in the same building as the Gestapo, so they can't help us unless they can find the room where the Gestapo are shooting at us from."

"How far is it to the car?" Barnes asked.

"About ten yards," Gunning said. "Maybe less."

"Can you make it?"

Gunning hesitated, then nodded.

"All right," Barnes said. "I'll give you what cover I can."

The captain resumed his position with his back to the wall beside the door and checked his weapon. When he was satisfied, he looked up at Gunning. "Whenever you're ready."

Gunning, who had been waiting a few feet back from the door with the car keys in hand, took a deep breath, then nodded. Barnes reached across the door, grasped the handle and pulled it wide open.

At first Gunning remained motionless, hoping the Gestapo sniper would let off a reflex shot, but none was forthcoming. Then he hurtled through the doorway and sprinted out into the street.

A rifle fired, but the shot went wide by over a yard and smacked into the pavement. Before the Germans could get off another shot, Barnes swung round into the open doorway and fired his pistol in the general direction of the snipers, one shot, then two more in quick succession, before ducking back under cover just as the German rifle fired again.

The goal, of course, had been to draw the Gestapo fire away from Gunning and toward Barnes, but that was unsuccessful. Quinn watched Gunning, midway between the front door and the car parked along the curb across the street, jerk violently to the side as he was hit and clutch at his upper arm. His momentum carried him the last several yards forward before he dropped to his knees and collapsed against the side of the car, sheltered by it now from the German sharpshooters above.

But the car keys had gone flying out of his hand when he was hit. Quinn had watched them skitter along the asphalt before coming to a rest, gleaming in the center of a pool of bright orange light cast by a streetlight. Gunning was safe for the moment behind the car, but he had no way of getting into the car, nor of starting it.

Quinn sprinted out the front door and was down the steps and into the road before Barnes had time to let out an inarticulate cry of protest. There was a rifle shot, and the bullet bounced off the asphalt between his feet but miraculously missed him. He did not slow down as he approached the car keys, maintaining a full sprint while bending to pick them up.

He scooped the keys up then, hideously off balance, spun on his heel and lunged toward the safety of the car a few yards away. Another bullet hit the road where he would have been if he had been any less agile, but he was unaware of it. He had stumbled as he lunged, staggered forward and rolled hard to a stop against the car, next to Gunning.

The sergeant was breathing shallowly and sweating, and blood welled between his fingers where they were clasped against his upper arm. "How are you?" Quinn asked.

"I'll be fine," he said. "Just winged me." He nodded to where Quinn had picked up the keys. "Nice work."

Quinn grunted, reached up and unlocked the car door. He got in, reached back and unlocked and opened the back door, then started the engine as Gunning climbed into the back seat. A bullet tore through the roof of the car but missed both of them, burying itself in the leather of the passenger seat. Through the doorway across the street Quinn could just see Barnes and Cokeroft arguing. He could imagine about what—Cokeroft was probably insisting that Barnes leave him behind.

He put the car into gear and pressed down on the accelerator, turning in a fast, sudden arc and pulling up at the opposite curb at the bottom of the steps leading up to the front door. He reached across, unlocked the passenger door and pushed it open as Gunning did the same in the back.

Ellie came dashing down the steps and into the backseat, slamming her door closed behind her; the Germans had just enough time to get a shot off at her, but it went wide. Barnes and Cokeroft were still arguing in the doorway.

"Barnes!" Quinn yelled. "He'll be all right. Come on!"

Barnes looked at Quinn, then back to Cokeroft, who nodded at him. Reluctantly, he turned and sprinted out the doorway and down the steps, diving into the car and just escaping the bullet that smacked against the steps behind him.

"Go go go!" he screamed, but Quinn had already put the car in gear and slammed down the accelerator, and they sped off into the night.

CHAPTER XX

AT FIRST no one said anything. It took several minutes for the adrenaline to stop pumping, for their bodies and brains to register that the immediate crisis had passed and that they were, momentarily at least, out of danger. The only sound was that of the engine's growl shifting constantly as Quinn changed in and out of gear, taking random turns without any specific destination, merely trying to put as much distance as possible between themselves and Ellie's building, while he and Barnes kept a careful watch to make sure they were not being followed.

At last, after several minutes of peering intently over his shoulder out the rear windshield, Barnes shifted his gaze to Gunning sitting in the back seat. "How are you, Sergeant?"

The sergeant had his good hand clasped over his wounded bicep and was sitting with his head resting against the car window and his eyes closed. At Barnes's inquiry, he opened them.

"I'll live, sir," he said. "Bastard just winged me. Amateur, he was."

Barnes smiled slightly. "You'd have done better if you'd been up there in his place, Sergeant, I'm sure. A proper professional, you are."

Gunning made a wan attempt at returning the smile. "Yes, sir. Thank you, sir."

Barnes reached under his seat and pulled out a first aid kit, turned and passed it to Ellie, sitting next to Gunning. "Fraulein," he said, "please see to him."

Ellie, wide eyed, had taken the kit automatically when Barnes proffered it to her and at first simply stared blankly at it. Then, visibly recomposing herself, she looked up at Barnes and nodded. Without saying a word, she turned to Gunning and gently began prying his hand away from his wound so she could take a look at it.

By now Quinn was heading generally south. He was satisfied they had not been followed, but he was still keeping an eye out for any *Orpo* patrol cars. Barnes, once he had satisfied himself that Ellie knew what she was doing and that Gunning's wound was indeed fairly light, turned back to face forward in his seat and lapsed into brooding silence.

"He'll be all right," Quinn said. When this elicited only a disinterested glance from Barnes, he elaborated, "Your man back there. Cokeroft. He'll be all right. The Gestapo were there for me. Now that I've gone, they won't go hunting for him. Your men across the street will be able to go in and get him out."

Barnes offered at first no response, then only a nod. After a few more moments he said, "You can't take the autobahn."

Quinn nodded. "I know. I'm going to take the back roads out of the city. We'll have to figure something out, though. Without the autobahn it'll be at least twenty hours to Linz."

After some time they passed from the city into the extensive maze of suburbs that ringed it. When after half an hour they had covered only about twenty kilometers, Quinn said, "Do you have a screwdriver?"

Barnes had been continuing to keep a lookout for the Gestapo; it took him a moment to process the unexpected question. "Yes," he said.

Quinn nodded and pulled into a side street of residential houses. He crawled along the dark, silent street, looking carefully about to make sure there were no signs of activity, and pulled up before a darkened house with a Volkswagen Karmann Ghia sitting in the driveway and turned off the ignition.

"What are you doing?" Barnes asked.

Quinn nodded in the direction of the Karmann Ghia and said, "The number plate." Barnes followed his gaze, then turned back to him, understanding on his face. Wordlessly, the captain got out of the car and walked round to its rear, opened the boot and removed something, then headed toward the Volkswagen.

Quinn glanced at the backseat. Gunning, his upper arm now bandaged, was sleeping lightly. Ellie had been asleep, too, but she had woken when he had cut off the engine. Quietly, Quinn opened his door and got out of the car, scanning up and down the street for any movement.

After a minute or two he heard Ellie's door open, followed by the sound of her footsteps as she walked around to join him.

He felt her settle herself against the side of the car next to him, her upper arm touching his. He glanced down at her and smiled reassuringly.

With her eyes she indicated Barnes, kneeling behind the Karmann Ghia and unscrewing its number plate. "What's he doing?" she asked.

"The Germans will have our registration number," Quinn explained. "If they didn't get it back at your building, they'll have got it from the British Embassy. That's why we've stayed off the autobahn, because they'll be watching it."

"So he's switching out the number plates?"

Quinn nodded.

She was silent for several moments. Abruptly, she asked, "Where are we going?"

"Linz," said Quinn.

"Why?"

"To try to contact Heydrich. Himmler negotiated the treaty with Britain, but the Führer's will names Heydrich as his successor. Himmler is going to use the treaty to have the will overturned."

She paused before responding, absorbing it all. "That's why they were so desperate to have Garner killed? So he couldn't get to Heydrich?"

"Yes."

Another pause. Then, "Are we going to die?"

He turned to her and stared levelly into her eyes. "Yes. I think so."

She nodded and looked away. He was unsure what he might have expected her to say now, but nevertheless he was surprised at her next question. "Do you know their names?"

"Who?"

She nodded behind them, at the car and in the direction of Barnes beyond it. "Them."

He gestured to Barnes. "That's Captain Barnes. And," a gesture towards the backseat of the car, "Sergeant Gunning. I don't know their given names."

"They're the men who—the men who took me. This morning."

He nodded. "Yes. They're also the ones who rescued us at Denlinger's flat." He hesitated, but did not add that they were the men who had killed Richard Garner.

All told it took Barnes about fifteen minutes to remove the two sets of license plates from the Karmann Ghia and their own car, and to replace the Karmann Ghia's plates on their car. He was about to toss their own plates on the backseat, but Quinn stopped him.

"We should put them on the Karmann Ghia," he said. "It might take him longer to notice that way."

Barnes let out a sigh of annoyance and looked pointedly at his watch, but then said, "All right, then." He tossed Quinn the screwdriver and held out the plates. Without a word Quinn took the plates and headed for the Volkswagen.

The captain stood over him as he changed the plates. When he had finished, the two men headed back to the car. He made to get back in the driver's seat, but Barnes shook his head and said, softly but authoritatively, "No." Quinn looked askance at him, and the Royal Marine gestured toward the passenger door. He thought about arguing, then shrugged and got in on the indicated side.

Barnes started the car and pulled away from the curb, but did not head in the direction Quinn had expected. "You're going west?"

Barnes nodded. "We're already so far off the southbound

autobahn as it is. We'll head toward Magdeburg, then turn south. They'll be looking for us to be coming from Dresden, but we'll actually be coming from Erfurt."

"That's a good idea."

They lapsed into silence after that, Barnes concentrating on the road signs as he made their way through the unfamiliar suburbs towards the westbound autobahn. Quinn, no longer in the driver's seat, had nothing to do but sit and stare out the window. Soon he found himself suspecting that Barnes hadn't taken the wheel just to emphasize that he remained in charge, but to avoid the same tension that Quinn himself now felt starting to build in the silence as Germany rolled by.

After they got on the autobahn and were heading in the direction of Magdeburg and Hannover, however, Quinn felt his frustration subside, but just a little. At least now they were traveling at high speed, in a straight line; as the countryside streamed past them, he could at least feel as if they were making some sort of progress. After a while, he dozed.

Their faces floated before him once more: broken, hopeless, their bodies so gaunt it was impossible to tell man from woman. Had one of those faces been a cousin? A family friend? His parents' rabbi? If not for a simple twist of fate, one of them would have been him.

He came awake with a start, blinking and rubbing at his eyes in an effort to wipe away the sallow faces. Barnes looked at him curiously, but said nothing. The emaciated images continued to tug insistently at the back of his mind; there was a thought there, something that wanted his attention, but he brushed it aside. Now was not the time.

It was after three a.m. when they swung south at Magdeburg;

by the time they passed through Halle, the sky in the east had begun to lighten.

Quinn checked his watch. "What time is the funeral?" he asked no one in particular.

"Noon," Ellie said when Barnes offered no answer.

"Bugger," Quinn said.

A little after seven o'clock they stopped outside Regensburg for gas. By now, as they drew nearer both to Linz and to the middle of the morning, they were beginning to encounter other traffic on the autobahn.

Quinn watched Barnes fill up the car, then head inside to pay. As the Royal Marine disappeared through the shop's front door, however, a sudden thought occurred to him, and he got out of the car.

"Where do you think you're going?" demanded Gunning, who had woken up a few hours before, but was looking pale. Quinn ignored him, swinging his door shut and hurrying across the plaza in pursuit of Barnes.

A small bell chimed as Quinn swung the front door open, causing Barnes, standing at the cash register with money in his hand, to look up. The captain's eyebrows raised in enquiry when he saw who it was. Quinn glanced around, picked up a morning newspaper from the stack just inside the door and held it up for Barnes to see. Barnes gave him a slightly perplexed frown but turned back to the cashier.

"Another twenty pfennigs," said the bored-looking young man, and Barnes counted out another two coins from his palm, then turned and headed out with Quinn.

"I can tell you already what the day's big story is going to be," the captain commented dryly as the two men headed back toward the car.

"It'll have an itinerary for the day," Quinn explained.

As they got underway once more, he leafed through the paper, looking for any public events that morning. The situation looked unpromising.

"Well?" Barnes asked after a few minutes. "What have you got?"

"It doesn't look good," he said. "Though I suppose I can't say I'm terribly surprised. Before the funeral starts, there's nothing going on in Linz except for the ceremony at ten when the will is removed from the Führer's palace and transported to the great hall for the funeral. He'll be sure to be there for that, but..."

"But," Barnes finished, "the security will be impossible to get through. And it'll be mainly Gestapo."

"Exactly."

Quinn gave up and deposited the paper on the front dash. Deggendorf went by, then Passau; all the while, the traffic was becoming thicker, and their progress was becoming slower. At last, shortly after Eferding a few kilometers west of Linz, they reached a jam and were forced to come to a halt.

"Damn," said Quinn as they rolled forward three meters for the fourth time in ten minutes, then stopped again. "Damn. Damn." He raised himself up in his seat, trying to see an end to the twin lines of inching Volkswagens stretching out along both lanes ahead of them, but he could not. "They can't all be bloody arriving for the bloody funeral this morning."

There was nothing for it. They sat meekly in their place and inched along toward Linz as precious minutes ticked by.

Quinn saw the cause of the holdup first. "Hell," he breathed.

"What?" Barnes and Gunning asked in unison.

Quinn nodded ahead of them. "Up ahead there," he said. "About seventy meters."

Both men strained to follow his gaze. "Christ," Barnes said when he saw it; a few moments later, Gunning let out a considerably stronger oath.

There were eight Waffen-SS troopers: four by the side of the road, checking the cars in the outer lane; and four in the median, checking the inner lane. They were stopping each car, talking to the driver and examining his papers.

"Do you have papers?" Quinn asked.

"In the glove compartment," Gunning said. "But they're a bit rudimentary."

"It wouldn't do us any good, anyway," Barnes said. "They'll have descriptions of all of us. A woman and three men, one of them," he nodded at Quinn's legs, "in German uniform trousers and jackboots, and another with a bloody bullet wound. We'll never make it past them."

Ellie had dozed off, but the sudden tenseness of their conversation had awoken her. "What's going on?" she asked.

"There's a checkpoint up ahead," Quinn said. "SS." He paused, then said to Barnes, "Turn around."

"Pardon?"

"You have to. We can't get through. Turn around."

"And just what are we going to accomplish by driving *away* from the city?"

"You'll have to get off the motorway at Eferding. Take the smaller roads into Linz."

"But that could take an hour."

Quinn nodded in the direction of the stormtroopers. "Better than being shot."

Barnes gave a dissatisfied sigh, then nodded. He turned the steering wheel, pulling out across the median and turning into the opposite lane. Quinn turned and looked back over his shoulder at the four stormtroopers in the median. One of them had seen them turn and walked forward slightly, staring after them, hand poised to unsling the automatic rifle at his shoulder. He said something over his shoulder to his fellows, one of whom came up beside him to stare after them as well. The newcomer said something, shrugged, then went back to checking drivers' papers. The first trooper continued to stare after them uncertainly as he receded out of Quinn's view, but by then, there was nothing he could do.

They got off the autobahn just before returning to Eferding and turned in the direction of Linz, following a narrow, single-lane roadway that had probably been in use since the Middle Ages as it wound its way through the forested slopes of the alpine foothills. Quinn was thankful that they encountered no traffic coming the other way, because there was simply no way two cars would have been able to pass each other on this road without one of them knocking the other off the track and down the side of the mountain.

Barnes's estimate of how long it would take to reach Linz on the side roads turned out to be very accurate, and it was almost nine o'clock when they rounded a bend in the road and found the city spread before them.

Barnes changed gear and cautiously slowed down as the road turned into a sharp, downward slope toward Linz. "Into the belly of the whale," Quinn heard him murmur.

CHAPTER XXI

OF ALL the German cities the Führer had rebuilt since the war, Linz had been his most personal project. It had been his cherished dream to turn this, his home city, into the cultural center of all Europe and to supplant Vienna and Budapest as the greatest city on the Danube. He filled it with massive, monumental architecture— the art gallery, the weapons museum, the communal hall, the Party and government centers; all carefully planned and arranged by the Führer personally to fit seamlessly into his vision of a city that rose along the banks of the Danube as if that were exactly what God had intended to be there.

From their vantage, elevated slightly above the city as they descended toward it from the hills, they could see the countless white stone monuments and galleries rising beyond the residential suburbs that ringed the city. Quinn picked out the spires of the Party headquarters, the bell tower whose base contained the Führer's parents' mausoleum, and the towering stories of the famous Strength through Joy Hotel. The entire effect, however, was spoiled by the cloud of grey industrial smog that lay over the whole city, rising from the Hermann Göring Works steel plant on the river's far side, which the Führer had insisted on placing there over the objections of his architectural planners and the Linz city officials.

They entered the city to find it predictably bustling. The streets teemed with pedestrians and parked cars lined every curb, while large notices proclaimed the boundaries of the large central section of the city that had closed to car traffic as of sunset yesterday evening. They busied themselves trying to find a parking space, which quickly proved none too easy a task.

Finally Quinn pointed to the open mouth of a narrow alley. "Just park in there," he said. "I rather doubt we're going to be needing the car again, anyway."

Barnes nodded and pulled into the alley. He cut the engine off, then, while the other three got out, opened the glove compartment and pulled out the car's registration papers. He tore the papers up thoroughly as he got out the car and slipped their remains into a dustbin sitting against the alley wall.

Gunning still looked slightly pale, and sweat was beading on his forehead. "Are you all right?" Barnes asked, but the sergeant just nodded.

"I'll be fine, sir," he insisted.

Barnes regarded him reluctantly for a moment, then turned to Quinn. "Well then. Which way?"

"For the removal of the will?" At Barnes's confirmatory nod, Quinn said, "It's being held at the *Führerhaus*. It's—I think it's towards the city's outskirts." He had never been to Linz before. He addressed Ellie. "Do you know the city?"

She nodded. "I've been here several times. With school, and with my family."

"The Führer's palace. Which way?"

She looked about at the street off which the alley opened to get her bearings, then nodded toward one end. "This way, I think. Yes, this way. Come on." Without waiting, she set off. They followed.

She led the way through the crowded streets, but soon they all knew where they were going due to the ubiquitous signs pointing the way to the city's major monuments. The four of them received a number of curious glances from other pedestrians, especially Gunning and Quinn with his jackboots, but they were fine so long as they were careful to escape the notice of the Waffen-SS patrolmen on most street corners.

The Führer's palace stood on a hill overlooking the river and the city center, situated so that the Führer could have a sweeping view of the monument to himself that he had built out of the city of Linz. He had always claimed to friends and subordinates that, when his work was done and he had secured Germany's destiny, he would lay down the burdens of office and retire here to spend his twilight years tending to his "garden"—the unparalleled collection of art housed in the art gallery he had built here—but that had never come to pass. Now, his will was held here under the strongest security in the Reich, and, after his funeral at the city's communal hall at noon, the Führer himself would be interred in a mausoleum beneath this, his favorite palace in his favorite city.

They could hear the low murmur of the crowd before they

turned the corner into one of the streets leading up to the *Führerhaus* plaza and saw it: a tightly packed mass of people spilling out of the plaza and into the street ahead of them, thousands in number, assembled for the removal of the will.

The four of them drew up when they saw the crowd. "Bloody hell," said Gunning. "How are we supposed to get through *that?*"

They walked forward to the edge of the crowd and stopped again. Quinn craned his neck, peering over the tops of heads into the plaza beyond. It formed a broad upward slope leading to the Führer's palace at the top, and right now it was filled with a seething mass of people pressed tight against each other.

"There must be fifteen thousand people here," he said.

"We need to get up there?" Gunning asked dispiritedly, nodding at the palace at the slope's summit.

Barnes nodded. "Yes."

Ellie gave Quinn's elbow a gentle tug. "What's going on?" she asked.

He glanced down at her. "We need to get to the palace," he said.

"Why?"

"To reach Heydrich. He'll be there for the removal of the Führer's will in—" he checked his watch "—twenty minutes. We have to let him know about the Columbia-Haus treaty."

Quinn went back to staring bleakly at the crowd with Barnes and Gunning. Ellie's eyes flicked between the backs of the people in front of them, whom she was not tall enough to see over, and her three companions, each of whom was much larger than she.

"I can do it," she said at last.

It took a few moments for the statement to register with the others. Quinn and Barnes turned and looked at her.

"Pardon?" Barnes said.

"I can get to Heydrich," she said. "I can get through the crowd and past the guards in twenty minutes."

"No," Quinn said. "I don't want you doing that."

Barnes held up a mitigating hand. "You're sure you can get there quickly enough? This is our only shot."

Ellie looked at the crowd, then back to the two men and nodded. "Can you think of anything better?" she asked.

"She can't go off on her own like this," Quinn objected. "It's too dangerous."

"I don't see what choice we have," Barnes said. He turned to Ellie and nodded. "All right."

"Does anyone have a piece of a paper?" she asked.

Quinn went to pat his pockets, but before he could, Barnes pulled out a small notebook and proffered it to Ellie. She took it and waited expectantly for a moment before prodding, "And a pen?"

"Ah. Yes," Barnes said. He produced a pencil and held it out to her. "Pencil all right?"

"Thank you," she said, taking the pencil from him. She scribbled a quick note, tore the page from the notebook and slipped it into her pocket, then handed the notebook and pencil back to Barnes. She brushed her hand lightly against Quinn's. "I'll be back," she said.

"Be careful," he responded.

She nodded, took a deep breath and plunged into the crowd.

Ellie was a small-framed woman and found it easy—much easier than any of the others would have—to slip through small spaces in the crowd and make her way across the plaza. Every once in a while someone would bridle when she accidentally gave him a slight shove as she tried to slip by, but she would quickly apologize and smile the same smile, widening her eyes ever so subtly. That always worked such wonders on her father or—when there was absolutely no other course open to her—on the Gestapo investigators at the office. At such times the affronted man would either frown gruffly or smile indulgently, but he would always give way.

As she made her slow way toward the *Führerhaus*, she could hear around her accents from every province of the Reich— Prussia, Westphalia, Bavaria, Austria, Holland, Norway, Denmark, and Poland all had representatives in the crowd. It had been a cornerstone of National Socialist policy ever since the Party had assumed power in 1933 that the happiness of the German people and the ascendancy of the Aryan Race could both be achieved through travel. The National Socialist government had worked hard to ensure that every family could afford its own Volkswagen, had built the *autobahnen* to facilitate easy movement across the country, and had required that every father received enough holiday time to spend a few weeks each year touring the great sites of the Reich with his family.

Ellie stopped when she found a portable metal railing barring her way. With another railing about six meters beyond it, it formed a narrow corridor of empty space, the crowd pressing in against it on both sides. She looked to left and right. Twin chains of portable railings created a clear passageway through the plaza, with Waffen-SS troopers spaced every few dozen paces to guard it, starting at the entrance to the palace and disappearing down the main road leading to the city center; no doubt this was the route the Führer's will was about to take to the communal hall, and the route the Führer's body itself would take when it was brought here from the hall to be interred following the ceremony.

She made her way along the cordon toward the palace, trailing her palm along the top railing to guide herself on her route. This made her going quicker: now she was able to maintain a straight route toward her destination, and people seemed a little more willing to give way to her as she made her way along the edge of the crowd than they had been when she had been trying to force her way through the middle.

She was about ten meters from where the cordon widened outside the palace's main entrance when the sound of sirens approaching behind her made her stop and turn. A Waffen-SS trooper on a motorcycle sped past her toward the palace, followed by a municipal *Orpo* patrol car, a sleek black Mercedes with tiny swastika flags flying from its front, and an armored Gestapo car. The whole convoy pulled up before the palace, with the Mercedes coming to a halt at the foot of the broad flight of steps leading to the building's main entrance. A Waffen-SS trooper got out the Mercedes's passenger door and opened the back door, and two men in National Socialist Party uniforms got out. The first looked to be in his sixties, though he was too far away for Ellie to tell if she recognized him; the second was younger. The two men headed up the steps into the building.

Ellie turned to the group of people next to her: a family of seven, with the five children—two boys and three girls—ranging in age from fifteen years to about eighteen months. All were dressed in their finest clothes, all had swastika armbands on their right upper arms and all—except the youngest child—were craning to catch a better view of the men entering the *Führerhaus*. The mother had her Bronze Honor Cross of the German Mother, recognizing that she had given the Fatherland more than four children, draped proudly at her throat.

"What's going on?" Ellie asked.

The father glanced at her, then took a slightly longer look before returning his attention to the palace. "Dignitaries arriving for the ceremony," he explained. "Top Party officials. Ministers. We saw the Reichsführer-SS go in a few minutes ago."

"He was *old*," contributed one of the girls, who looked about five. Her mother quickly shushed her.

"What about Reinhard Heydrich? The Reich Commissar-General?" Ellie asked. "Have you seen him?"

The man shrugged. "I don't know," he said. "I don't think so."

Ellie murmured her thanks and continued making her way forward as the small convoy sped away from the palace and back down the plaza. In a few minutes she reached the front of the crowd, pressing against the barricade where it widened before the palace's main entrance to create space for the convoys to drop off their passengers. She found herself a space in the front rank where two of the portable metal barricades stood end to end.

"Who was that who just went inside?" she asked the man next to her.

"*Reichsminister* Speer," he said.

"Have there been many others to arrive?" she asked.

"Oh yes, lots," said the man importantly, pleased to be in the know for a pretty girl. "Martin Bormann, Heinrich Himmler, President von Thadden from the Reichstag, Count Ciano the Italian, a couple of generals, an admiral, a Waffen-SS general. They're all here."

"What about Reinhard Heydrich?" she asked.

The man frowned momentarily, then shook his head. "No. No, haven't seen him yet." Then he added hurriedly, "But I'm sure he'll be coming, mein Fraulein."

As if on cue, the sound of sirens began to grow behind them, coming rapidly up the plaza. In unison the crowd turned to try and see the newcomers. Ellie strained her neck but was too short to see anything over the heads of those in front of her.

"There, this is probably Heydrich now," said her companion, who was taller than she was. "See, he's being escorted by the Army, not the SS."

Indeed, Ellie saw as the convoy pulled into the front area, the two motorcyclists leading the way wore Wehrmacht field grey rather than SS black. They were followed by an *Orpo* car and no less than three black Mercedes, all with windows that were tinted and, Ellie would imagine, bulletproof. An armored car bearing the red and black eagle logo of the Wehrmacht's Eastern Command, the forces under Heydrich's command, brought up the rear.

A cheer rose from the crowd as they realized who they were about to see. As the Mercedes pulled up at the foot of the palace steps, Ellie glanced down at the two metal barriers that met in front of her. A gap of about thirty centimeters separated the two of them. Not quite large enough. She glanced from side to side: a Waffen-SS trooper stood eight meters away on one side of her, and another six meters away on the other. While everyone was concentrating on Heydrich, she surreptitiously stuck out her toe and poked at the base of one of the barricades, widening the gap another five centimeters.

It was heavier than she had expected, making her toe throb, and it let out a grating shriek that seemed hideously loud to her but that no one else seemed to notice over the roar of the crowd.

At that moment the crowd became even louder as they saw Heydrich emerge from the second Mercedes, pulled up right at the base of the steps. Ellie looked quickly about to make sure neither of the stormtroopers had noticed her, then joined in with the crowd, clapping and bouncing up and down excitedly on the balls of her feet.

She did not see Heydrich clearly, but she knew it was him: a flash of black in his SS uniform before a forest of field grey surrounded him as his aides, all in Wehrmacht uniforms, closed in around him. He must have had a dozen attendants with him.

The group gathered itself for a moment, then started up the steps, Heydrich at their head. Ellie panicked. They were too far away for her to attract anyone's attention; she had banked on somebody being closer to her so that she could catch his eye. She felt her heart pounding in her chest and wondered what she was going to do.

Then she saw her chance. One of Heydrich's clutch of aides, a grey-haired colonel in his fifties, turned and barked something at one of the others, a younger man on the periphery of the group. The younger man saluted in response, turned and hurried to the armored car parked just a few meters from where Ellie stood. He was in his mid-twenties, with close-cropped auburn hair and an old dueling scar across his chin, and bore a captain's epaulettes. He spoke quickly to the driver of the armored car, then turned to rejoin the officers ascending the stone steps into the palace.

While the captain had been relaying his message, Ellie had briefly patted her hair to make sure it was properly in place. Now, as he returned past her, she timed her move perfectly. Just before the captain crossed her position, she jabbed the man she had been speaking with next to her sharply in the ribs.

He grunted in surprise and instinctively shoved her back. She let out a shriek and stumbled forward, throwing her weight into the gap between the two metal railings. She slipped between them but stubbed her toe hard against one of their bases, clouding her eyes with tears. She dropped to one knee, reaching out and clutching onto the passing Wehrmacht captain's sleeve for support.

The captain whirled angrily at the contact, then stopped and instinctively caught Ellie by the elbow with his free hand. The stormtroopers to either side reacted instantly as Ellie fell through the barrier, unslinging their automatic rifles and bringing them to bear on her.

"Thank you," Ellie panted, glancing up at the captain. "Thank you, Herr *Offizier*." She allowed the captain to help her to her feet, then gestured to the man behind the barricade, who was staring at her with a mixture of surprise and anger. "I-I don't know..."

"She struck me," he cried accusatorily, and the tone of his voice was hurt, but he was also affronted that she should have rejected his proffered friendliness of a few moments before in so unprovoked a manner.

Ellie gestured helplessly at the crowd and smiled apologetically at the captain, her soft blue eyes wide and guileless. "I'm sorry, Herr *Offizier*. We must have been caught in a press." Her hand still rested on his forearm.

The captain looked at the angry man behind the barricade, down at the hand on his arm and back up at the smiling, doe-eyed, golden-haired girl staring up at him, and Ellie could see in his face how instantaneously he chose sides. He smiled reassuringly at her. "It's quite all right, mein Fraulein," he said, patting her hand. Absently he waved away the two Waffen-SS troopers, who reluctantly reshouldered their rifles and resumed their positions at attention. "I am only glad I was here to catch you."

Her smile widened, then she withdrew her hand as if rather

embarrassed to realize she was still holding onto him. "Yes," she said. "I'm glad too." She glanced up the steps, to where Heydrich's entourage was disappearing inside. "Herr *Offizier,* do you—I'm sorry," she interrupted herself, glancing down shyly, "I don't know how to tell an officer's rank."

The captain's shoulders straightened with pride, and unconsciously he brushed the epaulette on his left shoulder with the fingers of his right hand. "*Hauptmann,*" he said. "Hauptmann Meier."

"Hauptmann Meier," Ellie repeated. "You are on Herr Heydrich's staff?"

Meier's chest puffed up even more. "As a matter of fact, mein Fraulein, I am personal aide to the Commissar-General." He did not add that he was probably one of half a dozen such aides, and near the junior end of the line.

Ellie was suitably impressed. "Is it—I don't suppose it would be possible to meet the Commissar-General?" she asked in a hushed, reverent tone.

Captain Meier's smile disappeared. "I am afraid not today, mein Fraulein," he said, reluctant to disappoint her—and possibly to seem less important in her eyes. "The Commissar-General's schedule is simply too full with the day's events. Another day, perhaps," he added hurriedly, "if you'd care to leave me your name and—"

"But it would just mean so much to me to meet him this morning," Ellie pressed, the hint of a pout playing across her lips. She laid a pleading hand on his forearm. "Please, Herr Hauptmann, is there *nothing* you can do? I would be ever so grateful."

She felt the captain's arm stiffen under her hand, and the scar on his chin rippled as his lips thinned. "I am afraid not, mein

Fraulein," he said, slightly frosty now. "It simply isn't possible today. The Commissar-General is too busy."

Ellie realized she was pressing her luck. "Of course, Herr Hauptmann," she said placatingly. "I understand." Her hand slipped down his forearm to clasp his gloved hand. "Thank you. You have been ever so wonderful." She kissed the tips of her first two fingers and brushed them against Captain Meier's cheek. The captain, mollified, nodded and offered her a warm smile as she slipped back between the gap in the barricade.

Abruptly, Meier realized he was now holding a slip of paper in the hand that Ellie had clasped. He opened his fingers and peered curiously at the note.

Gestapo to assassinate Heydrich at funeral. Art museum, central gallery, 10.45.

Meier looked sharply back up at where the girl had been standing, just beyond the barricade, but she had disappeared into the crowd. He scanned the faces of the crowd before him, but there was no sign of her.

CHAPTER XXII

QUINN PACED anxiously back and forth from one side of their small side street to the other, while Barnes and Gunning sat on the curb and waited. Once every circuit or so, Quinn would check his watch, then peer anxiously out over the heads of the crowd's rear rank into the plaza, trying to catch a glimpse of Ellie.

Barnes glanced at his own watch. "She hasn't even been gone twenty minutes yet," he observed reasonably. "There's no way she'll be coming back yet. You should relax."

Quinn shot him a venomous glare, opened his mouth for an argument, then decided instead on, "Bugger off." Barnes merely shrugged.

"I don't like the look of that Hun," Gunning murmured, and

Barnes followed his gaze down to the deserted end of the street, where a passing Waffen-SS patrolman was doing a poor job of concealing his curious glances in their direction. "That's the third time he's been past in the last five minutes," the sergeant added.

The patrolman passed round a corner out of view. "Let me know if you see him again," Barnes said. He raised his voice slightly. "Quinn. We might need to be ready to move in a few minutes."

Quinn paused his pacing and turned towards the two Royal Marines. "We can't," he said. "Not till she gets back."

Barnes shrugged. "It looks like we've been noticed. We'll be no good to her or anyone else in Gestapo custody."

"Well you can bugger off then," Quinn reiterated. "But *I'm* not leaving."

"I think," Barnes said, "that she's more resourceful than you give her credit for being. I think you know that, too."

Quinn glared at him but did not respond.

Suddenly Ellie emerged from the crowd, looking flushed and winded. Quinn ran to her but she waved him away. "We have to go," she said breathlessly.

"What happened?" Quinn asked as Barnes and Gunning got to their feet behind him. "Did you get to Heydrich?"

"I'll explain on the way," she said. "We have to get going. To the art gallery."

Without offering anything further she set off down the street, leaving the others no choice but to follow her. Quinn hurried forward quickly and came abreast of her. "What happened?" he insisted.

Before she could respond, the Waffen-SS trooper stepped out of a side street, barring their way. All four came up short.

"Just a moment, *Kameraden*," the stormtrooper said. "I am afraid I must ask to see your papers before you go any further."

For a moment they did not react. Then Barnes spoke from over Quinn's shoulder. "Actually," he said, "we're in rather a hurry at the moment."

The stormtrooper smiled thinly. Quinn, his hand resting protectively on the small of Ellie's back, felt her shiver slightly. "I am sure, *Kamerad*," the trooper said. "But I am afraid the business of the Reich takes precedence over your petty concerns."

"Actually," Quinn said, "we're *on* Reich business." He reached into his pocket and produced his Gestapo ID, knowing full well that if the stormtrooper had recognized them—which he clearly had—then he would already know the name on the ID.

Quinn held the ID out, a little too far in front of the stormtrooper for him to be able to make it out easily. The trooper leaned forward slightly, dutifully carrying on with the masquerade, but as soon as Quinn saw that he was off his balance, he reached out lightning quick with his other hand, grabbed the trooper by his helmet strap and jerked him forward.

He sidestepped neatly and sent the trooper sprawling past him, landing awkwardly, face down and unable to get to the automatic rifle slung on his shoulder. In an instant Barnes had dropped to one knee beside the trooper, pushed him onto his side, grabbed him by the collar and punched him hard in the face once—twice—three—four times. The trooper looked emptily up at them, blood streaming down his chin from his shattered nose. His arm twitched slightly as if he were trying to reach for them, and then he went limp, unconscious. Barnes let him go and stood up. He looked expectantly at Ellie.

"Lead the way, Fraulein," he said.

"Are we just going to leave him here?" she asked, glancing up at the rear ranks of the crowd, still just in view at the other end of the street. None of them seemed to have seen anything, but it would be only a matter of a few minutes before someone surely must notice the unconscious SS stormtrooper lying on the pavement a dozen meters away.

Quinn looked about. "There's nowhere convenient for us to hide him," he said. "Besides, it's not like it's going to matter terribly now."

Ellie shrugged uncertainly. "Well... I suppose." With a last glance at the stormtrooper, she turned and started walking again, and the rest of them followed her.

As they made their way through the streets toward the city's heart, Ellie explained what had happened with Captain Meier.

"It was my only way to contact the Commissar-General," she said, a hint of defensiveness in her voice. "I couldn't get any closer."

"That's fine," Quinn said. "You did well."

As they walked, the sound of bells drifted out over the city, playing an odd melody. "What's that?" Gunning asked.

"The carillon of the bell tower at the mausoleum of the Führer's parents," Ellie said, reciting from her school days. "Bruckner's Fourth, the *Romantic Symphony*. The Führer has it—had it play only on special occasions. It must mean his will has been removed from its vault."

Soon they emerged onto In den Lauben, the city's famous broad main avenue, which connected the complex of museums and cultural houses comprising the European Culture Center to the city's monolithic, glass and steel train station on the far side of the river. Ellie led them down the last hundred meters of In den

Lauben to where it opened into a broad, paved piazza.

Here was the heart of the city and the Culture Center; the city's library flanked one side of the square and the opera house its other, but it was the art gallery rising on the far side that dominated the scene. All three buildings were draped in red, white and black swastika banners that today alternated with plain black mourning banners. Normally bustling, right now the piazza held only a few dozen scattered tourists.

Barnes called a halt at the entrance to the piazza and checked his watch. "Just short of half past ten," he said. "Gunning."

"Yes, sir."

"How are you feeling, Sergeant?"

Gunning looked a little better, but was still visibly pale and clammy. "Never better, sir."

"Have a gander inside and check things over. If you're not out in five minutes, we'll know something's wrong."

"Aye, sir."

Gunning headed across the piazza while the others found seats on the benches scattered around its perimeter: Quinn and Ellie on a bench next to the entrance to In den Lauben while Barnes seated himself on one of the benches running along the face of the opera house.

For several minutes neither Quinn nor Ellie said anything. Eventually, Quinn broke the silence first. "I'm glad you're safe," he said. "I was worried about you."

Ellie patted him on the knee. "It was fine. Besides, it's not as if *any* of us are really safe right now, is it?"

Quinn sighed. "No, I suppose not."

There was another minute or two of silence, then Ellie said, "I'm sorry I called you a Jew."

"What?"

"At my flat. When I—when I didn't think you should fight this treaty yesterday. I'm sorry I called you a Jew."

The faintest of smiles played across Quinn's lips. "I *am* a Jew."

Ellie opened her mouth to respond, hesitated, and then before she could say anything, Gunning emerged from the museum and nonchalantly seated himself on the steps leading up to its entrance, a few meters below the two Waffen-SS troopers flanking the main doorway.

"Come on," Quinn said, cutting Ellie off before she could say anything beginning with "Yes, but—." He rose, and reluctantly so did she, and they walked casually across the piazza, converging with Barnes at the foot of the flight of steps. All three ascended the steps and entered the museum's entrance hall without a gesture of recognition toward Gunning, who remained sitting where he was.

Ellie led them through the entrance hall into the central gallery that opened at its far end. National Socialism venerated German art as a cornerstone of Nordic cultural and racial superiority, but it also celebrated the great masterpieces of the rest of western—Aryan—Europe. The central gallery of this, the Reich's greatest art museum, housed only a single work of art, the museum's crown jewel: the Mona Lisa, installed here when the Führer had personally first dedicated the museum in the late 1940s.

The Mona Lisa was displayed under a glass case at the opposite end of the gallery, with the intervening walls hung with swastika banners. Ellie and Quinn walked across the gallery and sat on a bench to the side of the painting. Barnes leaned casually against the wall just inside the gallery's entrance.

They did not have long to wait. It was only just after twenty to ten when a young Wehrmacht captain entered. He scanned the almost deserted gallery, and when his eyes fastened on Ellie he headed towards them. Ellie rose at his approach, and Quinn followed her lead, subtly placing himself between her and the captain. The captain's gaze shifted focus to Quinn when he saw this.

"Hauptmann Meier," Ellie said. "I'm glad you came."

The captain inclined his head slightly in acknowledgement and held up his hand. He held a scrap of paper between his first two fingers. "I received an invitation that was irresistible," he said, mustering an amount of poise but clearly nervous. Ellie smiled faintly at his remark. "But now," he continued before either of them could say anything, clearly trying to establish himself in control of the conversation, "I must insist on a further explanation." His eyes shifted back and forth between Ellie and Quinn, belying the apparent authority he was trying to assert in his voice.

Ellie gestured to Quinn. "This is my friend..." She trailed off, uncertain how to introduce him.

"Matthias Kaufholz," Quinn supplied. "Herr Hauptmann, I need you to take me to Reinhard Heydrich."

Meier blinked at Quinn's bluntness. "I'm afraid not, Herr Kaufholz," he said after a moment. "I've come this far on the strength of a scribbled note, but you get no further without providing me with a little more substance. Why would I believe that the Gestapo is planning to assassinate the Commissar-General? At the Führer's funeral, of all places. It's outrageous."

Quinn glanced at Ellie, then back to Meier. "It's eminently logical, Herr Hauptmann. It makes perfect sense. I don't know if they're planning to *kill* him, but whatever it is they do, it'll be just as good. At the funeral this afternoon, Heinrich Himmler must neutralize Heydrich so that he can overturn the Führer's will, which names Heydrich as his successor."

Meier blinked again, then let out a choked snort. "And just how do you come by all this information, that has remained secret to the rest of the Reich for the better part of a week now, Herr—Herr—"

"Herr Kaufholz," Quinn said. "It's all true, Hauptmann. And I have a document that proves it."

Meier's eyes narrowed as the stakes rose. "Where? Let me see it."

Quinn shook his head. "I am afraid not, Herr Hauptmann. I show this document only to the Commissar-General personally."

Meier let out a frustrated sigh, pursed his lips, and then finally shook his head. "I'm sorry, but no. If you're unprepared to substantiate such outlandish accusations, then I can humor you no more." He took a step back as if to leave, then paused, waiting for Quinn to concede.

But Quinn only smiled. "You would not have come here, alone, on your own initiative, Herr Hauptmann. You are here because you showed the note in your hand now to your superiors. Tell me, if you leave now and wash your hands of us, what happens to you when the Commissar-General is executed this afternoon? How do you explain *that* to your superiors?"

"Well—" Meier faltered, then visibly gathered himself. "Well—if that's true, if I am here on the authority of the Commissar-General's office, then what is to stop me from simply arresting the two of you, searching you for this putative 'document', and extracting whatever other information you might have—" he paused, then, a subtle menace lacing his voice, concluded, "—by persuasive force?"

Quinn smiled thinly. "For one thing, Herr Hauptmann," he gestured over Meier's left shoulder, "there are more than two of us." Meier turned to follow the gesture, then started when he found Barnes standing immediately behind him. "I am afraid," Quinn said, "that at the moment you seem to be in a little over your head."

The captain looked uncertainly from Barnes to Quinn to Ellie, all of whom were watching him intently. Ellie gave him a faint, encouraging nod. Finally, he sighed in concession. "Very well," he said. "If that is how you insist it be, then you must meet the Commissar-General."

CHAPTER XXIII

MEIER LED them back through the entrance hall and out the museum's main entrance, where a Mercedes with tiny swastika flags on its bonnet stood waiting for them at the base of the steps, its engine already running and a Wehrmacht private standing at attention at the front passenger door. Barnes's eyes met Gunning's briefly as the four of them descended the steps, but Barnes made no signal, and Gunning made no move to get up.

At their approach, the private swung the car's back door open for them. Meier stepped aside, inviting the three of them to go first. They hesitated, then Quinn made to climb into the car, but Meier stopped him with a hand resting gently on his shoulder and nodded toward Gunning.

"I think," he said, "that *all* of you should come along."

Quinn looked at Barnes, who sighed, turned and nodded to Gunning. The sergeant reluctantly rose and walked down the steps to join the party.

Meier's hand was still on Quinn's shoulder, blocking his way into the car. The captain fixed him with a meaningful stare. "Perhaps I am not in quite so far over my head as you surmised, Herr Kaufholz?"

Quinn returned his stare for a few moments, then broke it without responding and climbed into the car. Ellie came next, followed by Barnes, Gunning, and finally Meier. The private swung the door shut behind them and got in the front passenger seat, whereupon the car immediately pulled away from the art gallery.

They turned in a wide arc across the piazza toward In den Lauben, forcing several surprised tourists to hurry out of their way; automobiles were not ordinarily allowed in the piazza. As they sped up In den Lauben, they sat in silence and watched the buildings scroll past through the tinted windows, not wanting to speak in front of Meier.

Soon they had to slow down as they encountered a large crowd of tourists, and the Mercedes had to force its way slowly through, the pedestrians giving way reluctantly. Meier checked his watch and hissed impatiently.

Their crawl slowed progressively further as the crowd thickened and seemed to be having a difficult time moving out of the way. At last, when they were forced to come to a complete halt, they saw why: the road ahead was cordoned off. They had come to the communal hall, the site of the funeral, and ahead of them In den Lauben was blocked off because it became a part of the funeral's processional route.

Five stony-faced Waffen-SS troopers had gathered on the cordon's other side to see who was causing the commotion by driving through a prohibited area, but when they saw the Mercedes with its small swastika flags, their eyes widened and they immediately busied themselves hauling two of the metal barriers out of the way to allow the car to pass. A few moments later and they were on their way again, speeding down In den Lauben and crossing over the river on the massive Nibelungen Bridge. The bridge was named for both the mythical demigods and for the local factory, now demolished to make way for the Hermann Göring Works, that bore their name, where the Tiger tanks so critical to Germany's victory on the Russian steppe had been manufactured.

Then they were across the bridge, and a few moments later the car pulled off the avenue into a stretch of open parkway. Quinn looked out the window and saw them approaching a massive, imperious stone building, dwarfing its neighbors. The swastika flag fluttered proudly before the building's porticoed main entrance, with the Warsaw Pact flag flying slightly lower beside it, and then the flags of Germany's European satellites.

Quinn glanced at Ellie, who was peering past him out the window at the building. "Strength through Joy?" he murmured. She nodded without looking away from the view. This was the Strength through Joy Hotel, preserve of Reich ministers, Wehrmacht generals, industrial magnates, and foreign dignitaries.

The car turned into a square archway set into the hotel's base and descended the ramp into its parking levels. An SS guard in a booth stopped them at the entrance, but their driver flashed an ID and the guard nodded him through.

Their driver ignored several open spaces on the first parking level, instead heading unerringly for a space on the second. Quinn suspected that the hotel—which would currently be full of officials from across Germany and Europe—had assigned specific sections of its parking levels to all of its guests.

As soon as the engine was cut off, he tried his door but found it locked. Instead, the private got out of the passenger seat and opened the door on the far side.

Gunning waited for Captain Meier, sitting opposite him, to get out first, but Meier, all charm, gestured that Gunning should precede him. The sergeant shrugged and climbed out, followed by Barnes, Ellie, and Quinn. Meier was the last to get out.

The Wehrmacht captain led them to a well-lit corner of the level, where a Waffen-SS trooper stood guard at the entrance to the lift. Meier showed him a pass, and the stormtrooper pressed the button to summon the lift.

It arrived after a few moments. They all filed inside, and a bellhop, whom Quinn imagined was probably also Waffen-SS, asked, "Floor, Herr Hauptmann?"

"Fifth floor."

"Yes, Herr Hauptmann."

They rode up in silence. A bell chimed softly, the lift doors opened, and Meier stepped out into a foyer. Quinn, Ellie, Barnes, and Gunning followed.

A pair of rigid guards, Wehrmacht now, rather than Waffen-SS, with their rifles held across their chests rather than slung over their shoulders, flanked the lift doors. As the doors slid softly shut behind them, a lieutenant sitting behind an ornate wooden desk, seeing Meier, rose and snapped to attention. Out of the corner of his eye, Quinn saw the guards relax almost imperceptibly at the motion.

Meier did not even acknowledge the lieutenant, striding purposefully down a corridor opening off the foyer with the four of them in tow. Everything was a picture of Victorian grandeur, but subtly themed towards National Socialism: the lamps were held in gilt wall sconces shaped like eagles, and the brown criss-cross pattern on the beautiful red carpet turned out, on close inspection, to be subtle, interlocking swastikas.

At the end of the corridor, a door stood open, a Wehrmacht soldier standing at attention outside it. Meier led them through the doorway into what was quite obviously an antechamber. Three doors, all closed, led from the room; two of the walls were lined with wooden-legged, marble benches; and another lieutenant sat behind another desk.

"Hauptmann Meier to see the Commissar-General," Meier said.

The lieutenant nodded, rose, and headed over to one of the closed doors. He cracked it open and slipped inside, pushing it closed behind him.

After a moment or two the door opened again, wide this time, and the lieutenant stepped outside, followed by another officer. The newcomer was about sixty, grey-haired, with the red and gold badge of exalted rank on the collar of his field-grey Wehrmacht uniform. He had a sharp, triangular face and a confident gleam in his dark eyes as he surveyed the four of them. Meier snapped to attention, but the other ignored him. Quinn recognized him: Colonel General Otto-Ernst Remer, Heydrich's chief of staff and commanding officer of the Wehrmacht's Eastern Command.

"The Commissar-General will see you, Hauptmann," Remer said, stepping aside to allow them through the door.

Meier nodded formally and headed through the doorway. The others followed.

The office was large and spacious, elegantly but spartanly furnished. In the center of the room, three couches were arranged around a low, oval table. Beyond that, situated so as to catch the best of the light from the large windows on two walls, stood an ornate mahogany desk with a high-backed, gilt and velvet chair. Red curtains with fringed golden sashes framed the windows.

Two men stood over the desk, studying some documents laid out on it and conferring quietly. At the group's entrance they looked up, and Quinn recognized both of them.

The man on the left, in blue uniform, was the same age as Remer, though he looked slightly younger; despite a touch of grey at the temples, his hair and neatly trimmed mustache were still black. Under his right arm he held a marshal's baton. This was *Reichsmarschall* Adolf Galland, Commander-in-Chief of the German Luftwaffe.

But it was the man on the right who dominated. At sixty-seven Reinhard Heydrich was the oldest of the three men by almost a decade, but had Quinn not known that already, he might have pinned him as the youngest. He was tall and broad shouldered, dwarfing his companions, with eyes that were still a sharp, piercing blue, set over a prominent, bell-like nose, much like Quinn's own. His hair, parted high on his forehead, remained a pale, flaxen blond.

Remer was the last through the door, and he strode across the room to join Galland and Heydrich at the desk. The scene—the two men flanking, Heydrich in the center—tugged something in the back of Quinn's mind, but he could not place where he recognized it from.

The eye was naturally drawn to Heydrich, dressed all in black between the two men in field grey and military blue flanking him, for he still wore the black SS uniform to which he was entitled. Even though Himmler and the SS had become his greatest political foes, his official rank remained that of SS-*Oberstgruppenführer*, or SS field marshal, the highest rank the organization could bestow. Only Himmler, the Reichsführer-SS, outranked him in the SS hierarchy, and only his successor as head of the Gestapo, Ernst Kaltenbrunner, had ever received the same rank.

The Commissar-General nodded to Meier. "Thank you, Hauptmann."

Meier snapped his heels together and saluted, then wheeled about and strode from the room, closing the door after him.

It was on Heydrich that they all had their attention fixed, and he returned their attention curiously but coldly, resting his eyes on each of them in turn with his famous intent, unnerving gaze. Beside Quinn, Ellie shifted uncomfortably under the scrutiny. When Heydrich turned to regard Quinn, he met the stare levelly, refusing to flinch. Time began to stretch away as they held each other's gaze, and Quinn understood how this man inspired such fear—and such loyalty. But he stubbornly refused to give in.

And suddenly Quinn realized what he found so familiar about the image of Heydrich flanked by Galland and Remer—the statues outside the Purification Museum in Berlin. Three men: Adolf Eichmann and Hans Frank on either side, and in the center Heydrich, ultimate overseer of the Purification.

Unbidden, another face seemed to superimpose itself over Heydrich's—shriveled, malnourished, shaven-headed. Its sunken, black eyes stared at Quinn accusatorily. Involuntarily, Quinn took a step back, closing his eyes.

When he opened them again, Heydrich straightened up over his desk, the slightest hint of a satisfied smile on his face. The

Commissar-General pulled his tunic straight at the waist and sat down in his chair.

"So," he said at last. "You are the four English spies the Gestapo has been so desperate to apprehend for the past twelve hours." It was not a question. "Though my sources have been unable to ascertain why they are so concerned about you. I must confess, I am surprised to find you here in Linz, which on this day of days must be the most heavily guarded city in the Reich. But now to learn that you are here to find *me?* I am flattered." His eyes narrowed, and he leaned forward. "Tell me why I should not promptly hand you over to the SS for interrogation."

Quinn still felt a little shaken by the image that had come unbidden into his mind, but he spoke up. "You already know why, Herr *Generalkommissar.*"

Heydrich regarded him for a moment, then glanced back at the rest of the group. "Ah. Ah yes. This supposed 'assassination.' A rather curious claim, certainly noteworthy for its brazenness, though perhaps not for the weight of evidence supporting it." He sifted through some of the papers on the desk before him and pulled one closer to him, scanning it briefly. "According to what we have been able to monitor from the Gestapo—and for foreign spies, you do seem to be awfully well known to them—two of you are English soldiers, including one commissioned officer." He looked back up at Quinn. "You, I would imagine?"

Barnes stepped forward before Quinn could respond. "Captain James Barnes, Royal Marines, sir."

Reluctantly, Heydrich turned from Quinn to Barnes. "Well, Captain," he said after a brief pause, "you are out of uniform in German territory. You are aware, I have no doubt, that under the terms of your own Geneva Convention, I can have you summarily executed."

Barnes did not blink. "Germany has always made her adherence to the Geneva Convention... *selective*, Herr Generalkommissar, and in my experience, she has never needed a reason to shoot someone."

Heydrich's eyes flashed but he bit back any angry retort; instead, he pursed his lips meditatively. Finally he said, "Still, you have not provided me a reason not to turn you over to the Gestapo."

Quinn cut in. "You seem to have excellent sources of intelligence, Herr Generalkommissar. I would imagine that you are aware already that the Führer's will names you as his successor?"

Heydrich regarded Quinn, re-evaluating him now, and Quinn wondered what was going on behind those cold, magnetic eyes. At last the Commissar-General said, "Your own sources of intelligence would seem to be... not unsatisfactory. What is your name, *Kamerad?*"

"My name is Simon Quinn, Herr Generalkommissar, and I am an agent of Her Majesty's Secret Intelligence Service. Three days ago I was tasked to locate and neutralize an official of the British Embassy in Berlin who had disappeared with some sensitive documents, we believed in preparation for defection. The official was—" He paused, and out the corner of his eye he saw Barnes glance at him. "The official is now dead," he continued neutrally. "This is the document he was carrying." He nodded to Barnes.

Barnes pulled the Columbia-Haus file from his inside pocket and stepped forward to hand it to Heydrich, but Remer stepped out from beside the desk, blocking his path. Remer took the treaty, ran his gloved fingers quickly over it, then passed it to the Commissar-General, who began leafing through it.

He perused the treaty silently for several minutes, glancing up at Quinn periodically but then returning once more to the document. Galland and Remer waited patiently on either side of him, neither trying to glimpse the pages over his shoulder.

Eventually Heydrich passed the treaty to Galland, who began looking through it, and looked back up at Quinn. "It seems," the Commissar-General observed dryly, "that my intelligence is not quite so effective as I should like. My agents have been attempting to secure a copy of this document for some months now without success—assuming, of course, that this is genuine."

"It's genuine," Quinn said.

"Supposing for the sake of argument that I accept that," Heydrich said. "I see no reason to believe the accusation you made to Hauptmann Meier."

"Himmler plans to produce this treaty at the ceremony this afternoon," Quinn said, "where he will use the resultant confusion to overturn the will and have himself proclaimed Führer. In such a situation, Herr Generalkommissar, I would imagine the *best* possible fate you could suffer at Himmler's hands would be arrest and internment in a concentration camp." *But far more likely, death,* he left unsaid.

Galland had finished scanning the treaty and had handed it to Remer, who was leafing through it. Heydrich looked at the two of them. "Well?" he asked. "What do you two think?"

"About the veracity of the document?" asked Galland. "If it's a ruse, it seems a rather elaborate one. But the rest? About Himmler overturning the will?" He tapped his marshal's baton contemplatively on Heydrich's desk. Göring, the Luftwaffe's first Reichsmarschall and, after the Führer, the most powerful man in Germany in the 1930s and early 1940s, had worn a gaudy white uniform as a symbol of his rank. After his death, the Führer had appointed as Göring's successor his aide Erhard Milch, a sycophant whose career had been spent at the Air Ministry and whose Air Force rank was purely political. He had adopted Göring's white uniform as his own. But Galland was a soldier, a veteran fighter pilot who had received decorations for valor in both the Spanish Civil War and the Second World War, and when he had been promoted to Reichsmarschall following Milch's retirement he had chosen to retain the standard military blue uniform of the Luftwaffe, used by all its other officers and men.

"I am only a soldier, Herr Generalkommissar," he said at last, "and I prefer to confront my enemies directly. I have always found strength and daring to be the weapons that come most naturally to me, and the ones most likely to secure victory. But in my experience, the Reichsführer-SS abhors these tactics, preferring subterfuge whenever possible. So such a plan as this," he made a vaguely disdainful gesture in Quinn's direction, "this *Englishman* claims does not seem to me to be at all implausible."

Heydrich nodded thoughtfully, but Remer added as he set the treaty down on the desk, "The Reichsmarschall is right, sir. The Reichsführer-SS is a master of subterfuge, intrigue, and deceit, and I wouldn't hesitate to credit him with such a plan. But for the same reason I also wouldn't hesitate to believe that he could concoct this entire scenario to provoke you into action. If you storm publicly into the Führer's funeral, Herr Generalkommissar, and arrest the Reichsführer-SS and proclaim him a traitor, and this treaty proves to be fictitious—then you will have hanged yourself for him." He glanced at Quinn and the others. "After all, even if this is all true, why are these Englishmen here, betraying their own country?"

"This is the only way to stop this treaty," Quinn said, then pressed on unhesitatingly, "We have dedicated our careers and our lives to defending Britain from Nazism, and this is the only way we can stop her from surrendering to National Socialist Germany."

Heydrich stared at him for a long time; Quinn could not tell whether the Commissar-General was regarding him with respect or simply disgust. At last, Heydrich turned back to Remer. "You have a valid point," he said, but then grinned wolfishly, the first hint of emotion he had exhibited. "Tricking me into discrediting myself at the Führer's funeral—before all Germany and the world—*would* accomplish all Himmler could ever hope for. But for the Gestapo to carry through such a plan would require not only deceit, but also imagination—and that is something Heinrich Himmler does not have."

The door cracked open, and the lieutenant from outside stuck his head in. "It is time to leave in five minutes, sir," he said.

"A change of plan, Manfred," Heydrich said. "We will be delayed momentarily."

The lieutenant nodded without apparent surprise. "Very good, sir." He vanished, closing the door once more.

Heydrich rose. "Gentlemen," he said, "we do not plan a coup here. We leave such action to the Reichsführer-SS and his staff. We seek instead merely to preserve the will of the Führer and see that those who wish to execute his final directive to the German people can do so faithfully. Should the funeral go as planned, and the Führer's final testament be honored and our new Führer acknowledged, then we need take no action. We act only to ensure that no one subverts the Führer's wishes." He turned to Remer. "What forces do we have available us?"

Remer shook his head. "Right now? Almost none. We are far from the Commissariat-General. If the will proclaims you the new Führer and Himmler tries to suborn that, then we will have the entire Wehrmacht with us. But by then it will be too late. In the city we have only our escort—a single battalion, against at least five divisions of Waffen-SS who are no doubt on high alert. We're outnumbered forty to one—conservatively. A military action would be hopeless. Besides, except for the company here at the hotel, even our battalion is barracked on the far side of the river."

"But if we can gather them at the communal hall," Heydrich said, "we'd have enough to hold it through the funeral, by which time we'd be able to start bringing in reinforcements. And we'd have surprise on our side. They might already be expecting a fight, but they're not expecting *us* to be expecting one, too. Besides, this is a very risky deception Himmler is planning. It's entirely possible that simply by arriving in force, showing him we know what he's trying to do, that he might be intimidated into not playing his hand."

Remer looked at him skeptically. "But I doubt it."

Heydrich sighed. "Yes, so do I."

"He knows he can't last long in a regime with you as Führer."

Heydrich nodded and turned to Galland. "Adolf, do you have anything available to you that can be of assistance?"

Galland shrugged. "The Luftwaffe would be of use to you if you wanted to *destroy* the city, Herr Generalkommissar, but I am not sure what we can do in a situation like this. There is an airfield a few miles from the city; it might have a small police detachment, but it won't be more than a few dozen men. And the aerodrome at

Salzburg might have a division of combat helicopters."

"Whatever you can give us, Adolf," Heydrich said. He pressed a button on the phone on his desk, and a moment later the door opened and Manfred came in. "Manfred, Colonel-General Remer needs to speak with our battalion commander at the city barracks, and the Reichsmarschall will need to contact the Luftwaffe bases here and in Salzburg. And notify the captain commanding our motorcade escort that his troops are to be on high alert, prepared for combat. We'll leave for the communal hall as soon as all the orders have been issued."

Manfred did not even blink. "Right away, sir."

He turned to leave, but Heydrich called after him, "Oh, and Manfred. Give our guests here a room where they can wait comfortably for the next few hours, and see that any requirements they might have are met."

Manfred nodded. "Yes, sir." He turned to the four of them and held his hand out in the direction of the door. "If you'd care to follow me?"

CHAPTER XXIV

MANFRED LED them back through the antechamber and down the hall. Though he gave no sign that he was tracking which doors they passed, he stopped unhesitatingly at one that was near the end of the corridor and opened it, leading them inside.

They found themselves in a well-appointed, two-room suite. The first room contained two large settees, a coffee table, and four gilt and velvet chairs around a larger dining table, all matching the hotel's ornate décor, as well as a kitchenette, television, and radio. A door opened into the second room, through which could be seen the foot of a four-poster bed.

"You should find both the kitchen and the toilet stocked with necessities," Manfred said. "I will have a guard posted outside within a few minutes; notify him if you lack anything." He looked them up and down, a tired, unwashed group, and his eyes lingered on Quinn's jackboots and torn uniform trousers. "And I'll have changes of clothes sent in for all of you, as soon as we can find something," he added. "Now please excuse me, I have urgent duties." He snapped his heels together and left, closing the door behind him. Quinn heard the key turn in its lock.

For several long moments none of them said anything; they simply stood staring at each other. Then Ellie walked over to one of the settees and collapsed onto it, expelling a great breath of air, breaking the spell. Barnes sat on the other settee, and Gunning seated himself on one of the chairs.

"So this is it?" the sergeant said. "We're done? Just like that?"

"It does seem rather anticlimactic," Barnes agreed.

Quinn massaged the bridge of his nose with his thumb and forefinger, but he did not sit down. Instead he wandered into the bedroom, passing the cherry-wood dresser to stand at the window. He pulled the curtain aside a crack and stared down at the view of the River Danube and, across it, the city bell tower and communal hall. Thousands upon thousands of people, all dressed in black, packed the park spread on the riverbank before the communal hall; he could see the straight line of empty space that marked the beginning of the processional route running across the park from the steps of the communal hall to In den Lauben.

After a few minutes he heard the soft padding of footsteps on the carpet behind him, but he did not turn.

"You should rest." Ellie. He had expected as much.

He waited a moment longer, then turned to her. She was leaning against the doorframe, arms folded over her chest, watching him with a slight smile playing over her lips; it was possibly the first time he had seen her happy. Her hair was bedraggled, she wore no makeup, and her clothes were those she had thrown on when Barnes and Gunning broke into her flat. She looked radiant.

She straightened, closed the door behind herself, walked over to him and kissed him. When the kiss broke off, they stared into each other's eyes. She was smiling, but he was solemn. Absently, he brushed a lock of blonde hair away from her face. She took him by the hand and fell onto the bed, pulling him down with her, and they lay there, he with his arm around her.

The low buzz of voices on the television or radio, Wagner playing in the background, emanated from the other room, and Quinn glanced at the closed door. "They'll have the funeral on," he said; there would be nothing else being broadcast. "We should join them. I imagine it'll be a fairly interesting show."

He made no move to get up, but all the same she rested her hand on his chest to keep him where he was. "What are we going to do?" she asked, still smiling.

"What do you mean?"

"After this. After... all this." She lifted her hand from his chest to make an airy gesture at the room around them. "What are we going to do after it's all over? Where are we going to go?"

He frowned. "Well, you heard the general. The most likely outcome is still that Heydrich will be hopelessly outnumbered, and Himmler will overturn the will."

"In which case the Waffen-SS will storm this floor and summarily execute all of us, yes?"

"Yes."

She made a face at him. "Then let's plan for the other eventuality."

He smiled. "All right. Heydrich will be willing to take care of us, but he'll probably want us out of the way. Won't want to broadcast that a group of British spies brought him to power. We can live quietly somewhere in the Reich, a small flat in Berlin or Frankfurt or Prague."

She considered this. "I'd like that. But you probably want to leave Germany."

He nodded. "Yes. But Britain won't take us. Even if another Government comes to power, one that repudiates this treaty, I've still crossed MI6."

"There's always the Warsaw Pact," she suggested brightly. "Germany will let us stay somewhere in the Pact."

"Yes," he agreed. "A cottage in the Italian Alps, or a Mediterranean villa in Marseilles or Barcelona." That made him think of Maurice and Karl, and he closed his eyes. He knew what would really happen, of course: even if Heydrich, embarrassed by their existence, did not simply have them killed, there was still MI6 to contend with, and disaffected followers of Himmler in the Gestapo. That had been the choice he had made: if he fought this treaty, even if he was successful, he would die. There simply was not anywhere on Earth they could hide from all the groups that would be out to get them.

But he did not want to think about that, especially did not want to think about that happening to Ellie, and all because of him, so he played along with her fantasy, because it took his mind away from what he knew to be the truth.

He opened his eyes, ready to continue, but saw that her smile had been replaced by a concerned, confused frown. Apparently his emotions had been a little clearer on his face than he thought.

"Are you all right?" she asked.

"Yes, yes, I'm fine," he said, mustering a wan smile. Then, to change the subject, he pushed on hurriedly, "We could go to America. Or Canada, or Australia. They'll all owe us a favor if we keep Britain from going over to Germany."

She closed her eyes and snuggled herself more deeply into the pocket of his shoulder, choosing to accept his assertion that he was fine. "I'll have to learn English," she said.

"Yes, but it's a beautiful language," he said. "And you'll have me to teach you. English can make you laugh. German makes you frown. It makes you sound angry." He ran his thumb tenderly along her cheekbone. "When you're forty, if you've spoken English you'll be much prettier." She giggled.

A forceful knocking sounded, but it was not at the bedroom door; someone must be at their suite door. Quinn got up, opened the bedroom door and entered the main room, followed by Ellie. The television was on. Barnes and Gunning were standing warily a few feet from the door. Quinn just heard the key turning in the lock, then the door swung open.

A Wehrmacht major stood in the doorway, the badge of the Eastern Command on his greatcoat lapel. Their room guard's shoulder and the muzzle of his automatic rifle were just visible in the doorframe.

The major strode into their room and took them all in with a quick, severe glance. He looked a little young for his rank; Quinn guessed he must be about thirty.

"You must come with me," he said simply.

None of them moved. "Why?" Barnes asked.

The major surveyed him with disdain. At last he said, almost reluctantly, "The Commissar-General's orders. He wishes you moved to a more secure location."

Quinn and Barnes exchanged glances. "We'd like to see the Commissar-General, then," Quinn said.

The major let out an exasperated sigh and spoke to Quinn as if he were a child. "The Commissar-General has already left for the Führer's funeral. You'll just have to come along."

Quinn did not like such a sudden change, and he could tell that neither did Barnes, but there was hardly anything they could do about it. Barnes nodded to the major. "All right."

The major strode impatiently from the room, and slowly, the four of them followed. Quinn was last out the door. As he was leaving, he caught a quick glance of the picture on the television: rows of hundreds of people seated in a large hall before a podium and, beside it, the Führer's casket draped in a swastika flag.

"The ceremony should of course have begun," the commentator was saying in a hushed, respectful tone, *"but we have been informed that this delay will last just a few minutes more. Apparently it is caused by the unexplained absence of SS-Oberstgruppenführer Reinhard Heydrich, Reich Commissar-General of the Eastern Territories."*

Quinn emerged from the suite, and the guard fell into step behind them. The major led them back down the corridor to the entrance foyer, where the lieutenant behind the desk rose immediately and snapped to attention. The major ignored him, striding to the lift and pressing the button several times rapidly to summon it.

It took a few minutes for the lift to arrive. They all got in, and the bellhop asked their destination. "Parking level four," the major said.

"Where are we going?" Quinn asked as the lift descended.

The major flashed him an irritable glance. "I told you. To a more secure location."

"Yes, but where?" Quinn asked. "In the city? Outside the city?"

The major hesitated, then said, "I haven't been briefed with that information. Your driver will know where to take you."

"But surely," Quinn pressed, "the most *insecure* place for us to be right now is in transit through Linz. The city is about to turn into a war zone. What's going on out there? Has the Commissar-General secured the communal hall?"

"You will be given all the information you need at the time you need it," the major snapped.

A bell chimed, and the lift doors parted, revealing the gloomy parking garage beyond. The major exited the lift and the four of them followed him, filing past the Waffen-SS trooper on guard at the lift entrance.

The car park was empty except for a single armored van a dozen meters away. "This way," the major said, heading purposefully toward the van.

They followed him. He covered the distance between the lift and the van in quick, even strides, then walked around the van's front and gestured down its far side. "This way."

Once again Quinn was bringing up the rear, and so he was the last to round the van's fender except for their guard and almost walked into the other three, stopped there. They had stopped when they had seen the Waffen-SS lieutenant and three Waffen-SS stormtroopers standing concealed around the van's other side.

"Oh, hell," Quinn said.

The Wehrmacht major had stepped neatly away from them

and unholstered his sidearm, which he now pointed levelly at them.

The guard rounded the van's rear behind Quinn. He halted suddenly, taking a step back and raising his rifle when he saw the Waffen-SS troopers, but the major had been ready for him. He fired two quick shots, and the guard collapsed backward, his rifle clattering on the ground.

Ellie whimpered. There were several moments of silence. "I don't suppose any of you are going to turn out to be Royal Marines?" Quinn asked.

This time the major didn't even both to glance in his direction. "Shut up, Englishman."

Quinn was the nearest of the group to the van's front fender and he had taken a cautious step backward, but suddenly he felt a rifle muzzle pushed hard into the small of his back. He turned to find the Waffen-SS trooper who had been standing guard at the lift waiting behind him.

The major had taken a step back toward them and was surveying them, his lip curled in disgust. "Englishmen," he muttered. "You sicken me. Servants of Jewry." His eyes fell on Ellie. "And you. Treacherous bitch." The words were barely out of his mouth when he struck her hard across the face with the back of his hand.

She screamed in pain, her hands flying to her cheek, and dropped to her knees. Quinn snarled and made a lunge toward the major, but suddenly his world exploded in a flash of orange and white pain as the stormtrooper behind him slammed the butt of his rifle into the back of his neck. He dropped to all fours beside Ellie, struggling to remain up, not to collapse face down in front of these Nazi German bastards.

After a few moments the pain had subsided enough for him to look up, though his head pounded like the worst hangover God had ever bestowed on man. The major was staring down at him, his Luger leveled inches from Quinn's face.

"Now, now," he said. "Don't do anything foolish and you will at least have the opportunity to die like men, instead of being shot in the back like common Jews." He gestured with his gun toward the wall of the deserted car park. "Against the wall. All of you."

CHAPTER XXV

ELLIE HAD gotten back to her feet, and she, Barnes, and Gunning obediently walked toward the wall. Quinn was still in pain, gulping air on all fours. When he was too slow to get up, the major kicked him in the ribs.

That was all the opening he needed. He recoiled from the kick, using the motion to reach up and grasp the major around the calf while his foot was still in the air. He jerked hard, pulling the major off his balance and knocking him awkwardly to the ground. He heard the major's Luger clatter across the pavement.

He threw himself sideways, pulling the major on top of him, wrapping his arms under the major's shoulders and around his neck, then rolled to his feet, pulling the major up with him. He heard the major gasping for breath as he struggled to get his feet under himself so that he could rise with Quinn.

Quinn saw the stormtroopers and the SS lieutenant staring uncertainly at him, their rifles trained on him, and he took a step to the side, positioning himself so that the major's body shielded him from both the row of three troopers and the stormtrooper who had been behind him.

"Drop your weapons or I break his neck," he ordered. When the troopers hesitated, he screamed, "Drop your weapons!"

He increased his pressure on the major's neck; the major gurgled and let out a rasping, "*Do it!*"

Obediently the troopers deposited their rifles on the ground, and the lieutenant unholstered his pistol and threw it away. "Now step away," Quinn ordered, and they all took several steps back from the weapons in front of them.

As soon as the troopers were clear, Barnes and Gunning gathered up the firearms scattered across the ground. Each took an automatic rifle and pointed it at the group of SS troopers; as soon as they did so, Quinn released the major and gave him a hard shove in the direction of the group. The major staggered forward, then stood there gasping and rubbing his neck.

Quinn nodded to the other stormtrooper, the one who had come up behind him. "You too," he said. The stormtrooper stepped over to join his comrades.

"All right," Quinn said, "take your clothes off." They stared at him. "I said take your clothes off. I want you all naked." When they did not respond, Quinn bent down, picked out a Luger from the small pile of weapons and leveled it at the major. "You really think I need a reason right now?"

Reluctantly, the major began unbuttoning his greatcoat, and

the other soldiers followed suit. While they were undressing, Quinn turned to Ellie and gently pried her hand away from her cheek. It looked red and would probably bruise painfully, but it did not seem to be anything more serious than that. Tears had run down her cheeks.

"Are you all right?" he asked.

She sniffed but nodded determinedly. "I'm fine."

Looking over her shoulder and past the van, he saw an electrical closet near the lift doors. "Come on," he said.

He led her across the car park. The closet was locked, but he smashed the lock in with the butt of his pistol. Inside he found several large coils of electrical cord. He took a coil and handed it to Ellie, then took another for himself.

He led her back over to the van, where the naked Waffen-SS men stood over their uniforms, shielding themselves with their hands. Quinn handed his coil of cord to Ellie. "Tie them up at the wrists and ankles," he said. "Make sure they're secure. Be careful— have whoever you're tying stand separate from the rest. One of us will cover you, but the other two will need to be changing."

While she set about tying the first soldier up with Barnes covering her, Gunning and Quinn changed. Quinn took the lieutenant's uniform; he was happy to discover that these jackboots fit him more comfortably than the ones he had taken from the Luftwaffe sergeant yesterday. Gunning put on one of the stormtroopers' uniforms. When they were changed, they covered Ellie while Barnes changed, also into a stormtrooper's uniform.

The Waffen-SS officer who had disguised himself as a Wehrmacht major was the last man Ellie bound. Before she could bind his feet, Quinn took him aside.

"How did the SS find us?" he asked.

The major stared at him balefully. "Go to hell," he said.

Quinn belted him across the jaw. The major, his hands tied behind his back, staggered back. When he had regained his footing, he hawked and spat something at Quinn's feet. Quinn looked down to see a gobbet of bright red blood, a tooth sitting in its center.

He grabbed the major by the jaw, feeling him flinch at the rough contact, and held his face up to force eye contact. "I don't have time for this, you Nazi pig," he said. "For every question you don't answer, you lose a finger. How did you find us?"

The major just stared at him, a rivulet of blood dribbling from the corner of his mouth. Quinn shrugged, released his jaw and spun him round. He unholstered the lieutenant's pistol, grabbed the palm of the major's right hand and fired a single bullet into his little finger.

The major screamed and tore away from him, dropping to one knee and writhing in agony. Quinn took a step forward, grasped him by the hair on the top of his head and jerked him round to face him. He put his mouth to the major's ear. "*How?*" he demanded.

"I—don't—know," the major ground out through clenched teeth. "I just—follow my orders." He took several large gulps of air, visibly composing himself. "The order came down to get you—I went and got you."

Quinn shoved him forward, releasing his hair and sending him sprawling across the ground on his stomach.

He turned to walk away, but the major called after him, "He's finished." Quinn stopped and turned back to face him; he had raised himself up onto one knee and was staring after him. "Heydrich's finished," he continued. "We have him already. We had you all the whole time. We orchestrated everything you've done. You can run now, but this is the SS. We'll hunt you down."

Quinn took a step toward the kneeling man and kicked him savagely in the face, sending him sprawling onto his back. Then, as the major scrambled to lift himself onto his elbows, Quinn raised his Luger, aiming it directly between the major's eyes. For a long moment both men remained utterly motionless, staring at each other.

After several seconds that lasted an eternity, Quinn blinked, then turned his head to see Ellie a few meters away from him. She was staring at him, her eyes wide. He craned round a little further, to where Gunning and Barnes were also looking at him.

Without looking back at the major, he lowered his pistol and replaced it in its holster. Abruptly, he turned back round, dropping to one knee beside the major and grabbing him by the hair again. "I spare your life, because you're not worth it, you stinking piece of Nazi filth," he hissed in his ear, loud enough only for the major to hear. "*I'm better than you.* Always remember that."

He rose, turned his back on the major and strode away. "Ellie," he said over his shoulder, "bind his ankles."

They left the six Nazis, naked and bound, in a far, darkened corner of the parking garage. The lieutenant had been carrying the keys to the armored van, so they threw their own clothes and the uniforms of the other three SS soldiers into its back and left in it. Barnes drove, and Quinn sat next to him in the front seat.

"Do you believe him?" Barnes asked. It was the first time any of them had spoken, other than to give an instruction or report information, since Quinn had walked away from the major.

"About them already having Heydrich?"

"Yes."

"About everything we've done being planned by them?"

"Yes."

"Not a word of it."

"Why?"

"Because if they had him already, they would have simply stormed the floor we were on," he said. "No, they knew we were there, but not because Heydrich has already lost. They were desperate to figure out what we were going to do and would have been even more desperate to stop us if they'd known we would go to Heydrich. Now that he knows, they're scrambling to stop him."

He pursed his lips. "They disguised themselves and snuck in to get us. That means they still haven't got him, though they'll be ready for him." He paused. "And it means we were betrayed."

"I agree," Barnes said, "but I'm hardly surprised. Heydrich has some pretty efficient sources inside the SS; it stands to reason they have some of their own inside his hierarchy. We must have walked past a dozen of his people on that floor, and God knows how many others knew we were there."

Quinn shook his head. "No. This was someone highly placed enough to understand who we were immediately. Heydrich's secretary, or Captain Meier. Or Galland or Remer."

"Who?"

"The two generals with him. You didn't recognize them?"

Barnes shrugged. "I'm not MI6. German domestic politics isn't my brief."

When the guard at the booth saw their black SS uniforms, he waved them through without checking their IDs. They sped up the ramp out of the parking levels and onto the parkway leading to In den Lauben—

Into total chaos. They could not tell right away what had happened, but they could see that things had gone horribly wrong. The crowd that had thronged the roadside a half hour earlier had thinned considerably. It was still thousands strong, but those that remained were running desperately away from the direction of the bridge and, on its far side, the communal hall.

As they turned onto In den Lauben, they saw why. A hundred meters ahead of them, where the avenue led out onto the Nibelungen Bridge, was a war zone. Someone had set up a roadblock of three armored cars, blocking passage onto the bridge. In the intersection before it were several wrecked vehicles—Mercedeses, motorcycles, and an *Orpo* Volkswagen. Bodies littered the ground. Several other vehicles were sitting at the intersection, and Waffen-SS troops were using them for cover as they exchanged fire with someone out of view.

"Good God," said Barnes.

"Take us closer," Quinn said. "Stop about fifty meters back."

Obediently, Barnes pulled forward and stopped where Quinn had indicated, pulling up to the curb beside the building complex on the side of the street opposite from the hotel; a plaque proclaimed it to be the offices of the Hermann Göring Works. "Wait here," Quinn said, opening his door.

"Where are you going?" said Barnes.

Quinn paused. "I'm going to go find out the situation," he said. "It's best I go alone. I don't want us all getting pressed into combat."

Reluctantly, Barnes nodded. Quinn slipped out of the van's cab and hurried along the pavement toward the skirmish. As he drew closer, the fighting seemed to be dying down; gunfire was becoming more sporadic.

He approached half a dozen stormtroopers and a sergeant

under cover behind an armored truck. As he came up behind them, he could see further round the corner of the Hermann Göring Works. In the middle of the narrow road running between the river and the Works, about thirty meters beyond the intersection with In den Lauben, an armored personnel carrier bearing the eagle badge of the Eastern Command lay on its side, smoke issuing from under its bonnet. Motionless bodies, clad in both black and field grey, littered the ground around it, and its hull was pockmarked and dented from the attack it had just sustained.

Quinn scanned the bodies, checking the ones in black to see if Heydrich was amongst them, but he did not see him. Another body did catch his eye though, the only one wearing a blue uniform. At first it was the uniform's color that drew his attention, but upon closer scrutiny he recognized the face: Reichsmarschall Galland, a large dark stain across the front of his tunic.

Next he surveyed the bodies scattered around him in the intersection, searching still for Heydrich. Here the bodies were mainly Wehrmacht, though, with a fair number of civilians mixed in. The two motorcycles that had led the Commissar-General's convoy had smashed into the wheels of the armored trucks, blocking the way onto the bridge. Both their drivers lay lifeless half a dozen meters from them, limbs splayed at unnatural angles.

He turned back to the sergeant and his men a few meters away behind the armored truck. "*Scharführer*," he snapped, and the sergeant looked up.

"Yes, Herr *Obersturmführer?*"

"We have them holed up in that vehicle?" He nodded toward the personnel carrier.

The sergeant shook his head. "No, Herr Obersturmführer.

The survivors managed to reach cover in the building here." He gestured toward the Hermann Göring Works.

Quinn surveyed the building. "And Commissar-General Heydrich is amongst them?"

"Yes, Herr Obersturmführer."

Quinn nodded. "Who is in command here?"

The sergeant pointed, and Quinn followed the gesture to a parked staff car at the far corner of the intersection. An SS officer—too far away for him to make out his rank—surrounded by a pair of aides stood next to the car's open door, talking into the mouthpiece of the car's radio. "The *Sturmbannführer*, Herr Obersturmführer."

"Very good, Scharführer," Quinn said. "Carry on." He left the sergeant and his troops and headed toward the major at the staff car. As he approached, the major completed his conversation on the radio, turned to one of his aides and issued an order. The aide saluted and hurried away. Quinn came up, stopped and saluted neatly; the major turned to him.

"Obersturmführer," he said. "I do not recognize you. What is your name?"

Quinn's pause lasted only a heartbeat. "Obersturmführer Kaufholz. I have just arrived on the scene, Herr Sturmbannführer," he said. "I have a platoon with me. I understand the Commissar-General and his men have taken refuge inside the building."

The major nodded. He had turned his gaze from Quinn to stare instead down the street running between the river and the Works. "Yes. They seem to have taken refuge there—" he pointed, "—on the ground floor opposite the river. At the moment we have something of a stalemate, but we have reinforcements coming up from the opposite direction. They'll get behind them, and soon we'll be able to squeeze them in a vice." He grinned wolfishly. "In the end it should seem a rather pathetic attempt at a coup."

"I see you seem a little thinly manned, Herr Sturmbannführer."

The major bristled. "That was necessary," he said, a touch defensively, "to ensure surprise—and given the short notice that we had on this operation."

"I apologize, mein Herr," Quinn said. "I had not intended a criticism. I merely make the observation that you probably do not have enough men to secure the rest of the building—" he gestured back up In den Lauben at the Hermann Göring Works offices, "—and prevent the enemy from escaping that way while we await reinforcements. May I request that I lead my platoon to reconnoiter the rest of the building?"

The major had followed his gesture, turning from the street and the personnel carrier to stare at the long face of the Works, which extended a good three hundred meters back along the avenue. After a few moments' consideration, he nodded and turned back to Quinn. "Very well, Obersturmführer. But be careful—their situation is too hopeless for there to be any necessity for us to lose a dozen men in a room to room fire fight."

"Of course, Herr Sturmbannführer," Quinn said. "Thank you." He snapped his heels together, saluted crisply, and walked back up In den Lauben toward their van.

He climbed into the cab. "Take us back up the road," he ordered Barnes, "and round the corner back behind the building here." He gestured at the Works.

Barnes obediently put the car in gear and pulled around, heading back up In den Lauben. "What's going on?" he asked.

"Heydrich and a few men are holed up at the other end of

the building," he explained. "The SS commander thinks I have a platoon with me; I'm to reconnoiter the building and make sure Heydrich stays confined at that end while the SS waits for reinforcements to hit him from the other direction. It doesn't sound like there were many survivors from their ambush."

Barnes pulled round the far side of the building and up onto the curb. They both got out. While Barnes got Ellie and Gunning out of the back of the van and explained the situation to them, Quinn tried the doors.

"All locked," he reported. "Makes sense. It's a Day of National Mourning. The whole place will be deserted."

Gunning shrugged. "Only one way in, then," he said and, at Barnes's nod, slammed his rifle butt into one of the building's windows, shattering it with a loud clatter.

Quinn gave Gunning a boost up so he could scramble through the window, then, after Gunning had called the all clear, gave another to Barnes. Next came Ellie. Quinn frowned as she stepped up to him. He did not want her coming with them, but neither did he think she would be safe if she stayed behind.

She read the expression on his face. "Don't bother saying anything," she said. "I've come this far, and you wouldn't have gotten nearly so far without me. I see this through."

He hesitated, then extended his interlocked palms out to her. She put her foot in them and pulled herself up by the window frame; Gunning reached out, grasped her under the shoulders, and pulled her in. After she was through, Quinn climbed in after her, helped by Gunning and Barnes.

They were in a small office, its walls lined with filing cabinets. A desk with a typewriter sat immediately beneath the window to catch its light. The office was deserted, and no sound came from the other side of its frosted glass door. As Quinn slid off the desk, Barnes and Gunning took up positions on either side of the door. As soon as Quinn nodded that he was ready, Gunning reached out with his foot and pushed the door open, and Barnes stepped through into the hall beyond, rifle at the ready.

The Royal Marines captain scanned the hallway quickly in both directions, visibly relaxing when he did not see anything. He beckoned them after him. Gunning followed, but Quinn caught Ellie by the shoulder before she could follow too. She looked at him quizzically.

"Be careful," he said. "Stay near us. Stay in the middle of us. Please."

She seemed about to retort, but then changed her mind and nodded instead. "I will," she said solemnly.

They set off down the corridor after the two Royal Marines.

CHAPTER XXVI

THE CORRIDOR'S green linoleum tiled floor and stark white walls gave it a depressingly antiseptic feel. They followed it to the large doorway at its end and emerged into a stairwell. A door led into the street outside, and on the wall next to it was a simple schematic of the building.

Quinn studied the schematic. The building was square, shaped into four hollow squares around four large, open courtyards within its walls, rather like the outline of an oblong four-leaf clover.

Barnes came up behind him and looked at the diagram over his shoulder. Quinn pointed to the clover's top bar. "We're here," he said. He moved his finger to the bottom of the clover, on the far side of the building. "Heydrich and his men should be somewhere down here." He turned back to face the others.

"We'll need to be careful in these uniforms," Barnes said, addressing both Quinn and Gunning. "They got us past the SS, but they could get us killed when we come up on Heydrich's men." He glanced quickly at all three of them, then nodded. "All right, let's go."

They moved slowly and carefully through the building, pausing at every intersection and checking any open or ajar doors they passed. Gunning and Quinn took point, Ellie came next, and Barnes brought up the rear. They were able to move in a straight line, following the main corridor running all the way down one side of the clover; they would have been able to see right down the entire length of the building but for the closed doors leading to intersections and stairwells every twenty meters.

As they approached closer to Heydrich's end of the building, they became even more cautious, and their going became slower. They had penetrated deeply down the building's side; the stairwell they were approaching now must be either the last or second to last before the building's corner. And yet there was still no sign of the Wehrmacht.

Quinn and Gunning took up positions on either side of the double doors leading into the stairwell. At a nod from Gunning, Quinn reached across and pushed the door open, gently but firmly. They waited: nothing. Gunning took a step through the doorway, rifle held ready—

A loud, staccato burst of automatic rifle fire greeted him. He screamed and fell back through the doorway clutching his left forearm, his rifle clattering to the ground. The door swung shut.

Barnes had taken cover in an open doorway, pushing Ellie through ahead of him. He and Quinn stood stock still, waiting for the sounds of pursuit. Gunning had propped himself up on his good right elbow—the arm where he had taken another bullet wound not twelve hours ago—and was panting heavily.

When he heard nothing after a few seconds, Quinn bent down, grasped Gunning under his right arm and helped him to his feet while Barnes continued to cover them. "Fucking bastards," the sergeant said. "Got the other bloody one." Together, the two of them walked through Barnes's doorway into what looked like a conference room, with a long table surrounded by a dozen chairs. Quinn sat Gunning down in one of the chairs, then returned to the hall as Ellie knelt next to the sergeant and began gently prying his hand from the wound on his arm.

"I'll go," Quinn said, and Barnes nodded.

They were definitely Wehrmacht; they had had time to see Gunning's uniform and would not have shot if they were Waffen-SS. Quinn walked back up to the doorway at the end of the corridor and placed his pistol on the ground, then opened the door a crack and kicked the pistol into the stairwell.

"I'm unarmed," he called. "I'm coming out."

He raised his arms over his head and stepped slowly into the stairwell, stepping over Gunning's rifle. The door swung shut behind him. Turning, he found himself staring up at three Wehrmacht infantrymen midway up the flight of stairs above him, automatic rifles trained on him.

"We're not Waffen-SS," he said. "We're friends of the Commissar-General. My name is Simon Quinn. He knows me. I'm an Englishman."

None of the infantrymen said anything. One of them stepped rapidly down the stairs and patted Quinn down. Finding nothing, he nodded to his fellows.

"I have three other people in there," Quinn continued, nodding to the closed door. "We'll surrender ourselves to you."

"Have them come out here," one of the soldiers up the stairs ordered.

"Barnes," Quinn called, "all of you come out here. Unarmed."

There was a pause of several long moments, and then the door opened and Barnes, Ellie and Gunning filed out. Barnes and Ellie held their hands above their heads, but Gunning was clutching his wounded forearm. The infantryman who had frisked Quinn patted them down, then, at a nod from the infantryman who had spoken, headed back through the door into the corridor. He re-emerged a few moments later carrying Barnes's rifle.

"Who are you?" the lead infantryman asked.

"I told you," Quinn said. "We're known to the Commissar-General. We're here to render assistance."

The infantryman regarded him skeptically, then shrugged and turned to his fellow on the stairs with him. "Stay here." He descended the stairs and said to Quinn, "You will come with us," then headed over to the doorway on the opposite side of the stairwell. The four of them followed him.

The infantryman holding Barnes's rifle gathered up Gunning's rifle and Quinn's pistol, then brought up the rear. He made to rest a helping—and securing—hand on Gunning's elbow, but the sergeant shrugged him off, snarling in English, "Keep your fucking hands off me, you filthy Nazi. You fucking shot me."

The commanding infantryman led them down the next corridor. Quinn was next to Ellie as they walked.

"How is he?" he asked, nodding back at Gunning.

"It's just a flesh wound," she said. "I think he'll be fine. But it must be intensely painful."

The lead infantryman paused at the door to the next stairwell and gave a coded knock before he walked through. In the stairwell, they were met by a sergeant and another infantryman.

The sergeant looked at the four prisoners with surprise. "What are these?" he asked.

"They claim to be English," the lead infantryman said. "They claim to know the Commissar-General."

"Or Hauptmann Meier," Quinn added. "If he's here."

The sergeant eyed them suspiciously but then nodded. "All right. Return to your post. You four, come with me."

He led them through the door into another corridor. Here they found Heydrich's command center: every door down one side of the corridor was open, and Wehrmacht soldiers hurried back and forth between them.

The sergeant went up to one open doorway. "Hauptmann Meier," he said into it, "I have a matter here that requires your attention."

Meier emerged from the doorway. He started when he saw the prisoners, reaching for his sidearm, but paused when he saw Ellie. His eyes widened and he scanned the others' faces, recognizing them.

"They say they know you, sir," the sergeant said.

Meier nodded dumbly. "They do." He visibly took hold of himself and turned to the sergeant, authority reasserting itself in his voice. "Thank you, Feldwebel. That will be all."

The sergeant saluted and returned through the doorway to his post. Meier turned back to the four of them.

"How did you get here?" he asked.

"The Waffen-SS set a trap for us," Quinn said. "They disguised themselves as Wehrmacht and snuck onto your floor of the hotel to kill us. Someone tipped them off, Herr Hauptmann—they had advance warning of the Commissar-General's plans."

Meier gave him a curious look. At last he said, "Well, now that you're here I'm not sure what good you can do. This looks like a losing fight to me. But the Commissar-General will want to know you're here. Come with me."

He led them down the corridor to a closed door on the opposite side from the row of open doors. He knocked once, then opened the door and stepped inside. Quinn and the others followed.

They were in another conference room. Heydrich and Remer had been staring out the window at the paved courtyard outside, and the building's opposite wall on its far side, but at Meier's entrance they had turned. Their eyes widened when they saw Meier's charges, as they thought first that they were SS, and then recognized them.

"Herr Generalkommissar," Meier said. "They say they escaped from an SS assassination attempt." He made a vague gesture, as if to convey that he knew that did not cover all the information it needed to, but that he was helpless to expand more.

"I see, Hauptmann," Heydrich said slowly. "Return to your duties." Meier turned to go, but Heydrich hastily added, "How does it look out there?"

Meier paused in the doorway, half turning back to face them. "Still quiet, sir," he said. "The men are nervous, but they are determined to fight for you."

Heydrich nodded, very solemn. "Very good, Hauptmann."

Meier saluted and left the room, closing the door behind him.

Heydrich turned his gaze on the four of them. He focused on Quinn. "You seem rather old for a lieutenant, Herr Quinn."

"I was the best fit for it of the three of us, Herr Generalkommissar."

Remer was staring at them with his eyes narrowed. "How did you come by those uniforms? And how did you get here?"

Quinn spoke slowly, considering his words. When he spoke, he addressed Heydrich. "I believe that someone on your staff betrayed you, Herr Generalkommissar. A Waffen-SS officer disguised himself as a Wehrmacht major and removed us from the rooms in which you had placed us, claiming he was acting under your orders. He took us to the hotel parking levels, where an SS execution squad waited. We—" He paused again, then said, "We were able to disarm them. We had hoped to come to your aid, but..." He gestured toward the door. "Your situation seems rather bleak."

"It does indeed," Heydrich said. "Though perhaps not hopeless. We had a battalion expecting to rendezvous with us at the communal hall across the river; they will surely discover what is going on and attempt to relieve us. And we have been under cover here for almost half an hour without sustaining any attacks from the SS; I am beginning to wonder if they have the force to overcome us."

Quinn gestured to his uniform. "I was able to survey the SS lines a little while ago, Herr Generalkommissar. The forces outside are too few to overcome you without heavy losses, yes, but they are waiting to attack because they are expecting imminent reinforcements to flush you out from behind. They seem... very confident."

Heydrich stared at him, not reacting to this news at first. His face was typically inscrutable, but Quinn thought he detected a mixture of disappointment and defiance when the Commissar-General spoke. "Then our chances are not what I might have hoped, Herr Quinn. But one circumstance remains the same—at worst, we shall die here nobly, fighting for the Fatherland."

There was silence in the wake of this statement. Then Quinn spoke again. "Actually," he said, "there is another possibility. How many men do you have?"

"I had an escort of forty men," Heydrich said. "Fewer than half made it to safety here."

"We have an armored van at the other end of the building," said Quinn, "where the SS presence is currently very light. With the three of us in disguise, we can get you and your men out of the building and attempt to escape the city. You can return to the East and muster your forces."

Heydrich considered this, but before he could give an answer, Remer drew his pistol and pointed it at Quinn. "Herr Generalkommissar," he said, "this Englishman claimed we had a traitor in our midst, and he has just revealed it to be himself. First he comes here in this uniform, concocting a ludicrous story about escape from the hands of the SS. Then he suggests leading you into an ambush—into *another* ambush. It is exactly as I first feared, Herr Generalkommissar." He looked at Heydrich. "Their presence in Linz, their attempt to contact you, it has all been an elaborate ploy to provoke you into destroying yourself. And so far, they have been largely successful."

"Even if that's true, Otto-Ernst," Heydrich said, "why would they try to lead me into an ambush now? The SS seem to have us pretty well at their mercy right now."

Remer walked around the table to where the four of them stood lined against the wall as he spoke, never taking his eyes or his gun off Quinn. "To minimize bloodshed, Herr Generalkommissar. If the Reichsführer-SS can get you to walk yourself into the trap this,"

his lip curled in distaste, "*untermensch* proposes, he can kill you without losing a single SS soldier." By the time he had finished, he stood toe to toe with Quinn, the nose of his Luger stuffed painfully into Quinn's chest.

Several moments of tense silence followed. Quinn and Remer stared at each other. Then, without warning, the colonel general spun on his heel, brought his weapon to bear on Heydrich and fired. But Quinn had reacted lightning quickly, bringing his fist up and smashing it into Remer's elbow, and the shot went wide. Ellie screamed at the loud noise in the small room, and the windowpane over Heydrich's left shoulder shattered.

Remer slammed his elbow backward, ramming it into Quinn's neck, and Quinn was thrown against the wall behind him, gasping for breath, his vision blurring with tears. Remer had turned to him again, and Quinn felt the hot steel nose of his Luger shoved into his stomach underneath the ribs. Three shots rang out. Quinn's hand had grasped instinctively around the hot steel of the Luger's muzzle, and he felt a hot wash of blood run over his fingers.

CHAPTER XXVII

QUINN AND Remer stared unblinkingly into each other's eyes for a long time. The only noise Quinn could hear was a continuous, low-pitched ringing in his ears from the gunfire in the confined space.

Slowly—dazedly—he unwrapped his fingers from around the Luger's hot barrel and raised his hand before his face. It was dripping with blood. He looked at Ellie. Her hands were clapped over her ears, but she was staring back at him, her eyes wide and moist.

He turned back to Remer, who was still staring at him, and it was only now that he noticed the bright red gash of a bullet's exit wound in the colonel general's temple and the blood running freely from it down his face. Remer opened his mouth as if to say something, but instead collapsed against Quinn and crumpled to the floor. Quinn stared down at the body. A deep burgundy stain spread across the colonel general's uniform tunic.

Quinn looked up. Heydrich stood across the room, his pistol still leveled at where Remer had been standing. The Commissar-General focused on Quinn. "We seem to have found our traitor, Herr Quinn," he said, the sound only dimly penetrating through the ringing in Quinn's ears.

The door burst open, and Meier charged in followed by an infantryman, both men bringing their weapons to bear on Quinn and his companions. *"Hold your fire!"* Heydrich barked, and the two men froze, as did the other soldiers in the corridor behind them.

Meier took in the four of them, standing there apparently unarmed, Remer's lifeless body on the floor in front of them, and Heydrich holstering his weapon. "Herr Generalkommissar?" he asked uncertainly.

Heydrich spoke calmly, almost serenely. "Hauptmann, Colonel General Remer has expired from wounds suffered fighting nobly to preserve the will of the Führer."

"Sir?" Meier said.

"Return to your post, Hauptmann."

Meier hesitated, then nodded. "Yes, Herr Generalkommissar." He turned and, ushering the infantryman out ahead of him, left the room. He closed the door behind him.

The five of them stared at Remer's body. Absently Quinn wiped his hand on his trouser leg. "But—" Gunning said hesitantly, "—but why?"

Heydrich looked up at him shrugged. "The same reasons as

anyone else in my hierarchy might work for the SS. The same reasons my agents in the SS work for me. Money. Power. Treachery is a fairly simple matter in the Reich."

"But why now?" Ellie breathed. "What did he think he could accomplish *here?*"

Heydrich glanced at Quinn. "He acted when you suggested escaping using your vehicle."

Quinn nodded. "You could escape, and he would be powerless to stop you without revealing himself. But if he could have gunned you down, and us, then he could say that one of us wrested his weapon from him and killed you before he could get it back and kill us. Then he could order the rest of your men here to surrender."

A distant *crump* interrupted their conversation. Several long seconds of silence followed, and then the walls and floor shook with a great explosion coming from the other side of the door.

Quinn was the first through the door; the other four followed right after him. Dust and smoke filled the corridor outside, pouring from one of the doorways on the opposite side of the hall. A Wehrmacht infantryman staggered out the doorway, coughing, his face blanketed in grey concrete dust matching the color of his uniform. The bright scarlet blood spilling down his face from the cut on his forehead made a startling contrast.

Ellie went to help the staggering infantryman as the rest of them filed through the doorway. Two more infantrymen lay lifelessly on the floor. The room's exterior wall had blown away, and a deep crater extended out into the pavement of the street outside.

Quinn shielded his eyes, staring out across the river. He could see movement and some sort of emplacement on its far bank, but he could not tell what it was. He turned to Heydrich. "Do you have lookouts in the upper stories?"

The Commissar-General shook his head. "We couldn't spare the men."

"We need to see what's going on."

He turned and headed back into the corridor, the other three in tow. He hurried down the corridor, now filling with troops from the other rooms, and into the stairwell at its end. Heydrich and Barnes followed, but at a barked command from Barnes, Gunning remained behind. Ellie was still kneeling beside the injured soldier, tending to him.

Quinn sprinted up the stairs two at a time, Heydrich and Barnes right behind him. He went up three flights before turning down a corridor and hurrying into its first doorway. From here they had a much better view across the river.

"Damn it," he said, staring at the far bank.

"Field artillery," Barnes observed.

"Herr Generalkommissar," Quinn said, "your men aren't going to last ten minutes against an artillery bombardment."

As if to illustrate the point, the artillery fired again, another distant *crump*, and the building shook again. A cloud of dust and smoke rose past their window from the impact of the artillery shell at the building's base.

"There's still our armored van, Herr Generalkommissar," Quinn said. "We can get you and your men out of the city."

Heydrich, still staring out the window, did not say anything at first. Then he pointed out over the river. "Look," he said. "There is smoking rising across the river. From around the communal hall."

Quinn followed the Commissar-General's finger. "Yes, sir," he said uncertainly.

Heydrich glanced at him. "My battalion is putting up a fight," he said, a hint of pride in his voice.

"Herr Generalkommissar, we need to leave now."

Heydrich shook his head. "We are not retreating."

"You intend to die here? You intend your men to die here?"

"Quite the contrary, Herr Quinn," the Commissar-General said, a curious gleam in his eye, "I intend to die on the far side of the river." He paused. "Remer said that the Wehrmacht would rise with us once they discovered that Himmler intended to suborn the Führer's will, and he was right. By now word must have reached the local bases about the fighting in the city. If I can get to my battalion, we can take the communal hall and I can contact the local forces and move them into the city. The SS divisions in the city can't storm the communal hall or obliterate it with artillery. Every minister in the Reich is there right now, heads of state from all fascist Europe, dignitaries from all over the world." The expression on his face had set defiantly.

Quinn gestured at the intersection below them, where three armored trucks still barred the way onto the Nibelungen Bridge. Waffen-SS vehicles still littered the intersection, but the Waffen-SS soldiers had pulled back to the far side of In den Lauben to keep out of the way of the artillery.

"But how are you going to get there, Herr Generalkommissar? Your way is blocked, and the nearest other bridge is far too far away."

"That is where your armored van comes in, Herr Quinn. Those are heavy trucks they're using as a barricade—" Heydrich pointed at the trucks blocking the bridge, "—but they've left them completely unguarded. Someone at the wheel of your van could ram their roadblock and clear the way onto the bridge."

Quinn stared at the Commissar-General for a long moment, then looked at Barnes, who seemed just as stunned as he felt himself. "But you still have to get your men past the SS troops and across the bridge, sir," he pointed out.

Heydrich's sly smile reminded Quinn of a predator. "That's the beauty of it. The attack on their roadblock will cause enough commotion amongst the SS forces down there that they'll be completely disrupted and focused only on the barricade and your armored van. This will allow my men to commandeer one of the vehicles in the intersection while they're not looking and escape across the bridge. It's a tactic we're very familiar with in the East."

Quinn looked at him sharply. "The East, Herr General-kommissar?"

Heydrich nodded, too caught up in the prospects he was seeing to notice the edge in Quinn's voice. "A loud flash and bang at one end, then you attack with the bulk of your forces at the other while no one is looking. It's how the vermin operate—the *untermenschen* who infest the forests and the hills out there." He glanced at Quinn, a hint of pride in his voice. "It is those of us in the East who have remained strong, Herr Quinn. In the East we must continue to grind them into the dust, every day, because if we give them even a moment's latitude, a moment's hope, then they might believe that they can again be anything more than what they are now, what they are meant to be—which is *nothing*. It has kept us blooded, and it has kept us vigilant. But these—" he gestured again at the Waffen-SS troops down in the intersection, a brief, contemptuous flick of his fingers, "—these who have stayed here in the West, they have grown soft. That will be their undoing."

Quinn had not heard much of what had been said, for his mind had been somewhere else, three hundred miles to the East; and he was not aware now that Heydrich was staring at him expectantly, waiting for his answer. Uncertainly, Barnes stepped forward. "All right, sir," the captain said.

Heydrich's smile widened, and he clapped Barnes on the shoulder, apparently oblivious to Quinn's turmoil. "Excellent, Herr Hauptmann. Come then."

He led them back out into the stairwell and down the stairs. Shaking himself out of his reverie, Quinn followed. As they descended, the building shook with another explosion. Plaster and concrete fragments rained down around them.

"They're not firing very often," Barnes observed.

"They're trying to force us to surrender, or soften us up for an assault," Quinn explained in English. "They don't want to obliterate the building and risk not being able to recover a body that's identifiably the Commissar-General's. The last thing Himmler wants to do is create a legend. Do you know if there's a NATO consulate in the city?"

Barnes blinked at the unexpected question. "There's a British one, definitely."

"Other than the British."

The captain pursed his lips in thought. "There's an American consulate, too. I'm sure of it, but I've no idea where it might be. Why?"

But Quinn only nodded in acknowledgement of the information.

They reached the ground floor to find Heydrich's men falling back through the stairwell to the next corridor. Dust billowed through the doorway from the corridor behind them, and several men seemed to be nursing slight wounds. Captain Meier was standing in the doorway, hurrying his men through. He looked up as Heydrich, Quinn, and Barnes approached.

"The corridor collapsed, sir," Meier reported. "We've had a couple of men seriously wounded under falling debris, but we pulled them to safety."

"Ellie," said Quinn. "Where's Ellie?"

"The woman?" Meier jerked his head back in the direction he was sending his men. "Through there, with your other man."

Quinn hurried through the doorway, followed by Barnes. Ellie and Gunning were standing against the wall a few meters down the corridor. Gunning had found the weapons that had been taken from them earlier and was holding the two automatic rifles while Ellie held Quinn's pistol awkwardly.

Quinn strode over to her and put his hand on her shoulder. "Are you all right?" he asked, taking the pistol from her. She nodded.

Heydrich and Meier entered from the stairwell, the last to come through. Two Wehrmacht soldiers had taken up positions on either side of the door, covering the stairwell.

"Herr Hauptmann," Heydrich called to Barnes. "Are you volunteering to drive your van?"

Quinn looked at him and nodded before Barnes could answer. "Yes, Herr Generalkommissar."

"Then I wish you luck."

Heydrich turned to Meier and began issuing orders. "Come on," Quinn said, leading them down the corridor. Gunning handed Barnes his rifle, then shouldered his own; Quinn saw him flinch at the action.

"What's going on?" Ellie asked.

"You'll see," said Quinn. "Just keep moving."

They abandoned caution, hurrying as fast as they could back down the corridor and through the stairwells. Barnes and Quinn

went first, with Ellie and Gunning behind. As they went, Quinn
hurriedly told Barnes what he planned; the captain agreed.

They came to the office where they had first entered the
building. Barnes stuck his head through the window to make sure
the coast was clear, then climbed through into the street outside.
Gunning went next, but before Ellie could follow, Quinn caught
her by the upper arm.

"There's an American consulate in the city," he said. "Do you
know where it is?"

Her eyes narrowed. "Why?" she asked suspiciously.

"Because you're going there. Do you know where it is?"

"I am not," she said. "I'm staying with you."

Quinn shook his head. "No. You're going to the American
consulate with Sergeant Gunning and requesting asylum."

"I've told you before," she said firmly. There were tears in her
eyes. "I follow this to the end. I follow *you*."

He smiled sadly. "Ellie, this *is* the end." He gestured in the
direction of the armored van out in the street. "Barnes and I are
about to charge that van into a company of Waffen-SS and hope
we can distract them long enough for Heydrich to escape. God,
Ellie, this is hopeless." He brushed away the first tear as it rolled
down her cheek. "We'll meet later—I'll meet you at the American
consulate. But for me to do this, I need to know that you're safe."

"I'm not going if you won't come with me," she said, her voice
choking. The tears ran freely down her face now.

He smiled sadly and kissed her forehead. "No, Ellie, this is my
fight. This is what I have to do. But it's not yours. You've been
amazing—you've been more than I could ever have dreamed. But
now I need you to go."

There was a long pause. Then Ellie opened her mouth to say something, but all she could do was choke back a sob, so instead she just nodded. They embraced.

"Thank you," he murmured. "Thank you. At the American consulate. I'll find you." She sniffled a little as they stepped back from their embrace. "Do you know where the American consulate is?" he asked again.

"No," she said, "but I can find it." He nodded.

He helped her through the window, then followed her out. He caught the tail end of the conversation between Barnes and Gunning.

"You're no good to me in a fight, Sergeant," Barnes was saying kindly. "You've been shot in both arms. You're going. That's an order."

Gunning nodded glumly. "Yes, sir."

They saw that Ellie and Quinn had emerged. Barnes headed for the van's cab, while Gunning joined Ellie on the pavement.

Quinn went over to the back of the van and opened it. "Sergeant," he called. Gunning came over. Quinn had pulled the sergeant's civilian clothing out of the van. "You'll need these," he said, passing them to him. "And we should switch weapons."

"I prefer the rifle," Gunning said.

"I'm sure you do," Quinn said. "But it's going to look rather out of place on a civilian."

Reluctantly, Gunning traded his automatic rifle for Quinn's Luger.

"Best of luck, Sergeant," Quinn said quietly. Gunning nodded and turned to go, but Quinn said, "Sergeant." Gunning turned back to him. "What's your Christian name?"

Gunning looked at him before answering. "Michael," he said at last.

Quinn nodded and extended his hand. "Simon."

"Simon," Gunning repeated. He shook the proffered hand, a little awkwardly with the clothes and pistol in his arms, then turned and headed back over to Ellie.

Quinn closed the back door and went round to the van's front, where he climbed in next to Barnes.

"Ready?" Barnes asked, starting the engine. Quinn nodded. "All right." He put the van in gear and pulled away from the curb.

They turned the corner and trundled toward the trucks blocking the bridge, several hundred meters away. Though the other SS vehicles had been parked haphazardly at that end of the avenue, they seemed to have left a clear path for them through the intersection to the barricade. A cloud of smoke and dust rose from the Hermann Göring Works, and though Quinn and Barnes could not see the far end of the building, the edge of the cascade of rubble to which they were reducing it came into view as they drew closer.

No one seemed to have noticed their approach yet. Quinn felt them pick up speed as Barnes depressed the accelerator. They were drawing ever closer now, less than a hundred meters away. Amongst the SS ranks under cover at the far side of the intersection, the heads nearest to them were beginning to turn in their direction, but none of them seemed to have figured out what was about to happen or, if they had, what action they could possibly take against it.

"If nothing else," said Barnes, "this is going to be *very* satisfying."

The barricade of trucks hurtled toward them—Barnes was

aiming for the juncture where one truck's nose met the rear bumper of the next—the intersection passed by in a blur—they slammed into the two trucks—

Quinn had the fleeting impression of at least one truck careening wildly away like a plastic bag in a breeze before everything went crazy. For an instant only sky was visible out the front windshield, but then he could see the bridge again—only it was tilted wrong, with the bridge occupying the left third of the windshield, the river running down the middle third and the sky on the right, and everything seemed to be scrolling from the top of the windshield to the bottom. And then there was a jarring crash, and they stopped moving—there was a momentary, sickening sensation of tilting, and then they were still.

For a long moment Quinn just sat there. His head throbbed, and his neck hurt. The bridge had almost completely disappeared from view at the left end of the windshield, replaced by the river and the sky, sideways.

He heard Barnes stir next to him—below him—and he turned awkwardly to look at him. "Are you all right?" he asked.

The captain nodded stiffly. Gingerly he placed a hand on his side and winced. "Think I cracked a rib."

Quinn reached out and opened his door, pushing it wide open above him, then, bracing his feet against the cab's floor, he unbuckled his seatbelt. He wedged his arms into the open doorway and levered himself up and out of the cab, seating himself on the doorway's lip.

One of the trucks they had hit had been pushed aside and overturned; the other had gone spinning wildly across the tarmac of the bridge until, like their van, it had collided with the bridge's railing and now lay half over the water. They had made a gaping hole in the roadblock onto the bridge.

The intersection, eighty meters behind them, was still mostly empty, but a few Waffen-SS men had started to appear in it, surveying the damage. It would only be a few moments more, Quinn knew, before the rest of them shook off their inertia and swarmed into the intersection like ants. He suddenly felt very exposed up here.

He looked back down at Barnes. "We have to get out of here."

Barnes looked up at him and nodded. He had already unfastened his seatbelt. He passed their two automatic rifles up to Quinn. Quinn took them and dropped them down the side of the van to the pavement below, then scrambled out of the doorway so he could reach down and give Barnes a helping hand up. The captain winced as he clambered out of the cab.

They dropped down the side of the van onto the tarmac and scooped up their rifles. The chatter of automatic gunfire had begun at the intersection. Quinn motioned for Barnes to take cover at the far end of the truck, then hurried forward and dropped to one knee behind a two-meter shard of the bridge's concrete railing that the van's impact had knocked loose.

Most of the Waffen-SS men seemed to be engaged once more in combat in the intersection, exchanging fire with someone in the rubble at the end of the Hermann Göring Works. A few dozen meters further down In den Lauben, though, Wehrmacht soldiers were streaming out of the building toward an unattended armored personnel carrier parked in the street, unnoticed by the Waffen-SS. It looked as though one or two men had volunteered to stay behind and distract the Waffen-SS while the rest made their getaway.

There were also about twenty stormtroopers hurrying through the gap onto the bridge toward Quinn and Barnes. Quinn raised his rifle to his shoulder and gave them a short burst of fire, scattering them and forcing them under cover.

Heydrich was one of the last to cross from the building to the personnel carrier, unmistakable even at this distance in his black uniform. All told, not more than a dozen Wehrmacht men could have left the building. The gunfire from the Wehrmacht position had stopped now, and the Waffen-SS were advancing cautiously on where they had been. A few moments later, two last Wehrmacht infantrymen crossed from the Hermann Göring Works to the personnel carrier. Some of the Waffen-SS had seen what was going on now, but it was too late for them to do anything about it. The personnel carrier had started to move, picking up speed as it made its way toward the bridge.

Quinn and Barnes were under fire now from the Waffen-SS on the bridge. Quinn returned fire, and over his shoulder he heard Barnes doing the same.

Heydrich's personnel carrier rolled through the intersection and through the gap they had made, its armored hull impervious to the bullets bouncing off it. It trundled up the bridge towards them, eventually rolling to a stop just beyond Barnes's position at the rear of their overturned van. Its backdoor popped open and Captain Meier was there, beckoning to them.

Barnes waved to Quinn to go first, then began laying down covering fire for him. Quinn backed cautiously away from his cover, then turned and hurried along the edge of the bridge toward the van, crouching low as he ran.

Suddenly he felt the blinding, searing pain as the bullet slashed through his left upper arm, spinning him around and sending him staggering. He felt his left foot slip off the jagged edge of the bridge where their van had knocked the railing away—

He felt the bullet punch through his shoulder, a freight train slamming into him from behind. A fraction of an instant later, barely long enough for his brain to register that it had hit him in the first place, it exploded through the front of his jacket in a small shower of bone and blood. His pistol dropped to the ground.

Instinctively he reached out with his left hand and grasped onto a bent, twisted spike of iron railing, his right foot sliding to purchase on the bridge's edge and preventing his fall. His left arm screamed at him that it could not do this, could not support the whole weight of his body like this, it had just been *shot*, but he refused to let go, refused to grab on with his right hand instead because that would mean letting go of his rifle. Bright spots of white and orange exploded in his vision.

He looked back toward Heydrich's personnel carrier. At least fifteen meters to get back to Barnes, then another ten past that to get to where Meier waited anxiously at the carrier's open door. He turned and looked back at the SS. They were advancing slowly up the bridge. They were still under fire from Barnes and from the Wehrmacht soldiers at the mouth of the personnel carrier, but they were simply moving too rapidly for Quinn to reach Meier before they reached him first.

His pistol dropped to the ground. The bullet's impact knocked him to the side and carried him forward, one step, two steps, three, and he fell over the railing and plunged into the open air beyond.

Barnes had come out from his position and was hurrying toward Quinn, but Quinn shook his head and yelled "No!" All Barnes could succeed in doing was trapping them both on the bridge instead of just Quinn.

The Royal Marines captain ignored him and kept on coming, so Quinn braced the butt of his rifle against his hip and fired a wild burst in his direction, far too high over his head to have any possibility of hitting him. Barnes stopped and looked at him uncertainly.

"Get going!" Quinn yelled.

"Not without you," Barnes called back.

"Don't be daft!" Quinn looked pointedly down the bridge, and Barnes followed his gaze. The Waffen-SS were approaching. The captain turned uncertainly back to the personnel carrier, where Meier's gaze was flitting anxiously between the oncoming SS and the two of them, trying to judge how long he could wait for them.

But Barnes was too good an officer to decide that easily to leave a man behind. He turned hesitantly back in Quinn's direction.

"Don't worry about me," Quinn called. "Just go!"

They locked eyes, and Quinn nodded reassuringly. Barnes lifted his hand in a gesture of farewell that was at the same time a salute of respect.

"Barnes," Quinn called, and the captain paused. "Thank you."

Barnes nodded, then turned and, crouching low, hurried back along the van's length. Quinn turned back towards the Waffen-SS and opened fire on them, covering him.

Out of the corner of his eye he saw Barnes reach the personnel carrier and clamber inside, Meier slam the door shut and the carrier start moving away across the bridge. He turned and gazed back down the bridge at the Hermann Göring Works, the Strength through Joy Hotel, and the city beyond them.

Ellie was out there somewhere, and she would be safe. He had made sure of that. He did not know if he had managed to overturn the Columbia-Haus treaty, but he thought the British Government would probably have to repudiate it now after all this bloodshed—all this public bloodshed in a city full of the world's media—even if Heydrich lost his fight.

The Waffen-SS were nearing him now, screaming at him to drop his weapon, but he did not hear them. Ellie would be safe. That was the most important thing.

Thinking of another bullet and another river, in another time, he let go of the railing and plummeted into the open air beyond.

PART 4

REDEMPTION

In my end is my beginning.

—MARY, QUEEN OF SCOTS

CHAPTER XXVIII

AT FIRST, he was aware only of bobbing—of mild, repetitive motion up and down, up and down, as the empty, sunken, envious eyes set into gaunt faces with shaven heads floated away into the recesses of his mind. Then he realized, distantly, that he was wet; that he was immersed in water. But not all of him—the water came up only to his chest. He was lying on his back, on some sort of angled concrete surface. It felt jagged. Steps, maybe? They pressed painfully into his back.

That led him to the realization that he felt pain. Pain in his back, but also pain in his neck, which was stiff. And his left arm hurt. It stung, but not as long as he did not move it.

Voices. He heard voices. A voice calling, and then others, further away, answering. They were all male. Then the voices were just above him, and he felt hands, strong hands grasping him under the shoulders and lifting him from the water. His arm hurt more. His arm hurt *a lot*.

Hands grasped him by the ankles now, as well. They carried him up the steps and laid him out on the ground. One of the voices was speaking to him.

"Can you understand me? Can you tell me your name?"

His eyes were open now, but his vision was blurry. It was night, and he could see shapes above him in the eerie glow of streetlights or headlights, but he could not differentiate them into individual figures standing or kneeling over him.

He shook his head and closed his eyes again. "No," he murmured. "Wrong. Not—supposed to be. Supposed to be dead..."

"Sir," the voice said again, "are you English? Are you an Englishman?"

Reluctantly he opened his eyes. The fuzzy images were coming into sharper focus: three or four Wehrmacht infantrymen in field-grey coalscuttle helmets. One of them knelt over him and stared at him intently.

"Is your name Simon Quinn, sir?"

He frowned. "What?" It came out as a croak, and he cleared his throat.

The infantryman smiled patiently and helped him sit up. "I said, are you Simon Quinn, sir?"

He stared at the infantryman, only just processing the question. After a long moment, he nodded. "Yes. Yes, I am."

The infantryman's smile widened, and he and one of his fellows helped Quinn to his feet. Quinn's upper arm exploded in pain, and he gasped, clasping it with his other hand.

The infantryman looked concerned; he gently pried Quinn's hand away so that he could look at the wound through the tear in Quinn's sleeve.

"That looks nasty, sir," he said. "We'd best get you back to our checkpoint. We have a medic there."

They were on a narrow street overlooking the river. A jeep stood with its engine running a few meters away, and they ushered him toward it. As they were climbing in, he heard the distant *crump* of artillery fire, very faint.

"What's going on?" he asked. "What's that firing?"

"We've cleared the city center, but there are still a few pockets of resistance on the outskirts, sir," the infantryman said. "Nothing to worry about. We'll have the traitors all pushed up into the mountains in a few hours."

The darkened streets were deserted and, except for the occasional distant gunfire, eerily silent as they made their way through the city center. Every once in a while they would pass physical evidence of the day's fighting: an artillery crater, an overturned vehicle, soldiers' bodies lying in the street.

On one street corner dozens of bodies, both Wehrmacht and Waffen-SS, surrounded the burnt-out hulk of a tank bearing the SS's twin lightning bolts, the building beside it reduced to rubble. A small work crew had arrived. A pair of Wehrmacht guards stood over two Waffen-SS prisoners carrying away the bodies while four more searched through the rubble, trying to find anyone who might have been crushed underneath.

"We're coming up on the checkpoint now, Herr Quinn," the infantryman said.

They turned a corner as Quinn opened his eyes, but immediately he had to shield them from the harsh light. Floodlights blanketed the street leading up to the checkpoint to prevent anyone from sneaking up on it. Quinn tried blinking rapidly to adjust his eyes to the light. Out the corner of his eye he could see them passing sandbag barricades topped with barbed wire.

The sentry waved them through and they entered the checkpoint, where the light was much more bearable. They were in a small city square with a fountain at its center. The square looked to be used as a vehicle park, while the Wehrmacht had commandeered the ground floors of the buildings enclosing it— mostly small shop fronts.

The jeep pulled into a parking space, and the lead infantryman hopped out and helped Quinn climb out. "The medic's station is this way, sir." He led him over to one of the buildings; the glass of its front door had been smashed, and someone had propped the door open with a beam of wood.

They went inside. This was obviously some sort of souvenir shop ordinarily. Its shelves had all been pushed up against one wall. Shattered plastic figurines of the Führer and small pewter models of the city's bell tower littered the floor. The Wehrmacht had set up several rows of foldout cots. Wounded soldiers sat or lay on many of them, with their arms in slings or with crutches propped against their beds.

The infantryman led him over to a vacant cot and had him sit down, then hurried off to find the medic. Quinn waited patiently.

"Hey," someone called from a far corner of the room, "the radio's back on."

"What do you mean, the radio's back on?" came an answering cry.

"The *civilian* radio. *Deutschlandsender* has started broadcasting again."

"Well turn it up then!"

There was a pause, and then a staticky voice filled the room.

"*. . . and have now restored order in the city of Linz after acting to prevent an attempted coup by the leadership of the SS. A spokesman for Reich forces in the city said that at the current time details of the conspiracy are unclear, but it appears that the Reichsführer-SS and a few key aides had entered into an agreement with the English government whereby England would back the overthrow of the Führer's will and the rule of National Socialist law, in exchange for which the Reichsführer-SS, once vested with the Supreme Power, would make Germany a virtual English vassal, capitulating on all substantive sources of tension between the two states. The English foreign minister Lord Home was in Linz for the Führer's funeral but has not made himself available for comment. Once again, for those of you across the Reich just joining us after the interruption of service early this afternoon...*"

The infantryman returned with the medic, a lieutenant, who ordered Quinn to remove his shirt and sent the infantryman off for some dry clothes.

The medic pressed his fingers gently against Quinn's wound, causing Quinn to jerk his arm back in pain and eliciting a trickle of runny yellow pus. The medic tutted. "The bullet went clean through," he said, "but it is unfortunate that you spent so much time in the river before we could clean it. This might be a painful one."

Quinn glanced down at the inflamed purple and yellow skin surrounding the bullet wound. "I've had worse."

The medic glanced at the scar on his upper right chest and

nodded. He set about cleaning and disinfecting the wound, an extremely painful process, and was just finishing bandaging it when the infantryman returned with a clean change of clothes and a sergeant, both for Quinn.

"I have orders to take you to headquarters immediately, sir," the sergeant said.

"It will be just one minute, Feldwebel," the medic said, not taking his eyes from what he was doing. "I have to give this man a sling."

The sergeant was clearly unhappy with any delay, but he wasn't in much of a position to gainsay the medical assessment of a doctor who also outranked him. Thus it was that a little less than ten minutes later, Quinn exited the makeshift field hospital with his arm in a sling and clad in a civilian change of clothes the infantryman had found somewhere, with—blessedly—shoes instead of jackboots.

Quinn and the sergeant got in a jeep and headed out from the checkpoint. They wove their way through the darkened, silent streets, occasionally passing a patrol in another jeep or an armored car. As they trundled across the piazza overlooked by the art museum and the opera house, a combat helicopter glided overhead, its searchlight methodically criss-crossing the terrain below it.

"We remind you that the city is under curfew until further notice," the helicopter's loudspeaker blared at the city in general. "Remain indoors for your own safety. Not all fighting in the city has stopped. Anyone discovered out of doors not in Wehrmacht uniform is subject to summary military judgment."

They turned off the piazza and headed up In den Lauben. Soon they came to the great square before the communal hall that earlier in the day Quinn had seen from the window of the Strength through Joy Hotel, packed with tens of thousands of ordinary Germans awaiting their Führer's funeral. Now a barricade of sandbags and barbed wire enclosed it, with only a single gap to allow the entry and exit of vehicles.

The sergeant pulled up to the gap, where the sentry checked their pass carefully, then stared intently at Quinn while the sergeant explained that he had orders to deliver him immediately to headquarters. After the sentry spoke with someone on his field telephone, he waved them through.

They headed across the square to the communal hall on its far side. The bell tower over the mausoleum of the Führer's parents rose just beyond it. The sergeant weaved deftly through the vehicles scattered haphazardly around the square. There had obviously been a significant skirmish here: bullet marks scored and pockmarked the paving in places, there were several burnt out and overturned military vehicles, and bodies—both Wehrmacht and Waffen-SS—lay piled in a far corner.

The sergeant pulled up at the foot of the broad flight of steps leading up to the communal hall. The square fronted onto the riverbank, and Quinn stared out across the water at the silhouette of the Nibelungen Bridge a few hundred meters away, black against the inky blue of the night's sky.

"Mr. Quinn!"

Quinn turned to see a Wehrmacht officer—it took him a moment to recognize him as Captain Meier, silhouetted against the light spilling out from the communal hall—approaching down the steps, his arm raised in greeting. Quinn climbed out the jeep, feeling a slight twinge of pain in his arm, and ascended the last few steps to meet him. They shook hands.

"It is good to see you well, Mr. Quinn," the captain said. The English title sounded oddly accented from his lips. "I must say, I was positive you had died at the bridge."

"I'm as surprised as anyone, Herr Hauptmann," Quinn said.

Meier chuckled, then gestured toward the hall above them. "Come. Let's go inside. The Commissar-General will be eager to see you."

They ascended the steps and walked past the half dozen Wehrmacht sentries into the building's antechamber. Meier led him across the chamber and through a tall, arched doorway.

This was obviously the hall's main chamber. Rows and rows of seats, many of them now knocked over, had been arrayed to face the dais at the far end of the room, where the Führer's coffin, draped with a swastika flag, still stood, ringed by at least two dozen Wehrmacht guards. Eight or ten Waffen-SS bodies lay scattered about the room, but one in particular caught Quinn's attention. He was tall and thin, in his late sixties, lying on his back and staring emptily at the ceiling, a bullet hole in his forehead and blood puddled around him. But where the other Waffen-SS soldiers all wore common troopers' coalscuttle helmets, this man had on the uniform of a senior officer, and a pistol rather than an automatic rifle lay a few feet from his outstretched hand. Quinn recognized him immediately.

Meier, realizing that Quinn had stopped, turned to learn the cause. He followed Quinn's gaze, nodding sagely when he saw. "Ah, yes. SS-Oberstgruppenführer Kaltenbrunner. The Führer's body had a Waffen-SS honor guard here in the chamber. When our forces secured the building, Oberstgruppenführer Kaltenbrunner attempted to lead them in an attack from the inside." He paused, considering. "We would have preferred to take him alive, of course. For interrogation." A shrug—*But it couldn't be helped.*

The matter now closed as far as he was concerned, Meier turned and continued on his way. But, before following, Quinn stared a few moments longer at the corpse of Ernst Kaltenbrunner, commander of the RSHA and second in the SS hierarchy only to Heinrich Himmler.

Meier led him through a doorway into a side corridor, then down a cramped flight of stairs into a narrow hallway whose cinderblock walls, unadorned concrete floor, and flickering fluorescent lights contrasted starkly with the expansive marble floors and walls draped in swastika banners upstairs. Closed iron doors were set into the walls every few meters, and four of them had armed Wehrmacht sentries; one had two sentries and a lieutenant.

"The Commissar-General is currently questioning one of the senior SS officers we detained today," Meier explained. He nodded to the lieutenant, who opened the door he was guarding a crack and slipped inside, closing it after him.

Meier and Quinn waited. Intermittently, the sound of blows, whimpers, screams or stern questioning escaped from the doors that had sentries posted at them.

"Where's Captain Barnes?" Quinn asked, partly to cover the noise.

Meier seemed to come out of some sort of reverie. "He's at the municipal hospital," he said. "Wounded in the leg when we stormed the communal hall. He should be quite fine. I imagine you'll want to see him tomorrow."

The door opened again, swinging wide this time, and Heydrich and the lieutenant emerged. Before it swung shut again, Quinn caught a glimpse of the figure inside, a man in his sixties who had probably looked rather distinguished before they had stripped him to the waist and suspended him by his wrists from the ceiling, blood running freely from his nose and mouth: Hermann Fegelein, Himmler's personal deputy and Maurice Beauchamp's controller in the SS.

"Herr Quinn," Heydrich said warmly, extending his hand. "So good to see you survived."

Quinn shook the hand. "Herr Generalkommissar."

"I have the press assembled in two rooms upstairs, sir," Meier said. "Foreign and domestic."

"Then lead the way, Hauptmann," Heydrich said. "I'll see the domestic press first, then foreign. Then we'll return to the hotel for the night."

Meier saluted, turned and headed back down the corridor. Heydrich, Quinn, the lieutenant, and one of the soldiers who had been standing sentry outside Fegelein's door followed.

They ascended the steps to the hallway upstairs, and Meier led them to a closed door and stopped. Heydrich paused, taking a deep breath, then opened the door and went inside.

He did not close the door behind himself, and Quinn heard the scrape of chairs and the rustle of a large group of people getting to their feet, then Heydrich began to speak.

"You must excuse me, Mr. Quinn," Meier said. "I need to have the Commissar-General's car brought round."

"Of course, Herr Hauptmann."

"I am as surprised and shocked as all Germans must be—in fact, more so," Heydrich was saying as Meier walked away. "I worked closely with the former Reichsführer-SS during the years of our great struggle to secure the future of the Reich, and in the decades since I have always held great respect—admiration—for the devotion and tenacity with which he has served the German people and, most of all, our late Führer. Now, to discover that foreigners seduced him into conspiring to subvert our beloved Führer's last, and most essential, commandment to us all—I would expect it of a Jew; I would not expect it of a man who marched at Munich in 1923."

Quinn stepped away from the doorway; he did not wish to hear anymore.

CHAPTER XXIX

HE FOUND himself a bench to sit on and waited while Heydrich spoke with the press. After about ten minutes the Commissar-General moved from one room to the next, speaking now to the foreign press.

"In the East we must continue to grind them into the dust, every day, because if we give them even a moment's latitude, a moment's hope, then they might believe that they can be again anything more than what they are now, what they are meant to be—which is nothing. *It has kept us blooded, and it has kept us vigilant."*

The Commissar-General, ruler of the Commissariat-General. The Commissariat-General was the East, the broad, endless expanses of fertile plains and empty, abandoned shells of cities and towns. That had been Heydrich's fief. Thirty years ago that land had been the Soviet Union's most populous region. But its population had been Slavs, and the Germans had dispersed throughout the Reich as slave labor those few who survived having the most destructive war the world had ever seen fought in their homeland. Some remained in the East as farmers, feeding the German population in the west; many more had been sent west to work on assembly lines or as house servants.

"A Jew," Ellie murmured. "You're a Jew." Her eyes fastened on his and she stared at him, her face inscrutable. He reached out slowly and gently touched her shoulder, but she jerked away from him as if he might be contagious.

Jews had replaced the Slavs who had been deported from the East; the Jews of Germany and the conquered and allied territories had found themselves first confined to cramped, crumbling ghettos within their cities, then deported to work camps scattered throughout German Europe during the latter half of the war, and finally, after the fighting finished, relocated to a network of camps in the East, in the custody of the Commissar-General, Reinhard Heydrich.

Large black and white photographs of emaciated inmates arriving at the camps in cattle cars, being sorted into male and female, healthy and unhealthy groups by SS doctors, dominated the walls. Prisoners classed as troublesome had large targets sewn onto their backs. Quinn searched their gaunt, emaciated faces, shaven heads, and sunken eyes, looking for any resemblance to himself, wondering if he was staring at his own family.

A sudden peal of laughter jerked him out of his reverie, and a young girl—four or five years old—ran past him, clutching something black in her hand. A moment later another child—a boy, a year or two older, clutching something grey—followed. He turned to follow them with his eyes. The boy caught up with the girl and grabbed her by the upper arm, reaching for the object in her hand, and Quinn realized it was a Waffen-SS figurine, possibly from the museum's gift shop; the grey toy in the boy's hand was a figurine of a partisan fighter, one of the groups of Slavs or Jews who had taken to the hills and fought the German conquest. The girl was managing to keep the Waffen-SS figurine just out of the boy's reach, and giggling uncontrollably.

Reinhard Heydrich, as head of the SS under Heinrich Himmler, had first been responsible for the registration of Jews in conquered territory, for their confinement to the ghettos, and for their relocation to the initial camps, and had then, after his appointment as Commissar-General at the beginning of 1944, directed the camps to which Europe's entire Jewish population had eventually found themselves transferred.

Their relatives abroad, those who had emigrated from Germany in the 1930s, had grown old or passed on, and there were very few left who still tried to drum up international awareness of what had happened to the Jews, to bring about the condemnation of the Reich. And what can we do then, their children tiredly asked them. Turn Germany into a pariah state? It happened; it was evil, and we *already* condemn them for it. But the Germans are the most powerful country in the world, and we *have* to deal with them.

But Quinn—Quinn, who had been East, Quinn, who had followed his brother into the army to honor Isaac's sacrifice of his own life to stop the Nazis—had done more than simply deal with them. Quinn had just placed the man responsible for the Purification at their head.

My God. What have I done?

Heydrich, followed by his bodyguard, emerged from the press room and strode purposefully down the corridor toward the main chamber, Meier falling into step behind him. Quinn shook himself from his reverie and rose, joining the small entourage as it passed. They crossed quickly through the chamber into the building's antechamber, then out onto the entrance steps.

A Mercedes waited at the bottom of the steps, an infantryman standing by its open back door. Two Wehrmacht troopers on motorcycles sat idling ahead of it, while behind it there was an armored personnel carrier.

Heydrich descended the steps briskly and climbed inside the Mercedes. Meier gestured for Quinn to go next, then got in himself. The infantryman closed the door, and the whole convoy pulled away from the steps and set off across the square.

There was silence until they turned onto In den Lauben, heading in the direction of the Nibelungen Bridge.

"Where is Himmler?" Quinn asked.

Meier stirred, but Heydrich spoke before he could answer. "He is currently before a tribunal. Behind one of the other doors in the corridor where you found me interviewing SS-Obergruppenführer Fegelein."

"What will happen to him?"

"The tribunal should return its verdict some time after midnight. I imagine the Reichsführer-SS will come before his firing squad around dawn."

"Will you be present?"

Heydrich smiled. "No. I will be sound asleep at that time. As, I imagine, you will be." He cocked his head at Quinn's quizzical expression. "You wish to say something, Herr Quinn."

"I'm surprised," Quinn confessed. "You don't want a public trial?"

"That is the last thing I want. A public trial, a public execution—those will only create a martyr. On the other hand, I could simply brush him aside, intern him in a work camp in Kiev or the Volga, try to hold him out of the public eye. But alive, he would become a focal point of resistance for any disaffected officers in the SS hierarchy. No, the best thing is to dispose of him quietly, without fanfare. It won't be public knowledge; there will be no mention of his fate in the press. Eventually, after long enough without being heard of, he will simply be forgotten."

Quinn turned and stared out the window as they crossed the Nibelungen Bridge. The armored van still lay on its side on the edge of the precipice, as did the trucks he and Barnes had knocked out of the way earlier in the day; none blocked passage across the bridge, so none was an immediate priority for clearance. Work crews *had* cleared, however, the intersection beyond the bridge, though the entire end of the Hermann Göring Works overlooking it remained a pile of rubble.

They pulled into the Strength through Joy Hotel, though this time, instead of descending into the parking levels, they pulled up at to the hotel's main entrance. A doorman hurried forward to open the door, and the three of them got out and headed inside.

Heydrich strode straight through the lobby and directly toward the lift, where a waiting bellhop had already pressed the button to summon it. The guards scattered around the hotel, all Waffen-SS earlier, had now been replaced by the Wehrmacht.

The lift arrived. The three men entered and ascended to the fifth floor. The lieutenant at the reception desk jumped to his feet and snapped off a salute, but Heydrich ignored him and headed down the corridor to his office.

Manfred was waiting at his desk when the three men entered. He too immediately rose and saluted. Heydrich waved him impatiently to his ease.

The door to Heydrich's office was ajar. "Herr Quinn," the Commissar-General said, "why don't you wait inside? We'll be in in a moment."

Quinn nodded. "Of course, Herr Generalkommissar."

As Quinn crossed the room, Heydrich began speaking to the other two. "Manfred, before I forget. There will have to be a thorough honors list drawn up, and I'll begin earnest consideration of that tomorrow, but make a note for Hauptmann Meier: promotion and—" he paused, considering, "—Iron Cross, First Class."

Meier snapped proudly to attention as Quinn slipped through the door, pushing it almost shut behind him—closing it all the way would have seemed odd and drawn attention to himself.

He did not have more than a few moments. The room was dark. He crossed the room quickly, striding over to the window behind Heydrich's desk and unlatching it. Then, keeping half an ear on the low murmur of conversation from the other room to make sure all the speakers remained stationary and were not heading in his direction, he started trying the desk drawers. Two were locked, and he found nothing in the others that could serve for what he needed.

There was the door back out to the others, but there was also another door leading off the office. This one was closed. He tried the knob and found it unlocked. Silently, he cracked the door open. Heydrich's bedroom. A nightstand stood just inside the door. He began trying its drawers.

Perfect. Lying inside the second drawer was a dagger. He picked it up and examined it in the moonlight spilling in through the window. It was an SS dagger, a swastika tooled into the leather sheath, twin SS lightning bolts embossed on the haft. He slid it a half inch out of its sheath. Even in the slight, pale light, the blade reflected purely. He pressed his thumb against its edge; it was sharp. Satisfied, he slipped the dagger into his pocket.

When Heydrich and Meier entered the office, Quinn was sitting peacefully on one of the settees, and the bedroom door was closed.

"Why on earth are you sitting here in the dark, Herr Quinn?" Heydrich asked as Meier turned on the light.

Quinn shrugged, rising to his feet. "A moment of quiet reflection, Herr Generalkommissar."

"Ah," said Heydrich, satisfied. He seated himself behind his desk while Meier drew the curtains. "And on what were you reflecting?"

Quinn pursed his lips. "On the strange turnings our lives can take, in but a matter of hours. Or even minutes."

Heydrich snorted. "I see. How very... appropriate to the moment." He favored Quinn with a slight smile, but then his gaze became more purposeful. "I apologize for keeping you waiting for a few minutes, but I wanted to make sure I had the opportunity to express my appreciation to you this evening."

Quinn nodded in acknowledgement. "Waiting was no trouble at all, Herr Generalkommissar."

Now Heydrich rose. "You did what you did out of patriotism. You are not German, but patriotism of whatever ilk is something I can respect deeply. Nevertheless, without you, not only would I not have achieved what I have today, but I very likely would not have lived to see this night. You, Herr Quinn, have been responsible today for my achievement of supreme power in the Reich."

"Of that, Herr Generalkommissar," Quinn said, "I have been very much aware tonight."

Heydrich seemed not to hear the edge in his words, and continued, "After the day's events, I suspect you might currently be unable to find a welcome in your own country. Germany, on the other hand, will be more than happy to provide for you." He yawned slightly and checked his watch. "But that, Herr Quinn, will be a matter for tomorrow. Manfred will have a room waiting for you."

Quinn nodded at the dismissal. "Good night, Herr General-kommissar." He turned and walked from the room.

Manfred was sitting at his desk. He looked up when Quinn walked in. "Ah, Herr Quinn. Please, this way." He rose and led Quinn from the antechamber into the corridor, then stopped and opened the very first door on his left.

Quinn followed him in. This suite was much more spacious than the one he had been shown to with the others earlier in the day.

"Is there anything else you need tonight, Herr Quinn?" Manfred asked solicitously.

Quinn shook his head. "No, thank you."

"Very good then," Manfred said. He gestured to the telephone sitting on the desk. "If you are hungry, the phone has instructions for reaching room service. Good night, Herr Quinn." He turned and left the room, closing the door behind himself.

For a long time Quinn stood there, counting silently in his head. When he had reached six hundred—ten minutes—and no one had disturbed him, he turned and headed through into the bedroom.

He walked straight over to the window and unlatched it, pushed it open and slipped out onto the ledge outside. It was cold up here, twenty meters above the ground in the middle of the night, and the breeze bit bitterly into his skin.

Slowly, cautiously, he edged his way down the ledge to Heydrich's office window. He could hear voices coming from inside.

Heydrich was speaking. "We shall have to draw up shortlists for Reichsmarschall and Commissar-General soon, but the main priority must be the new commander of the SS. We must ensure he is *loyal*, and that he is not a Himmler sympathizer."

"Yes, Herr Generalkommissar," Meier said.

There was silence for a few moments, then Heydrich spoke again. "It has been a very long day, Hauptmann, and I think that for tonight that will be all. Tell Manfred I am not to be disturbed till I rouse myself. Good night, Hauptmann."

"Good night—" a pause, then, "—mein Führer."

Heydrich did not respond at first; after several long seconds, he said only, *"Heil Hitler."*

Quinn heard Meier's heels snap together and could imagine him saluting. *"Heil Heydrich!"*

After that there was silence; a few minutes later, the light went off. Quinn began counting again.

When he had reached three hundred, he gently pried the window open and slipped inside. The office was deserted, but Heydrich's bedroom door stood ajar. Quinn padded softly over to it, his hand in his pocket with his fingers closed around the dagger.

The lights were off. Heydrich stood before his bedroom window, looking out over the city. Quinn stood in the doorway for a long time, just watching him.

At last the Commissar-General turned. He started when he saw Quinn.

"What are you doing here?" he demanded, trying to cover his surprise with indignation.

Quinn withdrew the dagger from his pocket, removed it from its sheath and dropped the sheath on the floor. "Don't call out, mein Führer." The title sounded mocking on his lips. "You'll be dead before anyone can get to you."

"What do you think you're doing here?"

Quinn started crossing the room slowly, approaching Heydrich. "You killed my family, mein Führer." His voice was menacingly quiet.

Heydrich's mouth worked for a second without any sound emerging, then he managed, "What are you talking about?"

"You killed my grandparents, my aunts and uncles, my cousins. And my brother. My brother died trying to stop you, trying to avenge them, mein Führer. You killed the Jews." He stopped, standing toe to toe with Heydrich.

The Commissar-General frowned at him in confusion. "I don't understand. The Jews? What do you care of the Jews?"

"You said a little while ago, through there—" his eyes flicked toward the door leading back to the office, "—that I'm not German. That's true, though not because I was born in England. I was born in Germany, mein Führer. But I'm not German, because you—because the National Socialists—took away my German citizenship before I was three years old."

Heydrich's eyes had widened as he began to realize what

Quinn was saying. "No," he said. "No, you can't be."

"I lied, mein Führer. My name isn't Simon Quinn. My name is Mordechai Rosenhoch."

"Ros-Rosenhoch," Heydrich repeated numbly. But then he seemed to straighten. "And what of it? What do you think to accomplish here?" The slightest hint of a sneer touched his lip. "Do you think to give your family justice?"

Quinn shook his head sadly, even wearily, and seemed to falter for an instant. "Justice? No. They can never have that." But then his eyes glinted. "I come here for a simple act of vengeance."

The movement was quick—just a mere flick of his wrist—and powerful, and he had buried the knife in Heydrich's stomach. He twisted hard, turning the blade ninety degrees, and then removed it.

The Commissar-General did not make a sound, just clasped his hands over the wound, blood welling through his fingers. He looked down, then back up at Quinn, and crumpled silently to the floor.

Quinn tossed the bloodstained knife down on the bed, strode quickly back across the room, and slipped out through the open window into the night.

EPILOGUE

THE AMERICAN consulate turned out to be only a few blocks from the Strength through Joy Hotel. It faced onto a small square with an equestrian statue of Frederick Barbarossa in the center. Quinn, his arm throbbing intensely from the climb down the face of the hotel, settled himself in a darkened alleyway on the opposite side of the square, whence he had a good view of the consulate entrance, and waited.

It was possible she was already inside, of course, but he doubted it. Gunning would have had the good sense simply to get out of sight during the day's fighting, and only now that things had quietened down would he have started making his way here.

He had less than an hour to wait. He spotted Gunning first,

appearing out of the shadows at the square's far corner and surveying the square to make sure it was safe to cross. Then he turned and beckoned, and there she was. Ellie came out of the shadows after him, and the two of them hurried across the square toward the consulate's front entrance.

She paused at the base of the statue and looked about, searching for him, hoping he would be there waiting for her. Gunning saw she had stopped and turned back impatiently, waiting.

Quinn had been sitting with his back against the alley wall; now he rose, preparing to run to her.

"She would be much safer if you left her alone."

He whirled, and there was the familiar figure, face in shadow, standing just a few meters behind him, watching him.

The old man stepped forward, bringing his face into the pale light. "The Gestapo knows who she is," he said, "but alone, she's no threat to them. If you were to rejoin her, however..." His voice trailed off, and his eyebrows rose significantly.

"You expect me to just let her walk away?"

"I expect you to put her safety ahead of your own gratification, Simon."

Talleyrand came forward to stand next to him, and he turned back to see Ellie reluctantly following Gunning towards the consulate. They stood shoulder to shoulder and watched the two of them talk to the American marine at the consulate's entrance. In reality it probably took only about a minute, but to Quinn it seemed an eternity—an eternity during which he did not run to her, did not call out to her. At last someone in plainclothes came out to meet them, and the Marine let them pass. The two of them disappeared inside.

Quinn and Talleyrand continued to stare at the consulate entrance. At last the old man said, "I'm proud of you, Simon. That was a very noble thing."

No bitter retort about hypocrisy leapt to his lips; instead, he asked, "How did you know where to find me?"

"Oh, it wasn't a very difficult deduction. You couldn't very well send her to the British consulate, nor could you leave her with the Germans until you knew who'd won. This was really the only place left to you."

"So what happens now?"

"To her? She can go with the Americans, if she wants, as can Sergeant Gunning and Captain Barnes—I've already spoken with my opposite number at the CIA to ensure that. I imagine she'd be readmitted to Germany as well if she wanted. Or she could even come to England—I'd see to that, though I doubt it would require extensive intervention. The day's events have brought to light some... activities of the Government of the day that are causing quite the stir in Britain. I daresay we shall have a new Government by the end of the coming week, if not sooner. One that will welcome your Fraulein Voss, once I put a word in."

"And Barnes and Gunning?"

"The new Government will welcome them home as heroes. A good sort, Captain Barnes. He's impressed me. I shall have to keep my eye on him—I think he would fit in well with our organization."

"That was your intent the whole time, wasn't it? To bring down the Government?"

"Not necessarily bring down," the old man said. He turned to Quinn. "That is far beyond our remit, Simon. You know better than that—we don't interfere with domestic politics, nor should we have any desire to. But that insidious treaty? I could not permit it to come to pass."

"And we've been dancing to your tune the whole time, yes? This has all been your plan all along?"

"Well..." Talleyrand looked back over his shoulder at the dark silhouette of the Strength through Joy Hotel rising into the night sky, and beyond it at the smoke still visibly rising in the city center. "Perhaps not planned down to the minutest detail. But you certainly managed to catch my general gist. You did extraordinarily well, in fact."

"A good man died."

Talleyrand cast his eyes down a moment. "Richard Garner. Yes." He looked back up at Quinn. "I did not know he was going to run, and I would have saved him if I could. But you must understand, Simon, that even I have masters to whom I must answer, the Government, our supposed friends at the Gestapo. I did not want Garner to die, but if they had realized what aim I was truly working for, then all the sacrifices we *all* made would have been for naught." He paused, then added quietly, "And while I'm sure you look suspiciously on everything I say to you, I doubt you will have trouble believing that Richard Garner's death is far from the blackest mark on my conscience that I will someday have to explain to my Maker."

Quinn sighed. "No. I believe you." There was silence for a moment, then he asked, "What about my crew? And my boat?"

"Both have been released. We have the boat's title—the Greek customs police found it when they searched the craft. Would you like it back?"

He shook his head. "Give it to one of the crew. Giglio. He's one of the Sicilians."

"Very well." Talleyrand cocked his head inquisitively. "And you? Where will you go now?"

Quinn's eyebrows arched. "You know, I'm famished. I think I'll go find something to eat."

This elicited a faint smile. "And then?"

He gazed contemplatively up at the stars. "Oh, to the East for a time, I think," he said at last. "See if I can't find some old ghosts. Put them to rest."

The old man nodded sagely. "I see. Then I suppose this is good bye, Simon. Or would you prefer Mordechai?"

Quinn shrugged. "Either. Neither. It doesn't really matter now." He turned and walked away down the alley. After a dozen or so paces, though, he paused and turned back. "Why?" he asked. Talleyrand raised his eyebrows inquisitively. "Why did you do it? That peace treaty, whatever else it may have done, solved a lot of Britain's problems. Why was it worth all our lives to end it?"

The old man tutted. "Come now, Simon. What is the very first lesson we taught you? We seek neither victory, nor even peace. We seek only *stability*, for only stability can guarantee our safety from apocalypse. We need the Americans in order for us to continue fighting this Cold War, but the Americans have never been enthusiastic about it. Europe is much too far away for them to see Germany as an immediate threat, and the last time they came here, the Germans sent them home with their collective tail between their legs. They'd much rather forget the whole thing; it's only the British will that keeps them in it. If Britain were to suddenly forsake them and go over to the other side—why, then they would find themselves twice bitten. And with neither the Americans nor Britain here to oppose Germany—well then, who would be left?"

Quinn was staring off at an indeterminate point in the distance, nodding in understanding. "Stability. The preservation of order. Fair enough." He focused back on Talleyrand. "But in that case, I'm afraid everything might not have turned out quite as you were hoping for."

Talleyrand stared at him a moment, frowning, not understanding. Then, suddenly, his eyes widened, and he turned and looked toward the Strength through Joy Hotel, where Heydrich remained. Then he turned back to the shadowy alley, but Simon Quinn was gone.

POSTSCRIPT

HITLER DID indeed intend to demolish and reconstruct the great cities of the German Reich. Like many of his fantasies, these plans started out on a moderately manageable scale—only five cities—and then ballooned to more than two dozen cities as the war dragged on and German reverses began to mount. When the Führer finally retreated to his Berlin bunker in the early months of 1945, still convinced of an imminent, glorious victory as the Russians, Americans, and British closed in from two directions, he took with him his massive scale model of his plans for his most cherished reconstruction, that of the city of Linz, and would spend hours studying it as Berlin was reduced to rubble above him. Kaltenbrunner—like Hitler and Adolf Eichmann (with whom

Kaltenbrunner had attended school), a Linz native—arrived at the bunker intending to try to persuade the Führer to surrender, but was admitted to the room housing the model of Linz, a mark of special favor. Hitler declaimed for hours on his plans for the city, and Kaltenbrunner walked away a fervent convert to the approaching German victory.

Of the three reconstructed cities I have dealt with in detail, two—Berlin and Linz—are as much as possible based on Hitler's actual plans for them; as regards Munich, Glory Way is entirely my own invention. Plans for the new Berlin are taken from their architect Albert Speer's memoir *Inside the Third Reich*, the most influential primary source we have about the inner workings of National Socialism's upper echelons. For the reconstruction of Linz—and other discussion of the Nazi rebuilding of Germany, such as the great north-south autobahn linking Klagenfurt, Austria, to the projected German colony of Nordstern ("Polar Star") near Trondheim, Norway—I have drawn on Frederic Spotts's excellent study of *Hitler and the Power of Aesthetics*. I should note that Hermann Giesler, Hitler's principle architect and also the director of the reconstruction of Linz, vehemently disputed Speer's assertion that Hitler intended to be interred in Linz with his parents.

Several characters appearing in the novel were historical personages, chief amongst them Reinhard Heydrich. Heydrich was assassinated outside Prague by Czechoslovakian nationalists operating under British auspices in 1942. As head of the Gestapo's parent organization, the RSHA, Heydrich was responsible for the beginning of the Holocaust. He chaired the Wannsee Conference in Berlin in 1942, attended by Adolf Eichmann, at which the blueprint for the Final Solution was established—including the mass deportation of Jews to the East for the purposes of slave labor in the early stages of building the infrastructure of the Reich occupation.

Adolf Galland, who once famously told Hermann Göring that the best way to improve the Luftwaffe's performance would be to equip it with British Spitfires, was released as a prisoner of war in 1947 with the proviso that he was not permitted to pilot an aircraft. He worked as a forest ranger and served as a general in the Argentine air force before returning to Germany where, after the West German government passed him over for command of their new Luftwaffe, he worked as an independent aerospace consultant. He died in 1996.

Otto-Ernst Remer became a hero of National Socialism when, as commander of the Wehrmacht garrison in Berlin, he was instrumental in suppressing the coup attempt of July 1944 by arresting its leaders before they could gain control of the German capital after their attempted assassination of Hitler. After the war he became active in the Socialist Reich Party, one of West Germany's first neo-Nazi parties, and fled to Egypt in 1952 when he was sentenced to three months' imprisonment for denouncing the members of the German resistance as traitors. In 1992 a German court sentenced him to twenty-two months in prison for publishing neo-Nazi propaganda and denying the Holocaust. He died in 1997 in exile in Spain.

Heinrich Himmler shaved off his beloved mustache and covered one eye with an eye patch as part of his disguise as Heinrich Hitzinger, a sergeant-major of the Secret Military Police, when he left Flensburg shortly after the Germans had surrendered.

Captured outside Bremen, he committed suicide at Lüneburg on 23 May 1945 by biting down when a British doctor discovered the vial of potassium cyanide he had wedged between two of his teeth.

Ernst Kaltenbrunner, who did indeed succeed Heydrich as commander of the RSHA, was found guilty of count 3 (war crimes) and count 4 (crimes against humanity) by the Nuremberg tribunal and hanged on 16 October 1946.

Hermann Fegelein, brother-in-law to Hitler's mistress Eva Braun, was stripped of his rank and imprisoned in the guardhouse of Hitler's bunker beneath Berlin on 26 April 1945. With the city's fall to the Red Army imminent, he had slipped away to his apartment in Charlottenburg and changed into civilian clothes, preparing to flee to Sweden with his mistress, when the SS caught up with him. The circumstances around his death by firing squad remain murky: some sources say he was examined by a military tribunal, others that Hitler ordered his summary execution. Some say that his sister-in-law Eva Braun pleaded for clemency, others that she said nothing in his defense.

I have deliberately avoided introducing any historical British politicians into the novel. The only British minister named is the foreign secretary, the Earl of Home, and historically by 1971 there no longer *was* an Earl of Home. The fourteenth Earl, foreign secretary from 1960 to 1963 in the Macmillan Government, disclaimed his peerages in 1963 after the Conservative Party selected him to replace Harold Macmillan as party leader, so that he could be elected to the House of Commons for Kinross as Sir Alec Douglas-Home and assume the office of Prime Minister. He lost the General Election of 1964 and was replaced as Leader of the Opposition a year later by Edward Heath, in whose later Government he served with distinction once more as foreign secretary. He re-entered the House of Lords in 1974 as Baron Home of the Hirsel of Coldstream and died in 1995.

Integral to my understanding of Nazi Germany were Louis L. Snyder's *Encyclopedia of the Third Reich* and *An Illustrated History of the Gestapo* by Rupert Butler. Inevitably, I have taken creative liberties with the material in both volumes, as I also have with the material by Spotts and Speer on Hitler's grandiose plans for the reconstruction of Germany. Such liberties are even more necessary with alternate history than they are with conventional historical fiction. Responsibility for any and all inaccuracies in the novel lies, of course, with me.

ACKNOWLEDGMENTS

THE FIRST idea of what would eventually turn into this book came to me when I was fifteen. Between that point and this, many people have read portions of the manuscript or simply listened to me talk about parts of it (either with or without the context they needed for me to make any sense). They gave me thoughtful criticism or simply encouraging enthusiasm, and they have my gratitude: Andy Giglio, Kelly Gunning, Nikki Berger, Lee Berger and Diane Ashoff.

My thanks also to Andy Zack, my agent, who not only took me on but also whose feedback on the manuscript's first draft led to a lot of the ideas that are now among my favorite elements in the story.

And most importantly, my thanks to my wife, Lisa, for thoughtful criticism, encouraging enthusiasm, and so many other things, but in particular for saying, "You know, I hear a lot of talk about how you're going to write books someday, but I don't ever see any *writing*."

CPSIA information can be obtained at www.ICGtesting.com
Printed in the USA
BVOW041418300512

291402BV00001B/4/P